Among the Saints

A Novel from the Lapland Series

JARI TERVO

Translated by Daniel H. Karvonen

Published by
Ice Cold Crime LLC
5780 Providence Curve
Independence, MN 55359

Printed in the United States of America

Cover by Joanna Górecka

Photograph © Veikko Somerpuro

© Jari Tervo and Werner Söderström Ltd. (WSOY)
Original title "Pyhiesi yhteyteen"
First published in Finnish by Werner Söderström Corporation
in 1995, Helsinki, Finland

© Jari Tervo and Ice Cold Crime LLC 2014
for English version

Ice Cold Crime LLC gratefully acknowledges the financial
assistance of:

FINNISH LITERATURE EXCHANGE

Library of Congress Control Number: 2014941360

ISBN-13: 978-0-9824449-9-3
ISBN-10: 0-9824449-9-0

The People

Part One: A one-legged shoeless man

1. Marzipan Räikkönen
2. Taisto Toikka, Ambulance Driver
3. Sara Skinner
4. Laina Räikkönen
5. Aarne Sirkiä, Ambulance Driver
6. Sakke Löysä
7. Police Officer Jussi "Rosebush" Rosenström
8. Sarlotta Root, Housewife
9. Ossi Kaukonen
10. Detective Sergeant Osmo Nauris
11. Inkeri Feodoroff, MD
12. Police Officer Mauri Kildenstamm
13. Paul Ansalanka
14. Esa Skinner, Butcher
15. Kassu Vartio
16. Paavo Karhu aka the Grizz
17. Stella Gavia, Director of Nursing
18. Sebastian Räikkönen

Part Two: They rarely need to be opened from the inside

19. Laura Pahka, Shopkeeper
20. Aila Kildenstamm, Head Union Representative
21. Pipsa Skinner, Pedicurist

**Part Three: The leaves are playing house
in the birch tree**

**Part Four: The face of Jesus Christ appeared
on the ceiling**

Part One:

A one-legged shoeless man

1. Marzipan Räikkönen

I was killed the first week of May.

It wasn't even ten o'clock in the morning. I don't know how it happened. The whole damn night I'd been trying to scrape together cash for Parmesan. He was collecting it for some Russian, who was probably getting it for another Russian. It was a complicated deal, but for me everything is simple now.

I looked out the window at the birches in the distance. Their branches carried a hint of spring green. I took a dump, puked, washed my hands, and flipped through the paper, then went outside to get a closer look at the birches and realized they were still bare. I pulled a branch down, crushed a bud in my palm, smearing green gunk all over my hand. It made me think of Dimwit sucking on his green hard candy, and his green drool running down his chin, all over the floor, and onto my socks. Once I stepped in it, my sock got stuck in the green goo, and was pulled off my foot. It looked like the sock belonged to a one-legged shoeless man who had ascended to heaven from smack in the middle of our living room.

I used to slap Dimwit for making such a mess. My mother warned me that I shouldn't hit my own son, because it would make him a cruel grown-up.

"Then he'll be like me," I said.

Ma said he was already going to be like me, the way he dripped green crap on the freshly mopped floor, just like I did when I passed out after a drinking binge. At the age of eleven, he was too dumb for kindergarten. But he knew how to drool—about all he was good for. I told her she should've taught him then.

"Well, nobody else done it," Ma said.

She sure was running her mouth this morning, even though she knew my fist was ready to fly.

"You punk," she grunted and banged the coffeepot against the dented water pipe, reminding me that I'd hurled the pot against the wall the week before. Dimwit was still limping and had a dirty bandage wrapped around his leg from it.

"So, who raised *me*, then?" I asked, and tore the newspaper into shreds.

"What are you doing?" she snapped. She still needed to check which bingo hall she should go to. But not the one on Valta Street; she was sure that the woman there ran a scam.

"Who raised me then?" I yelled it this time, ripping the newspaper into even smaller pieces and tearing the photo from the soccer game in half. I looked to see if I recognized one of the spectators whose face I had ripped apart this fine May morning, but his face was too small, just a few black-and-white dots. When I moved it farther away, I could see it better until it got blurry again. Close up, he suddenly looked familiar, but I couldn't place him.

"You need glasses, boy? I can see just fine, and look at my age," Ma squawked.

She then remembered the question about raising me and said she gave up on me when I turned out to be such an animal at the ripe old age of seven. She said she should've put me in the doghouse with the dog or in a pigsty on a farm. Dimwit whined, drool dripping from his mouth, this time colorless. Ma threw him a bag of green candy, and he started flinging pieces around, whining and complaining.

"Flower," he said, pointing to the birch tree outside the window.

"It's a tree, stupid," I said.

"The birch tree's so pretty, it's a flower; it's a tree flower," Ma said, pressing her ear against the stove to hear if the water in the coffeepot was boiling. Her hair got singed, stinking up the whole room. She ran into the bathroom screaming. Dimwit stopped bawling and pointed his finger at her. I let out a *meep meep*, just like the Roadrunner in the cartoons.

"Ha," said Dimwit.

Ma returned, her hair wet and her cheeks smeared with makeup. I laughed, and Dimwit whooped ha-ha-ha for so long I had to shut him up with a little punch. He settled down and studied the candy wrappers.

"A grown man cackling over nothin'," she said and let out a long bellowing laugh. When she was done laughing, the silence made the room feel empty.

"Ain't no use for me to beat you, but mark my words, your son will break your spine when he grows up," Ma predicted. She then measured some coffee into the pot, poured off the foam, and set the pot halfway onto the hot burner so the grounds could settle.

"And what the hell are you rippin' up the newspaper for!" she exploded.

"We ran out of toilet paper, so I thought I'd make some," I said, as she set the cups on the table with a clank.

"A grown man who needs a hundred feet of tissue for one turd," Ma said, as she poured the coffee and grabbed some cardamom sweetbread from the cupboard.

I dug a dripping piece of candy out of Dimwit's mouth and peeled off the wrapper. He cried, thinking I'd stolen his treat. I shoved the candy back in his mouth, and his front teeth scraped my fingers.

"So, Dimwit's gonna break my spine, huh?" I retorted. "Whatcha gonna do to me...whatcha gonna do ...nothin'," I whined to him, and with just the tips of my fingers pushed him over on his back. Ma jumped up from behind the table. She managed a loud shriek just before Dimwit hit the floor. His head landed on a squeaky toy. He was hacking up the candy stuck in his throat, and Ma sat him up and slapped his back until the candy plopped out on the floor.

"Hecch, hecch," Dimwit gasped for air.

"A pig is what you are, grown man, you'll kill your own son yet," she hissed.

"Heh, heh," I said as Dimwit started to smile, and I peeled another piece of candy for him.

"Which one of you is the bigger idiot?" she asked.

"Dimwit, tell 'er," I said, "and don't say 'heh heh'."

"Heh," Dimwit said.

"Atta boy, Dimwit," I said.

"Get out of here, drink your coffee and go, and stay out with your whores until you sober up," Ma said, trying to sound tough.

"I ain't dumb enough to go into town with no money," I said.

"Well, you ain't gettin' it from me."

"But you see, if I don't ask, I'll be one of those guys who take without askin'," I said.

"Heh," Dimwit said.

"Drink your coffee," Ma barked, getting up and warning the boy not to fall with candy in his mouth. "It'll get stuck sideways in your mouth and stop you from breathin'." She showed him what could happen, but had to stop when Dimwit started to copy her. I drank my coffee and spread some butter on the cold sweet cardamom bread. It tasted good, and I remembered how things used to be.

I looked out the window at the birches and could tell that tomorrow, or the day after, they would sport little green sparks of spring. I said it out loud. Ma didn't say anything; she just kept studying the shredded bits of newspaper, turning them over in her hands. She'd never read the paper so carefully.

While Dimwit was bubbling with mucus, Sonny shot out of the bedroom to lick his face.

4

"Damn cat, get lost!" I yelled, and turned the cat into a fuzzy arrow that thudded into the wall of the shed out in the yard. That's what it sounded like anyway, coming from the shed, or else it was just a rake that fell over and rattled for a minute before returning to a rusty silence.

"Torturin' the poor cat, a livin' creature," Ma complained.

"That damn cat always gets diarrhea when he's on the prowl and then smears it around every room of the house. He always wants to mate when the female cats don't."

"He's neutered, the poor boy," she said.

"Then it's just diarrhea; could be the hooch I've been givin' him."

"Git!" she hiccupped. She sloshed the last dregs of coffee from the pot into my cup and put the butter away. I got up to leave and said that if anyone asked for me, I wasn't here and probably never would be.

"My fondest wish," she said while crossing herself with an exaggerated gesture. I grabbed her by the shoulders and slowly told her that this was no bingo bullshit; it was serious business. The guys that might come around asking for me didn't care what an old woman would have to say; they'd draw their own brutal conclusions.

"You done made a mess o' things again," she said, giving me a stern look. I looked away, at the birches outside and then at Dimwit, who pulled his tongue out of his mouth with his fingers to see if his candy was gone. I gave him another piece.

"Best if you know nothin' if someone asks," I said.

"Say what?" Ma asked, rinsing the cups under the faucet. She put them right side up in the cupboard. I pointed out they wouldn't drain that way.

"Now go. Looks like a car's comin'," she said. I was frantically putting on my second boot when she started to laugh. I threw the boot at her and she caught it, quite

5

nimbly for a sixty-some-year-old woman, and threw it out the window. It was a great shot—right through the small ventilation window and into the yard, not even grazing the frame. In a rage, I hobbled out to get my boot, slipping on the thin coat of ice that covered the stone steps. My side hurt like hell, and I wondered if I'd broken something. I slid my foot in the boot and bounded back up the wobbly steps of the house. Ma's gonna get it, I thought to myself, but just then I heard a car bumping through the potholes up our long, winding driveway. I couldn't remember where I put my leather coat, so I grabbed the nearest jacket from the hook in the entryway and scrambled down the trail. Just for the hell of it, I stopped by the shed door, and let out a scream. Then I ran into the woods and waited. I glanced at my bare wrist, wondering what time it was. I counted the seconds for ten minutes, then got back on the trail and headed toward town. Just before the pond I sat down on a rock. That's where I was killed; I'm just not sure how.

2. Taisto Toikka, Ambulance Driver

I was just trying to get a peek at Aarne Sirkiä's crotch when we got the call. I didn't think his could possibly be bigger than mine, but it was hard to tell with his loose-fitting pants.

We were called to the far end of Viirinkangas, where the Räikkönens live. As I was running to the ambulance, I wondered why any of the Räikkönens needed a ride—weren't they all either dead or in jail?

Sirkiä wanted to drive.

"My turn," he said.

We drove through the hospital gate and turned left in front of the church. Guess he had the right address.

"Is it?" he asked.

I hadn't told him how much his work habits irritated me, but I'd mentioned it to our supervisor Antti. Stuffing his face with a jelly donut, the boss acted surprised, and said that he'd never heard a bad word about Sirkiä before. There's a rumor that Antti is screwing the female CEO of Tasty Reindeer, Inc., who'd be way too much for pale Antti to handle, and too rich. Later I heard someone say that Sirkiä and Antti and two other guys own a shared fishing boat up on Lake Inari.

Sirkiä had an annoying habit of answering himself before he asked a question. If you gave the same answer as he had just done he'd nod and stroke his moustache as if to say, "That's what I just said." It was irritating as hell.

He probably forgot the pouches.

His job was to check that all necessary equipment was loaded into the "meat wagon." He often forgot the pouches we needed for collecting spare body parts of the injured or dead. Once I busted him for it, though we didn't even need them on that run. I mentioned the incident to Antti, who yelled back at me, "Who forgot to put gas in the damn ambulance last time?" It says a lot about Antti that it hasn't happened more than once or twice.

I didn't bother to ask Sirkiä about the pouches. If one of the Räikkönens has lost a foot, I'll just throw my arms up in the air. I had decided to talk to Limpström, Antti's boss. Maybe someone would finally get this place in order.

"Dammit! They're ignoring the siren."

A yellow Volga took off full throttle in front of us when they heard the siren. People are such idiots—they don't get they shouldn't race us when they hear the siren, they should just slow down and pull over. The Volga stayed in front of us up until Pappila Road, and the guy in the back seat kept glancing at us over his shoulder. I gestured how I'd shove my fist up their asses and twist it until it finally dawned on the driver that he should get out of our way. Lucky he didn't hit the kiosk on the side of the road.

"How does that Russian rustbucket go so fast?"

"That's one of those souped-up cars. A Ferrari engine inside an old frame."

No fucking way, I thought. If the guy's got enough cash to buy a Ferrari engine then he can afford a Ferrari frame too; he ain't gonna cover it up with surplus Russian sheet metal.

Sirkiä asked for the address again, stated it, and waited for my answer. I repeated the address, he wiped his moustache, and took the next turn so hard I wanted to point out we weren't in that big of a hurry to see what's bothering the Räikkönens.

I think we could've improved society's overall welfare by first enjoying a smoke and a leisurely cup of coffee while watching Eurosport before heading out to count the dead and wounded. That's what you get at the Räikkönens, not heart problems or broken legs. Half of

8

my taxes go to coddling that clan. If the city of Rovaniemi paid a million euros to the city of Kemi to take the Räikkönen family, we'd earn that money back in a couple of years: taxes would go down, and we could again afford to build community centers for hooligans to vandalize, and the shotput circles could get fixed.

We were almost there on that damn trail of potholes that rips your kidneys apart. I didn't see any smoke—at least the Räikkönens hadn't burned their neighbors' house down.

I looked at Sirkiä's crotch to see if his pants had gotten any tighter while he was sitting. I could ask Antti, or even Limpström, what Sirkiä did in his spare time. If it was sports, I could try to get on his team and bounce a ball around, and then in the sauna I'd finally see what kind of man he is. I couldn't imagine him as a ladies' man.

"What's in my crotch?"

"You spilled coffee on it."

"We didn't have time to drink any."

"There's some sorta spot there."

"I don't see nothin'."

"Who looks at their own crotch?"

"Who looks at another guy's crotch?"

I couldn't think of a retort, and I'll admit it pissed me off. I had to get to the bottom of it. I didn't want to wait too damn long wondering whether people thought of me as the town fool. The city paying me a joke of a salary to drive an ambulance was a façade, and the occupation on my tax return should say "a pansy drawing a steady paycheck for being the entire city's laughing stock."

The ambulance shook, bouncing over the potholes, and Sirkiä wobbled with it. It looked like he was exaggerating the shaking, pretending he had a woman under him instead of a pothole, making her scream so loud that the next morning all the neighborhood ladies would look at their husbands with jealous eyes.

"This is like a bucking horse."

A mare. Dammit, asswipe, just call it a mare. My wife, the mare, who can't wait for her husband to go to work, so hot and heavy to get some of Sirkiä's lusty dick, which drills her so hard the sweat pours out of her ears.

"I said a lot of potholes, man," Sirkiä said.

He knows he's been busted, he knows those kissy lips let the cat out of the bag. The girl at the hospital admissions desk—what's-her-name, it starts with an "M"—says she blushes every time she sees him. She actually lurks around at lunchtime to see which table Sirkiä picks so she can join him. You should see her licking her lips. An eighteen-year-old hottie the hospital had to hire as part of the back-to-work program, and she talks like a porn shop owner. I should bring it up with Antti; I'm sure I could come up with something about a hostile work environment.

Sirkiä propelled us to our destination.

"Ain't nothin' here."

I opened the ambulance door, and it hit the dimwitted Räikkönen boy right on the forehead. He let out a shriek. He was sitting on the ground wearing track pants, drooling what looked like swamp water. I yelled at him, "Whaddya sittin' there for, dumbass, we almost ran you over."

He started to howl. We could've put him on top of the ambulance, and he would've had a secure job as the siren until retirement age. I looked at Sirkiä, who was hiccupping, "Goddammit, goddammit."

"Now what?"

"Goddammit. I didn't see that little kid at all."

"He ain't that little, he just looks young because his head's not screwed on tight."

"Goddammit."

Sirkiä leaned his head on the steering wheel and hiccupped. He kept at it for a while until he finally killed the hiccups with some deep breaths. He shut off the engine and turned to get out of the ambulance. The front of his pants folded in such a way that you could tell he had quite a schlong, unless it was just a fold. I had to find out. I grabbed Sirkiä by the shoulder and cleared my throat.

"You're probably fuckin' my *spouse*."

3. Sara Skinner

I'm walking through the woods. The path splits the woods in two. Grandma says spring will be here soon.

Which part of the woods is spring?

When spring's over, and then when summer's over, I'll get to go to school. I'll get a backpack. I want a yellow backpack.

I'm walking along the path.

The trees have spread their roots onto the path. Roots are a tree's legs.

How does a tree limp?

I'm not going to the pond. I'm not allowed to go there.

Petteri from preschool went to the pond and sank. Grown-ups pulled him out, but he was completely filled with water.

If a boy gets filled up with water, he drowns. Petteri drowned.

I look at the sky. It's a bird's woods.

Right then a tree trips me and I fall. I rip the tree's skin off in revenge.

Dad said "sock" when my uncle asked what was on his foot. That was the wrong answer. Dad's foot was sore. Now it's not sore anymore.

I feel my foot. It's not sore even though the tree tripped me.

I have a green sock on my foot. My other foot has a green sock on it, too.

I'm not going to the pond. You get filled up with water there.

I start laughing. I fall even though the tree doesn't trip me.

I don't laugh long. Mom took Jonna to the doctor. Jonna's face was covered with spots. Her cheeks and ears and chins and noses. Even though she only has one nose.

I laugh a lot when Jonna comes back from the doctor. We laugh a lot when we spin around. We spin around even though we don't look for the pond.

I'm getting new shoes for school. If the shoes are brown and black, then they'll be like tree roots.

Then my legs get mixed in the tree's legs.

But the roots aren't brown and black. I look closely at the root and I pet it. The tree leg isn't any color at all. The tree leg doesn't have its own color.

The tree must be sad. Its leg doesn't have its own color.

I hug the tree and say "It's okay." The tree doesn't say anything. The tree says something, but in tree language.

I wonder where the mouth is on a tree.

It's so high up you can't hear it when it talks. If you grew really tall, it still wouldn't matter. You still wouldn't understand tree language even if you heard it speak.

Vertti lives at the end of the trail. Vertti is nice, but so childish.

Vertti is big and he's really messy. He drools all the time. He's much bigger than me. He's almost twice as big as Jonna.

He's as fat as a teddy bear.

Vertti is so childish. You can't pretend to slap him. He starts to cry. He cries for a really long time.

If you give him candy, he stops right away. We don't always have candy.

Once he ate all of Jonna's candy. Jonna cried. And then Vertti started to cry, even though he was the one that ate it all.

But he is nice. He can play for a long time. I like that his mom doesn't call him in to eat. Jonna's and my mom always calls us in.

Even if you forget to go in and eat, Mom calls us in again. She can keep calling for a long time.

My dad doesn't like Vertti's dad.

Vertti's dad smells bad. He smokes. Dad doesn't smoke. Sometimes late at night, when we have grown-ups over, I wake up by accident. They have cigarettes with them.

Once, Dad was going to say something, but then Mom interrupted, "Esa." Then Dad said, "Let's just say that Vertti's dad and I don't French kiss each other."

They're not really friends.

Vertti is our neighbor. In apartment buildings, neighbors are close. You don't have to go all the way outside when you go to the neighbor's.

Maire lives in an apartment building.

It's good that Vertti is our neighbor instead of Maire.

Maire's mom is my mom's sister. Just like Jonna.

My babies will then play with Jonna's babies.

Maire's mom once asked who are Sara's friends. Who are Sara's friends?

I didn't know.

Maire's mom then asked if Maire was Sara's friend.

I said, "Let's just say we don't French kiss each other."

Dad came home from work. Mom said she was so ashamed.

What's a French kiss?

Dad took me in his lap and said, "Daddy's girl, Daddy's girl." Dad gave me a euro. "And Daddy's girl won't tell Mom," Dad whispered. His breath was so hot it tickled my ear.

Vertti's dad drinks beer, too.

I'm walking toward Vertti's house. The pond is on the same side as the arm that doesn't have a watch on it.

I'll learn how to tell time in school. I already know what time it is when the hands are both pointing straight up and are on top of each other.

They're not doing that yet.

Vertti will for sure be able to come out and play. Vertti's grandma never says no.

Vertti's mom is never at home. She's been home once, or I don't remember how many times.

Vertti's mom is pretty. She wears beautiful makeup.

Mom got mad when I asked her why she doesn't wear beautiful makeup.

"Like Vertti's mom does?" Mom said angrily.

I heard Mom say to Dad that Vertti's mom is a whore. Whores wear beautiful makeup.

Maire's mom is a little bit of a whore.

Will Maire become a little bit of a whore when she grows up? I won't.

Now the pond is behind me. From the other side of the hill you can't see the pond at all. I didn't get filled up with water.

There's a curve in the path. Dad doesn't know why paths have curves.

I could say to Vertti, for example, "Come to that curve."

Curves must be different from each other.

I'm at the curve. Walking along a curve doesn't make me dizzy at all. Why not?

There's a man lying on the path. I'm a little afraid of him.

The man isn't moving at all. How can I get past him?

The man is sleeping differently than Dad. Dad always makes terrible noises.

The man doesn't move even when I yell. The man is wearing Vertti's dad's jacket. If it is Vertti's dad, then why doesn't he go home to sleep? He gives Vertti green candy.

I have to get close to see if he smells like Vertti's dad. Up close he doesn't smell like anything at all.

I nudge the man's shoulder like I do with Dad. He's a big sleeper. I nudge the man's shoulder and he turns a little bit.

The man has a big owie on his head. The man isn't crying at all.

4. Laina Räikkönen

It sure is flattering. I called Teddy Bear immediately after Marzipan left for town. I just wanted to talk, but right away he started begging to come over to visit. We call doing it "visiting." I told him that Marzipan had been so restless, going back and forth between here and town, that there was no guarantee that the monkey's ass wouldn't pop through the window right when we were "visiting."

Teddy Bear said he'd come in the evening, or maybe later that night. He figured Marzipan would pass out at some point. Marzipan had only slept an hour or two a night over the last few days or weeks, and even then it was at some bar. I guess a grown man knows what he's doing.

Marzipan left in the afternoon. Before his farting moped rattled past the curve in the road, he bellowed out, "When are you gonna move out of my place, you slut?" He thought I was making a big mistake if I thought I could live for free at his house until the judge declared the divorce final. I reminded him of the two grand I'd given him when he bought out his mother's share of the cottage. "Can you prove it?" he began. I didn't respond, since I could tell he was in a mood.

All day he had gone back and forth to town. A few times he tried to catch me off guard by turning off his moped down the road and walking it into the yard. He'd bolt into the cottage or the shed in the back. Mr. Empty Pants suspected something. One time he burst into the shed in a fury, and the cat startled him. He fell flat on his backside while the cat ran off. I laughed so hard, saying, "Has the man of the house noticed any tomcats hanging around?" He almost hit me, and then headed back to town.

At three in the morning he returned, a bit calmer. He smelled like soap, but not like our soap.

I was lying in bed, my heart thumping, because Teddy Bear had come through the woods fifteen minutes earlier and was waiting in the dark outside the window. Marzipan called a few people. I knew he wasn't calling the same person every time because I heard him introduce himself. At five in the morning he started to get tired.

It sure is flattering—having a young cock standing outside my window, waiting in the dark for the husband to fall asleep and the wife to get wet. It's flattering indeed. He's fifteen years younger than me, and eighteen years younger than Marzipan. I can barely fit his balls into the palm of my hand.

I told Marzipan to get some sleep so everyone else could too before dawn broke. I said it nicely. Apparently not nicely enough, though, since Marzipan asked me if he should put me to sleep for a really long time. I'd cracked the window open, and I got really nervous because I knew that Teddy Bear could hear us. Something rustled outside the window. Marzipan got up and looked out. I couldn't get a word out of my mouth— I was wet all over but my mouth was dry. The phone rang. Marzipan answered it, blurted out something, then sat down and spoke more calmly. When he put the phone down, he was shaking his head, thinking about something. He didn't go back to the window, he'd forgotten about it.

At 6:12 he fell asleep. I could see the quivering red digits in the dark.

He started to snore. Teddy Bear rapped softly on the window. I shushed him to stop.

At seven, I got up and walked into the living room, where my mother-in-law and Vertti slept. Vertti was slobbering all over his pillow. My mother-in-law was breathing deeply and chomping on something in her sleep.

I crept back into the bedroom. Marzipan was snoring like a platoon of soldiers.

I tiptoed into the bathroom, as if on pieces of broken glass, and wet down several wads of toilet paper. I wiped my face, my breasts, my armpits, and my crotch, which I really rubbed down. I didn't dare get into the shower, too noisy. I drank some water from the palm of my hand.

I checked once more to make sure everyone was asleep and silently opened the front door. Oiling the door hinges was the only chore Marzipan had managed to do the entire winter, and that was only after I kept nagging at him.

It made me laugh to think he had no idea why it was so important to me to keep them oiled. I slid into my slippers.

Teddy Bear appeared from behind the corner, and walked to the bottom of the steps. I had a long coat wrapped over my nightgown and slippers on my feet. In the dark I was shaking, but not from the cold. I went down to the second step from the bottom so that I was as tall as Teddy Bear.

He had a sheepskin coat on. He smelled like an animal, every last bit of him.

I asked if he was cold.

"We can use this as a cushion so the wood shavings don't poke you in the ass," he said.

I shoved the palm of my hand into his crotch and grabbed him through his jeans. He'd told me that he liked that. Girls his age wanted to first stroke his cheeks, hair, and neck, while faking heavy breathing.

"Let's go," he ordered me.

Crazy as I was, I went with him. He pulled me by the hand, and I wondered whether fucking his boss' wife made it hotter for him. I didn't mind if it did.

The shed door creaked as we walked in. Teddy Bear knew to stoop down under the saw hanging in the doorway. Marzipan had ordered him to chop wood for us last week, and he'd left a big pile of wood shavings on the floor along with some birch bark.

"A bed for us," he said, took off his coat, and threw it on the ground. He yanked his pants off in a single motion. I got goose bumps from seeing his briefs—even in the dark I could see the arc of his shaft. He remembered how I'd admired the briefs on that model in the magazine ad. He's a golden boy, my Teddy Bear.

He grabbed me as if he were grabbing life itself.

He was fresh shaven and his cheeks were like warm apples. I could still smell the shaving cream. I could've eaten his cheeks—both his face and his fuzz-covered butt.

I thrust my hand into his briefs and with a single squeeze he was completely hard. He wanted to get on top of me, and he shoved his fingers between my legs. I stroked the tip of his member with my forefinger and thumb before I lay down and let him get on top of me. He shuddered when he entered me, his nipples hard as plum pits.

He came quickly. As confused as always, he apologized and wondered how it could've happened. I patted his stomach, knowing that soon he'd be interested again, and then I'd get what I was looking for, too. I guess I dozed off for a bit.

Teddy Bear asked if he should do something— Marzipan had sounded serious.

"What?" I asked. He sat me up, sat behind me and squeezed my breasts, moaning into my ear, "What should we do about Marzipan?" I could feel his tool getting hard against the small of my back. He slowly lowered himself onto his back, and I got on top of him. I got to ride a couple of times before there was a thud at the door.

Teddy Bear pulled out, squeezed it in his fist and looked at me with eyes wide open. I burst out laughing when I heard the forlorn mewing of the damn cat.

"What?" he whispered.

"It's the cat," I laughed.

He was so scared he turned away and got soft. I scolded him for it. We sat side by side with our faces toward the door. Between the wide gaps in the slats in the door, we could see that morning had already broken.

I grabbed onto Teddy Bear's knee when I saw Marzipan between the slats, walking toward us. He stopped abruptly ten steps short of the shed. I felt he was looking right into my eyes, all the way through them and out the back of my head.

"Fuck," Marzipan bellowed. It was a big scream for a small morning.

"He knows, he knows, dammit, he knows," Teddy Bear whimpered and looked for something in his sheepskin coat. He had a hard time finding it, because he was lying on the ground.

"It's the cat, he's cursing at the cat," I whispered. "He hates that thing."

Marzipan stood still for a moment and then headed for the woods. Teddy Bear got his nerve back. Agitated, he asked what he should do, should he be a real man and bump off Marzipan, who was threatening his woman?

I said, "I'm still his wife."

"Only on paper," he said.

I got up and threw my coat on, wanting to get back to the cottage before Marzipan returned. The door squeaked; the cat wasn't anywhere to be seen.

In front of the shed, two slippers were lying on the snow-splotched grass.

"A grown man knows what he's doing," I said.

5. Aarne Sirkiä, Ambulance Driver

We arrive at the scene and Toikka grabs me by the shoulder.

"You probably forgot the *pouches*?"

He's always thinking about them, always mumbling about them. Toikka's hard to work with—he's a difficult person. I don't know anyone who likes to work with him, have a beer with him, or go anywhere with him. Not even his wife.

He always mumbles. It irritates me.

I push his hand off my shoulder. "I didn't forget."

"What?"

"Nothin'. I didn't forget nothin'."

"You're fucking with me."

I jump out of the ambulance and go around to the other side. The Räikkönen boy I nearly ran over is rubbing his head where the door hit him. He looks at me, surprised.

"You alright? You didn't get hurt badly, did you?" I say, fussing over him.

Toikka slams his door shut and stares at me.

"There ain't nothin' here."

Toikka scares the boy with his bellowing, and he starts wailing.

I ask the boy if anyone's hurt. We'll take anyone who's hurt to the doctor. The boy looks at me, confused. He ain't gonna talk as long as he's wailing.

I walk to the house. Toikka follows me, walking around the boy like he's avoiding getting shit on his shoes. The boy stops screaming.

An old lady comes out on the porch to meet us and asks if we've seen the cat.

"Someone called for an ambulance."

"Where's Sonny? Where's Sonny?"

"He's over there next to the ambulance."

"We didn't call for anything."

"Yeah, you did."

Toikka says he's gonna have a smoke, and does so. I tell him he sure picks a fine time to light up, dammit, on a job before we even find the customer. Toikka puts out his cigarette and gives me an angry look.

"You're fuckin' with me."

"No. I ain't got time for that."

"Where's Sonny?" the old lady asks.

"By the ambulance. He's playing there…eatin' candy."

"Sonny's a cat," she snaps.

I really feel like smoking. I ask once again, "Did someone here call for an ambulance or not? We've gotta know if we're needed here. Someone might be dyin' somewhere else, as we speak."

"No one here's dying."

The woman startles me when, out of the blue, she starts hollering for her cat, "Kitty-kitty, sonnysonny, come here kiiitty-kitty."

I walk back to the ambulance and check the address with Dispatch. They tell me that the call was made by a little girl. Sara Skinner, six years old, is how she had introduced herself.

"She said something about the Räikkönens and a pond and a trail. Look around now, use your brains," the dispatch operator moans.

"I'm with Toikka."

"Okay then," says Dispatch, ending the call.

The old woman spins around in circles, screaming for her cat. Toikka pivots in place, watching her. I try to talk to her, to get her to stop, but she's too fast. I grab her by the hand, and she stops.

"Where's the pond around here? Where's the trail?"

She points to the dense woods.

"The trail starts by the shed," the old lady says.

"Thanks."

"Let's get the stretcher," I say to Toikka, who bows to me submissively. There's always something bugging him. He was born with something bugging him.

Toikka says, "We're carryin' the stretcher for nothin'. Let's find somethin' to put on it first."

His own words surprise him.

He agrees to carry the stretcher anyway. The trail winds through the woods, roots crisscrossing it. I walk in front and Toikka deliberately pushes the stretcher into me. I don't say anything.

Toikka says there's nothing here and wants to turn back. He thinks I've got the address wrong, and they'll be laughing at us at the hospital.

"At you, not us."

"What?"

"Just carry it. That's what you get paid for, ain't it."

He was staring at my crotch the whole time we were in the ambulance. I wonder if he's gay. His wife told me that sometimes she's afraid of him. A couple of times she's woken up to him standing at the foot of the bed in the dark. Once he had a knife in his hand. He said he was on his way to make a sandwich, and then went back to the kitchen, and returned with a stack of rye crisps. He got crumbs all over the bed, and she couldn't sleep for the rest of the night.

I told her I wouldn't be able to sleep after something like that either, but I wouldn't blame the rye crisp crumbs.

"Who makes a sandwich that time of night?" I wondered.

"What?" Toikka asked.

"Nothin'."

"What sandwich?"

"You know; the sandwiches they make in porn movies? There's a woman and two men and…"

"Yeah, yeah…"

24

"I was just wonderin' why you were thinkin' about that."

"I just was."

"Why is it that you always think about sex when we're out on a job?"

"Toikka."

"What?"

"You sure are an odd guy."

"You sayin' I'm gay?"

"No."

"Who is then?"

"Nobody."

"Why are you goin' on and on about it, then?"

"I'm not."

"Yeah you are, and you do it all the time."

"Knock it off."

"Does my wife say I'm gay? Fuck if she does."

"No, she doesn't."

"You had a spot on your lap."

"Yeah, I did."

"You don't believe me."

"Yeah, I do."

"The hell you do."

Around the corner there's a man lying on the ground, with a halo-shaped pool of blood around his head. He looks dead. I stoop down next to him. The back of his head is bone soup, but his eyes are open.

He tries to say something. He's stammering, and I can't understand what he's saying.

"Fuck," Toikka says.

Standing farther away, he recognizes the man as Marzipan, and predicts that this is the end of Marzipan's criminal activities. His eyes light up, and he laughs and laughs. Just before we lower the stretcher to the ground, he kicks it, without making any move to lift Marzipan onto it.

"He's alive."

"Then let's wait a while."

"Eat shit, Toikka."

"The shit's lying right there. How do you know him?"

"He's fucked your wife, too."

The kick hits me in the side, cracking my ribs.

6. Sakke Löysä

I dunno what woke me up. Then it dawned on me I'd been sleeping with my ear folded over, and it stung like hell.

My pillow was wet.

I pulled my pants on and stepped into my boots. I was gonna push through the day no matter what.

I got some red soda from the fridge, gulped it down, and burped so loud that the stupid fridge light went out.

"Pig," Pop complained from the living room.

Mom came in to take a look at me.

"Ya gettin' something to eat?" she asked.

"The boy eats too much!" Pop yelled.

I walked into the living room, trying to keep my cool as the old man watched tennis on satellite TV.

"Millionaires slammin' a ball back and forth in the blazin' sun."

"Sabatini has a nice ass."

"What does the old man care about asses?" Mom quipped, looking in from the kitchen. She was gnawing away at a piece of cheese that she had cut with a small, sharp knife.

"I'm goin' into town."

"For booze," Pop snorted, taking a jab at his son.

"To see about work."

"More like watch other people work."

"Ain't gonna be home for supper."

"It ain't that hard to look at work when it ain't you bustin' your ass."

I went into my room and threw a sock at my Madonna poster. The radio was humming.

Suddenly I remembered.

I'd woken up to a call on the police radio. Kääpä Street 13. It was Marzipan's address.

That got the fire under me. I snuck into the hallway to make a call.

"Now the fathead's listenin' to work," Pop yelled from the living room.

I got a hold of Ansalanka and told him about the call on the police radio. It was tricky, talking over my old man and tennis, while making sure Mom didn't hear. I knew she was always listening.

Ansalanka cursed and said he'd pick me up.

"Got the key?" he crowed, as I was about to hang up.

"Yup," I said.

I put my jacket on.

"Your hat, too, it'll be cold tonight," Mom advised.

"I'm twenty-three."

"And it's ten below outside."

"Don't give him the key if he won't wear a darn hat," my old man yelled.

I relented and put the hat on. I had to give Mom a hug, the way she grabbed onto me and looked at me with such sad eyes.

I wondered if my old man had heard us talking about the key, but it was Ansalanka who said it, not me. The old man couldn't have heard it.

I jumped up and down in front of the house to calm my nerves until Ansalanka's delivery truck clanged and clattered into view.

I hopped in and Ansalanka stepped on the gas. He looked at me with his head tilted and spun the steering wheel around, his eyes ignoring the road.

"Does this thing rattle a lot?"

"Yeah. You can hear it all the way to the moon."

"Fuck. It's always something."

"Let's take care of this Marzipan thing first."

"But fuck, it's always something. Last week the exhaust pipe fell off in the driveway."

"Level the driveway, then."

"Fuck, I woke up in the middle of the night. I went to get a drink of milk and checked out the truck from my window to make sure nobody had kicked it. The streetlight shines right on it. Fuck. It was really quiet, couldn't hear a thing. Fuck. I was just watching the truck; you could see the back end of it from my window, and boom. The fucking exhaust pipe just fell on the ground."

"The metal wore out."

"Well, I'm worn out, too."

Ansalanka went on for a while about how exhausted he was. He finally shut up when I said we had other things to do besides bullshit. That offended him.

I told him that while he was out of town the last few weeks, Marzipan had been crazy as a loon. He was freaking out about everything and said that he was on the outs with the Russians.

I saw him one day at the bar, and he pleaded with me to understand that it ain't smart to fuck the Russians.

That's all he said, because a woman who people say is religious came up to the table, and Marzipan left with her.

"Fuck no," Ansalanka doubted me.

"Fuck yeah."

"Good-looking?"

"She looked like a real woman."

"Religious ones rarely are."

"You would know."

I told him I woke up to the police radio: a call to Marzipan's address. They ain't bringing him a birthday cake.

"It's his birthday?"

"Wouldn't matter if it was."

Marzipan had been so restless I was afraid he'd spill it all to the cops just out of pure exhaustion and booze.

"That's what this gig is about," I told Ansalanka.

"Dammit," Ansalanka said, finally putting it all together.

"Where are we gonna take them?"

"I dunno."

After we crossed the intersection he figured it out.

"We can't fucking bring them to my place, fuck no."

"Where then?"

"Not to my fucking place."

"Your dad's too old, you've said so yourself, he ain't gonna go to the cabin anymore."

"I dunno about that. Old folks can surprise you and perk up."

"Dammit, Ansalanka. He's connected to a tube in the hospital. Accept it, dammit."

"He's gonna leave me out of the will."

"No, he won't."

"Yeah, he will. He threatened to."

"You can't do that in Finland. You always get your share. You're a direct heir, dammit."

"I'm his son."

"A son is a direct heir. You're the only son. You'll get everything. Elsi's only a girlfriend, dammit. Legally, girlfriends don't inherit a thing."

"Dad calls her his half-wife."

"To me, he calls her a cow."

Ansalanka laughed. He wasn't capable of worrying about two things at once. We drove to the apartment complex parking lot. Marzipan had rented a garage there.

The kids in the yard loved it when Ansalanka maneuvered the big old truck back and forth trying to back it up right in front of the garage. The last thing we needed was a big audience—these little devils didn't even bother going to school.

Ansalanka got a little anxious again. "One of the wheels is probably gonna fall off," he cursed, "Damn if one hasn't fallen off already."

I got out of the truck and cursed at the kids to get them to move out of the way. They pointed at me and Ansalanka, taunting, "Nyah nyah nyah nyah nyah nyaaah."

"What a loooser, what a loooser, how's loser boy?" they started shouting at Ansalanka, who was smaller and friendlier than me. Ansalanka told the kids that his name was Aulis Moisander.

I walked up to the garage door to open it and saw a bike chained to the back bumper of the truck.

7. Police Officer
Jussi "Rosebush" Rosenström

When we arrived, the two idiots were in the middle of a fight. I could hear the thudding of their punches. One of them was Toikka. He lived in my building. Sometimes I'd see him in the courtyard, sometimes out on a job. It looked like he was winning, but his opponent was giving him a run for his money.

Mauri's jaw dropped—he cursed and asked why we always got the shitty jobs. He'd never heard of ambulance drivers coming to blows alongside a dead body. I hadn't either.

Toikka got hit on the cheekbone so hard that it snapped—half of his face would be swollen over by the end of the day. Toikka swayed, but didn't tip over. He shook his head, and big droplets of blood fell from his nose onto his white coat. The other guy was crouching and rocking back and forth, holding his side from time to time. He went after Toikka's neck with his right; Toikka clamped his jaw down onto his shoulder, and the other guy kicked Toikka in the groin. Toikka froze, but grabbed the guy's ankle and yanked him to the ground, plunging his knee into the guy's stomach.

Mauri pounced on Toikka, and locked him in a full nelson. Toikka shook his head angrily, and asked if he could please knock the teeth out of the shithead's mouth before Mauri ended the fight.

"Just kinda off the record," Toikka panted.

Mauri threatened to shoot Toikka unless he calmed down. He pulled his pistol out of the holster and shoved it in Toikka's ear. That did the trick.

"What the hell kind of ambulance drivers are you guys?" Mauri hollered.

I could see he was livid.

The other guy got up off the ground, rubbing his ankle. He looked to the right and swung with his left, hitting Toikka square on the nose. I'd never seen such a slick move before. Toikka slumped to the ground. The front of his jacket was now more red than white.

"Sirkiä," the guy said, extending his hand.

We shook hands.

Mauri ignored Sirkiä's outstretched hand and went over to check on the corpse.

"Tsk, tsk, tsk," he frowned and moved farther away to talk on his walkie-talkie.

He came back and said he'd called another ambulance and, more importantly, new drivers.

"I can drive," Sirkiä said.

"You'll be lucky if you drive a cartload of shit after all this," Mauri threatened.

Sirkiä said that driving cartloads of shit would be a promotion compared to working with Toikka, since shit doesn't talk.

Toikka lay still on the ground. It looked like he'd lost consciousness.

Mauri was examining the body, and Sirkiä said it was Marzipan. Mauri bent over again for a closer look, and confirmed that Sirkiä was right—the man was Marzipan.

"He was alive a moment ago."

"Until you guys found something more important to do."

Sirkiä went over to check Marzipan and declared that he was still alive. He apologized for what had happened, grimacing with each breath. I told him I figured his ribs were broken. Sirkiä asked if he could make up for what had happened.

Mauri asked how the fuck he thought he could make up for it when the patient died while two ambulance drivers were fighting.

"He ain't dead."

Sirkiä tried to grab hold of Marzipan, but Mauri shooed him away, fearing that Sirkiä would cause even greater harm. We lifted Marzipan onto the stretcher and carried him to the ambulance.

A woman came running from the direction of the pond and suddenly screamed.

Mauri stepped in front of the woman, raising his arm, ready to slap her if necessary. The woman stopped, and said she was done screaming, yet kept on screaming that she wasn't hysterical.

Since Mauri looked rather menacing, the woman approached me. She said she'd just gotten home. Her daughter had told her that something bad had happened to some man. She kept talking about some man.

The woman had called the emergency number. While she was on the phone, three men burst out of the woods into her yard, arguing loudly. They ran across the yard and stole the Volga, which they must've seen through the open garage door.

"Esa collects old cars. Fixes them up."

"Was it fixed up?"

"Yeah. But the brakes are pretty much gone."

"Oh, fucking shit," Mauri said, losing it and dropping his hand. He suggested we wait here for even more people to show up to report more murders and thefts. "Just so it doesn't get too peaceful around here," Mauri said. He was all worked up. A religious man, he rarely cussed.

The woman said the men seemed suspicious, because they came out of the dense woods with wet shoes and dirty clothes, despite the perfectly fine trail through the woods. The woman went silent, but kept her distance from Mauri.

"Yeah, and of course there was the car theft," the woman said softly.

We could hear the wailing of the ambulance. Mauri and I half-jogged with the stretcher to the Räikkönens'

34

yard. Sirkiä asked if he could do anything useful.

"Don't hit anyone," Mauri said, getting a better grip on the stretcher.

Sirkiä took off his jacket and shirt, huffing and puffing. One of his ribs looked nasty, sticking out, almost breaking through the skin. The woman stared at him and started to scream.

"Slap her," I said to Sirkiä.

Trying to keep a serious face, he said "But the officer just told me not hit anyone."

Mauri and I jogged into the yard. The ambulance arrived just as we lowered the stretcher to the ground. Marzipan was lying on his stomach. It seemed wrong to have the messed-up back of his head touching the stretcher.

"What's going on here?" the driver said, getting out of the vehicle.

"You tell me, you're the expert," Mauri said.

"I just drive."

"He's been killed. Marzipan's been murdered."

The man stood there, staring at Mauri. Having just moved from Tornio, he didn't understand that Marzipan was a first name. He was just learning the local dialect.

His partner came to help lift Marzipan into the ambulance. Mauri called Dispatch to report that we were now dealing with a murder, and asked for more men.

"What the fuck are you moving the body for, if he's been murdered?" the dispatch operator shrieked.

"The corpse is still breathing."

"Okay, gotcha."

Mauri ordered the dispatch operator to look up the license plate number of the car owned by a certain Esa, who lives next door to the Räikkönens. Patrols had to be careful when pulling the car over, because the men in it were suspects in a homicide case.

"Does this Esa have a last name?"

"Yes, but I don't know what it is."

"Oh, you don't, huh? With this much information, it'll only take me a few years to figure it out."

The dispatch operator hung up. Mauri cursed. That asshole had never carried a single wino to the drunk tank, yet he'd gladly fuck with a seasoned policeman over the radio waves.

I saw Marzipan's mother sitting on the steps with her cat in her lap.

Mauri could see where I was looking and nodded to me. He didn't want to deliver the news. He never did.

I walked to the bottom of the steps and introduced myself.

"Are you Jalmari Rosenström's son?"

"No. Ernest Rosenström's."

"Is that Jalmari's brother?"

"Yes."

"I danced with him in the fifties."

"Ah, um…"

"In Ounasvaara."

"I have some bad news to tell you."

"My son is dead."

"Yes… How did you know?"

Marzipan's mother told me how the week before the sun had shone through the window and projected the window frame onto her son's face in the shape of a cross. He hadn't noticed it. That's how the mother knew.

I told her I was sorry for her loss. I suspected that even though it was a difficult day, we'd undoubtedly have to ask her some questions later.

"Was my son killed?"

"Unfortunately, that seems to be the case."

"May the Lord forgive his killer."

I told her I wished the same, though for someone in my profession, it was difficult to relate to murderers compassionately. She said she understood that.

The cat had a fiery look in its eyes.

8. Sarlotta Root, Housewife

Pentti's nose started to drip, of course. When one of them gets a cold, they all do. A cold in our house lasts for a good five weeks. Pauli gets it first, then Pentti, then Laura, all before Auvo has to miss work, blaming us for his watery eyes, and then I start sneezing. But I don't get sick leave from all this. My God, sometimes I'd like to walk away from this house and lay in the hospital for a week. I'd even be happy to head out to the snow-filled woods to chop wood, and let my nose fill with snot, if only I could get away, even for a moment. Then after six weeks, Pauli starts complaining of a sore throat or an ear ache. Pentti's two years old, Pauli three, Laura four: too big of a forest for any lumberjack.

I love Auvo. He's a good man. I think it's so sweet when I see him playing with the children on a Saturday night, when he's finally managed to put aside the paperwork for his construction company. Pauli and Pentti look so much like their father that if there were ever any question, the judge wouldn't even bother ordering a DNA test. Pauli and Pentti are beautiful boys, but in my eyes they're also funny-looking. I see their faces as miniature versions of their father's, and Auvo's face requires a big canvas and a big palette. Laura got her features and personality from me. In our family portraits, we look like such a perfect little family that it's almost surreal.

Pentti's crying. Pauli digs out Pentti's snot with his finger and wipes it on Pentti's clothes. Laura hits Pauli in the head with a big hammer just as I'm rushing into the kids' room, and my heart stops. I laugh when I realize that Laura's thumped him with a toy sledgehammer that Auvo painted to look real. Pauli's startled by my sudden charge into the room and decides that the toy sledgehammer hurt after all, and he starts to bawl. Then Pentti has to cry even louder. He's the smartest of my children, and I realize that he's worried that his snot, the original cause of his distress, is in danger of drying up. Laura starts to cry too, because it seems like the most popular thing to do this morning. This happens a lot. Laura likes to cry as a hobby, not for any reason at all. If Auvo and I die before the children grow up, I know that Laura will take care of the boys and herself. I don't doubt it for a second.

I restore peace in our house. I wipe Pentti's nose—his skin will be raw by tomorrow at the latest, unless I remember to buy super-soft tissues. Our family doesn't save trees. I'm sure that in four years we've blown large holes into Finland's forests. I go back into the living room and slowly read a soft porn book by some French poet. It's my candy. When I'm lying on the living room sofa and the kids are making noise in their room, I feel like I'm free. It makes me feel dizzy. Three children tie you down tighter than a ship's anchor.

I have to put the book down in my lap. In a good place. I ponder once again whether I'd survive if I had more children. They'd come every year, because Auvo's a Laestadian. I have nothing against Auvo's faith—on the contrary. He doesn't drink, he's a decent man, and it feels really good compared to the situation I grew up in. My father's a tragic case, a bum, and my brother's a pig, a criminal. I love it when Auvo gets up early on his rare days off, makes coffee and oatmeal, and squeezes fresh orange juice. I know I'll never have to go out and fetch booze on a cold, frosty morning like I had to for my dad or my brother, until I refused to do it. In bed Auvo's affectionate and eager, because liquor and tobacco haven't dampened his sex drive.

We have an unspoken agreement that I go to services when I want. I don't have to act like some fervent daughter of Jesus, although on paper I'm Laestadian. My brother's mouthed off about it many times; he's hurt me so much that it's made my eyes sting. Auvo was raised in his faith, and he can't imagine life any other way. He makes crass jokes at work—you have to if you want to succeed in the construction business—but his heart isn't in it. He looked so wonderfully embarrassed once when I went to see him at a site near our home. I heard him yell out to one of his painters, Milla, who was carrying a can of paint in her arms, "Where are you taking those three big jugs?" She just laughed, but when Auvo saw that I'd heard it, he got so uncomfortable I had to kiss him through Pauli. Auvo can't kiss me in public. To him it's an insurmountable obstacle.

Auvo doesn't force his religion on anyone, but he can't understand what's so fun about going to some bar on a Friday night when the alternative is playing with the kids, taking a sauna, and romping with his wife. Auvo didn't mention the last part when he was talking about it once, but I know my shy husband.

I couldn't handle any more children—I'm just not up to it. But I can't talk to Auvo about it. That's where he draws the line. Children are gifts from God, and you accept as many of them as God sees fit to give you. Period. That's why I haven't told Auvo that I've made an appointment with a gynecologist, Inkeri's husband. She promised to mention to him that I want to get my tubes tied. I have enough work with these three. Auvo's God said to go forth and multiply, but He didn't mean that Sarlotta Root and her husband had to do it all by themselves. I'm not going to tell Auvo about it. He'll have to be happy to have the three. Pauli's screaming.

I put the book down on the table. I can feel myself snap; I run into their room and scream "QUIET" so loudly that the children jump. My heart aches as they huddle together because Mom's being naughty. They're completely silent. No one in our family yells, except for the children, except for the children. The kids start to cry timidly. I scoop them all up in my arms and calm them down, and blow into their hair that smells like babies. Is that the phone ringing?

I get up and go to the doorway with Laura in my arms; yes, it's the phone. I put Laura on the floor and tell her to give her brothers kisses, because they're feeling bad.

"Isses," Laura says.

I lift the receiver, and I know before she even speaks that it's Mom calling. She has an old phone that has a distinctive hum.

"I have some bad news."

"Dad?"

"Your brother."

"Which one?"

"Your big brother."

"Thank God."

Mom takes a breath. I can hear how her dentures move in her mouth. She moves them around when she's nervous. She asks breathlessly what kind of person I am and what kind of believer I am. Am I thanking the Lord for my brother's death?

"I'm thankful that Ensio is alive."

"It didn't sound like that."

"Mom. My condolences."

"Thank you. You're not grieving?"

"Come on now. Are you okay?"

"Don't worry about me."

"Of course I worry about you."

We're quiet for a moment, and I ask when my brother died. In the morning, this morning, just now, Mom says. She tells me that there's a police detective with a last name that starts with an 'N' at her place asking all kinds of questions.

"His stomach is rumbling horribly," Mom says.

I know that's one of her great amusements, but I don't say anything.

"Was it his liver?"

"Your brother was killed."

"Of course he was."

"Sarlotta. Is that how a sister talks about her deceased brother?"

"His liver or a knife. I've known for fifteen years it would be one or the other."

Mom moves her dentures around. The children come to witness the miracle of a phone conversation. "Who's calling?" Laura asks. "Tell Laura it's Grandma," Mom says. I tell them that Grandma and I have something important to talk about; please children, go back to your room. They go.

Mom asks, "Doesn't your brother's death mean anything more to you than your financial problems?" I say that there wouldn't be any financial problems if my brother hadn't created them. We had to pay the bank a ten-thousand-euro loan that we had guaranteed and Marzipan had defaulted on just at the time when nothing bigger than a playhouse was being built in the whole county. It bothers me, it bothers me so deeply that I remember we scraped together every penny and sold everything that could be sold.

"You made it through just fine," Mom said.

"Yeah, all by ourselves, all by ourselves."

Mom starts talking about the funeral. She doesn't understand, or she pretends not to understand, that she could've helped iron out the problems created by her son. Even a few hundred would've helped, if she didn't have any more than that, although I know she did. She always had enough money for my brother, even though everyone knew where the money went. Mom stops in the middle of thinking about what to offer the funeral guests.

"Did you go for a walk?"

"Every morning. Three miles."

"Where?"

"I've already lost ten pounds. What do you mean, where?"

"Did you go walking near our place?"

"Among other places, yes. Mostly in the woods. Why?"

Mom sighs.

"Your brother was found in the woods."

"So what?"

"Nothing."

"Goddammit, Mom!" I scream, "I can't imagine how any mother can first suspect her own daughter of her son's murder."

"If only you hadn't said it the other day."

"What?"

"That you were going to dig your brother's eyes out of his head."

"Well, were his eyes dug out of his head? Goddammit, it's a saying."

"His head was smashed to pieces."

"Goddammit."

"The police are asking everyone. This young man's been asking me things, and apparently his boss will be asking more."

"I'm coming over there. You're not going to discuss my walking routes with them."

"Come on over. This is really hard."

I hang up, and immediately call Inkeri. After a while, a man answers with a voice sounding like he just woke up. He says Inkeri's at work. I tell him what happened and ask if he can watch my children for an hour or two. He says he's leaving for work in an hour, says he's sorry, and gives his condolences. He explains he has to go tell an unmarried finance manager that she is indeed pregnant.

After a moment he suggests that his father-in-law could come watch the kids. "The man needs something to do," Inkeri's husband says. He promises his father-in-law will be there in a few minutes. I call for a taxi and get dressed.

I explain to Laura that Mom has to leave. I say that a nice man is coming to watch them.

"Laura will watch them herself," she says.

Laura asks why Mom's crying. I touch my cheeks, they're wet with tears. "Mom's just in a hurry," I say.

I hug the kids and go out front. The taxi comes. I get in the back seat and ask the driver to wait. When I see Inkeri's husband's car, a cream-colored Mercedes, turn into the driveway, I tell the driver the address. I wave to the Mercedes; two men wave back from the front seat.

Standing in front of Mom's house, I remember that I left the porn book on the coffee table.

9. Ossi Kaukonen

I saw a glimpse of the chick through the cabin window. Fuck, this to boot. My shoes were wet and my face was scratched up from the branches. I knew there couldn't possibly be bugs in this cold weather, yet it felt like they were all over the place.

Arkady mumbled something. His Finnish irritated the hell out of me—it would've pissed me off less if he'd just rattled on in Russian. I would've understood about as much of what he said—which was next to nothing. He swung his arms around violently, creating little breezes. He pointed to the garage, and when I walked closer I saw an old clunker in there. The car was so old it'd fall apart if anyone looked at it sideways. Arkady jumped in the front seat, splattering the inside of the windshield with his Finnish.

"What the fuck are you standin' there for, jump in!" Kassu yelled, shoving my shoulder.

"You!"

It was a fucking Volga. I guess a Russkie had to have a Russian beater; he must've found it by smell. I wasn't going to tell him that, though. Kassu pushed me and I pushed him back. Arkady grabbed me by the back of the neck and twisted me into the back seat. I swear his fingers were made of fucking metal.

My knees came up to my chin in the soft back seat. Arkady was messing around with the pedals, the steering wheel, and the gear shift. He was speaking some kind of mixture of Finnish and Russian.

"Hey, that dude…"

"Shuddup."

"Hey, that guy, was he…"

"Shuddup."

Arkady got the beater started, which was nothing short of a miracle. Shuddup, shuddup. That fucking accent! I knew Arkady was the fucking boss, but I wished I could get a gig with people who spoke my language.

Arkady and Kassu put their seatbelts on. I scrambled up to see, and yeah, believe it or not, this old clunker had seatbelts. None in the back, though. "Daddy, please drive careful now," I taunted. Neither of them said a word.

Arkady threw it in reverse and stepped on the gas. The car jumped backwards until the back bumper scraped the side of the garage door with a loud screech. Arkady yanked the steering wheel. He spun that piece of junk around pretty nicely—it felt like we were driving in the clouds, not hitting the ground at all.

I glanced at the porch, or whatever the hell they call it out here in the sticks. It had windows facing every direction. On the porch I saw the chick and waved at her. She looked nice. She had to have known how tough we were.

Arkady turned onto the road. The old beater jumped back and forth until Arkady got it under control, and then he floored it.

"Hey, that guy…"

"Shuddup."

"Fuck, I'm just asking…"

"Don't ask."

"Ossi, listen Kassu. Listen Kassu."

The Russian's horrible grammar made him sound stupid. Shit. He was such a dick. He rounded the corners like a race car driver and splattered gravel on the houses we passed. I remarked that this would get every fucking cop after us. Neither one said anything, but Arkady slowed down a bit.

Kassu started cursing softly. He was so smooth with his *fuck, goddammit,* and *motherfucker* that from the

45

tone of his voice you would've thought he was talking to a kid.

"What wrong?"

"Nothing. Let's go for a joyride."

"Zoyride. No understand."

It seemed to me like Arkady was driving around the gravel back roads of Viirinkangas in a big circle. In my opinion he wasn't the brightest bulb on the Christmas tree. I kept wondering if I should tell them about the chick that had spotted us. I figured she'd already called the cops if this was her clunker. It looked like she lived there. I told the guys about her.

Kassu immediately turned around and slapped me on both cheeks. He slaps pretty hard. He yelled so loud I could see his fucking liver through his mouth. Arkady instinctively drove faster, his head zigzagging between the road and Kassu. He kept hissing, "What wrong, what wrong, what the fuck wrong."

Kassu told him.

"Kill you."

"It ain't just me she saw. She saw everyone. Ain't my fuckin' fault."

"Kill you. Why the fuck no tell?"

"I did tell you."

"Kill you."

"I'll kill you, too. You fucking clown," Kassu said to me.

I was glad I was rolling around in the back seat where they couldn't pounce on me.

"If get caught. If get caught."

"What now?"

Arkady yelled, and his yelling got him so worked up that he drove even faster. He yelled that if we got caught, nobody would say a word. He hollered that he didn't have any doubts about Kassu, but if someone was gonna talk, he knew it'd be me. He said I'd end my time on this earth with a dick in my mouth, my own dick. He said that according to tradition, it would be cut off while I was still alive.

"The fuck I'll squeal. I never fuckin' have."

"You never know how it'll go."

"C'mon dudes. I ain't gonna fuckin' squeal."

Kassu said he believed me. He just finished saying we weren't caught yet when we heard sirens behind us. I turned to look, and goddammit, it was an ambulance. I told the front seat about it.

"Is it for that guy?"

"Shuddup."

I took a quick look at the ambulance. The guy riding shotgun flipped me off and shook his fist at me. Goddammit, where were his manners? Give them a fucking government vehicle and they think they own the road. What fucking losers!

Arkady raced away from the ambulance like he was running from the cops. Kassu yelled at him; he turned and almost hit a burger stand, and the ambulance flew past us. Arkady flipped a U-turn and went back the same way we came.

"Bad brakes."

Kassu started swearing again. We came to a wider road. I wasn't familiar with the area, but it seemed to me like Arkady was driving toward the city center.

"How the fuck are we gonna ditch the cops there?" I asked. Arkady told me to shut up. Kassu grabbed him by the shoulders and turned the steering wheel and we drove into someone's yard, the car slamming into a small cabin in the back.

We sat there stone quiet.

I saw three drops of sweat on the back of Arkady's neck before they disappeared under his collar.

Kassu was cursing.

Arkady was trying to figure out whether the old piece of junk was still alive. He jumped on the pedals so hard that the car rocked. It screeched and woke up.

47

Arkady coaxed the beater around to face the road.

Kassu said to him, "Don't, dammit, what are we gonna do on the road? Ain't it full of cops and ambulances, let's just hang out here." Arkady put the car in neutral.

Kassu got out of the car and picked the lock on the front door of the cabin. After what seemed like years, he came out and said the cabin was empty and we could stay there. Arkady wanted to know where he should park. The bright yellow paint job would be easy to spot from as far away as the fucking Kola Peninsula.

Arkady explained something at length to Kassu. He kept revving the engine so I couldn't hear them.

Kassu turned to me and ordered me to stay here. "Jump out," he said.

"What the fuck is this?"

"Just jump out."

"Guys, what the fuck is this?"

"Out."

"Why?"

"They're looking for three guys. Ain't gonna be but two after you jump out."

"I'll lie down on the floor."

A cop car passed us going a thousand miles an hour. Kassu said they saw us. Arkady swore in Russian. I didn't need a translator to know that.

He stepped on the gas and we got back on the road, flying like gangbusters in the opposite direction. I looked out the back window to see if they turned around to chase us, but I couldn't see around the curve.

Arkady was driving like a madman now.

Kassu was holding onto the dashboard with both hands. It seemed like Arkady was driving toward the center of town again; he didn't know these fucking backwoods any better than I did.

As we came to fucking Kemi Road, the spot where you turn toward downtown Rovaniemi, I banged Kassu on the shoulder. He tried to punch me.

Arkady was flying. We blew past a Nissan so fast we sideswiped its door panel. I saw the long scrape on the side of the Nissan just before it crashed into the ditch— the lady in the passenger seat grabbed her neck as it snapped back from the impact.

Kassu was startled, realizing what was happening.

He yelled, "Where are you taking us, damn Russkie?"

Arkady lost it. He shoved his hand into his breast pocket.

Kassu hit him on the cheek. Arkady's head banged against the side window.

He came to his senses, and screamed, "I turn to right, I turn to right." But he didn't slow down at all.

We all screamed at the top of our lungs. Then we heard the sirens again. None of us had realized how tight the curve was and Arkady should've slowed down if he wanted to turn right.

Where did that fucking ambulance come from?

Just before the curve Arkady hit the brakes, but the car didn't slow down until we were into the curve. We saw the ambulance heading fast as hell straight at us.

Arkady's late braking forced us to fly straight into the fucking oncoming traffic. The old beater turned and the left side headed straight into the ambulance.

In a split second the ambulance was huge.

I've never fucking been in an accident.

10. Detective Sergeant Osmo Nauris

The guys had taped off the entire area. Forensics was investigating the ground inch by inch. It sounded fancy, "Forensics," but around here it only meant that River-Jaakko was crouched down, staring at the ground, breathing heavily.

He's not gonna find a thing there, not even a rusty coin, that's for damn sure. Not after two cops and four ambulance drivers messed up the murder scene.

Yeah, and that little girl.

Rosebush was stunned when he called. He couldn't fathom that two on-duty ambulance drivers would come to blows on the job. It didn't surprise me at all. If I ever need an ambulance, I hope I give up the ghost first. I'd die anyway if Toikka was driving the meat wagon—it'd be my luck that he'd be on duty.

I walked up to the house and introduced myself to the lady. I told her I was leading the investigation into her son's murder until my supervisor Detective Lieutenant Rautapää returned from Sodankylä.

"And you are?"

"I'm Detective Sergeant Osmo Nauris."

"A boy."

"I'm 46."

A cat slipped out of the bedroom, and the lady picked it up. I looked at my shoes—they'd gotten dirty out on the path.

"Would you like some coffee?"

"Please."

The lady took an old-fashioned stovetop coffeepot out of the cupboard. At that point, I couldn't refuse, even though coffee cooked on the stove makes my stomach rumble like a volcano.

The lady didn't ask me to sit down, but I interpreted the invitation to have coffee as a request to do so. I was annoyed at myself when I realized I was sitting on the very edge of the chair, as if waiting to be told when to get up.

The lady put the water on. Moisture on the bottom of the pot hissed and popped angrily on the hot burner. The lady asked if I was going to question her now as to where she was on such and such day at such and such a time and who could verify it. Would she be asked to notify the police if she planned to go on a trip?

"No, not at all."

"I've seen that on TV."

"TV is actually quite different from real police work."

"It looks like every day's a party in America."

I told her that in my opinion TV police shows didn't do justice to regular, routine police work, which involves painstaking and exhaustive checking of minor details.

I didn't think they gave enough credit to what I called the middle stage of crime investigation. The glory always went to the officers who ended up in heroic gun fights or the detectives that Americans call lieutenants. The detectives questioned the rich people in their mansions and would finally catch the criminal because of some minor detail the killer let slip. The murderer would later call the detective a genius, and the detective would pat the killer on the shoulder, calling him clever as hell, but not quite clever enough. On TV the word "lieutenant" is often incorrectly translated into Finnish as *luutnantti*, the military term, though the correct word is *komisario*. I've written a couple of letters to the editor of the *Lapin Kansa* newspaper about these mistakes. My letters never get published.

The lady poured us coffee and smiled. I felt like I'd gotten a little too worked up.

I tasted the coffee carefully. The lady apologized for not having learned to make decent coffee despite her age. I had to actually drink the stuff.

I told the lady we were trying to gather information about her son's—her deceased son's—whereabouts over the past few days. That's why we had to talk to her, though we knew it was difficult. But our objective was to find the murderer, and to bring him, or them, to justice.

I remembered that I hadn't offered my condolences. I apologized for my poor etiquette and said that I was sorry for her loss.

"Thank you."

"I'm a little anxious about this case. I so rarely get to investigate a murder."

"How often is rarely?"

"Well… This is my first time."

"You're a nice young man."

The remark confused me. I had to drink some coffee in order to pull myself together, but I could feel the coffee attacking my gut, making it spin and roil with sharp pains. My cheeks got hot and my stomach gurgled. I coughed loudly to cover up the noise, which seemed to work pretty well.

"You have a spring cough."

"A little bit of one."

"Tell your wife to make you some mulled wine. It's okay to drink it at other times besides Christmas. You have a wife, don't you?"

"Yes, and three children."

"You're a nice young man."

I picked up my cup and blew on the coffee, hiding my hot face. The lady got up and went into the bedroom and I could hear cabinets being opened and closed. I thought I heard some faint weeping, but that could've been the cat.

I wondered if I could pour the coffee back into the pot. Would it make too loud a splash, and would the lady rush out of the bedroom, all curious? How then could I explain what I was doing? "Is my coffee really that bad?" the haggard sixty-something woman would ask dramatically from the doorway. "No, it's excellent," I'd say, my nose growing longer, while I poured the poison back into the pot. "Why aren't you drinking it then?" the lady would cry out with grief and humiliation, and then suffer a stroke, causing her nervous system to explode. Then she'd drop dead. When Toikka and that other screw-up came to pick up her body between the fourteenth and fifteenth rounds of their fight, the woman would return to the land of the living for a moment, lift her pitifully withered gray head off the stretcher, point at me with a trembling finger, and whisper the words I'd hear for the rest of my life, "That man killed me."

I decided to drink the coffee.

It was obvious the lady liked me. It was also obvious that she saw in me her dear departed son. I thought back to my police academy psychology class—easy to do since I could never forget the instructor.

Anja Huttu was made of cream and silk stockings. I sat in the front row, and Anja defied the laws of physics by somehow wriggling herself into a sitting position on the corner of her desk wearing a tight skirt and high heels. Sometimes she'd swing her leg real close to my face. I have to admit I had a crush on her, but I certainly wasn't the only one. I remember the class in great detail, especially one very embarrassing incident. At the end of one class, Anja asked if anyone had any questions or comments. As taciturn Finnish cops, we weren't up to discussing the quiverings and distortions of our young souls. Anja looked disappointed. I felt my hand shoot up in the air. Anja looked at the name tag on my desk and asked what was on the mind of Mr. Nauris.

"Legs," I answered.

The classroom, which had started to get lively as the class was about to end, fell silent. To my horror I realized what I'd blurted out. Vilfrid Remsu, who lives in Savukoski now, saved me. He was sitting next to me and started to laugh like an accordion. His laughter is still infectious. I know people who stop by the police station just to hear Vilfrid laugh. That's how folks in Savukoski care for their souls. Everyone in class laughed with Vilfrid and finally Anja laughed, too. The expression on my face seemed to amuse her—I was mortified as hell. She could've really complicated my life if she'd considered my wiseass remark to be a deliberate sexist provocation. Later at the police academy, some old lady squawked at us for two hours about hidden sexist attitudes in police departments. She used such strong language that one of my classmates told me he didn't dare have sex for two weeks, for fear of revealing some unfortunate hidden attitude.

Anja came to the next class wearing an old-lady calf-length skirt and looked at me out of the corner of her eye. The guys thought it was a clear invitation to approach her, but I didn't interpret it that way. The guys threatened to twist my nose off, since it was my fault that Anja had switched outfits from sexy to conservative.

Aside from the legs, I don't remember much of the psychology class. The old lady was nice to me, because I reminded her of her son. That could be useful in my investigation, but I vaguely recalled Anja saying that taking advantage of such a situation was unethical. Anja is married now and lives in Helsinki.

The lady apologized for letting my coffee cup get empty. She poured more before I could say no.

I asked what Marzipan had done the previous day. I had to remind myself to say "your son" and not "Marzipan."

"He didn't do anything."

"Nothing at all?"

54

"Dear Detective Sergeant, I know how my son made a living."

"I see."

"I never wanted to have anything to do with it."

"Was your son home all day yesterday?"

"He kept going back and forth to town all day."

"What about last night?"

"He stopped by here, fell asleep, went to town, returned, fell asleep."

"What time did he leave this morning?"

"He left half an hour before he was killed."

"How do you know that?"

"He left, and a little more than a half hour later Ernest Rosenström's son came to tell me that he'd been killed."

"Do you have any idea who wanted to kill him?"

"Everyone."

"Excuse me?"

"Everyone hated him. Those who knew him best hated him the most."

"Um, you...did you...?"

"He was a bad man. But he was still my son."

"I'm sorry, but I have to ask all these questions."

"It's okay. I understand."

"And his wife?"

"What about her?"

"What was her relationship with your son like? Where is she?"

"Wherever whores are. I threw her out this morning."

"At what time? What did your son think about that?"

"My son had already left."

"Why did you kick your daughter-in-law out?"

"She's a whore."

"Um... People use that term quite casually. It's used for women who sell their bodies for money, but also for women who have several...sexual partners..."

"I was using the term in the latter sense."

"I see."

"But I wouldn't rule out the other, either."

"Has your daughter-in-law engaged in...extramarital affairs...for a long time?"

"Always."

"Why today? Why did you tell her to leave today?"

"I'm embarrassed to say it. It's so shameful. It's the most horrible thing I can imagine."

"We're investigating your son's murder."

"I'm very tired. Ask that whore. And ask Paavo Karhu."

"Who's he?"

"Paavo Karhu, a thief. They call him the Grizz."

"How do you know him?"

"I'm very tired."

"We're almost done."

"He was my son's partner in crime in all kinds of things."

"Was this Paavo Karhu, the Grizz, here this morning?"

"Ask that whore. Or ask the Grizz."

"We'll definitely ask them."

"Yes, he was."

"You're sure about that."

"I'm very tired... Yes, I'm sure."

The lady sighed and poured me a third cup of coffee. She figured that I would help her empty the coffeepot—she was one of those old-timers who didn't want to let expensive coffee go to waste, even though coffee was always on sale these days.

I put my notebook in my pocket. I told her that she'd been very helpful. Since I'd left my walkie-talkie in the car, I asked if I could use her phone. She said yes and directed me into the bedroom.

I went back to the kitchen and asked if she knew the Grizz's address and where I could possibly find her daughter-in-law.

"They're at a bar, I'm sure."

I thanked her and called Detective Lieutenant Rautapää on his cell phone. I explained the situation, and he told me to bring both of them in immediately for interrogation. I made another call to Dispatch and gave the instructions.

"Which bar?" Dispatch asked.

"Some bar in Rovaniemi."

"There are only a few of them," Dispatch said sarcastically.

I went to shake the lady's hand and expressed my condolences again for her loss. She petted the cat and nodded at me. I asked what breed the cat was. As I spoke my stomach really rumbled, forcing a twisted and pained smile on my face. The lady looked at me.

"He's an ordinary cat."

"They're the best."

I had already pushed down the door handle when the lady called me back. She motioned invitingly back toward the kitchen table.

"Before it cools down."

I should have told her I was in a hurry, that I needed to take immediate follow-up action on the investigation. But I didn't, and went back to the table instead.

I ended up coughing a lot.

11. Inkeri Feodoroff, MD

As soon as I got to the hospital, all hell broke loose.

I got to work a few minutes after eleven, even though my shift didn't start until 11:30. I wanted to make a few calls. After my shift starts, I can't use the hospital's phone because Director of Nursing Gavia gives me a hostile look every time she hears me end a call with a friendly "Bye." She's convinced they're personal calls, and the city shouldn't have to pay for them.

She always thinks up some reason to walk into my office just when I'm on the phone. She can smell personal calls. She's been in the building thirty-two years; I've been here three.

I never managed to make the calls. They weren't all that important anyway. I just wanted to get away from home as quickly as I could—Dad was being so difficult. I worried I would hit him, and not just a light slap.

Don't get me wrong; I have loving feelings toward my father. He was a reasonably good father, and I thank him for that. Those who don't know him think he's captivating and charmingly primitive. But when Assar and I have our medical school friends over for an evening of wine and raclette cheese, reminiscing in front of the fireplace, I expect him to leave us alone. He's a seventy-something reindeer herder; what does he think he can talk about with a group of forty-something doctors? How to prepare authentic reindeer hoof soup?

My dad resolved the issue by making Tarleena, Erkki, and Soile examine and diagnose his every lump and bump. After they each gave him their opinion, my dad stared at them wide-eyed and told them the "real" diagnosis.

Dad woke up, after having passed out, just as our discussion on euthanasia had turned into a debate. It's possible that we'd raised our voices a bit. Dad came into the living room wearing a tank top and boxers that were much too tight for an older person. He had to show off his bravado, which he does by lifting himself with his hands up off the floor into a sitting position; and after swinging for a bit he scratches his nose with his toe.

His toenail was black and split.

Like any loving daughter, I was proud that my dad looked like he was in prime physical condition. The time and place of his demonstration, however were completely inappropriate.

My dad insisted that Tarleena, who had the larger breasts of the two female guests, squeeze his biceps several times. That made her laugh hard, and she also volunteered to feel his quads. I pointed out that she hadn't been asked to, and that also made her laugh. She told my dad he was as beautiful and muscular as an Italian lifeguard. I thought it was disgusting to flirt with an old man in his seventies. Erkki, her husband, wasn't laughing.

Assar was as quiet as a corpse. A lot of people think he's cold, but he's actually just matter-of-fact, sometimes painfully so. There was only one thing that got him excited. He was expounding to us about how supernovas, stars bigger than our sun, explode. When they do so, they send heavy elements out into space as dust and particles.

"Do you know what that means?" he asked everyone. "Do you know what's in each and every one of us?" he persisted, and in those moments you could just imagine what he had been like as a boy. He turned gloomy if he didn't get at least one chance to talk about it during our drinking sessions. Now my dad was stealing that moment.

As the flames reflected off Assar's face, I saw his smile harden. Dad dragged him onto the floor to demonstrate how a doctor could learn to scratch his nose with his toe.

"With that toe, no thanks," Assar said, trying to make light of the situation.

Dad grabbed Assar in a headlock and flipped him onto his back. Assar's head hit the leg of the table in the commotion, and wine spilled from the glasses.

Assar got up, red-faced. He didn't look very distinguished with his jaw hanging down. My dad, a foot shorter than Assar, got onto the table and blew on the top of Assar's head. He said he was curing the "owie" with an old home remedy.

"If Assar had any hair, he would've been okay, that's my *diiagnoosis*," my dad said. Everyone but Assar was laughing. He had lost his hair early on, and liked to wear hats. My dad's hair is pitch-black and as thick as the hair of a young Indian man.

Assar said he was going to check on Marko-Petteri. "He's been having some bad nightmares," Assar lied to the guests, without looking at me. If our son dreamt, he probably dreamt about drug dealers getting beaten up, and to him such dreams wouldn't be nightmares.

Assar disappeared into the library; he insisted on calling it the library because it had medical books, a desk, a leather chair, and a vaulted ceiling. He expected me to get the hint and follow him after five or ten minutes.

Dad threw a birch log weighing several pounds into the fireplace with one hand. On the first throw it thudded against the wall, and on the second it flew into the fireplace, spewing a cloud of sparks into the air.

"Dad. Shouldn't you be going to bed?"

"I've put you to bed many times, little Inkeri."

"Maybe I should put you to bed now."

"Don't go mixing up our roles; ain't it all clear to you by now?"

Tarleena rasped that there was no way my dad was going anywhere. In her opinion he was definitely the most erotic and fun of all the men in the room. Erkki snorted. My dad twisted Erkki's ear playfully, but hard, and afterward it stuck out on the side of his head like a bright-red amoeba. Soile put her hand on my thigh. This gesture of hers had irritated me for twenty years. She imagined it brought us closer together. She kept repeating that my dad was such an incredibly interesting person and had such an incredibly interesting personality. She looked into my eyes the entire time so that I'd absolutely understand what an animal my dad was.

Dad started imitating animals. He made funny noises and twisted his face into horrible contortions. Tarleena couldn't stop laughing. Soile egged him on. She wanted to make sure my dad completely humiliated himself and his family. She was so obvious about it that I asked my dad to show us his special skills.

Dad immediately understood what I was talking about. He said he could tell how much boobs weighed just by looking at them. He started with Soile, and stared at her breasts so shamelessly that we all fell silent, except for Tarleena, who was roaring with laughter. "1.1 ounces," my dad said. I burst out laughing. Soile pretended to be hard of hearing.

"What?"

"My dad figures your breasts weigh 1.1 ounces."

"Is this a joke?"

"Ask my dad."

"Is this a joke, Feodoroff?"

"Nope."

"My nipple weighs more than that."

"1.1 ounces. Both boobs together."

Soile started straightening out her skirt as if she was getting ready to leave. She declared that she thought the savages of the northern tundra had a barbaric and offensive sense of humor. Her bottom lip quivered. My dad had moved to the other end of the couch to evaluate Tarleena's breasts. He grabbed one of them and said it weighed at least two pounds. Erkki stared dumbfounded at my dad, who was massaging his wife's breasts. My dad estimated that the left breast weighed even more than the right. Tarleena crowed until she was on the verge of choking. She had nothing against a strange old man playing with her breasts with her husband sitting there glowering at them.

I realized that Assar had already been gone for half an hour. I said I was going to get more wine, and asked my dad to calm down. Dad asked Erkki to arm wrestle with him to decide who'd get Tarleena. Soile grabbed her breasts with a look of disbelief.

I hadn't been on my feet for a while. When I got up, I could feel the wine's effects. As soon as I walked into the library, Assar started yelling. He demanded to know what had taken me so long. I told him that I'd given him plenty of time to calm down Marko-Petteri, who was being disturbed by nightmares.

"Stop being so naive, Inkeri," Assar said. He took a bottle of brandy out of the cabinet and poured each of us a glass. I could see that he'd already knocked back quite a few.

Assar clinked his glass against mine. I could see how hard he was trying to control his emotions. He wanted to know when the elder Feodoroff was going to leave our house. He deliberately emphasized my dad's last name. It still bothered him after eight years of marriage that I'd kept my last name. I sat down and said as calmly as I could that I wasn't in charge of my dad's schedule. When he arrived, he said that he was dropping by. I wasn't able to say it very calmly. Assar said that my dad's visit, his "droppin' by," had already lasted a week. Assar didn't think he'd be able to make it through another week.

"Droppin' by," Assar said again. The dialect still bothered him; he's from Vehkalahti, down south by Kotka, where no one ever went *with* anyone, they went *wit'* them.

I've spoken proper Finnish ever since I started college. Assar can't say anything about the way I talk, but he always makes my dad the butt of his jokes. I'm not really sure whether the northern dialect is any more ridiculous than Vehkalahti's. Assar gulped down more brandy and demanded an answer.

"I don't know about my dad's comings and goings."

"Who does then?"

"Probably father himself."

"Oh, you mean the heavenly father? He wouldn't tell me even if he knew."

"Do you want me to kick my own father out?"

"Do I have to answer that?"

"Yes."

"Isn't a week of drinking in Rovaniemi enough?"

"Was that an answer?"

"Yes."

"It sounded like a question to me."

"It was an answer. Your dad's in his seventies. He's going to have a heart attack. Good God, even I couldn't stand getting pickled like that continuously."

"Was that a saying from Vehkalahti?"

"What?"

"Getting pickled. I'm sure it's not in the Modern Finnish Dictionary."

"I heard it from your dad."

"I haven't heard him say anything about getting pickled."

"Your dad doesn't talk about it, he does it. How in the hell can an old geezer like that take it?"

"Don't you call my father an old geezer."

"Your dad himself said that he's just a drunken reindeer geezer."

"He said it so we'd deny it."

"Well, *I'm* not going to deny it."

"Yeah, I know you're not."

Assar poured us some more brandy. I could feel it go straight to my head, adding to the wine already swirling around in there.

"Don't misunderstand me, Inkeri."

"You can't be misunderstood."

"Your dad is...colorful..."

"In other words, barbaric."

"I didn't say that... He's a man of the people in the...best sense of the word."

"You think he's a savage."

"No, I don't. Not at all."

"Your own wife's father, you're insulting our entire family."

"No, I'm not. I like your dad."

"Have you ever told him that?"

"Yes."

"Oh yeah, when?"

"Once."

"No, you haven't."

"He thought I was a homosexual."

"I'm sure he didn't."

"'Are ya queer? Are ya queer?' I interpreted that as homosexual."

"He was just joking around."

"A colorful man of the people often does that."

I had some more brandy. Assar said we should really get back to our guests. He actually had made some good points; I couldn't deny it.

"How about I talk to my dad tomorrow?"

"Yes... please."

The alcohol must have affected us both, because when we came back into the living room with our arms around each other's waists, we felt like we'd made a big decision.

The guests were gone. My dad had Tarleena's leather bra around his neck.

I woke up after nine. I felt like I'd drunk a bit too much. It didn't help that I remembered our guests had left without saying good-bye. I wondered if I should call them or send a note.

My dad was already sitting at the breakfast table, eating smoked ham with his fingers. On the table was a partially empty bottle of Koskenkorva vodka. I asked him where he'd gotten alcohol so early in the morning. He said he'd hidden the bottle among the fireplace logs. He insisted that the vodka hit the spot right now and offered me some, too. I refused, and gave him a piece of my mind about the fact that my old father was drinking like a wino.

Dad promised to cut his drinking in half. To me that seemed like a good start. Dad said he was going to halve his drinking by inviting his friend Niles Ahkiomaa to come visit.

"Invite him where?" I asked, although I was afraid of the answer.

"Invite him here," Dad said.

I didn't respond, but got up from the table, leaving my half-full cup of tea. I didn't say a word, but after taking a shower and putting on my makeup, I slammed the outside door shut and left. I hoped that said something.

I wasn't at all ready for the hell that broke loose at the hospital.

An orderly ran up to me and said, "Car accident, car accident." I told him to send an ambulance. He said he'd already sent one, the only one that was left. I wondered where all our ambulances were.

"Well, one of them was involved in the accident."

Doctor Rautio came up to me and asked if I could handle the case, since his shift was just ending. I kept my voice even and asked him to at least wait until we knew what kind of accident it was.

"An accident is an accident," Rautio said.

Within five minutes our cramped corridors were full of people. While hard to imagine, you had to believe it when you saw it.

We had four injured ambulance drivers, three injured patients, and one nearly dead patient. I told Rautio that the nearly dead one should be taken immediately to surgery in case anything could be done for him. That idiot Rautio then asked if that meant he couldn't leave when his shift was over. I asked him to count the number of the injured and to figure it out for himself. He left in a huff. The orderly came back and said there were now nine people who'd been hurt.

"Oh, no. What happened?"

"Rautio's feelings are hurt."

I would've punched the moron, but I had to run to the operating room. It turned out I was running for nothing, as all I could do was declare the man dead. It was a miracle he'd still been alive in the ambulance.

I ran to check on a young man who didn't appear to have any visible injuries. Even though I had worked in hospitals for more than ten years—three of them at this place (which Director of Nursing Gavia thinks she owns), it still took me aback when I realized the young man was dead. His eyes were still open.

Immediately I saw that his neck was broken.

"He wasn't wearing a seat belt," the orderly said.

The orderly took his hand out of his pocket and was about to point his index finger at the dead man when he realized how stupid it was. I asked him if it was one of the injured men who now appeared to be hightailing it toward the front door, surprisingly fast on one leg.

The orderly ran and caught up to him. The man stopped and leaned against the wall with one hand. He was drenched in sweat. With his free fist he socked the orderly in the face so hard that it dropped him to the floor. The injured man then bounced away, out of the front door of the hospital. I called for help on the intercom.

I checked our ambulance drivers. Timonen and Rämö had small cuts on their faces and arms from broken glass. They just needed a few stitches and bandages. It wasn't hard to tell that Toikka and Sirkiä had been in a fist fight, and Timonen confirmed it. There was a man sitting in a chair, holding his side, moaning and having difficulty breathing. I went over to him and told him my name.

The man cheered up and started moaning in Russian, which I don't speak.

12. Police Officer Mauri Kildenstamm

Rosebush complained for the hundredth time how we always seemed to end up with the shitty jobs. As soon as he finished, Dispatch called and assigned us a job.

Excited, Dispatch said that the murderers had been caught—they'd been in an accident with an ambulance.

"Christ," Rosebush sighed.

He glanced at me, alarmed, thinking he might have shocked me out of my pants with his cursing. I'm a religious man. These dumb cops don't get it; it includes words like goddammit, too.

We were driving to the station when Dispatch buzzed again, "One of the murderers has escaped."

"They're innocent until proven guilty."

"You guys can probably catch this killer."

"How do you mean?"

"He has a broken leg."

"Where did he escape from?"

"The hospital."

"Where is he now?"

"That's what you're supposed to figure out."

"Okay then."

"He left the hospital five minutes ago, so how far could a one-legged man have gotten? Think about that."

"He could have carjacked five vehicles by now. Think about that for a second."

I signed off and told Rosebush to drive to the hospital. We should look there first. Rosebush wondered why we always got the shitty jobs.

I love peace and quiet. This isn't how I imagined my last day before vacation. I had planned on catching up on paperwork, clearing my desk, and maybe leaving work a bit early. Aila and I had decided to head up to Lake Vikajärvi, to our "Shack," as soon as I got home.

We'd put twenty-five years of hard work into the Shack. Had I spent that time delivering newspapers instead, the money could've bought us a one-bedroom condo. I could've been a bouncer at a bar and bought us a townhouse. If only.

But who cares about any of that, we have the Shack.

Aila's a decent woman and she knows I never actually want to finish the Shack. A man's house needs just the right amount of chaos. It gives it a kind of artistic feel—not that I know anything about art.

Aila has been helping me. She's the one who came up with the idea to add a porch ten summers ago. I pretended to argue against the idea, but she insisted that all the nice summer homes have porches. I only pretended to argue. We both know that as soon as I'm on vacation, I go crazy sawing, planing, nailing, and varnishing. Then I stand on the shore with great pride, taking stock of it all. If I were a carpenter, maybe I'd use my vacation time driving around in a cruiser looking to rough up criminals.

I called Aila and told her what was going on.

"For Pete's sake! Will you have to work overtime?"

"Hard to say. You go on ahead. I'll take the bus, and you can come get me from the store."

"I'm not going without you."

"You'll be able to take a sauna as usual. I'll be there later."

"It's not the same without you."

"So Pirkko's not going, then?"

"She's sixteen. What do you think?"

"Think about what?"

"What were you interested in at that age?"

"Nothin'."

"Liar. I already knew you then."

"Of course I remember, Aila."

"And don't forget it."

We let the line go quiet. I could hear Aila smiling. I could see her leaning against the kitchen counter, looking out into the yard. She had her hair tied back, and a few strands had escaped onto her cheeks. I said I'd call later.

"Be careful."

"Always. Bye."

"Goodbye, handsome boy."

Rosebush was staring at the road so intently that I was afraid he'd heard what she'd said. Handsome boy. I'm a lot of things, but handsome is not one of them. I don't mind if Aila thinks so, though.

We got to the hospital, and I walked in. The entrance hall looked like a movie set: screams pierced the air and all around people were bleeding. The head nurse was going berserk—the one who always looked at me like I was about to crap in my pants when I came to interrogate punks. Last time I was here, interviewing Tomppa Saastamala, she very sternly informed me of his injuries: a concussion, a broken nose, several contusions, broken ribs, and he was in shock. She treated me like I was the one who'd kicked him, even though it was Tomppa himself who'd wanted to show off to those teenage girls. He'd jumped from the top of a moving car onto the back seat of a stationary convertible, but ended up hitting the wall of an electrical substation.

Though she was the big cheese, I could never remember that head nurse's name.

She was tall, too, which I noticed as she stopped in front of me. I had to stand up straight to look her square in the face. Rosebush had to look up.

"How can the police department screw up so badly?"

"Excuse me, what was that?"

"How can you let a man escape? A murderer, no less."

"He hadn't even been taken into custody yet. So we didn't 'let' him escape. He came here to be treated."

"He assaulted my staff."

"Could we talk to the assaulted?"

"He's being treated right now."

I could see the orderly being bandaged behind the head nurse's back. I told the head nurse that it wouldn't take long.

"What?"

I walked up to the orderly and asked him to tell me what had happened. He said the guy had bashed him in the face without warning. I asked the man to describe the assailant.

"It's Kassu Vartio," the orderly said.

"You know him?" I asked, a little foolishly.

"What do you think? He's my brother-in-law," the man said and fell silent. "That piece of shit," he said calmly after a while. It sounded like he'd thought a lot about the character of his brother-in-law.

The head nurse appeared behind me, asking what I meant. She said she was in charge here and wanted to know what wouldn't take long.

"Nothing," I said.

She spoke in a nasal voice, sounding just like children do with water up their noses. While Rosebush was writing down the orderly's contact information, I went outside to look at the asphalt-covered courtyard, the parking lot, the small plot of woods, and the sky, just beginning to show the first light. How far can you get on one leg? If Kassu hijacked a car, then I hoped he'd have the driver take him to Haparanda, across the Swedish border, or at least to another police district. Without a car he'd have no other place to hide besides that scrap of wet woods.

I called Dispatch with the details on the escapee.

"So Kassu's playing hopscotch at our expense?"

"Exactly."

"I've always thought that the criminals around here never grow up."

"Oh yeah?"

"We get so little light this far north."

The sun usually reached the Shack's porch at nine o'clock in the morning. The porch wrapped around the Shack so that we had sun all day long if the sun was out. We've never cared for lying on the beach. Aila would putter about, make breakfast, and I'd whittle away at something or go to the porch for a smoke. "Again?" Aila would say. "Keeping the mosquitoes away," I'd answer. Mosquitos weren't usually a problem on the windy porch.

Rosebush came up beside me and asked if Kassu had a gun.

"How should I know?" I said.

"Maybe the woman saw one," Rosebush said. "Let's call her; they never remember to tell you everything the first time around." It was a good idea. I asked Dispatch for the phone number of the woman who had reported the car theft.

"This is Sara Skinner," a child answered.

I asked if her mother was at home. "Yes," the girl said. We were silent for a minute before I realized I needed to ask her if I could speak with her mommy.

"Her name is Pipsa Eveliina, not Mommy," the smart-alecky girl said, dropping the receiver on the table.

"Skinner residence," a mother's voice said.

"Hello, this is Mauri Kildenstamm from the Rovaniemi Police Department."

"Hello."

"You reported an auto theft."

"Yes."

"Did you notice if the men had any weapons or packages? Were they carrying anything?"

"Just a minute…"

"I'm mainly asking about weapons."

"Don't break that lamp!"

"Um…"

"I don't remember… Oh, this is terrible…"

"It's not your fault, we're just checking facts."

"…terrible…it all happened so fast…just awful… they all looked like bandits… I'll bet they at least have knives…just horrible…"

"If you think of something later, would you please let us know?"

"Esa's mother bought that lamp."

"Goodbye."

Rosebush asked if Kassu had a weapon. I responded that if he did, it was probably a lamp. Rosebush raised his eyebrows at me. I waved my hand as if to say forget it.

I wondered if we should go have a look in the woods to see what Kassu was up to. Rosebush turned to me and said two able-bodied cops should be able to hold their own against a one-legged man. I agreed.

I called Dispatch and asked whether Detective Lieutenant Rautapää had arrived yet. Dispatch said no. I said I was going to call him on his cell. Dispatch questioned the sense in that, since they'd just tried to call him and hadn't gotten an answer.

"The smart ones don't respond, while the rest of us do all the work," I said, and asked for Nauris. Dispatch hadn't been in contact with Sergeant Nauris for a while, though according to building security, he was supposed to be in.

"Nothing else, then," I said, ending the call.

I asked if we should go get Kassu.

"Yep, sounds like a good idea."

"He could already be in Kemi, anyway."

We went up the hill from the hospital parking lot, staying about thirty feet apart, moving along slowly until I stopped.

"Rosebush, do you ever think you're stupid?"

"So now I'm stupid?"

"That's not what I meant. I mean right now, what are we actually doing?"

"We're going to get Kassu."

"Yeah, but I mean really."

"We're working, Mauri."

"I was just thinking."

"That's what happens when you've got vacation weighing on you…"

"We could be sitting on my patio drinking beer."

"Then two other guys would be looking for Kassu. And they'd wanna go get a beer."

"I was just thinking."

"Let's grab a beer after our shift's over."

"Yeah. Aila can drive."

We got to the top of the hill. The little patch of woods was about a third of a mile at its broadest point. It had boulders, hummocks, large trees, and old stumps that looked like lizard tongues. You could have hidden all of Kassu's relatives in there.

I started to yell for him, but not until I was at the bottom of the hill, so that I wouldn't attract a crowd. I yelled out that it was us. I assured Kassu that it was in his best interest to come out from hiding; nothing terrible had happened yet, and now was the right time to stop messing around so that we could go to the station to talk. Cars whizzed by on the other side of the woods. It would have made me happy to know Kassu was in one of them.

Rosebush took his turn shouting. He pointed out that he considered himself a professional, and in his opinion Kassu had a great deal of expertise in his own field. He wanted to talk to Kassu man to man, even though fate had placed them in opposite camps. He promised to make sure Kassu would get a fair trial. Rosebush has lungs of steel. I shouldn't have let him open his mouth.

Kassu didn't answer, if he was even here.

The lake at our Shack was still iced over, though there were a few areas where a bigger guy might fall through. Last week I cut a three-by-thirty-foot hole in the ice just off the dock, right in front of the sauna, for ice swimming. When I'm in the icy lake, Aila comes to the steps of the sauna and cranes her neck to see me. Craning her neck is her way of showing that she's worried. She's afraid that the icy water will make a widow out of her; she's had horrible nightmares about it many times. I've told her that's exactly why I cut a swimming lane into the ice, so that I wouldn't get lost under the ice and drown. Aila told me how in one of her dreams she can see me lying naked underneath the ice and then she comes on top of the ice and looks straight down into my dead eyes. I'm only two inches away looking straight into her eyes, but I'm already out of reach, gone. I'm in the land of the dead, and she's in the land of the living, and the ice is the gate of death—I passed through it via the hole that I cut.

Logic doesn't always work with women, not even with Aila. She's told me all her dreams since she was sixteen. It took me twenty years to get used to it, but now I'm happy to listen to them. Aila does a good job retelling them, except for these ice swimming ones. I don't dream. "Yes, you do," Aila says, "you just don't talk about it." "If I don't dream, I don't dream," I say. "You've been dreaming about something when you wake up with your tool all stiff," Aila retorts.

Rosebush said we should go back.

"I'll bet that piece of shit stole a car," he said.

I heard a groan, was it the wind? I looked in the direction of the groan, and saw a blue quilted jacket at the edge of a ditch, about two hundred yards away. You shouldn't be able to hear anything from that far away. The wind probably grabbed the sound and carried it to me. I heard the groan again.

I looked behind me and noticed a fat man trudging up the hill, huffing and puffing. I told him to leave immediately before he was charged with obstructing justice. The three-hundred-pound man stayed at the top of the slope, breathing heavily, unable to get a word out of his mouth. It clearly bothered him. He finally turned around, and it sounded like he was taking half the hill with him as he headed back toward the hospital.

Rosebush could also see Kassu in the distance. He suggested that we go get him, so he wouldn't catch cold in the ditch. We took off. We were protected by rocks, trees, and hummocks, but it didn't look like Kassu was a threat to us anyway. We stopped thirty feet away, and I asked Kassu if we should call it a day. He was lying halfway on his stomach, and had seen us approach over his shoulder. His ankle was bent at an unnatural angle. The little bit of his face I could see was sweaty and muddy.

"Let's go, we're all adults here," I suggested to Kassu.

"Who's there?"

"Mauri Kildenstamm."

"Are you alone?"

"You're not the kind of kid I'd wanna come and get all by myself."

"Oh, yeah?"

"Yeah, we know you."

"You're not alone, are you?"

"I'm here with Rosebush."

"You guys are doing things differently now."

"Whaddya mean?"

"You guys used to come with guns, or a billy club at least."

"Nice chatting with you, but my vacation's about to start."

"I ain't going nowhere."

"That's crazy talk. If we leave you here, you'll freeze to death overnight."

"I'm staying here."

"And then Rosebush and I will be charged with abandonment."

"Good."

"Kassu. Pull your head out of your ass. You got a gun?"

"That ain't none of your fucking business."

"Of course it is. You're gonna hurt yourself."

Kassu went quiet. He took a couple of wheezy breaths. He said that his foot hurt like hell. He'd twisted it again jumping over the ditch on one leg. He said he'd roll over onto his back so we wouldn't be charged with shooting him in the back. He told me he'd lost his gun in the accident. Even if he hadn't lost it, he couldn't have done anything with it, since two fingers on his right hand were broken. "You try shooting with that, dammit."

He lost consciousness as he rolled onto his back. I headed down into the ditch. All of a sudden Kassu turned quickly, and I saw a gun in his hand. Its muzzle was like a black sun, and it exploded.

13. Paul Ansalanka

Sakke was screaming. He screamed a lot lately. I felt like I'd aged four years in the four weeks I was gone.

Sakke was getting on my nerves. I'd started thinking that there must be better ways to make money than going around robbing places and raising hell. It wasn't fun telling Sakke that, though. He still reads *Commando* comics.

Sakke screamed again. I told the kids gathered around us that my name was Aulis Moisander. They thought that was funny; they couldn't believe anyone with that name wasn't in prison. I really like kids. I'm gonna become a kindergarten teacher, no matter what anybody says. Sakke thinks it'd be an excellent cover.

I went to see what was bothering Sakke. His screaming was pretty convincing. A bike, or at least what was left of it, was chained to the back bumper of the truck with a huge lock. I got to laughing about it.

"What the fuck you laughin' at," Sakke barked angrily. He'd also learned how to get mad while I was out of town.

Sakke thought I was a moron. The kids gathered round us, mocking us by pretending to honk a horn. They were running around us in circles. I thought we were starting to attract too much attention. I told Sakke to scream some more, so we could get the whole neighborhood to come over and look at what we were up to. Sakke was quiet, but not for long. He couldn't believe that I hadn't noticed I'd been dragging a bike all over town behind the truck. He was convinced that no one but me in the entire Northern Hemisphere could've done such a thing.

I suggested we saw the bike loose and leave it in the garage. We could haul it to the dump later. Sakke lit up a smoke. He told me to take note—he never smoked when he was hung over, but he was doing it now because he didn't think it'd be possible for him to feel any worse than he already did.

I took the key from Sakke and put it in the lock on the garage door. Sakke asked if I was crazy. He pointed to the pack of kids. He doesn't know a thing about kids. If you tell them to get lost, there's no way they'll ever leave. Sakke just didn't get it.

"I'm sure these kids would be nice enough to help us out and carry some boxes to the truck, ain't that right, kids?" I said. That got the bigger ones to saunter off, losing interest in us. Just a few of the little ones stayed behind, sucking on their mittens.

I opened the door and turned on the lights. Sakke kept twitching, and I remembered that he hadn't been there when Marzipan and I had put lids on the boxes. It was just before Marzipan started his binge, which lasted for weeks. Sakke thought we'd be carrying open boxes full of booze to the truck in broad daylight. I showed him the boxes and asked what the most talented criminal mind of our time would say about all this. He looked so relieved I thought he was about to pee his pants. I started carrying boxes to the truck, and told Sakke to go get a pair of bolt cutters or a hacksaw, so we could remove the bike from the truck. He didn't like me telling him what to do, but I felt that someone had to be the boss in this situation.

"The losers are carrying boxes, the losers are carrying boxes," two young girls chimed. I asked them to see for themselves how much the boxes weighed, and they rolled their eyes and sighed, "Oh, you're so strong." Sakke told me to stop hitting on them. The girls tittered. They demonstrated how they'd fall over on their backs if I hit on them. They held their hands up in the air and shrieked, "Aahh, aahh." They knew much more about boy-girl stuff than I did at that age. I'd have to watch out for them, they were wild. Then their brown-eyed friend appeared out of nowhere and started whispering something to them. That gave me a moment's peace to carry more boxes.

Sakke was complaining that he couldn't find a hacksaw or anything. He said we should saw off the bike only after we got all the boxes into the truck. I didn't like the idea.

"So you don't like the idea, huh? Well, too bad," Sakke hissed. With that he thought he'd become the self-appointed boss. I pointed out that a couple hundred people had seen our vehicle today, and some of them were surely unemployed, and they could've called the cops just to have something to do. Sakke shriveled up and looked so despondent that he had to sit down on top of a paint can. I comforted him by saying that we hadn't been hauled downtown just yet. I pointed out that the garage contained hundreds of gallons of paint, varnish, and paint thinner, and if they caught fire, the entire building would burn down. It'd get so hot that the groundwater would boil and we could make tea. He stepped on his unlit cigarette and started looking for a hacksaw again.

"Okay, boss," he should've said.

I carried boxes till I was dripping with sweat and stopped to catch my breath. Brown Eyes was telling a story loud and clear, and the other two girls kept moaning, "Horrible, horrible, is that true?"

"Of course it is, I was an eyewitness," Brown Eyes said. She flipped up the collar of her jacket. Eyewitnesses don't go walking around town sloppily dressed. I picked up another box. Something bothered me about her story. I could only hear a word here and there; then she raised her voice, irritated at the lack of appreciation she was getting. I left the box where it was.

"What's your name?"

"What's yours?"

"Paul."

"Paul, that's an apostle."

"Me and the apostle have the same name."

"I have the same first name as a famous actress."

"What actress?"

"That's what Daddy says."

"What name is that?"

"Sara."

"That's a nice name."

"Sara Skinner. I'm six."

"I'm Paul Ansalanka. I'm twenty-two years old."

Brown Eyes stretched out her hand and I shook it, straight-faced. I knew she'd be crushed if I laughed at her warm little hand and her "hello."

"Hello," she said. I said hello back. Sakke stared at us, but kept his mouth shut.

"Who's Vertti?"

"A boy."

"Is he your boyfriend?"

The girls giggled. I lifted the box into the truck and went over to Sakke to ask what Marzipan's son's name was.

"Dimwit," Sakke said. He remembered Marzipan telling him that as soon as his son was born, Marzipan could tell the baby was missing a few cards from the deck. So he started calling him Dimwit.

"Ah, I see."

"Why do you ask?"

"No reason."

I kept lifting boxes. Brown Eyes came up to me and asked how I knew Vertti. I said that I didn't know him.

"Yes, you do," she insisted. "His dad calls him Dimwit. My daddy says that it's not a nice name and you can't call him that," Brown Eyes said.

I put the box down on the floor of the garage and took the girl by the hand. I tried to look like I was just shooting the breeze with her. I asked her what had happened. She told me. It was a detailed story, and a good one. I started getting the chills and went to tell Sakke the story. He flew into a panic and ran to the truck. I had to yank him back out.

Sakke wanted to get out of there fast. Direction and destination were irrelevant; he just wanted to get as far away as he could. But there was nowhere to go.

"Get a grip," I told him. He babbled we were going to get killed, that the Russians were coming, and if not them then the cops, and that we were in deep shit.

"I called the ambulance," Brown Eyes said.

"You're a good girl," I said.

I took Sakke to the back of the garage. He had to be led like my grandma's old pooch.

"What're we gonna do, what're we gonna do?" he kept freaking out. I said we should sit down and think. Taking a second to think would make no difference between our getting caught or staying alive. He wiped the sweat from his face with both hands and brushed his hair back. It didn't look like he was thinking much. I knew it'd fall on me. He kept chanting, "The booze wasn't stolen from the state liquor store, was it?"

"Marzipan ain't around to tell nobody," I said.

"Goddammit," he moaned, "they killed the guy. I bet they tortured him before they smashed his head like a vase." He burst into tears.

He dried his face and asked me to figure out what we should do.

"Tell me what to do," he kept repeating.

"Let's pack that truck first," I decided.

We loaded the vehicle and Sakke calmed down. Every now and then he whistled happily—we had a simple and well-defined task. Humans are strange animals.

We filled up the truck. It took over three hours. I bent over and peered under the truck to make sure the exhaust pipe wasn't going to fall off, on top of everything else that'd happened. Sakke bent over next to me, and I could

smell both his sweat and his fear. One thing I do know—
fear smells like iron.

"What's up, guys?"

Sakke fell over on his ass. I looked over and got up
on my feet. A middle-aged man was tossing a key chain
up and down in his hand. He looked like he lived in the
building. And he looked familiar. Sakke got up, brushing
the wet sand off his pants. I wouldn't let him talk. He
would've made such a big deal out of it, wildly
explaining that we had a perfectly legal contract with the
housing association so don't bother complaining to us.

"You boys have a pretty big load there."

"We calculated that it ain't over the weight limit."

"Sakke. That's not what the gentleman means."

"Yeah, that's not what I mean," the man said.

"Exactly."

"It's those other guys who fuck with drivers, not me."

"Yeah."

"I was just gonna say something about that bike."

"It's as big a mystery to us as it is to you."

I told him my theory. The kids in the neighborhood
were restless, always coming up with different pranks.
They'd attached an old junky bike to my truck just for
the hell of it. They'd probably taken pictures, too, when I
was gunning the truck down the parking lot with that
piece of junk attached to my bumper. The guy laughed,
saying he doubted the kids in this neighborhood would
be that wild, though sometimes they were more trouble
than an invading army.

The older kids came back and said that given a
chance and a common area for their activities, they too
could take on anything. The man was the chairman of
the apartment association and remembered that the
suggestion for a common room was coming up at the
next meeting.

He expected us to be impressed, and I said "wow" in my best surprised voice. Sakke pointed out we were in a hurry.

The bigger kids were now blocking Sakke from the truck. He couldn't get to the truck without pushing them out of the way. The guy, too, was standing in front of the door and wouldn't budge. Then he started walking toward me. I considered my options and got out of his way. He took a look at the back of the truck and burst out laughing. He pressed his stomach gingerly.

"I shouldn't laugh, I shouldn't laugh," he laughed, while pointing at the bike like he'd just discovered it. It had suffered quite a bit. I'd seen the guy somewhere, but that wasn't unusual in a town this size.

"We better get going," I said.

"The police."

Though I heard him just fine, I stopped at the truck door and asked, "What?" The guy said we'd be pulled over within a block or two. He told us that terrible things had happened that morning and that the town was crawling with cops. If they weren't busy with something else, they'd pull us over for sure.

"You might get an overzealous cop, who'd start weighing the load, even if it's legal," the guy said. "Which it is, no doubt," he added.

Sakke cursed and yelled, "Do we have to hang out here until Midsummer because of some shitty bike?" He was afraid his wife would go into labor before we got our load to the cottage.

Sakke impressed me—he surprised me. The guy leaned on the truck. I didn't think he'd ever leave. He seemed to be deep in thought.

"I'm on sick leave the rest of the day."

"You look healthy to me."

"My ailment comes and goes."

"I didn't mean that."

"My boss said I should take the afternoon off."

"I believe you."

"I would've been happy to have stayed at work."

"I suppose anyone would've been."

"What do you mean?"

"If there's work to be done, then I suppose it should be done."

"Ah, that's what you mean."

"In times like these."

"Yeah, that's true."

The guy kept tossing his keys around. He had all the time in the world. He tapped the top of the truck lightly.

"I have a woodshop."

"And free time."

"Yeah, what I mean is, you won't make it all the way to the countryside with that bike there. No way."

"I suppose not."

"It's close by."

"Uh-huh."

"Three hundred yards away. I share it with a couple of friends of mine. We make chairs and bird feeders and stuff."

Sakke said now we knew who to call if we needed a bird feeder. The guy laughed and said he didn't sell them, but gave them away as gifts for Christmas and other special occasions. Sakke said we'd be going now.

"I was just thinking that I could easily remove it over there."

"What?"

"The bike. With a hacksaw."

"You have a hacksaw?"

"It's a nice tool."

Sakke looked at me with trembling lips, like he was trying to decide if this was salvation or damnation. The guy scrunched up his face into a friendly smile. He clearly wanted to do a good deed for two troubled travelers. He'd hoodwinked his boss and got the afternoon off and now he wanted to make up for it by helping us. I wasn't opposed to it. Sakke shrugged his shoulders.

"Um… That's really nice of you…"

"No problem. I've got nothing better to do. It's not far; it's the fourth apartment building in that direction."

"Let's go then. Thanks."

"I'll ride with you."

It bugged Sakke to no end that the guy slipped himself into the cab of the truck. He barely found enough room between the boxes of booze. They were everywhere. He tapped the boxes and shook them. They clinked. I saw Sakke clenching his hand into a fist. The guy asked what we were transporting.

"Empty glass bottles to the recycling center."

"Are they worth transporting anywhere?"

"You can get a good price for them in Murmansk. They don't have any across the border."

"The Russians screwed up their garbage, too."

The guy laughed and so did I. Sakke figured he should join in. I started the engine and looked at the guy in the mirror. He looked even more familiar with his face jiggling with kindness.

The truck moved along slowly. You had get it fixed up ahead of time to ever make it anywhere on time. The guy wanted to know who he was riding with—who was shipping recyclable glass to the Russians.

"Moisander," Sakke mumbled. I called myself Tauno.

The guy extended his hand, which he'd been sitting on.

"Osmo Nauris," he said.

14. Esa Skinner, Butcher

I was in the middle of carving up a calf for some Chamber of Commerce shindig, when the boss came to get me. I walked to the phone in his office. My old lady was screaming to high heaven. I yelled at her to shut up. The boss gave me a look, but didn't say anything. The wife managed to get out what she was trying to say between sobs. My face began to tingle, probably because the blood was running out of it. The boss said that if it was at all serious, I should go take care of it. I thanked him, left my bloody apron to soak, tossed my hat on the shelf, put my jacket on, and clocked out.

I drove fast. I put the radio on—someone was talking, which was good. Didn't matter what they were saying, I just swore back at the radio. When Whitney Houston, my old lady's favorite came on, I sang, actually screamed, missing every note.

There was an accident at the sharp turn on Kemi Road, just after the bridge. I didn't see the cars, because the ambulances were blocking the view.

The tire tracks in our gravel driveway showed that someone had left in a hurry. I parked and ran into the garage. The doorjamb had a big scrape of yellow paint on it. Goddamn fucking shit. I'd just painted the Volga the day before.

I ran inside. Shards of glass crunched under my feet. The wife was in the armchair, gasping for air. She can't breathe when she's upset. A fucking panic attack. I went over and hit her on the back. I got a glass of water and forced her to drink it. She started hacking and went to throw up.

I sat down in the armchair and lit a cigarette. She came back.

"Did they come inside?"

"Who?"

"The fucking Rolling Stones. Whaddya mean who?"

"No."

"Where the fuck did all this broken glass come from?"

The wife started bawling. She wailed that she'd buy a new lamp with her own money, that I couldn't tell my mother that she'd broken the old lamp to smithereens. I said I didn't give a flying fuck about lamps; I was only interested in my newly restored Volga.

"Jonna."

"What, what, what?"

"Jonna knocked it over by accident…"

I slapped her on the cheek. It had helped her come back to her senses before. She shut up and moved away. Then, slowly, she started telling me what happened. I said I was surprised that the car thieves weren't young punks.

"One of them was. He saw me on the porch. I was so afraid he'd come back…"

"Yeah, well, he didn't."

I patted my old lady on the ass. She came up next to me, trembling and sighing. I was getting horny, but first I had to deal with stuff that was a lot more important. My old lady noticed I was in the mood, and she teased me by softly blowing on my neck. I pulled back. She told me she'd called the police about the car, and Sara had called them about the dead body.

"All by herself just imagine, a six-year-old," she said proudly.

"Where is she?"

"She went to my sister's."

"You let her go, just like that?"

"I couldn't keep her here."

"What if she has some kind of fucking trauma?"

"She was just excited about it."

"I'm going to the station."

My old lady wanted to argue, but she kept quiet. She kissed me gently on the cheek and told me to control my emotions.

"Oh, so I'm the one who went nuts here?" I said. It's hard to yell when someone's kissing you like that.

I went outside, and got pissed off again when I saw the yellow paint on the garage door. I jumped into my car. At Kemi Road they were still loading the ambulances.

At the police station, Jaakkola was acting all important behind the counter.

"How're you, Esa?"

"The fuck you care."

"Well, I guess that's all then. Pretty busy here."

"Where's my car?"

"Someone lifted your car? I just got here."

He started leafing through some papers. He looked up, agitated. He told me that the murderers had stolen it. I said I knew that. Anyone who kills a Räikkönen is a friend of mine, but anyone who fucks with my Volga is my enemy.

"Esa, calm down."

"I'm so calm I'm about to fall asleep."

"Your car's been in an accident."

I slammed my fist down on the counter so hard I heard a crack, and I wasn't sure if it was the counter or my fist.

"Esa, calm down."

Jaakkola knew better than to try and bullshit me by saying, "The car's just metal and plastic, you can fix it up in no time." As I walked to the restroom, people stepped out of my way.

I went to the sink, ran some cold water, and scooped it onto my face. It didn't cool me off at all.

I heard loud huffing and groaning coming from one of the stalls. Someone was pulling tons of toilet paper off the roll, and then more groaning.

The restroom door opened, and a man marched in and banged on the doors of the stalls.

"Nauris, it's Rautapää," the man thundered.

"Yeah?" came from the stall with all the groaning.

"Where are the notes?"

"Didn't Jaakkola tell you?"

"He said they were on your desk."

"That's where they are."

"Someone wrote the word 'whore' on this pad of paper here; it's circled and someone drew a bunch of stars around it."

"Oh yeah?"

"Yeah. Then there's a drawing of a woman who looks like a whore."

Rautapää showed me the pad of paper. I said the woman looked like how whores look in the movies.

"Yeah... Marzipan's mother... The mother of the murder victim said that the victim's wife had lots of extramarital affairs."

"Nice notes."

"Isn't there anything else in there?"

"No."

"I've got an upset stomach. She made me drink..."

"We can smell it over here."

Nauris groaned one more time in the stall and then came out. I'd moved way back, but Rautapää was too close.

"Good Lord. What the hell did you eat?"

Rautapää showed the pad of paper to Nauris, who blushed. He figured he was already sick when he started taking notes. Rautapää voiced the opinion that if someone was going to be put behind bars for Marzipan's murder, Nauris's notes would hardly be the incriminating evidence. Nauris admitted that was true. Rautapää said Nauris's face was as pale as a maiden's ass; he was obviously sick, and he'd best go home and slurp up some chicken soup and weak tea. Nauris said he didn't want to leave now that they had an actual murder case in the precinct. Rautapää told him he didn't want to be responsible for his subordinate being on duty while sick, and Nauris' condition might get worse. Or when the police labor union reps show up in six months with their traditional list of grievances, Rautapää didn't want to give them reason to add "allowing an employee to work while ill." Who knows, by then Nauris might be dead or seriously injured and not remember wanting to work while he was sick. Rautapää figured he could get into a real heap of trouble.

"If it's an order, then I guess I'll go home," Nauris mumbled.

"Yup, it's an order," Rautapää told him. "Come back as soon as you're feeling better; we're not going to solve this murder today anyway."

Rautapää left, but at the door he looked at the pad of paper and laughed. Nauris looked at me.

"Pork stew," he said.

I left. At the counter I asked Jaakkola where my Volga had gotten smashed up. "Just past the bridge on Kemi Road," he said, and asked me to calm down. My hand hurt a lot. I didn't start cursing until I was in my car. It looked like the side of my hand was already turning purple. A fucking broken bone on top of it all.

I drove to the accident scene. The ambulances were gone. Some nosy people were checking out my Volga, which had been dragged onto the shoulder. I parked next to it and asked the onlookers which one of them wanted to get punched in the face first. I was there, ready, willing, and able to kick the shit out of any of them. An older guy, who'd been tapping on the windshield with the tip of his finger jumped farther away.

"What the fuck kind of cop are you?" whined a pimple-faced guy in a baseball cap. I slapped him on the ear with my healthy hand. I told him it was my car, and if even one twisted bolt was missing from it I'd sue every single one of the stinking people there, and keep filing appeals, ignoring all advice from my attorneys. And if I ultimately lost the case, I definitely wouldn't pay for anyone's attorneys' fees. Recovering them through any kind of collection procedure would take a really long time, and the interest they'd try to collect would be worth jack shit.

The onlookers left, muttering to themselves.

"Nice car," the older guy said. "Even now," he said quickly, as I glanced at him. My Volga was a pile of junk. The front of the hood had a foot and a half of crumpled-up metal. All the windows were broken to bits. I looked at the seats; they were stained with blood. Fucking hell.

Some guy pulled up on his motorcycle. He took his helmet off and circled around my dead car. I realized I was protectively dangling one of my hands. The guy stopped in front of me and said I was really lucky to escape with just a broken hand from such a terrible crash.

I am so tired.

15. Kassu Vartio

I turn and pull the trigger. Kildenstamm clutches his chest with both hands before falling onto his back. My ankle hurts. Rosebush grabs Kildenstamm under his arms and drags him to the edge of the ditch and from there to safety behind a rock. He starts yelling, calling me an asshole. I hear branches rustling and feet dragging on the ground, I know he's hauling his friend farther away. I ask how Kildenstamm is doing.

"Fuck off," Rosebush screams. He yells that you can tell from Kildenstamm's face that his life is hanging by a thread. Rosebush hollers that no one would blame him if he were to come over and shoot me now. He says he has an uncontrollable urge to do it. First he wants to shoot me in the balls while stepping on my ankle, then shoot me in the kneecaps and continue upward from there. Finally he'd shoot me in the head from far enough away so that blood wouldn't splatter onto his boots.

"Why don't ya come over here?"

"Should I?"

"Why don't ya?"

"I might just do that."

"Rosebush, we both know you ain't gonna come over here."

"You bastard."

"I didn't mean it in a bad way."

"What did Mauri do to you?"

"Nothing."

"You sewer rat."

"You wouldn't believe me anyway."

"Fucking scumbag."

"I don't even know myself."

"Explain that to the judge, if you live that long."

"Take Kildenstamm to the hospital."

"You son of a bitch."

"Get goin'."

Rosebush starts dragging Kildenstamm toward the hospital. Kildenstamm is gasping for air. Judging from the horrible sound he's making, he must have gotten hit in the windpipe. When I see that Rosebush has made it far enough away, I force myself up. The pain in my ankle is so excruciating I can't really feel it anymore. Once I broke my thigh bone and remember hoping it'd hurt more so that I'd lose consciousness. Now my ankle needs to hurt a little less, so I don't pass out. I make it to the road, and put the gun in my jacket pocket. Sweat soaks my sleeve when I wipe my face. I wave my hand at a car, but it drives on by. I wave at another one and hop to the middle of the road. The car stops.

"To the hospital?" a small gray-haired woman asks. Her hair makes her look like she's stood by the side of a dirt road in the blazing sun for a long time.

"Yeah," I say. She opens the door, and I work myself onto the front seat.

"What happened?" the woman asks.

"Drive to Kemi Road," I bark my orders.

"Aren't we going to the hospital? You should have your leg examined by a doctor," the woman says, mothering me.

I tell the woman to drive to Kemi Road. I pull the gun out of my pocket and push it squarely against the tip of her nose the way kids do with their fingers to make their noses look like pig snouts.

"Okay, I will," the woman says, wide-eyed. She speeds up, revving the engine. She quickly shifts into second gear, into third, and then into fourth. Before I can slow her down, she's punched it to almost sixty. As she jumps on the brake, my hands hit the dash awkwardly, and I hit my forehead on the windshield. I see pulsating spheres that go from orange to red. I hear a click as she takes off her seat belt, a clack as she opens the door, and a slam as she closes it, then the clattering of her heels and loud screams. I open my eyes and see my face in the rearview mirror. My nose is twisted to one side, broken, and my eyes look sick—I look like a monster. Blood is dripping onto my lips, chin, and neck. I sigh, and a tooth pops out of my mouth.

"What the hell's next?" I say out loud, lisping like a fag on a TV sitcom. Another tooth pops out of my mouth.

I wriggle myself over the gearstick to the driver's seat. My ankle hits the glove compartment—I groan. I want to cry, but there's just no time. I squeeze out a tear or two as I push the clutch to the floor with my bad ankle and start the car. Suddenly I feel warm, soft, and comfortable, but I shake it off. I know it means I'm about to pass out. I manage to get the car going. In the rearview mirror I see the woman stop a truck behind me and explain something to the driver with her hands. I can't see her mouth. I'm struggling to see small things in general. My ankle's so messed up it makes me scream every time I shift. When I get the car into fourth, I decide not to downshift; I'll ram right into the cop car if they try to stop me.

I struggle to keep the car from hitting the ditch all the way to Kemi Road, where I feel a big sense of relief. Then I realize that it's on this road they're most likely to nab me.

I try to figure out where I should turn. Do I know anyone out this way? I can't think of anyone between Rovaniemi and Kemi. Is Laurila around here? Or Koivu? What about Muurola? Goddammit, how can life be so difficult? I see a semi coming toward me, it's moving over into my lane, oh my God, it's so big, why is it in my lane, why is it going to run me over, oh Lord, oh Lord, oh fucking shit, I'm in his lane. I jerk the steering wheel and get back over to my own lane. I over correct and the wheels bite the slushy sand on the side of the ditch, slurping the edge of the ditch like some gourmet, the world's greatest womanizer who has found a really juicy pussy, then pours champagne on it and licks it. Great time to think about sex. The sand scrapes the bottom of the car, the steering wheel shakes in my hands, the car hits the bottom of the ditch, and then silence comes crashing down.

I lift my head up from the wheel and look at a red world through the shards that used to be the windshield. I'm aware that blood is running into my eyes, it's happened before. I wipe my forehead, and flinch when I realize a big flap of my scalp is hanging down. It's so big you could flip it and see the hair on the back of my neck. I shake my head. I feel nauseous; I drool onto my lap. I don't know how long I've been slumped over the wheel. Not long, it turns out, as a guy runs up to me, rips open the door and asks how I am.

"A vacation would be nice," I answer.

"You got hit on the head."

"Yeah, long ago when I was young."

"I'm gonna call an ambulance."

"Again?"

"What do you mean?"

"Nothin'. You ain't gonna call no ambulance."

"You're injured. You're confused."

"Call a taxi. I ain't goin' nowhere in an ambulance."

"You're confused."

"Ambulances are dangerous."

I search for it at my feet. It's under the brake, good. I take it out and push it against the guy's nose. I laugh at him; he looks just like a pig. I ask how Porky Pig's doing.

"What," the guy says, "Who?"

"He's the one whose birthday we celebrated yesterday," I giggle.

"Are you high?" the guy asks.

My head cocked, I look at him more closely; he doesn't look like the kind of guy who'd chat up junkies in the hot dog line about the chances of Finnish javelin throwers against the formidable Jan Zelezny. The guy complains he can't understand what I'm saying.

"*You* try to fuckin' pronounce Zelezny after your two precious, cavity-free front teeth have fallen out onto the floor mats. I didn't mean to say it out loud; I mean there was no reason for me to say it. The Lord, Lord Zelezny, His Javelinic Highness, is a name both mysterious and charming." I realize I'm talking gibberish.

I bite my lower lip in order to grab hold of my fleeting sanity. Biting down hurts my upper gums, where my two front teeth are missing. I tell the guy to open the door and help me out of the car. He does what I say. I get to my feet and see a crowd gradually gathering around to enjoy the entertainment. My gun's up against the man's back underneath his sweater. People who want to help crowd around us, and I growl at them to move farther away. Finns do as they're told—they don't want to witness a man dying right in front of their eyes.

The guy understands what I want. He takes me over to the passenger door of his own car. He dawdles and says he can't let me get in his car, because I'll get blood all over it.

I say to him, "Wouldn't you rather have my blood messing up your car, and not your own?" The sentence comes out of my mouth with stunning clarity and the guy gets it and almost lifts me into the car. While he's helping me in, I whisper in his ear, "It doesn't make a damn bit of difference to me whether I shoot you or not. You better get in the car nicely or you'll get a bullet through the window. If it's the last thing I ever do, then I..."

"What's your name?"

"Auvo."

"If it's the last thing I ever do, I'll shoot some guy named Auvo on Kemi Road."

Auvo says he believes me, goes around to the front of the car, opens the door, and sits down.

"Where are we going?"

"Drive toward town."

"Which town?"

"Rovaniemi. Get off this road as soon as you can."

"Okay."

"Turn on the windshield wipers."

"I can see without them."

"And stop them on my side of the windshield."

Auvo starts the car and does as I say. After a little while he gets it. "So the oncoming cars can't see your face."

"Yeah. You got a hat?"

"You don't want it."

"Give it here."

Auvo snatches a wide-brimmed women's sunhat from the back seat. I put it on. The flap of skin on my forehead hurts so much I shiver all the way down to my balls.

"Are you the one they're talking about on the radio?"

"I haven't had a chance to listen."

"They made a plea to you."

"I didn't say it was me."

"If it is you, they made a plea to you."

"A plea for…"

"For you to turn yourself in."

"Then how would they earn their paychecks?"

"Who?"

"The police…if criminals just went around turnin' themselves in on their own."

Auvo steers the car into an industrial area. I feel weak and nauseous. He glances at me. I tell him to forget everything he was just thinking about. I may look tragic, but I'm serious about killing a guy named Auvo if things

98

start getting fucked up. Auvo promises he won't try anything. He tells me he's a family man, with a wife and three young kids. He doesn't want to die a hero; he wants to remain a regular guy from Rovaniemi who's still alive.

"Don't think I'm gonna let you go," I say, "even though you keep going on and on about havin' a wife and kids. Doesn't everyone have them? Or do you think, Auvo, that I have the time to pick bachelors for drivers, so the police won't care if they get killed?"

In Auvo's opinion bachelors shouldn't get killed, either.

"Mauri shoulda been a bachelor."

"The radio said that cop's alive."

"He's alive, huh?"

"That's what the radio said."

"So you think I'm gonna turn myself in because I haven't murdered anyone?"

"I don't think anything. That's just what the radio said."

"You're lyin'. What did it say?"

"That a policeman was taken to the hospital in conjunction with an escape, and he's in the ICU."

"He won't be for long."

"Why not?"

"I shot him in the chest from ten feet away."

Auvo goes silent. I can see him sweating, I tell him to crack open the window and he does. The nausea comes back—when I spit into my lap, the hat tips down and covers my eyes, and when I push it back on my head it tears the flap of skin again. I curse so I won't cry.

As we drive past a bakery, I smell fresh sweet rolls and bread—my head is spinning, and I see the events of the morning like they happened to someone else on some other day. A picture of Marzipan appears in front of me; he's lying on the ground with his head crushed like a giant lingonberry. I have to be careful not to talk about it out loud. I look at Auvo, who's driving, staring at the road, and when he turns right he doesn't dare look this way. Marzipan's head rises up in front of me, and I already see flies and other shit-eating insects on it, even though I know I couldn't have seen them, since there aren't any flies buzzing around the Arctic Circle in early May. Not unless it's an unusually early spring, which it isn't. As long as I can remember, on the radio they always say that spring in the north is two weeks late and at this latitude it's never arrived on time. Well, if spring is always two weeks late, why in the hell can't they change the arrival time by two weeks? Then spring would be on time, people wouldn't get pissed off waiting for it and feel like they've been cheated out of two weeks of spring. Couldn't fall also be moved so it'd arrive on time, too?

Marzipan, Marzipan, a giant lingonberry that no one would sprinkle with sugar. If it had snowed this morning—and it could have because spring is late—it would've snowed like sugar on Marzipan's giant lingonberry. Wouldn't everything feel better then? I'm Marzipan's friend, and I didn't kill him. I tried to convince him all last night that you don't steal booze from the Russians, but he didn't get it. He didn't want to get it, the fact that times have changed; even though spring is late, times are different. You can steal booze from Parmesan, or you can try—and sometimes succeed—except when Parmesan's alcohol belongs to the Russians, but it ain't Arkady's. He's just the mule; he gets orders from so high up that he hasn't even seen the bottoms of the boots of those higher-ups. Sometimes Marzipan has such a thick skull that the only thing that works on it is booze. Booze worked and now Marzipan's head only moves in the direction the medical examiner turns it; his mouth opens up, but no words come out, and the man in the white lab coat checks his teeth against the records, so they don't end up reporting the wrong man as dead. Marzipan, Marzipan, Marzipan, why didn't you believe me? I don't buy it for a second that you're so broke you couldn't come up with twenty thousand euros. Why did you have to go pilfer the Russians' booze?

Will I ever see Miina? She's such a fat woman that I'm the only one who can lift her into bed. When I asked her whose tool she uses when I'm out of town, she said, "The Kemi River's. The river's melting soon, it's running fast, the river can lift me off the bottom where the current's fast." Miina laughed. "It's easy to be carried in the arms of such a strong river; in the old days it carried twenty thousand logs at a time, a few of them plunged into the water, and sank. They became submerged logs."

But will I ever see Miina again. Will she come and visit a murderer behind bars? I didn't kill Marzipan, he was my friend; but I did shoot that Kildenstamm, I don't know why. And I don't believe this guy is telling the truth when he says that Kildenstamm isn't dead—you die when you get shot in the chest from ten feet away. What's this guy sayin'? Nothin'. Who is he?

"Auvo," he said.

"Fuckin' drive, Auvo, drive the murderer to the police station, then we'll see who's who. Just like the stars in the sky have names, I'm Kassu Vartio."

My sister ain't gonna come see me this time either, she ain't even going to send me a postcard. I hit her husband, and he was the last guy I wanted to hit, but why did he have to be the guy that I had to hit to escape from the hospital, to get up the hill, then kill Kildenstamm. Kill this guy, what's his name… "Auvo," he says. I push the gun into his side, but he just says that Auvo's his name; a guy will tell you his name if you ask for it with a gun. I bounce around a little when we get to a curve. It's throwing me around, I've got a gun in my hand, and my hand is bouncing around. I could pull the trigger twenty thousand times, and it wouldn't straighten out the curve. Why, why didn't Marzipan just scrape together the twenty grand in the first place; it would've calmed Arkady down. But actually Arkady was calm, a calm employee, but his bosses weren't. Well, actually they were, because they're cold-blooded. If I kill them and slice a hole in their chests with a big knife, they'll bleed cold blood. If it freezes at night then a pink crust of snow will form underneath them.

Marzipan, Marzipan, Marzipan, I would've loaned you the twenty grand out of my own money, you should've taken my word for it. Marzipan, if you can still hear me, I can't turn into money. A man can't turn into money, though there are a lot of guys in this business who think that when you stab a guy, shoot him, or crack his head open, he becomes money in an instant: His eyes drop out of his head and onto the ground like coins, his hair rustles like euro bills, and when he gets stabbed with Esa Skinner's enormous butcher knife, his heart hardens into gold that you can carry away like gold bricks. It's no longer a man, he's turned into money. But that's not what happens. That's not what happens. Oh Marzipan, I'm a murderer. I shot Kildenstamm dead though I had nothing against him. Oh Marzipan, oh Marzipan, oh Marzipan, what was your real name? Does a man exist without a name; did you exist, since I only ever knew you as Marzipan? Will I ever find you in the great hereafter if I tell the gatekeeper that I once knew someone by the name of Marzipan? Oh Marzipan, oh Marzipan, where have you gone...and this guy, this Auvo, he stops the car. I realize he's driven me to the police station. I hit him in the cheek with the gun.

"Where the fuck did you drive to?"

"You yelled, 'Drive to the police station, drive to the police station.' That's all I could make out."

"Fuckin' idiot."

"Don't hit me. Don't shoot."

Cops pour out of the building. Of course they recognize the car, fuck. They take cover behind parked cars. Shit, my head's fucked up.

"Can I say something?"

"Fuckin' moron. I'm gonna kill you."

"I'm begging for mercy. Don't kill me."

I hit him on the mouth with my gun and tell him to go fuck himself and go plan his future children. He asks if I'm letting him go or whether I'll shoot him in the back. I tell him to find out. He gets up slowly, but the whole time he moves faster and faster. He leaves the door open and runs behind the nearest car. My head's all fucked up, fuck.

I raise the gun to my mouth, but my gums hurt so bad that my eyes cloud over. I put the gun to the side of my head and press it tightly in place. This is it. Then I pull the trigger.

16. Paavo Karhu aka the Grizz

Laina asks if *visiting* feels sweeter to me because I'm screwing the boss's wife.

"Marzipan ain't my boss," I insist.

"You didn't answer the question," Laina says, sticking her pinkie into my mashed potatoes. She picks some up and puts it in her mouth. Then she takes her pinkie out of her mouth and licks it by sticking her tongue way out to reach it. Next she sticks her ring finger into my mashed potatoes.

"Hey," I say.

"Well, hello there," Laina says, performing the same trick with her ring finger. The licking takes a long time because Laina has long fingers and her ring finger is the longest.

"You have your own mashed potatoes."

"Yours are better."

"Let's switch plates then."

"Yours will still be better."

I sigh and try to dance my knife and fork between my mashed potatoes and reindeer stew while avoiding cutting her fingers. I end up finishing her reindeer and mashed potatoes too, and now I'm stuffed. I clear my throat and ask why she called me.

"You didn't answer my question."

"What question?"

"Is it hotter, because Marzipan's your boss?"

"Keep your voice down."

"What are you trying to do now?"

I couldn't admit to her that it was more delicious because Laina's such a slut. She uses too much makeup, wears revealing clothing, and she doesn't know how to ask anyone with a dick over the age of eighteen what time it is without sounding like she wants to screw.

I say that what feels sweet to me is what feels sweet to her.

"What do you really mean?"

"Exactly what I said."

Laina's begging for a fight. She enunciates each word as if she's justifiably hurt. She turns her head a little and her mouth opens in an expression of amazement. Her eyeballs make quick movements, and I wonder if she can see something no one else can. Her upper lip twitches at irregular intervals. She just might do anything—throw an ashtray, pour beer in my lap, or stab me with a knife, if she can get her hands on one. I hate her when she's like this. I move our plates and silverware to the table next to us.

"What do you mean?"

"Laina!"

"C'mon, do you just think of me as a good lay?"

"Don't yell at me."

"Don't tell me what to do. You're not my husband."

"Go ahead and yell, then."

"I'll yell whenever I want."

"You want to all the time."

"Go ahead and fuck with me. You ain't gonna get a fuck by fucking with me."

"That was really clever."

"Fuck you, why don't you go fuck girls with master's degrees, then."

"Be quiet."

"An honest working-class pussy isn't good enough for the gentleman? Well, this one comes with sound effects."

The phrase "working-class pussy" attracts the attention of an electrician I know. He's in the doorway pretending to be glad to see me again, and starts coming toward our table, but I show him with a couple of flicks of my wrist just how much I'd like him to join us. Laina turns to see who I was gesturing at. The electrician manages to turn around, insulted, before Laina can get a good look at him. She always invites all kinds of guys over to our table and flirts with them to get me mad. Then I get to fight in the parking lot with the dumbest and horniest of them over Laina's ass, and it makes her laugh so hard. Sometimes I really wonder.

Ehnrooth shuffles over to our table. He's fiddling around with two fifteen-pound dumbbells. He looks like the kind of guy who could lift up one end of a giant bridge, then casually have a smoke, forgetting he's holding up the bridge.

"Paavo, the phone's for you."

"Who is it?"

"Didn't say. He's calling from a cell phone, though."

Laina gives me a nasty look, and asks Ehnrooth what his real name is.

"Susanna," he says and walks away. I go after him before Laina has time to start again.

Some unemployed guy is bouncing around restlessly by the phone in the coat check. Ehnrooth tells the guy that the phone's being used, and that it's impolite to dance around next to it when someone's talking. And, unfortunately, the pay phone is broken.

Ehnrooth sits on his stool, pulls out a book, and starts reading. I look at the cover: Jacques Derrida.

"What's it about?" the unemployed dude says fawningly, but Ehnrooth isn't listening.

I clear my throat into the phone.

"Grizz?" It's Torsti Rautapää.

"Hi."

"We were going to come get you in the patrol car, but then I thought that maybe it wasn't such a good idea."

"What?"

"And your girlfriend, too."

"What the hell?"

"Because we have this agreement of friendship, cooperation, and mutual assistance, I thought your friends wouldn't like us solving the case right after we brought you in."

"I don't like you talking about our deal."

"Like what you want. We have to meet."

"Tell me why."

"You don't know, huh?"

"No."

"You don't know?"

"Tell me, goddammit."

"Marzipan's been murdered."

"No."

"Um, yes."

"I saw him…there…"

"I know."

"No, you don't."

"Yeah, I do. You fit the bill for a murderer ready to stand trial."

"What the hell?"

"Passion and jealousy, professional envy, and who knows what else."

"You're sick."

"All the Helsinki newspapers would come to interview me."

"Listen. I don't know. I don't know anything about it. That's the gospel truth."

"Then you agree."

"With what?"

"That we have to talk."

"When?"

"Now would be good."

"No."

"Um, yes. I'll be in town in fifteen minutes."

"Where?"

"On the riverbank. Right where you bums like to watch the logs float down Kemi River."

"Why don't we go live on the local radio station while we're at it? Goddammit!"

"See you there."

"I can't make it in fifteen minutes."

"A man of action could get there and have time to kill in that amount of time. You'll be there or I'll have someone get you."

"Yeah."

Ehnrooth glances at me, over the top of his book, and asks if any monkey wrenches have been thrown into my life.

"Not too many," I say, and he goes back to his book as I head back to the table. Laina's putting on lipstick using a small pocket mirror. She raises her hands behind her head, looks me in the eye and asks if her breasts are too big. I have to look at them, they look like they're blowing hot air through her blouse—the top two buttons are open, showing the top of her cleavage. I can smell a mixture of her body odor and deodorant, which gets my thighs quivering.

"They're the best in the world," I say.

"But are they too big?" Laina asks.

"Only if too big means the best in the world."

Laina stops and tilts her head to think about it and tries to decide if she should get mad. I say that I have to go, and ask her to tell me what she wanted to say.

"I don't like your whore calling when I'm with you."

"Laina, not now."

"Not now, not now. When, then?"

"I'll be gone an hour. Wait here."

"The whore gets an hour, I'm lucky if I get five minutes."

"Stop it."

"Okay. It was eight minutes this morning."

"I'll tell you all about it when I get back."

"Tell me what? Greetings from the whore?"

"It was a guy that called me, believe me."

"Now I get to compete against guys for your dick, too. Are you bi?"

"Shut up now."

"I'm gonna start screaming like you won't believe."

"Don't. Please, Laina."

"Prove it to me."

"What?"

"That you're not going to see a whore."

"You can't come with me."

"In the restroom."

I have to stare at her for a long time before I realize that there's not a shred of rationality in her green eyes. She's serious.

"In the restroom, here?" I whisper. She nods and shows me the tip of her tongue between her teeth. I tell her she's weird, when I get back we can go to my place or to a hotel or even the summit of Mount Ounasvaara to do some grunting. She says that not only does she want cock now, she wants proof that I won't cheat on her. If I'm her man, I'll screw her in the restroom now; if I don't screw her, she'll announce to the whole world that the only thing hard on me is the top of my head. Laina raises her voice. I look at my watch, I have thirteen minutes. I ask how she figures we can both slip into the same restroom. Laina instructs me to go to the coat check to shoot the shit with Ehnrooth, then she'll call him over into the dining room. While Laina's chatting with Ehnrooth, I can slip into the women's restroom. She'll then come in after me. I ask her how I'll be able to slip into the women's restroom if there are other guys or waitresses smoking by the coat check.

"Use your head," Laina says. I look at her, she can't be talked out of it; she's already so far gone that words won't reach her.

"Damn it all to hell," I say. I go to the coat check, but Laina calls me back.

"The left stall, dear," she says.

At the coat check I ask Ehnrooth if he's been to the gym recently. He puts his book down on the counter, astounded by my stupidity. Laina starts yelling for Ehnrooth from the dining room. As soon as he's gone, I walk into the women's restroom, and I don't bother to look back to see if anyone's watching me because I'm in such a hurry now that I feel sick. At the door I sway back and forth a bit; in case the waitress sees me, I can chalk up the mistaken door to one too many beers. I go into the stall and wait. I drop my pants and start working on my cock. I tell it that I'll cut it off if it fails me now. And, if I don't cut it off, Laina will.

I don't hear Laina. I get down on the floor and peek to see if there are any legs in the next stall. None. Theoretically someone could be standing on the toilet, but why would anyone do that.

The restroom door opens.

Laina's humming. I recognize the sound of her steps. She knocks on the door, "Hey there, is my lover in there?"

I ask her to be quiet, and open the stall door. Laina looks at my cock in my underwear—it's half-ready and throbbing—and gets into my lap, sticks her tongue in my mouth; there's so much of it I feel like I'm about to suffocate. She slips her hand underneath my underwear, grabs my butt, and asks me to flex it. I oblige. Laina asks if I want to suck her breasts, and for the first time I start thinking that fucking in the restroom could actually be kind of fun. Laina takes off her blouse like we have all the time in the world; I tell her to hurry. I grab her breasts and bite her nipples softly.

"Harder, a little harder," Laina demands, and she gets what she wants. She sticks her hand down the front of my underwear and jacks my cock. She takes off her jeans—button-fly jeans of course, dang it—and right after that her panties. She slips her left leg, with her boots still on, out of her pant leg, and all of a sudden I realize that she might have planned all this ahead of time. She turns her back to me, puts her legs on both

110

sides of the toilet, leans toward the tiled wall, arches her back and wants tongue. Soon she's wet, and I go in like I'm going home.

I pound Laina hard. I want to come as soon as possible, no matter what she says. The door opens, dammit, and I have to slow down right when I'm about to shoot. A woman walks in. The treads of her shoes are filled with sand from the sidewalk, and the sand scrapes against the floor grating on my ears. She opens the stall next to ours, and Laina tries not to pant. The woman sits down on the toilet and lets out a squeaky fart that lasts a long time, rising at the end into a very high flute sound. Laina bursts out laughing.

"Is someone there?" the woman asks.

"Yes," Laina says, turning her head and motioning to me that I should continue.

"Do you have any hairspray?" the woman asks, "I had to leave for work in a rush, and my hair looks like a rat's nest."

"Yeah, wait a second," Laina says, turning again and showing me her tongue. The woman finishes her job; I wait for her to flush like I'm waiting to get into heaven, and when she finally flushes I shoot my load, my moans covered up by the rushing water. I extricate myself, pull up my underwear, and wriggle into my pants. Laina's managed to get into her clothes in the same amount of time. I go into the corner of the stall, and Laina opens the door, slips out, and closes it. The woman comes out of her stall. Laina says she forgot her purse on the table, and leaves to go get the hairspray from it. The woman stands humming in front of the mirror. The stalls can only be locked from the inside, and of course the door quietly creaks open, giving the woman a direct line of sight toward me, if she turns her head. I look at my watch. I'm four minutes late already. The detective lieutenant's so strict he'll throw me in the slammer for just being late if he's in a bad mood.

I open the stall door and walk behind the woman. She looks at me through the mirror, and her face gets stuck in a grimace as if the dentist were checking her gums.

"Hi," I say, "the wife called and said she dropped her wallet here, but I couldn't find it."

I continue to the restroom door, open it and am greeted by a look from Ehnrooth.

"Paavo, Paavo," Ehnrooth says.

"What?"

"Love," he says.

"Yes?"

"It should know its time and place…"

I give him a ten-euro note and walk out. Outside it seems like everyone's staring at me.

Running, I end up getting to the riverbank seven minutes late. Torsti's sitting on a bench. He looks at his watch when I sit down next to him, out of breath. He says I must be tough, because I had the balls to disregard Detective Lieutenant Torsti Rautapää's invitation.

"Goddammit, if you only knew," I said.

"So, what's new in the life of a snitch?"

"Not much."

"Who bumped Marzipan?"

"No idea. Torsti, I swear."

"Listen carefully, Grizz. The only reason I've cleaned up your shit is so you'd tell me about other people's shit. Is that clear?"

"Yes."

"You were at Marzipan's cottage this morning."

"What do you mean?"

"C'mon. I know."

"If I was there…"

"You were after Marzipan's wife's pussy."

"Was I?"

"We're not getting anywhere. How about I arrest you on suspicion of Marzipan's murder?"

"Goddammit, Torsti."

"You had a motive and the opportunity. Of course you had your gun with you."

"Was he shot?"

"Guns can be used for other things besides shooting."

"So he wasn't shot."

"Fuck off. I know that you couldn't kill a man. You're a cream puff."

"Thanks a lot."

"But I'll throw you in cuffs if I can't come up with anything else. Dammit, snitch, I'm not kidding."

"What do you want me to do?"

"Why was that Russian after Marzipan?"

"Marzipan stole their booze. Totally by mistake."

"That's why he killed Marzipan?"

"I don't know if he killed him."

"That's not enough."

"What, then?"

"The Russian probably threatened Marzipan."

"Probably. I don't know."

"Someone could tell the court that the Russian was threatening Marzipan."

"Dammit, Torsti. I can't do that, I just can't."

"Why not?"

"It'd be committing perjury."

"Would it?"

"You're the one enforcing the law here."

"And you get to decide what charges I'll bring against you?"

"What am I gonna do?"

"Stop whining. Either you find me the killer or I'll arrest you for murder."

Rautapää gets up, looks at the icy river and tells me to take care of myself. He takes off walking toward the old bridge, and I see him get into his car.

I think about the mess I've been thrown into. I didn't kill Marzipan. I know just as well that Rautapää's conscience won't suffer much if he frames me. He wants to be the county's top cop and wouldn't hesitate for a second to frame me.

There, on that wet bench, all I can do is bury my head in my hands. If I tell the court that Arkady threatened to kill Marzipan unless he got his booze back or cold, hard cash, I'll be knocked off within six months. Definitely, definitely, definitely.

I walk up Koski Street. I remember Laina, who still hasn't been told that she's a widow. At the corner of Korkalo Street, I see Laina walking toward me. I point out that I haven't even been gone an hour yet.

"What does that mean?"

"Nothing."

I take Laina by the shoulder and lead her under a shop canopy, away from curious eyes. She sees something in my expression and doesn't bitch at me.

I tell her that I don't know how she'll react to the news.

"Try me," Laina says.

I tell her Marzipan's been murdered. Laina says that it had to have happened right after that old biddy kicked her out of the house.

"Oh, she did?" I ask.

"She saw us fucking," Laina says.

"Well, anyway, Marzipan's been murdered." Laina's quiet for a moment. Then she has a fit.

"What kind of a guy fucks me in the restroom of a bar when my husband's been murdered!"

She slaps me on the cheek so hard that my head rings, then turns on her heels and stomps back to the bar.

She can't help but shake her ass.

17. Stella Gavia, Director of Nursing

Ambulance driver Toikka wanted to get up as soon as he regained consciousness, but I told Nurse Taavitsainen to make sure the patient kept still. It was obvious he had a concussion and needed to stay put to avoid serious complications.

I didn't hold Mr. Toikka in very high regard professionally. I was shocked to learn he had gotten into a fight with the other ambulance driver, Mr. Sirkiä, at the crime scene. In my opinion that was completely irresponsible. They were employees at my hospital and had to be held responsible for their actions; and unfortunately, the only possible outcome was to terminate both of their employment contracts. But at the moment, Mr. Toikka was hospitalized, and my primary responsibility, as well as that of all other hospital employees, was to provide the best possible care for him, just as for any other patient.

I returned to his room. It looked like Nurse Taavitsainen was having trouble handling the patient. I asked her if she was sure she could manage. She responded with a less-than-friendly look. I went to Mr. Toikka's bedside and told him that in light of his condition he needed to stay as still as possible. I advised him to forget about everything else for the moment and concentrate on healing. To me, accepting what had happened was a critical part of the recovery process. A patient has to make peace with his illness before he can heal. While dishonorably acquired, I believe his injuries from the fight were also an illness. It's not the hospital staff's job to judge a patient's lifestyle.

"You just focus on resting now," I told Mr. Toikka, offering him a kind smile. Nonmedical factors such as expressions, gestures, and atmosphere are certainly part of an effective recovery process.

Mr. Toikka responded very impolitely.

He claimed I was of the same profession as those young women from Russia who have been arriving here in recent years, and said that I charged considerably less. I would have left the matter alone and chalked it up to a post-injury state of confusion, but Ms. Taavitsainen let out a loud chuckle. I immediately demanded an apology from the patient. The way I see it, it's imperative to the proper functioning of any organization that the authority and irreproachability of those in management positions not be questioned within earshot of their subordinates. My demand for an apology seemed to anger Mr. Toikka further, and he called me a series of names I was unfamiliar with. But there was no mistaking the hurtful tone and meaning of his words.

Nurse Taavitsainen took Mr. Toikka by the shoulders and pushed him back down into bed. She said Taisto was still confused from the assault, and that I didn't need to take his rantings and ravings so seriously. Nurse Taavitsainen seemed to find the situation amusing, which confused me. I told her that I couldn't approve of her calling the patient by his first name. Patients were to be addressed formally by their last names, preceded by Mr. or Ms. Our goal at the hospital was not to create a relaxed coffee break or poker-night atmosphere, but to strive for the most efficient, effective, and safest care possible. This was also unquestionably in the patient's best interest. I had to wonder aloud whether this wasn't mentioned to Nurse Taavitsainen in nursing school. I assumed someone her age should still be able to recall that. Nurse Taavitsainen fluffed Mr. Toikka's pillow so vigorously that the patient let out a grunt. Soon I realized that I sounded unnecessarily strict and uncompromising in what was an altogether trivial matter. During the six months she had been working at my hospital, I hadn't found much to complain about in the quality of Nurse Taavitsainen's work, nor in her work ethic.

I asked her to come to my office at two o'clock so we could discuss the matter in a calmer setting. She said she would and curtsied to me as I stepped out. I thought that was unnecessary, and it came across as mocking. I didn't like it, but I wasn't sure whether it was her inadvertent lack of understanding of the nuances of the current situation or just poorly-veiled criticism of one's supervisor.

Mr. Toikka exclaimed loudly that he was content that the people of Rovaniemi had other things to laugh at besides him. He commented that there was room for improvement with regard to his wife's fidelity, then he mumbled something else and fell asleep. I nodded to Nurse Taavitsainen and continued down the hall.

The situation seemed to be calming down. I couldn't remember the last time things had been so hectic at the hospital, nor could I think of the last time two murder victims were brought in at the same time.

I wasn't totally happy with how the morning had gone. I had definitely smelled alcohol from the night before on Doctor Feodoroff's breath. I'm a tolerant person—I have the occasional drink, though only rarely. However, it was alarming that a doctor would consume alcohol knowing that she'd have to work the next day. We all had expected this to be a normal, peaceful Wednesday morning, but as I always say, you never know what the next day might bring. A school bus plunging off a bridge, a fire in a nursing home, a deranged bomber in kindergarten—it all sounds unlikely in this town, but could quickly become reality.

I fear the worst, but hope for the best. I've lived my life by that simple adage taught to me by my father, who was the manager of the city planning department. It's gotten me through the so-called "junctures" in life, as my father used to say.

Chief Physician Laulanne was walking down the hallway toward me. A busy and absentminded man, he looked up at the light fixtures and didn't see me until I raised my voice to wish him a better day than the morning had been. Doctor Laulanne shot me a friendly reply, apologizing for having to hurry. Laughing, I took his arm and asked if the chief physician could show a small gesture of gratitude to his employees, since they'd managed reasonably well through the rapid fire of the morning's incidents.

Doctor Laulanne was a handsome bachelor, always putting up with the young nurses who found excuses to get near him, and he laughed uneasily when I grabbed his arm. I am at least twenty years his senior, so I'm sure he understood I wasn't coming on to him. I was just showing a little camaraderie between colleagues and perhaps adding a bit of spice to our daily routine.

He cleared his throat and said that he didn't believe praise was necessary; it was reserved only for when performance exceeded expectations or when people went beyond the call of duty. He assured me that as long as Ms. Gavia, the director of nursing, was at the helm, he had every confidence the hospital could handle a murder, a couple of assaults, and several accidents in addition to the usual cases. Doctor Laulanne regretted that he had a budget meeting starting in fifteen minutes. I turned him to face me and straightened the knot of his crooked tie, scolding him for giving the hospital administrators the impression that we didn't take proper care of our chief physician—that was an impression I wanted no part of.

I loosened his tie a bit and smoothed out his jacket. I fixed the collar of his shirt and told him that he now looked like the kind of chief physician all of us at the hospital could be proud of. I'll admit I felt a sudden, strange fluttering in my chest when I saw him blush, and I touched his cheek with the palm of my hand to see how hot he was. I laughed and said that our chief physician should consider getting a housemaid soon, because it looked like he hadn't shaved this morning. He laughed and began to disentangle his arm from mine. I acted like I misunderstood his intention and danced a little waltz with him right there in the middle of the hallway. Teasing, I told him all the young nurses would be jealous to know he had asked an older woman to dance. The chief physician's dancing skills were not on par with his professional skills. He stepped on my foot, tripped, and almost fell flat on his face. I had to let go of him, and when he regained his balance, he stepped a few feet back, bowed, thanked me for the dance, and rushed off to his budget meeting.

I continued my rounds. We had survived a crisis situation under *my* leadership, and I started humming quietly, which rarely happened, since nature hadn't blessed me with musical talent. I saw two young nurses giggling in a doorway, but didn't give them the pleasure of seeing me embarrassed. Instead, with my chin held high, I broke into song, as horrified as I was to hear my own voice bounce off the shiny walls.

My song was cut off by a scream.

The orderly who had been assaulted by the escaped murderer came running down the hall. I've always emphasized that my hospital is a place of dignified behavior, but I had to excuse him as he breathlessly explained that a police officer had been shot in the woods next to the hospital. I smiled, and it confused the orderly. I wasn't smiling at the violence directed toward the authorities, but at the feeling of my blood tingling. My city planner father used to say that a person is tested in crisis situations, and I can say—without flattering myself—that I'm in my element during a crisis.

I asked the orderly to show me the way. He took off running, and I followed him at a brisk pace. He ran into the lobby and straight outside. I saw a police officer, whose name I didn't know. He was yelling from the edge of the embankment, "Mauri's been shot, someone help me!" I knew that Mauri was Police Officer Kildenstamm. I'd often had differences of opinion with him. In my mind, he didn't treat the hospital staff with due respect. I don't mean that everyone should kowtow to us, but in my opinion professional decorum had to be maintained. Even when the police, although understandably, wanted to interrogate victims of accidents or perpetrators of crimes immediately. I may sound self-righteous, but as soon as I heard who'd been shot, I forgot his profession and title, and instantly he became my patient, Mr. Kildenstamm.

I told the orderly to get the stretcher and carry the shooting victim into the emergency room. He set off. I went inside to the front desk and told them to immediately contact a surgeon as we had a shooting incident on our hands, probably serious. Ms. Manner, the receptionist, earned a little gold star because she waited until after she called the surgeon to sigh "horrible, totally horrible." Though she was young, Ms. Manner had no trouble prioritizing her tasks.

I went back outside. The orderly and the other police officer were carrying Mr. Kildenstamm down the embankment with difficulty, as their shoes kept slipping on the gravel. I yelled over to them and asked where the patient had been shot. The police officer answered that he'd been shot in the chest. I returned to the front desk and told them that the patient's name was Police Officer Kildenstamm. I told the receptionist that the police department should be notified immediately that one of their own had been shot. Ms. Manner nodded, and I asked her if the surgeon had shown up. She said Doctor Feodoroff, who'd been paged from the cafeteria, was on her way. I didn't say anything, but walked down the hallway toward the cafeteria to meet Doctor Feodoroff.

She ran right into me. I told her that Officer Kildenstamm had been shot in the chest. She nodded and thanked me for the update. We walked together to the lobby, as Doctor Feodoroff didn't dare run. I inquired whether she felt she was ready to treat a serious gunshot wound. Doctor Feodoroff stopped and wondered why I thought she wouldn't be ready, and asked if I doubted her professional competence. I denied that I did, because I believed that in crisis situations professional assessment took a back seat to more urgent issues. Doctor Feodoroff asked me to get the patient prepped for surgery, and she rushed off to the operating room. I told her I approved of her delegating skills.

The orderly and the police officer carried Mr. Kildenstamm into the first vacant room. I called in two nurses and ordered them to remove his clothes.

"Why?" Nurse Laaksonen asked. I told her that I would discuss with her later whether it was appropriate to question your superior's orders in a crisis situation.

The nurses started removing Mr. Kildenstamm's clothes. My mind was working on two levels. On one level, I was dealing with the shooting and the immediate procedures it required; on another level, I noticed that, despite being considerably overweight, the officer was quite attractive for such a hairy man.

I ordered the nurses to prepare the patient for surgery and returned to the front desk, where I asked Ms. Manner to call Mr. Kildenstamm's family.

Back in the room I saw that he had been prepped. The nurses pushed him into the operating room. I led the way with the orderly and the police officer walking beside me. The officer was rattling on incessantly about two things: In his opinion, it was strange, impossible even, that Mauri had been shot, as he had a long vacation coming up. In between rants, he kept vowing to take revenge on Vartio, the gunman. He knew that as a police officer he shouldn't pass judgment, but instead patiently wait for the court's verdict. He kept asking about Kildenstamm's chances for survival; the possibility that he might be permanently disabled preoccupied him as we made our way to the operating room. It was obvious that the police officer was hysterical, and that we might have to prescribe a sedative for him once the situation was under control. In any event, I wouldn't let him return to work today.

We arrived at the operating room, and I handed Mr. Kildenstamm over to Doctor Feodoroff and the operating room staff.

"The doctor is welcome," I said, heading toward the door. At the same time I reminded the orderly and the police officer that only authorized staff were allowed in the operating room. The police officer kept peering over my shoulder as if he'd never been to a crime or accident scene before.

I was almost out the door when Doctor Feodoroff called me back.

She asked me where the police officer had been shot. I reminded her that I had already told her once that the patient had been shot in the chest. I then repeated my question about whether or not the doctor felt she was ready to handle a serious gunshot wound. Doctor Feodoroff asked me to come to the operating table and point to the exact spot where the police officer had been shot. The situation already resembled a grotesque comedy, but I nonetheless went up to the operating table. I was quite surprised when I examined the police officer all over and couldn't find even the smallest scratch, much less a bullet hole. Doctor Feodoroff stared at me, with an expression that seemed to mock me, yet all I could see of her face were her eyes, eyebrows, and a narrow strip of her forehead. The OR staff didn't look pleased with me, either.

I told Doctor Feodoroff that I'd only passed on the information Mr. Kildenstamm's colleague had given me. Doctor Feodoroff asked me if I would have done the same thing if the colleague had said the patient's head had been cut off. She didn't wait for an answer, but instead pulled off her rubber gloves, making her point by loudly snapping them, and wondered how the director of nursing hadn't noticed that the victim wasn't bleeding from a gunshot wound in the chest. Unfortunately Doctor Feodoroff was right; in my haste I hadn't checked for bleeding. Doctor Feodoroff examined Mr. Kildenstamm's face and diagnosed him as currently suffering the aftereffects of a moderate heart attack. Doctor Feodoroff gave the OR staff instructions for treating the heart attack and asked all unauthorized personnel to leave the operating room. She was clearly referring to me, and it stung.

The police officer rushed past me to the operating table and smacked a kiss on Mr. Kildenstamm's lips before the staff pulled him away. The officer let out an enormous howl and fell to his knees to thank the Lord— he considered the event a miracle. He yelled that he'd heard a shot, and said that he'd even seen the evil look on Vartio's face just before the shot was fired. The officer yelled "miracle" so loudly that people started congregating in the doorway. The officer believed that the Lord had placed a steel-winged angel between Vartio and Kildenstamm at just the right moment, and the angel had plucked the bullet from mid-air like a little flower and placed it underneath her wing, The Lord apparently considered his life worth saving. Tears were flowing down the officer's face.

Despite the serious and confusing situation, I was moved by the fact that the officer fell to his knees to thank the Lord right in front of a group of complete strangers. Doctor Feodoroff didn't doubt the officer's observations about what he'd seen and heard, but thought it more likely that Vartio's bullet had simply missed Kildenstamm. Although Doctor Feodoroff's interpretation was cool-headed and likely correct, I felt sorry for the officer, who insisted that he knew Vartio couldn't miss from three paces away. Not wanting to get into a long discussion, Doctor Feodoroff repeated that all unauthorized personnel had to leave the room. It wasn't difficult to figure out that she'd directed the unnecessary jab at me.

I shooed away the officer and the curious onlookers gathered near the door, closed it, and asked Doctor Feodoroff if in light of all this she was now going to dismiss my more than thirty years of nursing experience. Doctor Feodoroff said she didn't want to do that, but pointed out quite rudely that in more than thirty years even the densest head would have absorbed a few basic concepts about the principles of nursing. I didn't dignify her comment with a response. I left the operating room and, keeping the patient's well-being in mind, quietly closed the door.

Out of my window I saw Doctor Laulanne walking to his car. I dialed his extension on my phone and his rather unsophisticated secretary answered. She quickly informed me that Doctor Laulanne was still in a meeting. I thought it inconceivable that he could have given his secretary such instructions. I felt a burst of satisfaction thinking about the secretary getting in trouble when I reported her actions to Doctor Laulanne.

I wondered if I should inform the administrative deputy chief physician that Doctor Feodoroff was working under the influence of alcohol. Many hours had already passed since morning, but if she'd consumed enough alcohol the previous evening, she would still have some traces of it in her blood. However, it was difficult for me to be proactive about the issue because news of the events in the operating room had undoubtedly already spread, with perverse delight, to every corner of the hospital. I could possibly get Nurse Parkkila involved, though. She worked in the OR, and if I could convince her that there was alcohol on Doctor Feodoroff's breath, she could report it to the administrative deputy chief physician. Even a blood alcohol content of .001 would be devastating to her reputation as a doctor, in terms of the Hippocratic Oath. I wasn't after personal revenge, though it might seem that way. Rather, my goal was to ensure the safety of our patients.

I tried to reach Nurse Parkkila all afternoon, but she was busy with her duties. At two o'clock, two nurses appeared in my office for a meeting which I had completely forgotten about. I gave them brief reprimands and asked them to tell Nurse Parkkila to come to my office immediately. She arrived a moment later. I asked her whether she'd noticed the smell of alcohol in the operating room, especially near Doctor Feodoroff. Nurse Parkkila's reaction to this serious matter was, in my opinion, rather nonchalant. She said she hadn't smelled alcohol. I asked about her career plans and told her I could help her out if she showed courage and a sense of justice. Admittedly it would be difficult for her to relay unflattering information to the administration about a much-admired doctor.

I thought I detected a hint of relief on her face when she said that both she and Doctor Feodoroff had worn surgical masks, and regretted that her nose would not be able to act as a witness. She promised to keep an eye on Doctor Feodoroff's alcohol use in the future. She added that the staff was aware that working under the influence was prohibited for the sake of patient safety and the hospital's reputation. I thanked her for making every effort to follow the rules, and sent her on her way.

A headache was building inside my head, and I didn't feel like meeting anyone—I was quite displeased with my day.

As soon as the clock struck four I put on my street clothes, walked out of the building staring straight ahead, and went directly to my car. I put Albinoni's *Adagio* into the cassette player, and its timeless strains calmed my mind as I drove home in the short Rovaniemi rush hour traffic. As I parked my car, Albinoni had significantly alleviated my headache, and I was able to put the day's tribulations into broader perspective. After a thorough review, I was convinced that both my work and its quality were beyond reproach.

I took off my shoes. This was one of the most enjoyable moments of the day. I took a shower and threw on a robe. In front of the mirror I lifted up my arms, and my breasts were still perky enough that I could imagine a mature man being interested in them.

I put Mozart's *Magic Flute* into the CD player and when its melodies had filled every corner of my one-bedroom apartment, I climbed into my recliner. I allowed myself a glass of Madeira, which was nowhere near what Doctor Feodoroff had consumed the previous evening.

In moments like this I didn't deem my life to be sufficiently fulfilling; I wanted to feel the touch of a living being. For a long time I'd thought about getting a cat, but they're such independent, capricious creatures. They bond to places, not to people. In any case, I had no intention of moving out of my apartment.

In the middle of Sarastro's solo the doorbell rang. I often just let it ring, because I don't want to get involved with Jehovah's Witnesses, deal with peddlers selling May Day publications, or donate to the building association's events. But this time I decided to open the door.

My shy neighbor, a retired elderly lady, told me that from her window that morning she'd seen some boys from the city-owned apartment building down the street steal my new bike. She didn't know how they'd gotten into the bike storage. She knew it was my bike because she happened to be at her window when it was delivered to me two weeks ago.

I thanked my neighbor and said I'd report it to the police. It might still be possible to get the bike back undamaged. The lady hesitated, and said she didn't think that would be possible, since the boys had tied my bike onto the back bumper of a truck, which had been driven off. She'd seen my bike suffer significant damage even before the truck left our parking lot.

The news shocked me.

18. Sebastian Räikkönen

We're sittin' at the edge of the town square, right next to the liquor store. Arvi's gone to get booze. He left just a bit ago. Can't remember when that was…

I go behind the transformer shed to puke. It helps, gets the bad juices out.

There's no sign of Arvi. We scraped together all our coins for him. He's the best at gettin' liquor.

My bones are frozen.

And I've got black gunk under my fingernails. One day I tried to clean them, but Arvi said not to, it keeps you warm. Arvi's funny.

I haven't pissed my pants for a week now. The skin on my thighs is so raw they bleed easily.

My wife comes, not Arvi.

The wife says I'm a miserable sight. Tauski says to her, "Get the fuck outta here, you skank." He's young. He doesn't know she's my wife.

"Shuddup," I say to Tauski. He settles down. He got some sauce first thing this morning, so he's feelin' sleepy already.

My wife says that my son's dead.

"Naah, he ain't…he was just here."

She says I've drunk my brains out.

I get mad. Tauski starts going off on my wife again. "Shuddup," I say.

"He was here, what day was it? We ate some sausage."

I ask Tauski what day we ate sausage. Tauski says it was yesterday. That's when he got money from social security. He remembers days. He's young.

My wife says my son was killed in the morning.

I say it wasn't yesterday morning.

"This morning," my wife says.

My son was with some woman. She looked like a young Laina. But she didn't look like a whore.

"The heck you saw him with some woman," my wife says.

I get mad. I ask Tauski if he saw my son, and that woman, too. "You saw what you saw," Tauski says.

I wonder if I remembered seeing him fifteen years back. I wonder if that woman was Laina when she was young.

"Anyway, he was killed," my wife says.

My son gave me money. Now I remember, it was forty euros, in tens. He said he was giving me small bills so that if I lost one, it weren't no big deal.

"He's never given anyone money," my wife says.

He'd thought it out beforehand. He was thinking of his father.

Some bums nearby saw the money.

My son went over to them and said, "You'll answer to me if anyone messes with my dad's money."

They were afraid of my son. They said, "The fuck we'll try to take anything from Sebastian."

My son told them that even if someone else steals the money, they're the ones who'll have to answer for it.

"For every cent," my son said. Now I remember.

"You and your memory," my wife says. She asks me when I was last sober.

"Before Easter I was."

"How long before that?" my wife asks.

Tauski gets into it again and says, "Go to hell, bitch." My wife slaps him on the cheek.

Tauski falls down on his ass. From there he slowly rolls onto his back.

We look at him. Then he starts to snore.

That's how Tauski is.

Who went to get liquor? I don't feel good.

"Who was the woman?" my wife asks.

The woman said, "Oh, my goodness," when my son pushed those bums around. She was classy.

I don't feel good. I wipe my face.

My hand is black. I need to wash it in the gas station bathroom.

If the fat brunette is working the counter, she won't let me in. The blond boy will. He says it's okay as long as I don't pass out in there.

Once I passed out in there while the dark-haired fatso was working. That's what she's mad about. I pissed all over the place.

I need to wash the black off my hand. Otherwise you won't be able to see the frostbite on it, and it'll have to be cut off.

I often dream that a snake's licking my feet. The snake's tongue is like a saw blade and that's how it saws off my feet.

That's how I know to wake up and get the blood moving. Otherwise I'll get gangrene.

I hope the dream wakes me up.

The snake has red eyes. You can hear its voice comin' out of the tunnel, or actually the snake is the tunnel.

I don't feel good. Arvi's missing in action.

My wife asks if I'd be able to drink a beer. I can't always get it down, because of the acid. Today I can, but I prefer booze. She tells me not to go anywhere.

I yell after her to make sure it's from the refrigerated section.

Tauski's snoring. I drag him under the bench. He's behind my legs, and the cops won't see him from the cruiser. Tauski doesn't like the drunk tank.

Now I remember. That classy woman said hello and shook my hand.

My son had said, "This is my dad. Don't he take after his son?"

The woman, or girl I guess, she was so young, said, "Hello." She said she was my son's friend.

She said it very nicely. My son has a friend. I felt like crying. Lately nice words make me feel like crying.

"Who said what nicely?" my wife asks.

"The woman," I say, "She's my son's friend."

"Our son's dead," my wife says. She gives me a bottle of beer. I bite it open.

I gulp almost all of it down, then burp. My wife says I sound like a pig.

"She was a slut," my wife says.

"She was a classy person," I say. My wife's jealous, green-eyed, though she's got blue eyes. I had a dream last week and in my dream the woman had green eyes. She grabbed my head and pulled it underneath her shirt and laughed. She rubbed my nose on her breasts. I took one of her nipples into my mouth and sucked on it.

"What're you mumbling about?" my wife says.

"Classy person," I say. "She wasn't introduced to you. My son introduced her to me."

And he gave me money to boot.

In ten-euro bills.

Arvi's missing, and I don't know why. Arvi went to get sauce. I don't feel good.

My wife takes another beer out of her purse. She says she won't give me anything more to drink. It's from the refrigerated section. My bones are frozen. They're frozen because I'm living in the refrigerated section.

I say that my bones should be put in the beer cooler.

"You can't handle even one bottle of beer," my wife says.

Now I remember.

She put her soft hand in the black palm of my hand. Her nails were clean and shiny like the beak of a baby bird.

There's a rattle in Tauski's throat, but he keeps on sleeping. But Arvi's taking his sweet old time.

I raised baby birds when I was a boy.

The crows were like chimney sweeps. I thought when my baby birds grew up they'd come to the roof of our shed and caw, "Hello Sebastian, how are you?"

I still know how to caw like a crow.

"What got into you?" my wife asks.

The second beer's gone. Where did Arvi go? Maybe he pulled a fast one on us.

Tauski's young. The old guys wouldn't dare pull a fast one on him.

He's said it many times. I believe him.

He protects us from the bums. "Tauski, security guard," he introduces himself to the ladies when they pass us on their way to the store.

I laugh like an old crow.

My wife asks if I'm aware of what she told me.

I'm aware. Tauski's not.

I tap him on the shoulder with my boot. He rolls onto his back, his eyes roll back, too.

He wriggles himself out from under the bench.

My wife grabs her handbag with both hands.

"Dammit, my entire cheek's swollen," Tauski says. He asks who hit him, and when.

"The bums did," I say. "Tonight they're comin' back to the corner by the station and the store."

"I don't remember," Tauski says, and tells my wife to go fuck off.

"Shuddup," I say. "She's my wife." Tauski shakes his head.

He says he'll make those damn bums pay for this. "Where are they?" Tauski asks.

"They're comin' tonight. They always come at night."

"I'm going to fuckin' make them pay and they'll fuckin' remember it, too," Tauski says. My wife says people are staring at us.

Tauski rips his winter jacket open. Underneath it's just his hairy chest.

Older women start quickening their steps. Tauski's teasing them.

My wife just stares at him.

"She was a classy person," I say.

Tauski yells off in the distance. Would he get any sauce if Arvi came now? Where's Arvi?

"Thanks for blaming it on the bums," my wife says to me. She puts a crumpled twenty into my hand.

She doesn't give it to me in ten-euro bills.

A little while later she says she doesn't have anything smaller. Was it a little while later?

"Sausage," I say.

My wife asks if there's anything moving inside my head. My eyes, my mouth, my tongue. My nose and my ears a little bit. And the back of my neck, if you count that.

My wife says that I'm in no shape for a funeral.

But I'm not even dead.

And all the relatives will be kicking dirt in my face.

Is it the inheritance they're after?

My wife starts to laugh. She has to work hard to hold her purse against her chest. Otherwise the power of her laughter would toss it to the ground.

I laugh, too.

"Inheritance," my wife laughs.

Gotta get some sausage.

My wife says, "You've got a twenty, go buy some." They ain't gonna let me in the store. One time they thought I drank one of their beers right next to the beverage cooler.

My wife asks if I fully realize that my son is dead. I show her that I can still laugh like a crow. My wife leaves. At the bus stop she turns back and looks at me.

I wave. She waves, too.

What's taking Arvi so long? And Tauski's gone, though the bums'll be here soon.

I won't be feeling good in a moment. Some guy walks up and says I should be ashamed of myself, that I should get a job.

He speaks to me in a formal way.

My son's dead. They killed my little boy.

Part Two:

They rarely need to be opened from the inside

19. Laura Pahka, Shopkeeper

Mäentaka drops me off at my apartment building, and in front of the correct door even. He gets out of the car, pulls my suitcases out of the trunk, and sets them on the ground. The sun's rising. I thank him and let out a big yawn, so I won't have to invite him in, with all that would entail. I tell him to give me a buzz the next time he comes to town, and we can go out and wiggle our bodies to the tango. During the trip I found out that he's a dancer.

I know Mäentaka will call. By next weekend at the latest, he'll call, all surprised that something urgent just came up that he needs to take care of here in Rovaniemi. He won't remember that as the plane took off from the Palermo airport, he told me he only has to do business in Rovaniemi once a year, even though it's just sixty miles away from his office and almost all of his customers are here. That's how the male brain works, and also the brain of a log cabin salesman.

As he's leaving I ask if I can keep the *Lapin Kansa* newspaper he bought at the gas station in Kemi. Mäentaka says, "Fine," folds it over a few times, and predicts that before long he'll be dancing the tango to the beats of *The Fabled Land* with me. I laugh politely. He's pretty handsome, and he's kept himself in good shape. And he was so adorably embarrassed when I squeezed his bicep after our first drink on the plane and asked him if he got that by going to the gym or by lifting logs.

Once I'm at home I kick aside the mail that's accumulated on the floor underneath the mail slot. I carry my suitcases into the bedroom and go take a shower. I look at myself in the bathroom mirror, happy that I kept my breasts out of the sun. Men like tanned women who seem especially naked when their breasts are glowing white.

I stroll wet and naked through my apartment and reclaim my home. I read the article in *Lapin Kansa* one more time.

I make up my mind to actually do what I had already decided as we were leaving Kemi, and I get dressed, despite being exhausted. I turn the radio on to blast me awake.

The radio plays several syrupy, passionate Italian songs in a row. I'm amused that I can't remember my Sicilian bed partner's face. I rated him a C-minus, which really should have been a D-minus because he didn't know how to behave afterward. The next afternoon he showed up at the street café near my hotel and tried to force himself into my arms to kiss me, but I pushed him off, said a polite hello, and went to leave. He grabbed me by the wrist. I remembered what I had learned in a self-defense class and twisted his arm behind his back, forcing him to squat down, moaning. I kicked him in the ass and told him I'd cut off his balls if he ever crossed my path again.

He was left with two alternatives. He either had to take off or kill me. He chose the former. I had looked up the word for castrate in Italian, just for this sort of occasion—*castrare*.

After such a repulsive incident, I didn't feel like practicing *pasta erotica* anymore, so I just wandered around town in a bit of a buzz. I knew that the wine would keep any stomach bugs at bay.

Mäentaka was on the same tour company's trip, but we didn't actually meet until the return flight. I wouldn't have minded meeting up with him earlier. It would've been funny if I'd gone all the way to Sicily to get between the sheets with a log home builder from Kemijärvi.

Mäentaka was good looking, well-built, a Finnish male powerhouse. He wanted company for the long drive from Helsinki to Rovaniemi, and I knew I'd be safe with him. I had taken the train down to visit my sister in Helsinki, and getting a ride back with Mäentaka saved me quite a bit of money. He was a good guy.

I put on a modest dress and flat shoes and dabbed on a bit of makeup. In my line of work people tend to shun a shopkeeper who looks too flashy.

I walk the quarter of a mile to my store, and the brisk spring weather perks me up. I remember how I missed this clean air when I was in Sicily.

I open the front door and look around. No break-ins. My mom always comes by to check on my store when I go out of town, even for one night. "So the store doesn't go belly up," she says. It's been five years and she's still amazed that her little girl can run a business. She goes to the library regularly to read business magazines and makes copies of the gloomiest articles to show me, just to keep me on my toes.

I air out the place and stand by the front door to call my mom on the cordless phone. I tell her I've returned safely. She's surprised. She was sure I'd be raped and killed. When Mom starts going on about the long-term cycles of the global economy, I move the door with my foot to ring the customer bell. I tell her I have to go help a customer.

"Try to make a sale," Mom advises me, and we end the call telling each other "kiss, kiss."

I get the cash register ready and wait. I smoke a cigarette amidst the hum of the range hood in the back room, then walk into the display room, take off my shoes and put them behind the counter. Using a stool I climb into a casket. I cross my arms over my chest and stare at the water damage on the ceiling.

I close my eyes.

The casket is a peaceful place, but that's probably because I'm tired.

I wake up to the sound of banging on the front door. The lid of the casket accidentally slams shut. I can faintly hear the customer bell buzzing.

I start to sweat. I can hear a distant conversation. I freak out when I realize I don't know if the casket's airtight, and if it can be opened from the inside. Obviously, they rarely need to be opened from the inside.

I hear puzzled voices, and then another buzz of the customer bell. I push the lid open and gasp for air. My face is sweaty. It's hard to get out of the casket—the cushion has sucked in my rear end so tightly that it makes a reluctant slurping noise when it finally lets me go. I quickly put on my shoes and run out to the street.

I yell after two women, an old one and a young one. They turn around and slowly walk back. I ask them if they were coming into my store. I explain that I was in the back alley emptying the garbage, and I thought I heard the customer bell ring.

The older lady takes stock of my reddened face, but doesn't say anything. The younger one says, "Yes, we need a casket." I ask them to come back into the store, and apologize that they had to traipse back and forth. I tell them I just returned from vacation. The younger woman says she can tell that from my face.

I recognize the younger one; her name is Sarlotta. She was three grades below me at Korkalovaara School. I envied her name back then. It's still a beautiful name.

The sidewalk's slippery from the morning dew, and I warn Sarlotta about it. This way I engage her in conversation, and it's more difficult for her to decline the invitation to come into my store. Sarlotta mumbles that the bottoms of her shoes are worn smooth and new shoes cost too much. The older woman doesn't say a word. I sense that if it were up to her, they wouldn't come back in. Older women consider so many things to be personal affronts.

I lead the women into the store and lock the door behind us. When the older woman raises her eyebrows as if to ask why, I realize she does it the same way as Marzipan. I know now that she's his mother, and I say that now we can talk without any interruptions.

I take the women into the back room. I spread a white tablecloth on the table and tell them that I haven't even had time to drink my morning coffee yet, and I'm guessing the ladies would like some, too.

"Thank you," Marzipan's mother says, accepting the offer, and I know I've won her over. I put a lot of coffee grounds into the coffeemaker. Coffee was hard to come by in the 1940s, and expensive in the 1950s, so to older ladies it's always expensive and hard to come by. Strong coffee is a sign of respect.

Sarlotta asks where I went on vacation, and I have to walk the tightrope between being good-naturedly polite and being ready to share the grief of someone who's recently lost a loved one. It's a precise, but shifting boundary. I tell Sarlotta about the food, the hotel, the cleanliness, the sun, and the friendliness of the locals and the unbelievable brashness of the shopkeepers. I play down my Italian language skills just enough. During the conversation, I keep studying Marzipan's mother's expressions.

When the coffee's ready, I pour it into cups that sit on dainty saucers. Marzipan's mother isn't the type to drink coffee out of a mug. Sarlotta asks for milk or cream for her coffee. I give her cream. Marzipan's mother tastes the coffee, and for the first time gives me a friendly look.

We all drink another cup, and when the women have politely turned down cardamom rolls and a third cup of coffee, Marzipan's mother clears her throat.

She introduces herself as Mrs. Räikkönen. Her son died suddenly yesterday morning.

"My brother was killed," Sarlotta says. Marzipan's mother clears her throat again and asks if her daughter thinks it was necessary to share this fact with the shopkeeper, and if she thinks they make special caskets for those who have met a violent death. I assure her that the casket doesn't ask how someone died.

"Shall we go into the display room?" I ask.

"A proper casket," Marzipan's mother says.

"The customer won't complain, even if it isn't," Sarlotta says.

"Your brother isn't the customer, we are," Marzipan's mother snaps back.

I pretend not to hear them, because it's clearly the seed of an argument, and I shouldn't take sides. But if I had to, I'd side with the mother.

Marzipan's mother and Sarlotta start checking out the caskets, feeling them, fingering the tassels. The mother moves the same way her son did, like a large cat. It's rare in an old woman.

Marzipan moved that way from the time he was a boy. When I was a girl I knew all about boys' sports, just as I know all about men's sports now. In gym class, the boys always picked a nerd or a girly guy to be the goalie. Marzipan wanted to be the goalie, but no one ever thought of making fun of him. He'd jump around and stalk the ball like it was a mouse. When we girls were running endless laps around the field, I would imagine Marzipan pouncing on the ball, and with a flash and a bang the ball would give up the ghost.

Marzipan was my hero. He's the one who'd get me hot. My imagination would dress him in an unbuttoned shirt, revealing his muscular hairy chest. He'd wear boots that smelled like leather…and I'd fantasize about him in his underwear. A dreamy teenage boy.

In class that thirteen-year-old shy girl didn't see the lanky, slightly big-boned yet amazingly graceful boy, but instead her secret nightly lover, whose greatness only grew because he was the first one in school wild enough to wear a leather jacket, and because he royally beat up an older boy who teased him about it.

My family had moved from Kemi to Rovaniemi over Christmas, and my first day of school I heard about it from everyone—I was told that people from Kemi and Rovaniemi were eternal enemies, because the people in Kemi were Communists. I told them that no one in Kemi had ever heard of such a feud, but they just kept making fun of me. Mom couldn't understand why I refused to wear my red sweater.

I couldn't tell them, and didn't think to tell them, that my dad had always voted for the Center Party and my Mom however she was told, except once right after Dad died she accidentally voted for the Social Democrats, carried away by her newly-found freedom of choice.

In retrospect, I'm convinced that a thorough accounting of my family's political views wouldn't have helped. My class simply lacked a suitable target for their bullying, and I fell right into it as if on cue: A shy, modest, average student, who once drew a pirate with stars for his eyes in her math book. The teacher showed my drawing to the entire class.

Marzipan's mother asks me about prices. I give her the price list and tell her that we offer installment plans. Sarlotta blows on her fingernails, like she used to twenty years ago. When the girls in our class talked about boys during recess, often about Marzipan, I could see Sarlotta blowing on her fingernails out of shame within her own circle of younger girls. I didn't get it. I would've been beside myself with giddiness if Marzipan was my brother—or even better, my boyfriend.

I don't remember any other girls from Korkalovaara School three grades below me, but I do remember Sarlotta. I memorized things about her. The clothes she wore, what rock star's photo she had in her schoolbag, when she began wearing makeup, and how she cut her hair. Eavesdropping at recess, I learned what she liked and what she hated. I got much closer to Marzipan that way.

And I remember the moment when I fell in love with Marzipan.

Viinikainen, the worst bully, got the bright idea to start calling me names. One day he kept repeating it over and over. A group of ten kids waited for me outside after class, and pushed me into the middle of the group.

"Wet-ass Laura," they taunted me. My backpack landed on the ground, spilling its contents, which got soaked in the snow. I started to cry, but that just egged them on—they smelled blood.

Marzipan came into the schoolyard, swaggering and swinging his schoolbag. Viinikainen, who became a waiter, yelled to Marzipan, "Come take a look, here's a Communist from Kemi, whose name is Wet-ass, ain't that a hell of a name for a Kemi Communist."

I'll never forget it. Marzipan blazed a trail toward me through the circle of kids, wiped my tears, gave me a kiss on the cheek, which was completely over the top for a thirteen-year-old boy, and said, "Laura is a perfectly fine name."

The group broke up. Never again did anyone from school call me names or pester me about being from Kemi. Marzipan's status was unchallenged; he had accepted me, and he went so far as to accept me in a way that shocked our fellow classmates.

From that moment on, I loved Marzipan and still do to this day.

Any psychologist would say that I suffer from childhood regression or fixation or projection or whatever, but that wouldn't change anything. I suppose I know that. I know why I love him, but it doesn't change my love for him. If Marzipan were alive, and if he walked through the front door of my store and wanted twenty thousand euros, I'd close up shop, walk to the bank, and take out a loan. I'm absolutely sure of it.

I'm not beautiful.

It doesn't hurt as much now as it did when I was a teenager.

The incident on that March afternoon taught me to work on myself. I've played sports and taken care of my body and mind, doing the best I could with what I had.

I'm not smart, but I've worked hard to educate myself.

All this because Marzipan, a thirteen-year-old pubescent hoodlum, gave me life. Just like that.

Marzipan's mother asks if I'm still here. I apologize for being lost in my thoughts. Sarlotta says that choosing a casket shouldn't take this long. Marzipan's mother asks if they can take the brochure and call me if they find a casket they like.

I offer them a discount if they decide right now. They huddle in the corner to talk.

When he was fifteen, Marzipan disappeared from school. He'd been held back a grade. Rumors went around that the principal went to Marzipan's house to bring him to school, but Marzipan punched him so hard that the principal had to take a week of sick leave. The principal didn't have the nerve to take legal action. I thought the rumor was credible.

After that I only saw Marzipan once. When I heard about the line of work he chose, I worried about his fate.

Five years ago I spent an evening with a loudmouthed computer analyst. I probably would've gone to bed with him, but he got so drunk that the police had to drag him out of the pub.

Sort of amused, I decided to stay and have a few more beers at the bar.

Marzipan sat down on a stool around the curve of the bar. I would've recognized him through the pub window in the middle of the night, because he still moved like the world's largest cat.

I was terribly nervous. He was alone, so I went over to talk to him. I told him we were in the same grade in school.

"Minna Perttilä?" he guessed. He was pretty drunk. Later some of his friends joined him, all skid row alcoholics, and I shied away. When Marzipan and his group went to play the slot machines, I gave the bartender two hundred euros and asked him to give it to Marzipan. I said he'd dropped it. "I don't think so," the bartender doubted, but I made him swear he'd give it to him.

With my two hundred euros in his pocket, Marzipan stumbled out of my life. Nonetheless, I was ready to help him out if he ever needed it.

A rough life spent at the bars had aged him, but I was sure that if I ever went to his place, took his hand and placed it on my cheek, he'd tell me that Laura was a perfectly fine name—just like he had before.

Marzipan's mother clears her throat and complains that she never knew caskets were so expensive.

"Mom thinks making a thousand euros a month is good money," Sarlotta says, lifting her purse and getting ready to leave.

I ask if her name is Sarlotta.

"Yeah," Sarlotta says, surprised.

"How do you know that?" Marzipan's mother asks.

"We went to the same school; I remember your name," I say.

I ask Marzipan's mother if Räikkönen, the murder victim mentioned in the newspaper, was her son. She says her son was indeed the murder victim.

"He was in the same grade I was," I say.

"What's your name?" Marzipan's mother asks.

"Laura Pahka," I say.

"Ah," Marzipan's mother lies, as if she remembers; older women always pretend to know their children's classmates.

"He was a real hero," I say.

The women go quiet.

I realize they've misunderstood me, thinking I was being sarcastic and really calling him a hoodlum, a schemer, a low-life, or a criminal. I didn't know how to fix it.

Marzipan's mother says she'll be in touch about the casket.

They're already at the door when I say, "What about this brown one?"

"What do you mean?" Sarlotta asks in a huff.

They sense something and come back inside. They walk around the casket and check it out, peering inside. Marzipan's mother asks if something's wrong with the casket. I tell them no.

"It's a fine casket," Sarlotta says.

She goes on to say that all the caskets are good, but her mother doesn't want to part with her money; to her it's like she's throwing money into a hole in the ground.

Marzipan's mother shoots Sarlotta a furious glance. Sarlotta looks at her mother as if she doesn't recognize this angry woman who's silently fuming.

"I'm saying that you can have the casket free of charge, completely free," I tell them.

"Why?" asks Sarlotta.

"For an old classmate," I say.

"You shouldn't pay any heed to what my daughter's saying," Marzipan's mother says, but stares at me intently.

"I absolutely insist," I say. I tell them the business is going well and that one casket isn't a big deal. "Besides, Marzipan was a good friend of mine," I say.

"Oh, okay," Marzipan's mother says.

"Thank you very much," Sarlotta says.

"What do we do now?" Marzipan's mother asks.

Sarlotta tells her mother they shouldn't offend me. If a shopkeeper wants to donate a casket to her deceased classmate, then she can do so. She says they have no right to rob me of that joy. Marzipan's mother mumbles something about making the arrangements.

"Well, okay then," I say, and we arrange the details. They leave and I lock up, dead tired.

I've warmed up the casket for Marzipan. I fall asleep on the sofa in my office, hoping for no dreams. Mäentaka, however, will somehow sneak his way into them.

20. Aila Kildenstamm,
Head Union Representative

I haven't slept in three days, unless I've done so with my eyes open. I've sat until my back was sore, and I've walked miles of hospital corridors. Fatigue is starting to weigh me down now, as the strength that accompanies shock fades away.

I smell myself. When I'm nervous, I sweat, and I haven't showered for three days. Pirkko said she'd bring me a change of clothes and other necessities in the morning. It's now six in the morning on May 1, May Day. We had planned to drink a bottle of wine at the Shack on May Day, and I'd bought silly, red May Day noses. Mauri probably would have peered out the window to make sure no one accidentally caught him wearing one.

I'm holding Mauri's hand. I give him strength that way. Every now and then I squeeze his hand hard, but Mauri hasn't responded yet. Now I'm squeezing it again. Nothing. I get up from the chair and walk over to the window.

The birch trees have almost leafed out. The sun woke them up yesterday. I so wanted to greet spring at the Shack with Mauri. I still want to.

I won't cry. It takes energy, energy that I want to give to Mauri.

When they called from the hospital and told me Mauri had been shot, I wanted to know how serious it was. "Unfortunately we have no information here at the front desk," a woman's voice had said slowly, and I knew right then that it was a matter of life or death.

I was worried about having enough cash for the taxi. As I called for the cab, I kept saying that I needed a taxi that would accept a credit card. It's weird how your brain functions when in shock.

Once I got to the hospital, a woman came up to me and said that my husband hadn't been shot. He'd had a heart attack that at first appeared to be moderate, but now some complications were developing.

I wondered aloud whether there's a loud bang in someone's chest when they have a heart attack. The doctor introduced herself with a Russian name and said she didn't understand what I meant. I asked how the hospital staff could get confused between a heart attack and a shooting victim, when no one outside the hospital would. "Tell me about it," the doctor sighed.

It seems like that was just a moment ago. The doctor's sigh stays with me in these rooms. That was three days ago.

I go to Mauri's bedside, sit down, take his hand, and squeeze it.

I caress his cheek; it feels scratchy. He's so helpless, and he's such a man.

The first afternoon, evening, and night I kept calling home, in case Pirkko had gone there. She'd given me her girlfriend's number, but of course I left it at home. I got hold of her the following afternoon. She said she'd come right away.

When I saw Pirkko, I had to hold back tears. Within twenty-four hours she'd become a child again, frightened by every hospital bed, tube, device, and every person in a white jacket. She told me she was afraid one of them would come and tell her that her father was dead. I held Mauri with one hand and Pirkko with the other. I was about to split in two.

Pirkko's neck looked terrible, covered with hickeys. I touched them and asked her if she liked the boy a lot, and if she remembered what I've told her about birth control. Pirkko started crying. The hickeys weren't from a boy; but from clothespins. She and her girlfriend wanted to have something to brag about at school. She regretted being so deceitful, and now it was even more horrible, since this had happened to Dad. She assured me, with tears in her eyes, that she wouldn't let clothespins pinch her neck anymore.

She cried for a long time and then pulled herself together. She went home that evening and returned later with a thermal lunch box full of liver gravy, mashed potatoes, and cooked carrots. I ate all of it. It tasted so good—I'd forgotten to eat. Pirkko started bringing me food every day, and she threatened to give me a sponge bath this morning if I didn't start washing myself.

I go to the window, come back, and squeeze Mauri's hand again.

I'm a tough old lady—that's what Mauri says—and I know it, too. But when you whack a tough old lady in the right spot, she'll shrivel up. I'd feel empty if Mauri were taken from me. I can't imagine having to build a life with someone else. If all Mauri did was wheeze in bed and fill his pants, it would be good enough for me. I could keep him clean and squeeze his hand.

I caught the head nurse by my husband's bed yesterday, caressing his chest. I think it was yesterday—the light confuses me this time of year. I got back from walking the halls, and she was lost in her thoughts, but to me it didn't look work-related.

I stood in the doorway and didn't say anything. The head nurse broke the uncomfortable silence. She said she was washing my husband. I didn't respond. She looked at her hand and was startled. She apologized, saying that she was so scatterbrained during these busy times that she'd forgotten to put on a washcloth. She criticized the younger nurses, who spent all their time discussing parties and the escapades of international playboys and weren't interested in the welfare of their patients.

She probably intended that as an answer to my unspoken question as to why the director of nursing would be washing a patient in the first place.

She said she was going to get a washcloth, but she never returned. Later I asked one of the nurses about her, but all I got was a long look and a longer sigh.

The sigh from the nurse joined the one from the doctor and they wander the halls with me.

The door opens.

Rosebush walks in with a bouquet of roses. He enters sideways and holds the flowers far away from himself. I have a sudden fluttering feeling inside. I realize that I've missed having someone else to talk to besides Pirkko, who doesn't actually talk all that much. She's now decided to become the mother of the family, since Mom is so consumed with worry. Mothers *do* rather than *talk*, and when they're engaged in a conversation they spend most of their time listening.

Rosebush is startled to see me. I nod to him and try to smile.

"A few flowers, for Mauri…"

Rosebush doesn't know where to put the flowers. He tosses them on the bed, and a few land on Mauri's face. Rosebush sits on the edge of the bed and starts pondering life and its random events. He tells me how, after his friend and colleague was shot, he dragged him out of the woods. He expected to get some recognition for his heroism, but felt that everyone was pissing on his shoes. At the station, Rosebush overheard some snotty-nosed peon with a desk job complaining to his boss about having to go to the doctor because he'd been shot. The ridicule went on for a good fifteen minutes and only got louder when they realized Rosebush was standing in the doorway, steaming.

I tell Rosebush that I'm grateful to him. In my mind he saved my husband's life.

His eyes fill with tears, and he thanks me. He tells me he was upset when the hospital staff treated him like a moron. He thought Mauri's narrow escape was a miracle. He looks at me intently and says he still believes that a steel-winged angel plucked the bullet shot by Kassu Vartio right in midair. He's relived the shooting in detail, the moments before and the moments after. He's sure he saw a steel-winged angel. He realizes that the angels in the Bible are men, but this angel was a plump woman with golden hair and light makeup. She looked a lot like world champion weightlifter Karoliina Lundahl. As the angel was leaving, she showed Rosebush the bullet she'd snatched and placed under her wing. Then she winked at him, raised her wings, and swooshed away. The longer Rosebush pondered the matter, the more certain he became that he'd seen the angel and the wink, and he thought of the resemblance between the angel and the weightlifter.

I ask Rosebush if he's still on sick leave.

Rosebush gets up off the bed and takes several quick steps, turns his back to me, then abruptly turns to face me. He's considering suing the people that forced him to take sick leave. He tells me he went to the doctor, who just muttered something and nodded, and wrote him a month's worth of sick leave. Rosebush laughed at the guy, telling him he didn't need a single day of leave, he needed to work. He said he'd rather some young lazy punk use his sick leave, but the doctor said it wasn't optional, and the leave would be effective immediately.

Rosebush remembered the last time he was sick, thirty years ago in the spring, and it was over the weekend, so he didn't have to miss any work.

I try to console him, suggesting that he enjoy the spring and read some books.

Rosebush suggests that I think he's crazy. He raises his hand, waiting for my denial. He doesn't want to talk about it; he only wants to talk about Mauri's condition. I tell him that Mauri hasn't regained consciousness yet.

Rosebush reminds me about the flowers he brought for Mauri. I thank him and tell him they're beautiful. Red roses are my favorite.

Rosebush is concerned about the flowers being the right color. He says he doesn't know much about flowers. At the florist he checked a couple of books about the meanings of different flowers, but it ended up only confusing him more. He first selected yellow flowers, because the color was supposed to represent loyalty. But while the clerk was wrapping them, he browsed through another book, which claimed that yellow flowers symbolized intense, passionate love, so he changed his mind.

After thinking about it, he decided that because Mauri meant a lot to him, the yellow flowers represented what he wanted to convey after all, but by now they were all sold out. He ended up with red, and he told me he didn't know anything about their symbolism.

I tell him the flowers are beautiful and that's all that matters. I assure him that Mauri knows what he wants to convey.

Rosebush squeezes Mauri's foot and says he has to go. He plans to go straight home. At a time like this, he wouldn't even enjoy watching and making fun of the May Day parade. He makes me promise to call him the moment Mauri returns to this world—so he can immediately tell Mauri how he was saved.

I promise to call.

Pirkko comes in, and we hug. She looks into my eyes, and I shake my head. I get up and go to the sink to brush my teeth. They feel like new after brushing. I wash my face with the familiar-scented soap.

I glance in the mirror. I look terrible. I've lost weight, but mostly I look broken down.

"Put on some makeup," Pirkko suggests, and I put a little color here and there. I go to the hallway to stretch my legs and come back.

I sit down next to Mauri and take his hand. Pirkko looks out the window and tells me she was hiding behind the door so she wouldn't have to face Rosebush.

"He's just in shock."

"Hasn't he always been that way?"

"No."

"Really?"

"No, he hasn't. Policemen can't be nutcases."

"He seems scary."

"You don't know him."

"I'd be more scared if I did. If he really hasn't always been like that."

"He's a sweetheart of a guy."

"Did he bring roses?"

"Yes."

"Red roses?"

"He told me a long story about it."

"Men don't understand anything about anything."

"He's just in shock."

"I'm not dissing him."

"Come here."

"What?"

"Let me hug you."

We hug. Pirkko tells me she's going to bring me a veal cutlet this afternoon. She made it herself. She's going to put canned asparagus on top; she remembers that I had a dish like that on our first trip abroad.

How can it stick in a three-year-old's mind that her mother ate Veal Oscar at the Stockholm train station? I hug her again. She gets up and says she's going to get us some coffee and sandwiches.

Before I get a chance to ask, she says, "Yes, I have money."

She's gone for a good while, and I'm about to go looking for her.

"Take these goddamn weeds off my face."

I turn and look into Mauri's tired eyes, and fling the roses to the floor. He squeezes my hand like an eighty-five-year-old. I laugh and immediately tell him about the clothespins that sucked on our daughter's neck.

21. Pipsa Skinner, Pedicurist

Esa's sleeping. His vacation starts tomorrow. He always takes his vacation in May so he can get his car ready for summer.

A moment ago we were still at it, but with less enthusiasm than before. He's been after me ever since his Volga got smashed up. For days on end now, dammit, even though we're not teenagers any more. Well, that's what he's like.

At first I was afraid of him. The first time we went to a dance together, a neighbor boy asked me to dance a schottische. I looked at Esa to see if it was okay. He nodded a tenth of an inch.

When we got to his car, I was shocked because I thought he was having a seizure. He was shaking and quivering and snorting, and then started licking me all over, and he then had me. When I got out of his car afterward, the roof was steaming in the cool early morning. And the car wasn't even running.

I lost my earring in the tussle. Esa brought it back to me several days later. He said he'd washed it. I was dumbfounded as to why he would've washed it. Then I realized the poor guy had been so horny that he hadn't noticed swallowing it. And it wasn't a small earring.

When he gets mad, all the blood goes into his shaft. From what I've heard from my nurse friends, that's unusual.

Sometimes I get scared.

When his yellow Volga was towed into our driveway, I cried. Esa had pampered that car so much! I didn't try calming him down by petting him, he would've just blown up.

If his yellow Volga had been bashed up ten years ago, he would've screwed me to death. I'm absolutely, positively sure about that.

He's calmed down with age.

Every now and then I say to my sister with a laugh that the day will come when I'll get him mad on purpose. I still haven't needed to, since a lot of things make him angry, mainly the taxes on cars and the price of gas.

Yesterday I caught him whistling angrily.

He'd been cursing for many days that his Volga was an unrepairable piece of shit. And yesterday, at one-thirty in the morning, he was wondering whether the frame could be straightened out after all.

I hope so. I got some *again*.

I get up and sit on the edge of the bed so I can hear better.

Sara hasn't woken up yet tonight. She's woken up every night since the poor thing found Marzipan beaten to death.

She sits up in bed and mutters, "The man isn't crying at all, the man isn't crying at all." It lasts for a while.

In the morning I've asked her about waking up, but I stopped as she doesn't seem to remember. Hopefully it won't affect her development. People have had their development affected by smaller things—there are many good examples of that in the city's public housing.

I tiptoe into the kitchen. In front of the refrigerator door, I drink some lingonberry juice straight out of the pitcher. I sit down on a chair, then head to the bathroom when I realize that Esa's juice is running down my thighs. I wipe the chair off with toilet paper and put it in the toilet.

I just sit and hum; Esa's on track again.

I just hope Sara isn't permanently scarred.

I decide to stay at the table, in case Sara happens to wake up.

I wake up with my neck twisted like a corkscrew, thinking about Veera Jaakkola's horrible heels.

Part Three:

The leaves are playing house in the birch tree

22. Detective Lieutenant Torsti Rautapää

I called the hospital on the first business day after May Day, and got stuck talking with that fucking Stella Gavia. She claimed that the chief physician was in a meeting.

It turned into an argument. The fucking director of nursing wouldn't agree to anything.

"Can't the police ask the murderer any questions?" I bellowed.

"Not until the end of the week, at the earliest," Gavia argued back. Apparently I should've already gone looking for her stolen bicycle. I told her that on Friday I'd be interrogating Arkady Wolfovich Arkhipov or arresting Stella Gavia.

The line went silent. I used that to my advantage and slammed the phone down in her ear. I like old office phones. It's hard to slam a cell phone in someone's ear.

Clearing out my lungs was invigorating. I called Officer Vauhkonen into my office.

She was dressed in loose-fitting clothing, but couldn't hide her stunning body. I welcomed her to the Violent Crimes Unit.

She thanked me, shifting her position on the chair. I wanted to be that chair.

I promised her there would be plenty of work, and good investigators were highly valued. The salary was what it was, but someone who wasn't afraid of hard work could make more with overtime.

She said that hard work puts food on the table.

I said my name was Torsti.

"Marja-Leena," she said with a slight smile. Dammit, it made my neck tingle.

I told her that the police department traditionally had been a man's world. And, it wasn't just about strength. If the boys start talking inappropriately, you come tell me. We'll figure out some way to keep them in check.

Marja-Leena said she'd be fine. She had four brothers. Her mother always had to protect them from her.

"Good," I said, and offered her a cigarette. She said she was trying to quit.

I lit up. She stared directly into my eyes through the smoke.

I told her I didn't know how to put it, but as an older man I had to try. The young guys wouldn't have the nerve to say it.

"What do you mean older?" Marja-Leena said.

That felt so good I had to pretend to cough out smoke so she wouldn't notice the look on my face.

I said that machismo was expressed at the police department through shouting, stupid stories, and hidden aggressiveness. I asked whether she'd noticed that.

She said she'd had very little experience with it. But there was a lot of truth to what the detective lieutenant was saying.

"Torsti," I said.

"That's right," she said.

I told her I was glad to see anything that would help me get rid of the macho attitude around the department. It was the little things, like how people dress.

Marja-Leena raised her eyebrows.

I quickly told her I would not be giving orders about dress code. But if any of the women wanted to dress in a feminine way, I'd definitely support it.

"I see," Marja-Leena said.

I pointed out that the men who weren't required to wear uniforms dressed like men around here, so why couldn't women dress like women?

"Uh-huh," Marja-Leena said.

I remembered how at my first job, in the late sixties, one of the office girls wore a miniskirt. The old dinosaur of a police chief almost had a heart attack and chewed her out. From then on the poor girl wore such long skirts that she kept tripping over them walking down the hallway.

Marja-Leena let out a strange giggle, then quickly stopped and asked whether I wanted her to wear a miniskirt.

I told her it was up to her, and that I wasn't going to stand in the way of modern fashion.

"I see," Marja-Leena said.

"Please don't get me wrong," I said.

"Of course not," Marja-Leena said.

I said I believed it was the little things that could change the atmosphere in the department. They were also bound to advance gender equality.

"Uh-huh," Marja-Leena said.

"Maybe you'll become the first female detective lieutenant in Rovaniemi," I said.

"Well, I don't know," Marja-Leena said. She complained that my room was hot. She took off her jean jacket and folded it in her lap. Jesus Christ.

I asked Marja-Leena to walk around the unit and introduce herself to everyone. If anyone acted condescending to her, my door would always be open.

Marja-Leena got up. She extended her hand to me across the table. I shook it and then pulled it in front of my face.

Boasting, I said that my unit definitely arrested bad guys. Marja-Leena thanked me.

She slowly walked to the door.

Once the door was closed, I got up. I turned around and looked President Martti Ahtisaari right in the eye. I'd had the photo put up at exactly that height.

I took a step to the side and looked myself in the eye. The mirror was the same size as the photo of Ahtisaari. I'd also chosen the same frame.

I smiled.

"A modern policeman," I said aloud.

I sat down and punched the Grizz's number into the phone.

He answered, timidly. I advised him to either answer the phone or not answer at all. Sighing into the receiver doesn't befit a snitch.

The Grizz whined that he hadn't found out much.

I asked him if he knew what I had sitting in front of me. "An arrest warrant," I said.

"Torsti," the Grizz said.

I said that all I had to do was find a name to put on it.

The Grizz swallowed. It didn't sound like he had anything to swallow.

"Hello!" I yelled, asking if there was anyone on the other end of the line.

"Arkady's wife," the Grizz said.

That troubled me. "What about her?" I asked. The Grizz asked me if I knew the woman. I didn't.

"I was thinking because of your hobby," the Grizz said. I asked what he knew about my hobbies. He assured me that all he knew was what I'd told him.

"And you've shouted that from the rooftops, you piece of shit snitch," I yelled, just to see how he would react.

The Grizz muttered that he wasn't so dense as to tell everyone in town that he talked to a detective lieutenant daily. I admitted he was right.

"She's as dumb as a box of rocks," the Grizz said. He believed the woman could be helpful if she was cleverly interviewed.

"Will she open her mouth?" I asked.

The Grizz answered that she definitely would. He asked if I had a pen.

"Talk, snitch," I said. He said the woman's name was Aurora Arkhipova.

I asked if the woman was Russian. The Grizz said he'd heard that the woman was Finnish, but bilingual.

"Wow," I said.

"Sorry," he said, surprised.

I asked how I could get in touch with her.

"There aren't too many with that name in the phone book," the Grizz ventured.

"Fuck off," I said, ending the call. I put my feet up on my desk.

Someone knocked on my door and I told them to come in. From the doorway, that boneheaded Jaakkola said I had a customer.

"A customer, huh?" I said. He fussed and said that the customer wanted to talk about Marzipan. I told him to send the man in.

"It's a woman," he hastened to clarify.

Marzipan's mother came in, looking somewhat dignified. I motioned for her to take a seat, and she extended her hand before sitting down, introducing herself as Mrs. Räikkönen.

"Mr. Rautapää," I said.

"Excuse me?"

"If you're a Mrs., then I'm a Mr."

The old lady got up, straightened her jacket and the skirt underneath it. She extended her hand again.

"The mother of the murder victim, Mrs. Alfhild Räikkönen."

"Detective Lieutenant Torsti Rautapää."

The old lady sat down again. I asked if she wouldn't get too warm with her jacket on. She didn't answer.

We sat in silence for a while.

The old lady gave in. She asked if there was anything I wanted to ask her. I told her there wasn't, but I knew she had something to say.

She stared at me across the table, irked, and then broke down unexpectedly. "It's true, it's true," she kept whispering.

I waited for her to wipe her nose, and said I was waiting. The old lady stuffed the dripping tissue into her purse.

"Immediately after the murder I spoke with Detective Lieutenant Nauris," the old lady said, her voice quivering. I corrected her, saying that Nauris was a detective sergeant.

"A very nice young man," the old lady said, blowing her nose again. I made no comment.

The old lady regretted having told Nauris that the Grizz had been at their home just before Marzipan was murdered. It was true. However, the old lady was afraid of having given Nauris the impression that the Grizz was the only one who'd come to their place.

The old lady asked for some water. I went to the door and asked someone to get some coffee for her.

"Thank you," she said.

She fell silent, and I realized that she was waiting for the coffee. It came five minutes later. I asked how far they had to go to get it. Jaakkola said he'd made it himself.

"It's very good," the old lady said.

I wondered if I had to wait till the end of the entire coffee ceremony until we could get down to business. I did.

I could see the old lady covering up her burps as she started talking.

She said she wanted to cast suspicion on the Grizz, because she hated him and her daughter-in-law Laina Räikkönen to the core of her being. I asked her why.

The old lady looked at me with a face begging for pity and asked that the matter stay between the two of us. I promised her that it would.

She said she understood that marriages go sour. That's up to the Lord. What she didn't understand was why they had to commit adultery in her home while the husband was sleeping.

166

"I was awake that night because I had a hunch," the old lady said. "When my anxious son finally fell asleep, his wife sprang into action."

The old lady told me how she had pretended to be asleep when her daughter-in-law came in to make sure she was sleeping. Through the window the old lady saw her daughter-in-law go right into the Grizz's arms. They scampered around in the yard and then went into the shed.

The old lady said that even though she was an old woman, she knew what they had gone there to do.

"You can't be sure about that," I said.

"I was listening on the other side of the shed door."

Daggers were shooting out of her eyes fast and furious. I wondered how I'd seen tears coming out of those same eyes a moment ago; maybe they were made of glass and she could carve daggers out of them as needed.

I started to think that this old lady was made of hard wood, right down to the core. She was a tough old bird, not some nice grandma.

"Go on," I urged her to continue.

She told me how her son had woken up and went outside. When she heard him cursing out there, she was afraid someone was about to get killed.

"And for good reason," I said.

The old lady said she was afraid her son would kill the Grizz. In any case, her son headed off into the woods, and a little while later the woman saw the Grizz bound off into the woods in the opposite direction.

"I'm sure that's not all," I said.

"No," the old lady conceded.

When her daughter-in-law came back to the cottage, the old lady was waiting for her. She whirled her daughter-in-law around so she could see her back—the sight of wood shavings and dirt from the floor of the shed enraged her.

The daughter-in-law argued that there wasn't anything there. And the old lady called her a whore. "You're imagining things, just like your son."

"Get out of here, you whore," the old lady said, shoving her so forcefully that she crashed into the wall. The coat rack swiveled, and a fur hat fell off, landing on her daughter-in-law's head at a ridiculous angle.

The hat infuriated the daughter-in-law more than the shove. In her opinion the fur hat was premeditated humiliation.

The old lady realized what was going on in her daughter-in-law's head and started to laugh. Her daughter-in-law tried to attack her, but the old lady grabbed her by the hair and hauled her into the bedroom, told her to pack, and warned her not to steal anything. The old woman gave her five minutes. She didn't think there was any chance her son would beg for her to come back. It was all over.

"I've paid money for this place," her daughter-in-law said.

"Send the bill to your stud," said the old lady.

Her daughter-in-law cried with rage. The old lady asked if she should call a cab or if the whore was going to walk. Her daughter-in-law didn't answer, so the old lady called a cab.

The daughter-in-law lugged her bag to the top of the steps and walked to the cab. From the back seat she hissed something. The driver got out of the vehicle, took her bag, and put it in the trunk.

"That's how I got rid of her," the old lady said.

"I'm sure that's not all," I said.

The old lady told me that then she started cleaning the cottage. After a little while, Vertti came in.

"Vertti?" I asked.

"My grandson," the old lady said.

Vertti knocked on the window. The old lady went to look. Three men were walking toward the cottage down the rutted road.

Initially, the old lady had figured the men were her son's partners in crime, and she became worried because the men didn't look drunk. The clinking bags were also missing.

The men came in without knocking.

"When you enter a house, you're supposed to knock on the door," the old lady pointed out.

"Tough chick," the youngest in the group said in a nasal voice. The old lady figured he was from some city down south.

An older man, who seemed to be a local, nudged the young one on the shoulder. The one who looked like the leader didn't say a word.

"Where's Marzipan?" the local guy asked.

The old woman said she didn't know. The guy said she'd better know.

"Better for who?" the old lady asked.

"For everyone," the guy responded. He sat down and told the lady she needed to know that this was a serious matter that had to be taken care of.

"Then take care of it, gentlemen," the old lady instructed them.

"The old bitch is fucking with us," the young one said.

The local guy warned the boy against using the term "bitch" before he got one for himself. The young one said he didn't realize he was working with marriage counselors.

"Young punks," the local guy said to the old lady.

"I know all about them," the old lady said.

The young one wondered who was on whose team here.

The old lady said that her son had long ago stopped informing her about his schedule. The local guy said that an attentive mother would be aware of her son's activities without him having to tell her.

The old lady looked at me, blew her nose again, and then said she'd made a terrible mistake. I tried to console her by saying that we all made mistakes.

The young one asked if she had lived a good life.

The old woman said it didn't concern boys she didn't know. The young one said she should think about her life since she was at an age where it might be over at any moment.

"What does that mean?"

"He's an idiot," the local guy said.

"Are you threatening me?" the old lady said.

The young one said he'd been thinking about life himself. He said he'd lived his life to its fullest, and he was ready to bow down in front of the Grim Reaper at any moment.

The old lady put her tissue back in her purse. She was afraid she'd passed a death sentence on her son. She had told the men that her son had gone off into the woods fifteen minutes earlier, and she pointed them in the right direction.

"Why did you tell them where your son went?" I asked.

The old lady said she felt like she was being threatened. She could take almost anything, but not the smallest mention of violence. "Oh no, oh no, does this mean that I had my own son killed?" the old woman lamented.

"I don't think so," I consoled her.

The old lady then wailed that the young one had shot a nasty glance at Vertti, who was clearly terrified, nearly choking on his candy. The old lady took the child into her lap and caressed his head. The boy was hiccupping.

"I kept thinking, what if they hurt little Vertti?" the old lady sighed.

I asked her if she would testify in court that the men who were after Marzipan were all riled up and out for blood.

The old lady thought for a bit. She said she just wanted to tell the truth, the whole truth, and nothing but the truth.

"I don't want you to perjure yourself," I said.

The old lady said she could testify that the men went into the woods very determined.

"How good is your vision?" I asked.

"I'd recognize them anytime," the old lady said.

I asked her to describe them, and she described them to a tee—she'd obviously seen Arkady Wolfovich Arkhipov, Kassu Vartio, and Ossi Kaukonen.

I asked the old lady if she'd met the men before. The old lady had seen Kassu Vartio, the local guy, a few times in Rovaniemi with her son.

"And the ringleader didn't say a word?" I asked.

"No," the old lady said. She figured that was part of the men's plan: the local one was nice, the boy from the south was mean, and the ringleader was quiet.

In the old lady's opinion they'd planned it so she'd be most afraid of the man who was quiet. She said that if she felt she couldn't communicate with him, the man could do anything.

"Was there anything else you remember?" I asked. The old lady suddenly looked sly. She thanked me for being a skilled policeman.

The old lady said she hadn't wanted to know about her son's criminal activities, but in a small cottage words were heard here and there. Even a spry old grandma could put two and two together.

"How did you put two and two together?" I asked. The old lady had begun to amaze me.

The old lady raised a finger and lectured, "The leader didn't speak, because his accent would've revealed his

171

identity." From that she reasoned that the leader was Arkady the Russian. She'd heard a few things about him.

"What kinds of things?" I asked.

"Reprehensible things," the old lady said. She understood that her son and Arkady the Russian were competitors in some business that she didn't want to know anything about.

I said that the newspapers hadn't indicated that one of the people held in conjunction with the case was a Russian.

"So, he is then," the old lady said, delighted. I had to smile.

"I didn't say that," I said.

"Of course you didn't," the old lady said, nodding like a bobblehead doll.

I asked if the men immediately went after Marzipan, and if they said anything. The old lady said that the men took off jogging toward the woods, and they stumbled onto the right trail.

"Did they have any guns?" I asked.

"The young one had a bag."

"What was in it?"

The old lady didn't know.

She possibly heard a little jingling coming from it, but she wasn't sure.

I said I was surprised by all the people who'd been at her cottage that morning, and wondered who else might've been there.

"Ambulances and the police," the old lady said. She asked if the murderers had confessed. I said the survivors hadn't been interrogated yet, but were being pampered with clean sheets in the hospital.

"Dear detective lieutenant, please put my son's murderers in prison," the old lady begged.

"I just arrest them; the court sends them to prison," I said, and asked if there was anything else she wanted to say.

The old lady thought for a moment. "No," she said, "I've told you everything," and she regretted any difficulties that the Grizz has faced because of anything she'd said.

I consoled her by saying that the Grizz always had something on his conscience. It was for the public benefit if he had to answer for something.

"Thank you," the old lady said and got up.

"Um…," I said, "my condolences." The old lady thanked me and said she would bury her son tomorrow. Then she disappeared out the door with her head held high.

I put my feet up on my desk.

A tricky case had started to solve itself beautifully. I was glad I'd resisted the Rovaniemi office of the National Bureau of Investigation, who had started sticking their snoopy noses into the case. They could smell headlines from miles away.

I got up, turned around, and looked President Martti Ahtisaari in the eye. The president's gaze met mine.

I took a step to the side, in front of the mirror. "'The case can be considered largely solved,' Detective Lieutenant Torsti Rautapää from Rovaniemi Violent Crimes Unit told *Ilta-Sanomat* early this morning," I said aloud.

It didn't sound that bad.

I made the most monsterlike face I could in the mirror. I repeated it ten times. It keeps the muscles in the face taut, and keeps the chin from sagging.

I shadowboxed for a moment and then sat down at my desk. I took out the phone book and looked up a number, then dialed it.

Busy.

I dug a ten-cent coin out of my pocket and flipped it. After I flipped tails five times, I tried the number again.

Busy.

I threw tails five more times.

"Aurora," a nice voice answered.

I stated who I was and said I needed some help.

I suggested that we meet, and mentioned a time and place. It worked for her. "I like miniskirts," I said, but apparently she'd already hung up the phone.

23. Ensio Räikkönen, Chief Executive Officer

I hopped onto the platform, walked through the train station, and got into a taxi. I asked the driver to take me to the Saarenkylä Nursing Home. En route, I glanced at Kari Huhtamo's twisted metal art sculpture sitting on the hill. I'd always liked it, and still liked it now, but I couldn't explain why.

It was overcast, which made me think about the sixties. I'd asked my father a few times before he went off the deep end if the weather in Rovaniemi in the sixties was always overcast. Dad said he remembered a few ladies from the fifties; from the sixties freezing weather and chicks who smoked and defiantly tossed back their heads.

My college roommate explained it to me once: the photo albums from the sixties are mostly black and white. Cloudy weather gives the landscape the appearance of a black-and-white photo, not all the time, but when the clouds are the right color and fairly dense. His explanation made sense to me.

Looking at a photo, you can place it in time not only by the way people dress, but also by its colors or hues. My roommate had a summer job as a reporter. He said he'd learned how to date a photo—even nature pictures. He could determine the decade based on granularity, how much the photo had faded, and even by the smell. I once saw him bet against some full-time reporters about the dates of photos they showed him. He won lots of money.

Later he wrote a story about me and my firm for his paper. It was about us winning some Chamber of Commerce award. He was disappointed when he found out what we did—plastic machine parts for manufacturers. It's difficult to explain to the layperson. I've tried to demonstrate it by saying that if a factory needs a fifty-foot-long exhaust pipe, which has two receptacles along its length, and the pipe has a z-shaped curve every ten feet, and the pipe is eight feet in diameter, then the factory calls us. The layperson often asks what the pipe is used for. I have to respond that it's not used for anything; it was just an example. It's difficult for the layperson to understand it all.

My reporter friend was disappointed when he realized that he wouldn't get a nice business gift from me. Of course I could've given him a suitcase full of plastic components, but few households need industrial parts. He kept laughing about it. For Christmas I sent him a bottle of brandy. His article was decent, but in the third paragraph my last name was misspelled as Räkkönen instead of Räikkönen. He got my first name right, though. He never wondered why I was named Ensio.

Last week I saw in the paper that he was named news director. I always had the impression that he was good at his job.

I looked out of the taxi window. Trees so rarely grow in straight lines, except when they're planted that way.

When we got to the nursing home, I asked the driver to wait. I walked up to the reception desk and asked for Mrs. Solske. The receptionist nodded over my shoulder; I turned around and saw Grandma sitting on a wooden bench next to a bunch of plants, even though there were comfortable armchairs nearby.

I went up to her and said hello. Grandma looked at me for a moment and then smiled. "Ensio," she said, and I stooped over to hug her carefully. It seemed like her bones hadn't yet turned brittle, even though she'd turned eighty a couple of years back.

I took her by the arm. Grandma released my grip and said she could still walk on her own, but that she wasn't quite up to leading a grown man by the hand any more.

Her cane had been leaning against a plant that looked like a palm. I picked it up and handed it to her. Grandma thought the cane made her look more dignified. I said that all dressed in black, she'd definitely be the most stylish woman in the cemetery. I suppose I could've chosen my words better.

Outside, Grandma praised me for having the sense to choose a yellow Mercedes for the trip. I didn't tell her it was a coincidence. When the taxi driver saw Grandma, he sprang out of the car and opened the door, making sure that neither her foot nor the edge of her coat got stuck in the door, and then he pushed the door shut.

I asked him to drive to Viirinkangas Cemetery.

"Certainly," the driver said and started driving more smoothly than I thought was possible with such a big car.

Grandma asked if I was making ends meet and whether I was behaving.

I told her our machines were popping things out and they were getting snatched up right and left. Over the winter we'd added a new production line. I gave Grandma a brief and nontechnical overview of it. I told her it seemed as though somewhere outside of Oulu there was an enormous hole in the ground that our factory tried to fill with our plastic industrial components, but we just couldn't make enough of them, even at a reasonable price. It wasn't impossible that in the next few years we'd need additional space—a completely new building—and we'd reported these plans and employment needs to the representatives of various municipal committees and labor unions. Several of my subordinates had had many late nights since these committees and unions considered any discussions without sauna and liquor to be frivolous.

As for me, I was considered boring company because I didn't party into the wee hours. I simply couldn't gulp down more than two pints of beer. That filled me to the brim. Hard liquor on the other hand tasted so bad that a couple of sips was all I could take, and only when mixed with lots of soda.

"And are you behaving yourself?" Grandma asked.

I told her I'd just said I'd never become much of a drinker. She admitted that was true, but it wasn't what she was talking about.

I didn't understand her. I told her I'd behaved extremely well. For a thirty-three-year-old man, I'd succeeded reasonably well. My new house would be finished in July, a home with 2,000-plus square feet, almost a mansion by Finnish standards. I owned half of a successful business. You couldn't yet turn it into cash, but in five or ten years I'd get a million or more if I were to sell my share of the business.

"What about girls?" Grandma asked. The driver's right ear turned toward the back seat. I didn't like it.

I told her I thought I'd look for a wife in a year or two. Grandma said it wasn't good for a person to be too well-behaved. The taxi driver nodded to her like it pertained to him and he had any say in the matter.

Grandma started asking the driver about his family background and where he was from. He was from an old Rovaniemi family, and they started talking about who all had died, and from what. I didn't participate in the conversation.

I didn't think I'd been too well behaved. I approached things in a matter-of-fact and rational way. Grandma was undoubtedly well meaning when she doled out advice, but it seemed to me her advice would've fit better right after the war. Different times, different ways.

I've taken several business management courses, which were painful experiences. Grown-ups doing group work just like back in elementary school. The group work was considered valuable in and of itself. But valuable it wasn't. In my own experience, precious work time was lost in recounting Mediterranean vacations and rehashing sporting events that had already taken place. People should talk about those kinds of things in a pub; when you're at work, you work. And I'm not a tight ass.

I pay a decent salary for decent work. It makes no difference to me if someone works on Monday morning or on Saturday night. The main thing is that the work gets done well and in a timely manner.

I once gave a project to a young man who had just come to work for us. He had a month to complete it. Young and enthusiastic, the guy worked sixteen hours a day and right through the weekends. After two weeks or so, he told me that the project was done and wondered what he should do next. I told him to go find a hobby; we wouldn't need him for a couple of weeks. The union reps came whining to me about it. Apparently, I hadn't treated my employees as their contracts required. I explained that we drew up a plan for each employee on the first business day of each month. If everyone were to finish their work in two weeks, I'd happily close up shop for the rest of the month. It would save money on electricity, too.

Nobody's more conservative than the average worker. Everything has to be done exactly the way it's always been done. All change is bad. What's worse is that the unions are proposing a heavy tax on new machinery so companies would have to hire more employees to perform manual labor. Why not destroy all machinery while we're at it? Just leave the shovels for digging into the frozen ground and you'll guarantee work for the entire country.

Of course that would put a damper on folks flying south on vacation.

I consider myself a straight-shooting Finnish man and business executive. The fact that I don't drink has nothing to do with religious beliefs or a moral standpoint. I simply don't enjoy it. I understand, however, that some need it to blow off steam.

Grandma told the taxi driver that she was going to bury her grandson. The driver said he was sorry for her loss. He said he'd read about it in the paper. He knew from experience that for a parent the toughest thing is the death of a child or a grandchild—it was so unnatural.

"The boy will enter into eternal bliss," Grandma said. The driver told her that faith was what helped him through the most difficult things in life also.

"Into eternal bliss, into eternal bliss," Grandma kept repeating and then fell silent. I could still see her lips moving, however. I decided not to tell her about my views on the management of mid-sized industrial companies.

"Into eternal bliss," Grandma said.

But, I'm not a tightwad. I looked up at the darkening sky. It seemed awful to think that snow might yet fall on my brother Marzipan's grave, even though it was May already. The word "tightwad" reminded me of an incident from several years ago. It was May then, too.

I was in Helsinki with my secretary, closing a deal. We had traveled by train because I prefer them. On an airplane you don't even realize you're traveling. We had some free time before returning home, so we went to the restaurant on the second floor of the Helsinki railway station.

I asked for the menu and my secretary, Kaija, was eyeing a noisy group three tables away. "In the middle of the day," she said disapprovingly. Three men and a woman looked like they were drunk as skunks, though it was only early afternoon. I ordered mineral water with my meal. I told Kaija she was welcome to have a beer, and I'd pay for it. Our work was done for the day. She ordered mineral water.

I was enjoying my Wiener schnitzel and she her chicken salad when one of the guys from the noisy table got up to go to the men's room, located on the first floor.

When he came back, I recognized him as my cousin Topi Räikkönen. He was drunk.

I thought for a minute whether or not to acknowledge him. We'd played together when we were kids, but went our separate ways when we hit our teenage years. I knew he was involved in criminal activities. Even so, there'd never been any discord between us. It bothered me a little to know I was usually considered to be boring company, and the lunch conversation with Kaija wasn't exactly stimulating, so I decided to get up and go say hello to my cousin Topi.

Topi seemed overjoyed to see me, and after he got over the initial shock, he cursed for several minutes. The waitress came out of hiding to see what was going on. Cousin Topi kept slapping my shoulder warmly, and I assured the waitress that everything was okay. I asked her to bring the group a round of whatever they'd been drinking. Cousin Topi emphatically insisted that we join them.

My secretary was beside herself. She couldn't stop asking if the man was really my cousin. I have to admit her reaction gave me a sense of satisfaction. After finishing lunch, we went to sit at their table. I asked the waitress to put another round of drinks on my tab. I ordered a beer for myself and an Irish coffee for Kaija. I'd noticed that women often drink them. Kaija hesitated, but I could see that she did so only out of habit.

The woman in the group saw Kaija as her competition. She wondered how Kaija had nabbed such a moneybags as me. My cousin Topi and the other men told Maisa to stop it. I couldn't imagine Kaija wanting to get acquainted with the men, so Maisa was worried for nothing. Kaija told her she was on a business trip; she was CEO Räikkönen's executive assistant. Maisa quipped that though she was rotting away on unemployment, she still had her self-respect—she hadn't yet sunk to the level of secretary.

At that point I was still sipping my first beer, though I'd ordered a second round for the group, including Kaija. The Irish coffee made her talkative. Kaija kept asking what Maisa meant by secretarial work, and stressed that she'd graduated from secretarial school, and in addition to Finnish, she spoke Swedish and English, and was studying German. By then, our table had become quite noisy, and I kept ordering more rounds. Maisa spilled at least two pints of beer and the waitress finally said she was cutting off everyone at the table until Maisa left.

Maisa's departure was messy. She somehow got the impression that Kaija accused her of being a paid woman. The men assured her that wasn't the case.

"In fact, quite the opposite," my cousin Topi said. The big guy in the group—I think his name was Toropainen—took Maisa to a taxi and came back.

"I'm Väinö Ewald," Toropainen said repeatedly, and wanted to shake hands with me over and over. He just couldn't believe that the Räikkönen family had "dough men" in addition to all the "pickled men." My cousin Topi had to explain to me the meaning of the terms, though I had a faint understanding from my brother's stories.

I ordered another beer for myself. By my count Kaija had had five Irish coffees. She was also smoking. She leaned toward me, brought her face very close to my face and asked if she should switch our tickets to a later train. It was a good idea. She opened one button of her blouse and asked me to feel how hot her cheeks were. They were hot. She blamed it on the Irish coffee, which indeed was served very hot. I felt her glass and nodded. She went to switch our tickets.

Topi suggested that as businessmen we could collaborate on something. I was surprised; I didn't know he had any experience in manufacturing plastic components. He tousled my hair and said he figured I'd never change. I asked when he was coming up north. If he ever had any business in Oulu, he should get in touch with me and we could take a sauna and reminisce about old times. Topi said he'd come, but he didn't think it would be before fall. He did come up north that fall, but he didn't visit me. I heard he went to Rovaniemi and Sodankylä and unfortunately ended up in jail on that trip.

I asked Grandma if she'd heard whether Cousin Topi was coming to Marzipan's funeral. Grandma looked at me surprised, and said, "Absolutely not. A cousin isn't a close relative." This was odd because Topi was in fact Marzipan's closest and dearest relative. I noticed the taxi driver looking at me, and I turned to look out the window.

My secretary, Kaija, returned to the table. I noticed she'd put on more makeup and looked quite attractive. Toropainen said he'd always dreamed about a job where he could travel around with a beautiful secretary. Kaija laughed and tickled Toropainen under the chin. "Väinö Ewald," he said, introducing himself to my secretary. The third man in the group didn't say a word during the entire conversation. He did take part in the rounds, however.

I managed to finish my second beer and Kaija her seventh Irish coffee. I said I was sorry, but we had to leave now. Kaija laughed as she told the men we were going to splutter our way toward Oulu. My cousin Topi wished me success in my business. He was going to think about what kind of collaboration there might be for us business-savvy Räikkönen men.

We got our coats. Kaija left her coat unbuttoned. The buttons on her blouse were undone and I asked her if she wouldn't be cold. Kaija said she doubted it. She said she'd reserved a private compartment for us for the six-hour train trip, because it was more enjoyable to travel that way. I said I appreciated such initiative from my subordinates. Kaija smiled.

She leaned on my arm as we walked on the platform and told me that the heel of her shoe had started to wobble. I got into the train first and helped her up the steep steps. She lurched into my arms, saying she should definitely get her shoe fixed in Oulu.

From the train window we watched Helsinki get dark in the early evening. We showed the conductor our tickets and retreated into our compartment. I took off my suit coat and tie. Kaija sat down on the lower bed and looked at me. I dug my laptop out of my bag and put it on the small table. Kaija asked what I was going to do. I told her I was going to write some notes about today's negotiations. I'd seen the scenery between Helsinki and Oulu so many times I didn't feel like staring at it again. Kaija stripped down to her bra and asked if it was okay if she lay down for a bit. It was fine by me. In an hour, at most, she'd fallen asleep.

The following days at the office were so hectic that I didn't notice the change in my secretary's behavior. When things let up, I thought I sensed that she had taken on an excessively professional manner and seemed cold at every turn. Normally she'd laugh politely at my jokes, which I got from the boys at the workshop, but now all she said was, "Oh."

Two weeks later she came into my office to resign. I wondered why she wanted to leave. She said she'd gotten a good job offer and mentioned the name of the company. I doubted the company in question could make a good offer to anyone; it seemed to me more likely they were headed for bankruptcy. I couldn't get her to change her mind, though. She wanted to advance, to potentially move from a position of recording decisions to one where she could make them. I said that I didn't consider that to be out of the question in our company, either. It didn't help. She wanted to leave. While we talked, she kept staring at a colorful painting that was on the wall behind me. I lost a competent secretary.

Later on I realized that she couldn't deal with my relatives who tossed back so much booze on a weekday. She might have also figured out my cousin Topi's profession. I let out a sigh.

We arrived at our destination. The taxi driver helped Grandma out of the car.

I saw my sister, Sarlotta, standing on the church steps with her husband. She looked like she had aged. I walked over to give her a hug.

"Into eternal bliss," Grandma mumbled. I offered my hand to Auvo.

24. Police Officer
Marja-Leena Vauhkonen

A woman entered the restroom as I was washing my hands. She was wearing a miniskirt. I was glad not to be the only one, but then I realized she probably wasn't an employee. Sometimes you can just tell.

She walked to the basin, washed her face and kept coughing up over the sink. She kept rubbing her face with paper towels. She was putting on makeup when I left. Her skirt was shorter than mine.

I went to my desk, sat down, and checked my inbox. Nothing new had shown up in the last ten minutes. I adjusted the position of my penholder.

That pig Rautapää came into the doorway to chat with a detective whose name I couldn't think of. It started with an N.

The pig looked at me and nodded. He listened as the detective explained something, his cheeks on fire. The detective said that he was really sick—it was his damn stomach.

"Then take sick leave, idiot," the pig growled.

The detective asked if he could go right into his summer vacation when his sick leave was over. He said his wife was insisting on it.

"Go ahead and take all of it," the pig said.

I hiked my skirt a bit higher and adjusted my posture so that I was sitting with my legs apart and my back arched. That way your ass sticks out more, even when sitting down. Nauris, that was the other cop's name.

Nauris left, and the pig walked over and sat on the corner of my desk. He asked me how things were going. *Go roll in the mud*, I thought, but out loud I said that I'd like some work.

"Here." The pig set a cassette tape on my desk. He said he'd just interrogated the main suspect, one of two suspects in the murder case.

"I see," I said. His eyes were bouncing around like the balls in a pinball machine. He tried to look me in the eye and ogle my legs at the same time. Pig.

He asked if I could transcribe the tape. He didn't know if transcription was part of my job description, but since there was nothing else to do, he thought it might help get me into a work rhythm. The case was far from being solved, and it wouldn't hurt to get me involved.

I said I'd do it.

The pig advised me to use the QA-method. I asked what that was. He smiled with his entire snout and said "Q" stood for question and "A" for answer. How the fuck could I have known that?

"Come and tell me immediately if you find anything unusual or interesting," the pig said. In his opinion, the interrogator could get so wrapped up in the interrogation—as he himself did—that it was hard to keep the questions and answers straight.

I said I'd let him know if I found anything. "Today," the pig said. *Go stick your head up someone's ass, but not mine.* "Okay," I said.

The pig got up from the corner of my desk and said that during his career he'd never seen an officer with more beautiful legs. *When you get a kick in the crotch from one of these beautiful legs, you'll change your tune.* "Nice to hear," I said.

The pig left.

I went up to Jaakkola and asked him for a tape player and headphones.

"You're so young, are you gonna be listening to the Top Forty?" Jaakkola blathered.

"I'm going to transcribe an interrogation," I said. What an asshole, I thought.

Jaakkola gave me the tape player. When I turned to go, he said, "Walk slowly then, girl, give an old guy a chance to have a good look."

I turned back around and stood right in front of him. I asked him if he knew what sexual harassment was.

A muscle in his cheek started twitching. I said he'd get to learn all about it if he kept up this bullshit. He tried to smile, but he looked pitiful with that twitch.

I turned around and walked to my office, which was divided into four cubicles. I walked slowly, just to tease him.

I turned on the computer and created a file. I named it "Marzipan."

I slipped the cassette into the tape player and put the headphones on, then rewound the tape to the beginning and hit play.

I hear a chair creak, furniture getting shuffled, and the sound of chair legs scraping the floor.

The pig's voice announces the date and time of day and his name. Also present are Arkady Wolfovich Arkhipov, a citizen of the Russian Federation, and Detective Sergeant Osmo Nauris.

The pig starts asking questions.

Q: So, I'm Torsti. And you, I already know you.
A: We have not met.
Q: I know you by your reputation. You speak Finnish pretty well, I have to admit. We can get an interpreter if you need one or want one.
A: I understand Finnish.
Q: Sounds good. How do you feel?
A: I better now.
Q: You broke one of your ribs.
A: Bone punctured my lung little bit.
Q: That's not good. How is it now?
A: Okay, if you breathe right way.
Q: Marzipan breathed the wrong way.

A:	I know.
Q:	Oh yeah?
A:	I saw him lying there dead.
Q:	Did you see how he died?
A:	No.
Q:	Let's get started.
A:	Fine with me.
Q:	Where were you on the morning of April 28 of this year?
A:	What time at?
Q:	Between nine and ten in the morning.
A:	I was many places.
Q:	What might those places be?
A:	I was at home. Kassu and Ossi come there. We go out.
Q:	Where did you go?
A:	To town.
Q:	Where in town?
A:	We went to meet Marzipan.
Q:	To meet him…?
A:	To see him.
Q:	Why?
A:	Marzipan owe me money.
Q:	What for?
A:	I give him money. Marzipan doesn't give back.
Q:	What was the money used for?
A:	That not my business. My business is get money back.
Q:	Where did you get the money?
A:	That my business.
Q:	No, it isn't.
A:	I work.
Q:	What kind of work?
A:	I take stuff to Russia. Murmansk.
Q:	What?
A:	What?
Q:	What kind of stuff?

A: Video, tape player, electronic stuff. Good qualities stuff.

Q: You make money that way?

A: Business okay.

Q: Good enough that you can lend money?

A: They tell me Marzipan trust…trustworthy.

Q: Who said so?

A: He pays back.

Q: Who said so?

A: Many say.

Q: Names, names…

A: I don't mix up other people. Deal already mixed up without.

Q: How much did you lend him?

A: I can't say.

Q: It'd be better if you did say.

A: Business secret.

Q: How much?

A: A lot.

Q: When was Marzipan supposed to pay you back?

A: Middle April.

Q: With interest?

A: Small interest. Big loan.

Q: But he didn't pay?

A: Didn't pay.

Q: You were upset!

A: It's much money.

Q: You were furious!

A: Pretty upset.

Q: You went to collect. Marzipan didn't pay, so you killed him.

A: No.

Q: You'll be convicted of manslaughter, if the court believes the story about the loan.

A: I not kill.

Q: They could decide it was murder.

A: No murder, no manslaughter, no assault. Nothing.

Q: First of all, the story about the loan is bullshit.

A: No, is not.

Q: C'mon now, big guy. We know that Marzipan stole your illegal liquor, the liquor you sell to make your money. It pissed you off, because you have to give a portion of the money you get to the Russians. And because you were afraid of what would happen to you in Murmansk if you didn't pay, you panicked, and in the heat of the moment you killed Marzipan.

A: No, I not kill.

Q: It could be deemed murder.

A: No manslaughter, no murder.

Q: How come you forgot assault?

A: What?

Q: How come you forgot assault?

A: I not touch Marzipan. Not even with my pinkie. Not with knife, not with gun, not with club, not with nothing. I not have time to.

Q: We'll discuss that later. You were talking with Marzipan's mother.

A: Kassu and Ossi were talking with her.

Q: Tell me what you talked about.

A: Kassu and Ossi asked where Marzipan. The old mother was in another world in my opinion. She was petting cat and said stomachache.

Q: The cat had a stomachache?

A: I don't know. Either cat or old mother.

Q: Okay, then.

A: Or the boy, crazy from the head.

Q: You threatened Mrs. Räikkönen.

A: I not say a word.

Q: Your subordinates Vartio and Kaukonen threatened her.

A: Detective Rautapää…

Q: Torsti.

A: We have custom. Last names with strangers.

Q: Nonetheless, I'm Torsti.

A: If. I talk hypothetical situation, if. *If* I say to Kassu and Ossi, push old lady around, so that she says where Marzipan. Kassu and Ossi no have time to do. Not at all.

Q: So, there wasn't time to assault Mrs. Räikkönen.

A: Not physically, not mentally.

Q: That's not what I heard.

A: I tell truth.

Q: Of course. If you'd tell everything, it'd be a lot easier.

A: We come in. The old mother petting a cat. Kassu ask where is Marzipan. The old mother say he go in woods. We go in woods.

Q: Mrs. Räikkönen has a different view of the situation.

A: She sick.

Q: What do you mean?

A: She feeling bad already when we came.

Q: How so?

A: Her heart was hurting.

Q: Really?

A: The old mother brea…breathing heavy when we got there.

Q: I don't know anything about her ticker.

A: I tell truth.

Q: She threw her daughter-in-law out of the house. That might make an old lady pushing seventy a little out of breath. No matter how tough she is.

A: Kassu ask. The old mother answer.

Q: Ossi Kaukonen threatened her.

A: Ossi little boy. He pretend to be like gangster. No one notice, not even old lady.

Q: He was talking about the end of life. That's hard to misinterpret in a situation like that.

A: Sorry.

Q: What?

A: I speak bad about deceased. Sorry…

I stopped the tape. The suspect said something in Russian. I wrote down the numeric reading from the tape player to mark the spot. Someone fluent in Russian would have to translate it. I got a glass of water and drank it. I pushed play.

Q: I hope we can keep this in Finnish or else we'll have to get an interpreter.
A: I say that I'm sorry in Russian. That's all.
Q: Okay. Let's assume that Mrs. Räikkönen told you where her son went.
A: I tell truth.
Q: We'll get back to what you did later.
A: I can talk now.
Q: You'll have the opportunity to talk about it, both here and in court. Don't you worry.
A: I no worry.
Q: It seems to me that your wife should also be questioned about this.
A: She not know.
Q: A person doesn't always know what they know.
A: I tell everything. Everything true.
Q: Aurora could have heard all kinds of things.
A: Detective Rautapää. Aurora don't know.
Q: How can I keep her away from this case?
A: Believe me, Aurora not know.
Q: She could have unwittingly sucked up information from you and some other guys.
A: Aurora is good woman.
Q: I'd like to know if she sings well.
A: What?
Q: If she sings well, like a canary in an interrogation.
A: I tell everything. Aurora don't know.
Q: We'll see.
A: She is good woman. Good to me.

Q:	I don't want to bother her.
A:	What you want?
Q:	Let's talk about stolen liquor.
A:	Detective!
Q:	Torsti.
A:	Can I have a little tea, please?
Q:	Osmo, could you get some? I'd like some coffee.

I hear furniture shifting and a thud from the door closing, and a moment later the clinking of dishes. Nauris says laughingly that the cardamom sweet rolls are day-old; but compared to what we're used to here in our department, they're fresh out of the oven. The pig says that he doesn't drink tea, because there's nothing better than tea from a samovar, but you can't get it just anywhere. The suspect says that the department's tea is good. Nauris wonders why spring is so late. No one wants a second cup.

Q:	Okay, then.
A:	What?
Q:	I'd like to hear about the stolen liquor.
A:	Detective know if I involve in that stuff and I talk about it.
Q:	What do I know?
A:	How long I live.
Q:	A long time. If you have a clear conscience, you'll live a long time.
A:	How long I live then?
Q:	I don't know.
A:	A person not always know what they know.
Q:	All right then.
A:	I could tell story.
Q:	You should be telling facts, not stories.
A:	I tell story. Can detective imagine story could happen? It could happen. From Murmansk comes car full of booze. Driven by Russian man. It could

194

be for me. For one of my guys here. It could
happen.

Q: I don't know if I want to hear a hypothetical story.

A: Worth listening.

Q: That booze was bought in a liquor store in
Murmansk, obviously.

A: Not like that. The driver busy or stupid. He not
bring it to me, but bring to one of my guys. The
man don't listen to name carefully. He write down
name wrong. So, he take liquor to Marzipan. It
could happen. What name is close to Marzipan?

Q: What?

A: We can say some name is close.

Q: What kind of bullshit is this?

A: Is no bullshit.

Q: I don't know.

A: It could happen.

Q: Mm-hmm.

A: You can use this.

Q: The suspect points to his temple with his index
finger.

A: Right.

Q: I wouldn't have thought to use it otherwise.

A: What Marzipan do?

Q: What?

A: Takes booze. Gift from heaven. Hides it.

Q: And you want it back.

A: If that happen, I want. It mine.

Q: You'd go get it and then kill.

A: I not kill. I not murder.

Q: We're running around in circles here. You haven't
done anything, you didn't get any booze, you
didn't kill Marzipan. Why were you arrested,
innocent man?

A: I hear things in hospital.

Q: Nurses' gossip?

A: I hear everything.

Q: From Aurora. Your wife's involved in this.

A: No Aurora. She not involved. She is good woman. My woman.

Q: I guess.

A: I hear in hospital. Police go Marzipan house. His friends hide booze again, different place.

Q: You know the place?

A: I not know.

Q: Good. This is moving forward.

A: I know who hides.

Q: Who?

A: Three men.

Q: Their names?

A: Sakke and Ansalanka.

Q: Oh, fuck.

A: Ask. Probably find. Rovaniemi small.

Q: And the third?

A: I hear in hospital. Bike attached to Sakke and Ansalanka's truck. Bicycle.

Q: What?

A: Bicycle.

Q: Huh, what?

A: Bike chained to truck. They can't get it off. Man come, who has saw. He remove bike.

Q: Give me the name of the man with the saw.

I hear clattering on the tape. Nauris accuses the suspect of lying. I hear more clattering and then the sound of a dish breaking. The pig asks Nauris to clean up his mess and says that he'll let Nauris know if he needs any more help with the interrogation. The door opens, and I hear banging and clinking. Nauris asks if he can put the garbage in the pig's office. The pig yells that no one's gonna fill up his wastepaper basket with that stuff. Gradually, the pig gets worked up during the interrogation and his voice gets shrill. It's quivering a little. I wonder where the strange tapping sounds on the tape are from. I figure that the pig's tapping the surface of the table with his finger. The door opens again, and then it's silent.

Q: Sorry for the interruption.
A: I tell truth.
Q: What's the man's name?
A: I not know. I hear in hospital that regular guy. Not crook, not Marzipan's friend.
Q: How can we move forward here?
A: Arrest Sakke and Ansalanka. Young boys confess quickly. Then arrest men. Solve case. Get a lot of stolen liquor in your storage.
Q: Which you have nothing to do with…
A: You solve crime. The detective find big amount stolen booze.
Q: This isn't much to go on. What have you really told us?
A: Maybe they say bike is stolen.
Q: It's possible.
A: The detective solve much. The detective's boss thank him.
Q: Don't you worry about my career. That's my job.
A: Detective have career, I have career.
Q: I'm afraid your career is about to be finished.
A: Businessman. I am businessman.
Q: Let's get back to Marzipan's house.
A: I tell much truth to detective about stolen booze.
Q: I'll be exceedingly grateful for it for the rest of my life. But there's a murder to be solved here, too. Actually, you can forget about the liquor, if we can solve the murder.
A: The detective forget nothing. Never.
Q: Where did you go after leaving Marzipan's house?
A: We went into woods.
Q: Yes…
A: Along trail.

197

Q: Were you running?

A: Not running, slowly. If Marzipan gets wrong idea, he's sitting behind rock, with gun. We go slowly.

Q: And then?

A: Man lying on trail.

Q: Can't be true.

A: I have seen dead person before. I know dead person. I see man was dead.

Q: What did you do?

A: I get down on ground, man's face against ground. I look from side. It is Marzipan. He says.

Q: Says what?

A: I cannot understand.

Q: Of course you can't.

A: What does it matter? What does man do when dying soon? In Russia, man screams mother: Mother Russia and own mother.

Q: Keep going…

A: I say to Kassu and Ossi, it's Marzipan. What they do? They not believe. Kassu looks also. Ossi not feel good.

Q: And then?

A: What do you mean?

Q: What did you do?

A: I no understand.

Q: You called an ambulance and the cops, like anyone would do?

A: Detective understands perfectly.

Q: I don't understand, you tell me.

A: How we call police? We have been looking for Marzipan. Now man is dead. Who they suspect? Detective tells me, who they suspect?

Q: The fact that you high-tailed it out of there with a stolen car doesn't lessen the suspicion. On top of that, Kassu assaulted an orderly and almost killed Officer Kildenstamm as well as a certain Auvo Root.

A: I have not killed, have not murdered. And not Kassu or Ossi. No one has killed.

Q: I'm not so sure about that.

A: Why I kill? Why I kill? Marzipan in debt to me, how I get money? Detective tell me how I get money. I must pay.

Q: It's tough for all of us every once in a while.

A: Detective tell jokes. I have question about body.

Q: That's exactly what we're talking about here.

A: About my body. My life.

Q: You'd have a clear conscience if you'd confess.

A: Detective, dear detective.

Q: Thanks a lot.

A: I have difficulty. I have problem.

Q: Oh?

A: I not good man. Good Lord knows, I done bad in life, done much bad. Now I arrested, I answer for bad things. But I have problem. Bad thing detective say I did is not my bad thing. I not kill. And not Kassu or Ossi. I swear in front of Good Lord's eyes and I swear in front of Aurora, I not do bad to Marzipan. I admit it possible that I could do bad to him, I have bad temper and could have happened that I lose cool and hit him. But I would not kill. And I did not kill. Why I kill him? Who give me money now?

Q: It seems to me that you're capable of confessing to anything except for what you're being accused of.

A: I not craf…crafty, no.

Q: That's exactly what you are.

A: Detective. I swear. In front of everything holy, I swear.

Q: Let's not get so overly pompous. Just confess, and you'll get off easier.

A: I confess that I bad, but I not confess what I not done.

Q: It's a bit suspicious that in the same breath you say that although you didn't kill Marzipan, you could've killed him. That'll make the jurors sit up straight in their chairs.

A: I could kill person who kill Marzipan. He take my money, and he kill me same time.

Q: Oh really?

A: Yes.

Q: Let's see what you've given me.

A: Truth, much truth.

Q: So you didn't kill Marzipan. In addition, you told me a colorful story about the stolen liquor, which possibly happened, but possibly didn't. The rest of this has been a bunch of hooey.

A: Sakke and Ansalanka.

Q: Yeah, and their friend, this third guy, what was his name again?

A: I not know.

Q: Exactly.

A: I tell truth.

Q: Do you know how I see the truth here? First off, you go to collect money from Marzipan. It's a feud between two criminals, although you deny it. We don't even have to prove that the two of you were on the outs, because you've admitted that Marzipan owed you money, he didn't intend to pay you back, and you were furious about it. Second, you admit having gone to Marzipan's house on the morning of April 28 of this year with two of your accomplices. We have your statement, and in addition to all of that, statements from witnesses to the effect that Marzipan headed into the woods and all of you went after him. So, Marzipan was seen alive, you go after him, and after that Marzipan's found dead. These are indisputable facts. Third, Mrs. Räikkönen saw

Ossi with a heavy bag, which presumably contained the murder weapon.

A: But I not kill. We not kill.

Q: So you had the motive and the opportunity to kill Marzipan. We'll find the weapon, too.

A: We not kill him. But why detective think, if we kill, then it was me?

Q: You had the motive.

A: No motive. How I get money now? How?

Q: Things are looking pretty bad for you.

A: Blood. Where blood?

Q: What blood?

A: From Marzipan's head came much blood. Where blood? Not my clothing.

Q: The murder weapon will explain that, when we find it.

A: How?

Q: If the gun's long enough, then blood won't get splattered on the person holding it.

A: Detective quickly want blame Marzipan's death on me.

Q: Arkady, you've dug your own grave here.

A: No matter who kill, just quickly find someone who could kill?

Q: We conduct our investigations a little differently than you Russians do.

A: In Russia I give detective something, detective let me go.

Q: See what I mean?

A: No car, no booze, no woman. Money is best.

Q: What?

A: Money best. Money in hand, money in detective's bank.

Q: Are you proposing something to me here?

A: Your assistant also get money. But not as much as detective.

Q: Are you trying to bribe us?

A: I tell you how we do things.

Q: That sounded strange.

A: Much money.

Q: Oh yeah?

A: Tell different killer.

Q: What?

A: Tell different killer. Like Ossi.

Q: He's dead.

A: Killers die.

Q: Don't even go there. Pretty soon you're gonna get slapped with a charge of bribing a police officer.

A: I not trying. I tell what we do in Murmansk.

Q: Now I get it. Stop telling me about how things are done your way.

A: Detective decide.

Q: Decide what?

A: What we talk about.

Q: Good.

The tape lapses into silence. Nauris clears his throat nonstop. The pig hums and grunts heavily.

A: Detective red. What wrong?

Q: I have a bit of asthma.

A: Should take care.

Q: We should air out the room. Nauris, could you do that?

A: Treatment expensive.

Q: Arkady, I'm warning you.

A: What I do? Murder being laid on my shoulders. I not murderer. Still I must watch out. What I watch out for? That I get cold?

Q: Arkady, listen here. Now you'd better listen up. If you confess, then everything'll be easier.

A: For who?

Q: For everyone. Your confession and your willingness to cooperate in this liquor theft will be counted in your favor. It'll reduce your sentence.

A: Not so.

Q: It will, absolutely. Have you ever been in the slammer in Finland?

A: No.

Q: You'll probably get off with half of the sentence. Think about it.

A: What?

Q: You confess. It'll probably be deemed manslaughter—the heat of the moment. Eight years.

A: Eight years.

Q: Of which you'll be behind bars for four. Four years. That's not a lot.

A: It is a lot.

Q: For a clear case of murder, it's one hell of a short sentence.

A: I get different sentence.

Q: Goddammit. Just ask a lawyer. He'll tell you the same thing I'm telling you.

A: I mean different sentence. My boss give it to me.

Q: People are rarely killed in Finnish prisons.

A: But they still killed.

Q: I can't even remember the last time I heard of someone being killed in prison.

A: Bad memory.

Q: Ask anyone. More criminals are killed outside of prison.

A: Detective just talking.

Q: This isn't America.

A: Sun shines in America.

Q: I just can't get through to you. Not even with an axe.

A: I no believe lies.

Q: Did you get through to Marzipan with an axe?

A: Detective just talking. I not kill. I not kill.

Q: Four years. Four short years.

A: I cannot. Aurora making baby.

Q: Really?

A: My only child. I cannot. Have to see baby, look at me, say daddy.

Q: Good Lord.

A: Detective no understand. In Russia everyone love babies.

Q: Don't you get it, blockhead? Your choice isn't between four years or freedom here. The choice is between four years or life in prison.

A: I not believe you.

Q: Ask a lawyer. You get life for murder.

A: Detective offering death.

Q: That's what you offered to Marzipan.

A: Not me.

Q: Although he didn't place an order for it.

A: What?

Q: Nothing.

The men fall silent, the tape hums. The chairs squeak. Nauris clears his throat.

Q: Nothing. That's what you've told me.

A: Sakke and Ansalanka. Check them out.

Q: I just can't seem to be able to knock any sense into your head.

A: Already sense there.

Q: Make no mistake about it, with this information you'll get a sentence, and it won't be short.

A: That not right.

Q: It was murder.

A: This murder of justice.

Q: All right then, maybe we'll quit for now.

A: Thank you.

Q: You're welcome.

The pig states the time of day and the tape snaps to the end.

I notice I'm sweating. I feel like I've been sitting in the same room with those men. I look around, as if to see where they went.

I read the text on the computer and correct the typos. In my opinion, the pig did a good job of asking questions. The only thing that revealed his agitation was his voice.

I print the text and wait for it by the printer.

Jaakkola comes up to me.

"About what just happened," he says.

"Forget it."

"I didn't mean anything by it."

"I've already forgotten it, let it go."

He leaves.

I stack the sheets neatly, walk up to the pig's door and knock. The light flashes green.

"Well?" the pig asks.

"Interesting interrogation," I say.

"It is, isn't it?"

I ask if they're going to interrogate the Russian again. The pig says yes, definitely, but he doesn't think the stubborn mule will change his mind.

The pig asks if I heard anything out of the ordinary on the tape.

"I don't think so," I say. For some reason the pig laughs and puts his feet on his desk. I can smell the leather of his shoes.

He thanks me for the quick work.

"It was interesting," I say.

The pig asks me if I'll go out for a beer with him sometime. A married pig.

"Why not?" I say. The pig says we can talk a little less officially then. He suggests tomorrow.

I say I'm helping my cousin move, sorry.

"Some other time," the pig says, lifting his feet off his desk. I leave the room and close the door behind me.

When I'm back at my own desk, I think about how many cousins I have.

25. Auvo Root, General Contractor

Ensio came up to shake my hand while Sarlotta's grandma was singing the praises of eternal bliss. What she meant was that Marzipan was on his way there. I didn't have the heart to tell the elderly lady that to enter into eternal bliss you needed to have faith, which was something Marzipan absolutely lacked.

I asked Ensio how things were going in the plastics business. We saw each other once or twice a year, and it was our perpetual topic of discussion. He said his products were flying off the shelf, and they were lucky if they remembered to send invoices to the customers.

Sarlotta went to get a chair from the church for her grandma, who was looking pale. I asked Grandma how she was doing. She looked at me for a little while, and then recognized me. We hugged, and she asked if Sarlotta and I had any more little believers on the way. I told her more little darlings would come if they were meant to come.

Sarlotta brought the chair over and helped Grandma sit down. I told Sarlotta her grandma already asked if she should open a new savings account for a new baby Root. Sarlotta retorted that while all of us Roots had bank accounts, there wasn't any money in them. That was a little harsh.

Ensio told me about his new production line and kept asking me if I was getting what he was saying. After all, plastics manufacturing was very difficult for a layperson to comprehend. I just kept nodding.

Grandma said she wanted to go sit by the grave. She said she'd buried so many people that she didn't care to go into the church. Sarlotta tried to persuade her not to, for fear of her getting cold outside. Grandma opened the top button of her coat and showed us all the layers she had on. Ensio said he'd go ask where Marzipan was going to be buried. He came back right away, pointing with his hand, and took Grandma by the arm. I grabbed the chair. Sarlotta sighed and wondered why it was that as people age their will is the only thing they have left—and in this family, it was made of iron.

We walked at Grandma's pace along the gravel paths of the cemetery. Grandma pointed out that the clouds were breaking up, so you had to squint when you looked up.

"The sun's coming to my grandson's funeral," Grandma said.

Grandma was softly humming a hymn. Nobody spoke. Ensio pointed out where to turn at each intersection. Ensio has never asked me how my construction company is doing. Sarlotta says he's being considerate. I suppose he's read in the business section of the paper that the construction industry is in a slump.

We arrived at our destination. Ensio pointed like a salesman to a grave surrounded by a wooden frame. We set the chair down on the gravel path. Grandma sat down and loosened her scarf. She took her glasses off her nose and wiped her eyes with her handkerchief. She also wiped her glasses. Ensio put his hand on Grandma's shoulder.

"Can we leave you here, Grandma?"

"Yes, you can."

"You won't get cold?"

"No."

"We should go into the church. We're pall bearers."

"Go ahead, go ahead. I'll be fine here. The sun's coming out."

Ensio looked at the sky. The sun was poking out and seemed to be telling him that Grandma would be okay here. We started off toward the church. As we glanced back at Grandma, we saw her rocking quietly back and forth. Ensio cleared his throat.

"Old people sure do get ideas in their heads."

"She just wants a moment with her grandson."

"He's not there yet."

"But she wants to reminisce."

"Oh, I get what you mean."

Ensio fell silent. We walked back with measured steps. I felt like it wasn't appropriate to hurry. Ensio tried to match my pace, though it meant he had to slow his step in midair. Grabbing me by the sleeve and with an air of concern, he said that he'd heard that local hoodlums had tried to knock me off, too.

Ensio stopped to think and said he'd heard about the incident from Sarlotta. "What happened?" he asked, and I began telling my story.

I was on my way back from Kemi when I saw a car that had just gone off the road. At least two drivers witnessed the accident, but both continued on without even turning their heads. I recognized one of the drivers by his license plate; he was a member of the church council. I didn't want to reveal his name.

Ensio nodded and I was a bit irritated, but I understood he'd lived in Oulu so long now that he hardly knew any members of the Rovaniemi church council. Besides, I wasn't sure how Ensio felt about matters of faith. Sarlotta told me once that Ensio thought God was just a regular person.

I pulled over and ran across the road to see if everything was okay. A man covered in blood greeted me with a gun.

"Whoa," said Ensio in reaction to my story. He asked if I'd tried to run away. Run away to where?

The man covered in blood threatened to shoot me through the glass if I tried anything. He pushed the gun into my back, and we stumbled over to my car. He told me to drive to town. He wasn't making much sense.

Ensio asked if I'd begged for mercy. I put my hand on his shoulder and told him somberly how that never does any good with killers. Ensio nodded and wanted to know what happened next.

After driving around, I tried to talk him into realizing what a sin he was committing. It was difficult. He was delirious, and I suspected he was on drugs. But our conversation calmed him down. He was sobbing when I finally drove him to the police station. The tough guy was rattled by his sins. He let me go, saying he appreciated my reasonable yet forceful message.

Ensio couldn't believe I had stayed so calm. He imagined he'd have been completely soaked in sweat if a blood-stained killer had come at him with a gun.

"The Good Lord is all you can rely on in this life," I said, and Ensio jokingly replied, "Other than maybe Nokia cell phones." I thought his comment was in poor taste in light of everything I'd just told him, not to mention that his brother lay in a casket waiting to be buried.

Ensio must've noticed I was upset and told me I was the family's first hero since the war. It made me smile— I knew that deep down he was a decent man.

I scrambled out of the car and ran into the police station. When the officer on duty screamed, I ran out the side door. While I'd kept my composure, I was overcome by worry and started running for home. I was sure the killer would blow up our car or the police would shoot it to shreds. That would mean the end of my construction business, but it'd be a small price to pay if it meant a murderer was caught.

"Wow," Ensio said.

I kept running, and though I don't exercise much, I covered the distance quickly. I was on my way back from Kemi where I'd turned a new building over to its owner, so I was running in a dark suit and tie. People were giving me puzzled looks. I just waved to them, trying to convince them I was a stable construction contractor, and not an escapee from the loony bin.

As I kept running, the thought struck me that the last time I'd run that far was when I was a kid. I knew I had to get home right away to tell my family that Dad wasn't dead or injured. It didn't occur to me to take a taxi—in my mind only drunks needing rides home late at night take taxis. Even though I was out of breath, I couldn't stop.

Many of my neighbors saw me and called out to me, concerned. I gave them a happy smile and a wave to put their minds at ease. The Hattulas' Pekingese chased me for a hundred yards, yelping, before giving up out of exhaustion.

Ensio stopped at the bottom of the church steps. Funeral guests were arriving, and we stepped aside. I was pleased to see how intently he was listening to my story—I had gotten the impression in the past that he wasn't too interested in me, and only paid attention out of politeness. I continued my story.

When I got to the front door of our house, I was drained. I had to lean against the wall to muster the energy to press the doorbell. My house keys were on the keychain with my car keys, still in the car that was now probably on fire. I heard the doorbell ring inside.

I didn't know the old man who opened the door. He looked like a Laplander.

We stared at each other without saying a word.

A bead of sweat slid down my nose and fell onto the step. The old man's eyes followed it down and he said, "Oh, so that's how it is," and shut the door.

I rang the doorbell again. The old man opened the door again.

I asked him who he was. He told me his name was Feodoroff, a free nomad. I told him I was Auvo Root, a construction contractor and the owner of this property.

"Step right in," the old man said. I followed him and shut the door.

The whole situation was absurd. I didn't know the man, and he had no business being in my house. However, that afternoon I'd learned a few things about the peculiar twists of life, so I kept quiet and followed the old guy into the kitchen. He smelled like Sarlotta's father, Sebastian, who'd fallen into a sorry state. Other than that, there was nothing familiar about him.

Seated around the kitchen table, my children let out a joyful shriek when they saw me. Tears came to my eyes at the sight of their faces. I quickly took count to make sure they were all there. They seemed unharmed.

"Bring me some of that meat!" the old guy yelled, then turned to me meekly, as if he hadn't just roared the command. "Get me more meat!"

I noticed a fierce hunting knife in the old guy's hand, with liquid dripping from its blade. He leaned over to stir the pot with it. I heard the blade clink against the steel of the kettle.

I wondered how I could manage a surprise attack. I figured I could take him down from behind, even though he had a weapon. I was so confused it took me a minute to realize there was another stranger in the house, and the old man had been yelling at him, not me.

"More meat!"

The old guy didn't turn away from the kettle, but pointed with his knife. The children were noisily spooning gruel out of their bowls. I walked into the living room.

An obscene-looking reindeer carcass was sprawled out on the glass coffee table. It was the entire carcass, and judging from the smell, it was smoked. Another old Laplander in blackened pants was carving strips of meat off of it. While I realized he was sitting on our white sofa in those dirty pants, I just told him that more meat was needed in the kitchen.

"Sure thing," the man said, and scooped up four handfuls of meat strips off the table onto a newspaper, which he handed to me. He grabbed a bottle of booze from under the table and took a swig, then pushed it toward me. I shook my head, which seemed to surprise the man. He let loose a noisy fart.

I took the newspaper with the strips of meat into the kitchen. The nomad was drinking from his own bottle. He slid the strips off the newspaper into the kettle and stirred it with his knife.

"There'll be more soon," he said to the children.

The children were laughing—they must not have grasped the gravity of the situation. The old guy winked at me and told me I had some sweet little squirts.

Sweet little squirts?

I sat down at the table next to Pentti and stroked his hair. The old guy threw a bowl and a spoon down in front of me. Sweet little squirts—maybe the old guy was talking about my children. Maybe this was a kidnapping in progress; maybe the old buzzards had barricaded themselves in my house and taken my children hostage. Maybe my neighbors had tried to warn me not to go in. Maybe there were SWAT team sharpshooters in bulletproof vests tiptoeing on my neighbors' roofs. Maybe the old guy was waiting for the children to fall asleep so he could slit my throat with his saber-sized knife. Maybe the sun had made the men wild, after the long, dark winter, and so they first wanted to feed us and make us all drowsy and trusting, and then they'd suddenly begin the bloodbath. Maybe my wife had been butchered in the sauna, her delicate body strung up on a clothesline in the laundry room. Maybe my wife's spirit was turning into drops that formed into puddles, trickling down the drain and out of my life. Maybe I was going crazy.

Maybe I was already crazy. Maybe Sarlotta was bustling about doing her chores in front of the stove, the children were eating and banging the table with their spoons, maybe Sarlotta was beginning to worry about her husband, who just sat at the table quiet and morose, maybe she was getting afraid, maybe she was gripping the handle of the knife a bit harder, maybe she was getting ready to fight her deranged husband for her children's lives and for her own. Maybe a demon with a scaly tail had planted in my mind the two old Laplanders, who looked like sauna trolls who'd just arrived from hell.

"Wow!" Ensio put his hand on my shoulder. He looked worried and glanced at the familiar faces among the funeral guests. I realized I'd gotten seriously caught up in retelling the story. My forehead was sweaty and my jacket felt tight. My tie felt like a hand squeezing my throat. Ensio forced me to sit down on the side of the church steps. The cool stone felt calming.

I didn't know where I'd left off.

"With the sauna trolls," Ensio said, and a man coming up the steps glanced over at us. "The trolls," Ensio repeated, more quietly. He kept his hand on my shoulder.

I sat quiet at the table for a long time. The old guy ladled some broth in my bowl; it was smoked reindeer stew. I realized I was hungry, and tasted the stew—it was good; the meat was soft and tender. I spooned the entire bowlful into my mouth, and the old Laplander poured me more.

"Daddy's eating," my daughter said.

The old guy stopped in his tracks. He crowed like a rooster and stomped his foot. He said that now he believed I was the man of the house. I didn't know what to say to that. To the old guy, I had looked like one of the murderers the whole city had been hunting for since morning.

"It's Daddy," my daughter said.

It was the best compliment I'd received in my entire life. My daughter came over to pat my arm, to comfort me. My eyes filled with tears, and my voice came out muffled.

"I thought you were going to do something to the kids."

"I thought *you* were gonna."

"Me?"

"You looked like a guy lookin' for a fight."

"You let me in anyway."

"You wouldn't be able to handle me. I figured I'd make a package out of you and then mail it to the cops."

"Really? I was already thinking…"

"And you definitely couldn't handle Rankki-Niles."

"What?"

"I can't even handle Rankki-Niles Ahkiomaa."

"The guy in the living room?"

"That's him."

"Where's Sarlotta?"

"I don't know her."

"My wife. The children's mother, where is she?"

"She left when we came… I mean when I came. Rankki-Niles came over later."

"Left to go where?"

"She went to her mother's."

"Why did you come here?"

"Because we were asked to."

"So you don't know Sarlotta?"

"No, it was Assar who asked us."

"Who?"

"My daughter's husband. Assar; he looks at pussies for money."

My daughter burst out laughing, put her little hand in front of her mouth and giggled, chanting "looks at pussies, looks at pussies." The Laplander laughed along with her and winked at me. He said his son-in-law wasn't a real man; real men did it for free.

My daughter was singing out, "sex, sex." I was too tired to do anything about it. The stew had warmed me up, but it sapped all my energy. I asked how the men had fared with the children. The old man said he'd raised twelve children, he didn't think he needed much advice on how to manage for a few hours with three sweet-faced little squirts.

"My goodness," Ensio said. He looked surprised. I may have read more into his facial expressions than I should have, but I felt like he thought my entire story was just a figment of my imagination. I told him I wasn't finished yet.

"The minister's starting soon," Ensio said, and tried to get past me up the church steps. I pushed him down.

I asked the old guy if he could watch the children a little longer. I wanted to lie down, and then call Sarlotta and ask what happened. Rankki-Niles came into the kitchen, and they had a good laugh when the nomad told him who I was. They said they'd watch the kids. I didn't feel like telling them what had happened to me. I didn't even feel like lecturing them about the fact that I didn't allow liquor to be consumed in my house. I dragged myself onto the living room sofa and closed my eyes for a moment. I thought about the mess that Rankki-Niles had left on our sofa. I fell asleep thinking about that.

I woke up to Sarlotta pulling the nomad by the hair. From the light outside I could tell it was evening. Rankki-Niles was sitting in a chair convulsing with laughter. Liquor bottles were strewn all over the table. A couple of bottles had tipped over and spilled onto the shag carpet. I didn't see the children.

I got up and scolded Sarlotta for getting these men to be our babysitters. She froze in the middle of the floor, panting frantically, and a couple of buttons had popped open on her blouse so that her bra was showing. She started screaming "Get out!" I wasn't sure if that included me. Rankki-Niles asked for the number for a taxi, which surprised Sarlotta so much that she gave it to him. The men called for a taxi and got ready to leave. I

216

tried to collect the liquor bottles for the men to take with them. I asked them to also take the reindeer carcass, but the taxi had already arrived. The driver was waiting impatiently in the entryway and refused to take the carcass.

The old guys said they'd donate the reindeer to us and asked us to say good night to the squirts on their behalf. I said I would, but my promise got drowned out by Sarlotta's command for them to get out. In addition to the carcass, the old guys left us a porn book. I burned it in the fireplace—I didn't even dare show it to Sarlotta. I flipped through it enough to know it would have shocked her.

"Amazing the stuff that can happen," Ensio said, astonished. He quickly got up and pulled me up, too. My hands were shaking from the intensity of my story. Ensio dug some salt licorice out of his pocket and offered me some. I took a handful of it and threw it in my mouth. I've never had the desire to smoke, and I don't know what it tastes like, but if someone had offered me a cigarette right then and there, I might have lit up.

Sarlotta came out of the church to say they were waiting for us. She'd arranged for the minister to speak at the graveside and for us to sing one hymn there, so Grandma wouldn't miss out on everything. Ensio said he suspected Grandma specifically wanted to miss out, but Sarlotta disagreed. Ensio told her that I'd just told him about our escapades on the day Marzipan died. I realized that Sarlotta was right when she said that Ensio didn't get psychology or the intricacies of relationships. I could tell Sarlotta wasn't in the best mood. She hissed something at Ensio, and though I couldn't make out the words, I knew it wasn't nice.

Ensio wondered aloud whether we could have found more traditional babysitters in the city of Rovaniemi. Two reindeer herders drunk out of their minds sounded like the worst choice for little kids.

"I can't deal with this," Sarlotta said and asked how stupid her only brother thought she was. Ensio shrugged and said he considered Sarlotta an intelligent and sensible mother, with a few small reservations.

We went inside.

The church was full. That puzzled me—I wouldn't have expected Marzipan to be so popular. Then it occurred to me that perhaps some of the people were here to witness that he was in fact dead and gone. I glanced at Sarlotta, who was walking down the center aisle beside me, and I was ashamed of my thoughts. I asked the Lord to forgive me, especially since I'd had the thoughts in His house. I squeezed Sarlotta's hand. She turned to look at me, startled.

She pulled her hand away and slipped in front of me, stopping at the end of the pew where our family friend Inkeri Feodoroff was sitting. She was a doctor. It was still difficult for me to imagine her as the daughter of our babysitter. Sarlotta leaned over to her without bothering to lower her voice, which I found inappropriate.

"Where's Assar?"

"He asked me to convey his condolences."

"Where is he? I've been trying to reach him."

"In Helsinki, attending a training course."

"Oh, really?"

"He'll be back next week."

"Oh, okay."

"I have the number to his hotel."

"I want to talk to him face to face."

"About what?"

"Babysitters."

"Oh, about that. You won't be able to bitch him out any worse than I did."

"I can try."

"He paced around for three days without uttering a word after I gave him a piece of my mind."

"I'll silence him for the entire summer."

"If you want to do that, I'm all for it."

"It might help. It made me so mad then, and still does."

"And Assar, an educated man, he wasn't thinking at all."

"Men."

"Men!"

The women had a laugh and hugged, and we walked to the front pew. I thought their behavior was totally inappropriate for church.

26. Manta Solske, Pensioner

The wind is whistling. The sound comes from a low cloud passing through the trees. I hear the birds. As a young girl I could identify the species of a bird just by listening to its call; now I can't see them clearly, and all I can hear now is their distant singing. It could be a sparrow, a titmouse, or a lark. Names have a tendency to escape me. Sometimes in the nursing home, I find myself staring at my food and the thing my food is placed on, and I can't remember the word for it. The sun came to my grandson's funeral. It rose up from the grave where my little Marzipan will be laid to rest. I can't remember what kind of weather it was when my husband was buried.

A plate. Food is placed on a plate. There are dinner plates and bowls—you put soup in a bowl.

I have to wipe my eyes and my glasses again. I'm not crying. Sorrow is such a familiar feeling for me that at this age you don't greet it with tears. It's the wind that's making my eyes water, even though I'm wearing glasses. The wind makes me cry, and Marzipan comforts me. He's lying in the casket in the church, soon he'll come past me for the last time, and then he'll lie in peace in the ground.

Although the minister says so, the ground isn't a haven of peace. In my dreams I've seen that when a person leaves this earth, he goes to hell, under the ground. Marzipan will be lowered into the ground, and when the hymns have been sung, and the casket's been covered with dirt, and when the first cold night comes, then too will come the worms and the spirits of the underworld; they'll open the casket and lead my little Marzipan into caves filled with weeping and the gnashing of teeth. Marzipan will walk with his eyes wide open, and he'll see how people are punished: how a dog breeds with an adulterer, how a grunting pig eats a murderer's innards, how a child abuser is impaled on a sharp stake and is left there for the day, the entire next day, and for eternity, eternity which is so immense that when it all has gone by, not even a fleeting moment of it will have passed.

Marzipan will walk underground with his eyes wide open, and the sand will scrape his blue eyes. I hear the scraping sand as the mourners bring Marzipan's casket on a carriage. The young men have slipped the carrying straps over their shoulders, and are walking on both sides of the carriage. I recognize my granddaughter's husband and that daft Ensio, who turned out just as daft as predicted by his name. Sebastian, my dear son-in-law Sebastian, made that prediction. During Ensio's christening, while drunk as a skunk, he blurted out the prediction, and he was right, my wonderful son-in-law; the boy's name couldn't have been anything else besides Ensio. The minister didn't want to christen the child, but he did after I said, "Christen him or you'll be christened in the swirling icy waters of the Kemi River, right where the current is the strongest." The minister believed me, and he christened him. Ministers, they always want to call the shots during a christening.

The spirits of the earth and the little white wriggling animals... I grab a familiar-looking young man by the sleeve and ask him which animals are the ones that move with the dead in the underworld halls and light the way from chamber to chamber. The young man squats down next to me and takes my hand. He explains that Grandma doesn't need to be afraid, there's no need to trouble my mind with worms; they need oxygen in order to live and the casket is lowered so deep into the ground that the worms can't live there. He regrets that the church and the church employees don't enlighten the family of the deceased with this simple matter, which would undoubtedly comfort the mind of many a griever. The young man gets up, but keeps holding my hand.

Worms and spirits of the earth, worms and spirits of the earth.

The worms are small wriggling lamps on the walls of the underworld corridors, and Marzipan follows them as they take him from chamber to chamber. They are torture chambers, where fingernails and confessions are torn out of people, and the wretched want to confess, they confess to anything at all without realizing that no confession will absolve them from the pain. I saw it all in a dream. In dreams you're shown things that are true. In the underworld chambers Marzipan will have to relive all the bad things he did on this earth. He did bad things. As his grandma, I know that and I deplore it, but at his core he wasn't rotten.

After the chambers, desolation begins, covered with fog and smoke. An occasional burnt tree is left standing and steaming, its branches like charred arms. Arms, which even though dead still embrace their death, but they don't burn beautifully the way love burns. The ground is slushy and wet, and when Marzipan looks down at his feet he'll see that the ground is actually flesh oozing blood. Marzipan will be short of breath; he'll lean on a stone, which he'll think is a statue, but then realize that it's a petrified person who's been burned into a crouching position, and that's how the netherworld, or hell, is set up. Some poor soul lives there, all crouched down and petrified into stone; he seems alive and his eyes move. It's someone that Marzipan knows, dead, dead, dead.

Like a stone. The young man leans over to me and says that they'll take care of the gravestone later, as nowadays they never put up the gravestone immediately after the funeral. I say that Marzipan will turn into stone, we'll all turn into stone. The young man says, "In a way Grandma's right, what's left of us after a hundred years?

If we're lucky, there'll be a gravestone in the Rovaniemi Cemetery." The young man comforts me by saying that it's just how the law of nature works, and he knows that as a wise woman I know that.

The casket is lowered into the grave. The men carefully release their carrying straps, glancing at one another. A man's job at a funeral is to carry and glance around. I've lived through a hundred funerals, and the men always glance around. Never has a casket slipped and thudded, popping wide open, but at the funeral luncheon someone always tells a story about having carried a casket at exactly that kind of nightmare funeral.

The casket descends slowly. The sun's shining in my eyes now. That must mean something.

I get such a painful sadness in my heart when I think that my little Marzipan will soon be shown the horrors that an old woman was allowed to see in her dreams. I so want to take the little boy by the hand, before he's had a chance to fully grow up, when he's shown the bloody entrails of the world, what the world had for dinner. I remember holding him by the hand when I walked him to the sandbox, and I realized too late that it wasn't his usual sandbox. The boys there were strangers, and Marzipan whispered, his breath choppy, "Grandma, hold my hand, Grandma, hold my hand."

Oh my boy, my little boy. Grandma can't hold your hand on this journey during which nightmarish animals in the sandbox dismember and maul; it's the worst thing there is, and the worst thing is that it's the only thing there is. The dead of the netherworld never forget; a person can endure anything that comes to an end, anything can be measured in time. But in eternity, clocks are made into breaking wheels, which turn and smash incessantly. There, into Satan's trap my grandson will walk wearing his knickers, a bandage on his leg. There, a black bat will glide down and snatch his favorite purple cap off his head. He'll want to cry the evil away, but the tears won't come, the tears won't come to stifle the horror. And his voice, his voice will be lamenting it all. The young man leans over next to me.

The casket has been lowered into the grave, and the men toss the carrying straps down into it. I remember how they used to pull the carrying straps up. Sarlotta says something, throws a bunch of flowers into the grave and bursts into tears. "I'm sorry, I'm sorry," she mourns. What bad have you done to Marzipan? You haven't done anything. You just tried to toughen yourself against your brother, but because you're a good girl, you committed a crime against yourself, that's what's making you cry; go ahead and cry—that's how you'll remember your brother. You can't fight against your own blood. If you do, you kill yourself.

Some of the mourners toss flowers—each tossing a single flower into the grave. If only Marzipan could take the flowers with him on his nocturnal voyage; if only he could push the soft flowers into his ears so that he wouldn't hear the terrible sound of judgment while walking in the field of desolation, the sound that ceaselessly roars, the sound of judgment that turns into small arrows that pierce people's ears, and everyone's cheeks turn red from the blood which flows from their ears. The burning rank smell of crushed flesh clogs their noses, a smell that's shoved up their noses as if it were a doctor with one of his long tubes.

A bird is singing, and the young man says that he doesn't know birds. The birds down there are songless; what flies there are winged wounds, fresh, throbbing wounds that land, dripping with blood, on the branch of a burnt tree that's as slippery as a paralyzed snake. From the sky of the netherworld a boiling liquid rains down, boiling liquid sprayed out by shameless lizards that breed in midair; it's terrible to watch those silent creatures, which are the size of a large city. They all look the same; they're lit up inside, but they're still dark and terrifying. They fly with their stomachs open; in midair they turn onto their backs, pushing their long beaks into their stomachs to eat themselves.

"The minister's starting soon," the young man says.

My daughter goes to the edge of the grave.

My daughter, an old woman.

She walks with an odd posture right up to the edge of the grave, stops, says something, and turns. She has that old cat in her arms—I can't remember its name. I don't really give a damn about good manners or the strict observation of rules, because when you're old you can act however you want, and it's excused as senility. But to me, it's strange that someone would bring a pet to their son's funeral. I've never cared for that cat. I had to laugh once when Marzipan came to visit me in the nursing home and told me how he gave liquor to the cat. The young man looks at me, and I notice others looking at me, too. Maybe I laughed out loud.

My daughter walks back to where she was standing, sullenly and without swaying, true to herself. The cat yawns so widely it lets out a sound. Marzipan didn't like the cat, nor did he like heights. If only Grandma could hold little Marzipan by the hand as he walks with a bandage on his leg along a faint narrow path on the side of the mountain, on the brink of the bottomless abyss. Grandma got a ladder and rescued Marzipan from the tree when he climbed it with the big boys. Marzipan was so afraid. He asked Grandma not to touch him, please don't, Grandma. He could stay for the rest of his life lying on that thick branch; it was the most dangerous place in the world, but it was also the safest place in the world, because only the branch separated him from falling down onto the rocky ground. Did the little boy already know back then to fear what would be waiting for him underground, where he'd end up if he fell off the branch? The path is slick, the rocks slip under his feet. Marzipan knows he has to climb. He's not traveling anywhere, but he has to travel there. If only he could slip, and hit his head and fall into a kind of sleep; but it's not allowed, you can't fall, you must be afraid, afraid, afraid.

I have to tug to get my arm free of the young man's grip. He looks at me, surprised. Looking into his eyes, I see he's afraid that I'll go into a fit, crazy with grief, and he'll have to deal with it. I smile at him kindly. I take a handkerchief from my purse and dry my eyes and my glasses. How can there be so much liquid in such an old, shriveled woman. A runt of an old woman is what I am—nothing more, nothing less.

The mourners look confused. I clear my throat and ask if we should sing a hymn. My daughter looks at me angrily, and the old women mumble that the minister should speak first. I propose that we sing again after the minister has spoken, and it'll be even better after we're strengthened by his words.

I begin singing "A Mighty Fortress Is Our God," because to me it's always been a beautiful, simple, and majestic hymn. The mourners whimper along, and start singing properly only after the minister joins in. I know it annoys my daughter to no end that even here I thrust myself into the center of attention. She can think that if she wants, she's an adult. The singing swells fervently once it gets going. The minister is an imposing man with a vigorous voice, and he undoubtedly gets his congregation's hearts fired up and spews out sermons like avalanches.

After the hymn is over, the birds sing more beautifully. My hearing is so poor that I sometimes wonder if I hear live birds singing or whether they're dead birds from seventy years ago that are still singing in my soul. If that's the case, how is it that a little bird can be so strong against the passage of time? It's fascinating to think that the song of a small titmouse ceased seventy years ago, but still echoes within me—it'll echo in me as long as I live. But where will I take the bird's song? Underground, and then what? The song of dead birds is my bedrock on this earth. But Marzipan doesn't have any bedrock, he didn't listen. The minister starts speaking. I hum on top of him, so that I can't hear him.

"Excuse me."

I open my eyes. The minister is taken aback.

"Excuse me."

It's my daughter who's speaking. The mourners are frozen in place. The minister clears his throat and regains his composure. It's now very quiet; the birds inside me have become silent.

The cat turns its head and licks its owner on the neck. My daughter flinches.

"Excuse me, but would it be possible to cover the grave before the minister starts speaking?"

The mourners turn to look at the minister, who nods slowly. He pretends that this happens all the time at funerals.

Ensio and Sarlotta's husband look at each other. They take the wooden frame and lay it on top of the grave, on top of Marzipan. Ensio straightens his tie, and Sarlotta's husband looks to the sky as if to get permission for what they're doing.

People holding wreaths of flowers in their hands look at one another. Should they put the flowers down on the wooden frame? My daughter looks at her own wreath.

"Could we lay down the flowers after the minister has spoken? If it's all right."

The minster nods in assent.

He begins to speak, his voice rising up from the depths. I hum "A Mighty Fortress Is Our God," in order to cancel out his voice.

A fortress is peace that you can't find downstairs in the cellar. My Marzipan will soon be restlessly walking along the hallways of the cellar, where his dad, on those rare occasions when he'd lose his temper, used to lock

227

him up so he could think about the naughty things he'd done. Marzipan was so afraid of ending up in the cellar, he was afraid of the spider webs on the unpainted walls. He was afraid of the musty smell of the earth, and of the hallway that had the burned-out light, the hallway where you had to walk all the way to the end to get wood for the sauna. That twelve-foot-long hallway reached as far as the other side of the world. Marzipan told me that he was afraid because he couldn't see the floor; he was afraid that there was a hole in the floor that he'd fall through, a bottomless hole. I walked with him down that hallway with my hand in his little, soft, damp hand dozens of times, but he was so afraid that strange men would come and dig a hole in the floor at night, a hole that was open at both ends.

I told him that a hole can't be open at both ends, but he fervently believed in it. "Open at both ends," he repeated in the dark hallway, as we walked toward the stack of sauna wood. Nothing helped. I tried to joke around with him, tell him that everyone knows that it's not falling that's dangerous, but the abrupt stop. "Marzipan wants to stop," he'd say. He wanted to hold onto something.

I last talked to him three weeks ago just outside of the nursing home. He was in a taxi, and he had the driver stop when he saw me sitting there on the bench. The taxi waited and Marzipan came over to talk to me. We stood on the lawn, until he went over to the big rack for beating rugs and had to hold onto it, a big strong man on a calm day. I knew things weren't well with him. They never were.

"Do you have any money, my poor boy?"

"Yes."

"I'd lend you some if I could, my dear boy."

"I've got money."

"You take a taxi, even though you don't have a cent."

"Believe me, Grandma. It's embarrassing how much money I have."

"Hug your grandma."

And he hugged me. I can still recall the smell of cigarettes and sweat from his jacket. Then he kissed me on the cheeks, and then on the lips, which shocked me to my core, as he was so fresh and warm. Blood, which came from me, was still warm. As I stroked his cheek it made a scratchy sound—just like my husband's cheek a long time ago. The men in our family have wonderful cheeks.

"Be good."

"What else would I be?"

"Listen to me now."

"Don't worry, Grandma."

"I won't, but I'm not stupid."

He waved from the window of the taxi. Now that I think about it, he was waving goodbye to life.

The minister's talking. I have nothing against ministers, but I don't need a man to show me where heaven is and what God is thinking. I need a woman to do so even less. At my age I get to decide who I listen to.

The minister's finished, and looks perplexed. The funeral guests stare at him; he makes a move to leave, but then says something I can't hear. He takes a scoop, shovels up some earth, but notices that there's a wooden frame on top of the grave. In my opinion, funerals used to be better organized.

Ensio and Sarlotta's husband lift the wooden frame off the grave. The minister throws some sand from the scoop and says that Marzipan is dust, and unto dust he shall return. I can't hear the rest. The minister is quiet again. Ensio and Sarlotta's husband set the wooden frame on top of the grave again. To say their final goodbyes, the funeral guests begin laying flowers on top of the frame. Many also mutter something, or read the words on the ribbons attached to the flowers. Several just lay down their flowers and bow.

"All right, then," my daughter says quietly and puts her wreath of flowers on the grave. I can't hear her, but I can see her lips moving. She often says, "All right, then."

"The child went to be with his father," an older woman says in a loud, gravelly voice and hugs my daughter. It's such a strange thing to say; the woman doesn't know that at this very moment Sebastian is trembling and hallucinating on the steps of some shop near the local liquor store.

The father is drifting, the son is wandering underground; and I know, I was told in a dream that he'll be taken to the edge of a burnt forest, a forest where on every branch of every tree a baby has been hanged. The nurse came to check on me when I got to that part in the dream. It was such a terrible sight; the smell of the babies' skin was still wafting amidst the smoke. I know that it was shown to me because my second child died in the crib. Juuso Akseli, the laughing baby. I've stayed healthy, but I'll never be so sick that I want to die, because I know that I'll be led in front of all that cruelty, and I'll be left with the babies gently swinging there in the quiet breeze with their eyes open. The little ones still get rocked, even though sleep has already come to them.

The flowers have all been laid down. My daughter turns toward the loud woman as the minister comes to shake her hand. The minister transforms his attempt to shake her hand into a glance at his watch, although his watch is on his left hand.

"The funeral guests are welcome to our home for coffee and a light lunch."

People nod at the invitation from my daughter. I wonder whether I should go straight to the nursing home. The young man bends over toward me and asks if he can give me a ride. I thank him, and get up with his help. My daughter comes to ask me if I have a ride. I point to the young man, who says his name. My daughter says her name, nods, and thanks him.

I ask if I should leave the chair here. The young man says that funeral guests shouldn't be carrying chairs; that job belongs to the church and idle ministers. He's a pleasant young man even though I don't know who he is or his name. People speak so softly these days.

The young man knows how to walk with me. I don't feel rushed, and I don't need to catch my breath.

His car is amazing, because it's low to the ground and because of how brightly it shines. When he opens the door, I can smell leather. It reminds me of the horses in the country when I was a child. He adjusts the passenger seat for me so it fits me better and then turns toward me to ask if I'd rather sit in the back. I want to sit in the front. He comes around to my side of the car to help me in, and even so I let out a little yelp when I sit down, because it feels like I'm falling down on the ground.

His car makes me laugh. I make a joke about him having to buy new pants when the road scrapes holes in them. The young man chuckles, saying that it's never occurred to him until now that that's how you can tell who the race car drivers are. I take him by the wrist. I have to, he's so warm and my Marzipan is cold.

But Marzipan won't be cold for long; he'll receive forgiveness.

The day and moment will come when an angel will knock on the lid of my grandson's casket with his wing, and the angel will ask if he's ready. With a beat of his wing, the angel will wipe away the pigs eating his innards, the lizards breeding in the air, and the babies hanging from the burnt trees; he'll wipe away the darkness from the kingdom. The angel will knock and Marzipan will open his eyes; he'll reach out his hand and lift the lid off the casket from Laura Pahka's casket store; with the same easy movement he'll lift off the dirt, and with a single step he'll rise to the surface of the cemetery, which will be bursting into life.

All over the cemetery there'll be dirt flying up, and from the ground will emerge shining human beings, who know that the day of love has dawned. People will be dressed in long white robes that brush the earth, robes that purify every square inch of them. No one will be in the form they were buried in; rather, they'll simply be spirits, pure souls, but everyone will recognize their loved ones without fail. The wife will run up to her husband, the child to its mother, families will gather together and friends will embrace one another; nature will be clothed in its spring garb, the birds will be singing fanfares for the day of joy, and in the sky a cluster of suns will be shining.

Then I'll rise up from my husband's side; I'll throw dirt laughingly into his hair and then wash it out; we'll hold each other quivering with the joy that nothing will ever separate us again. I'll walk the lanes of the cemetery looking, and when I find my grandson, I'll take him into my arms, take him by the hand, and I'll never let him go. His eyes will be like two little heavens. He won't believe that he's been invited to this day, but forgiveness touches us all, forgiveness is a wind that blows out of God's lungs through the darkness of space and breathes life into it. Everyone will be breathing the Holy Spirit, who burns as our blood inside of us. The blood is a flame and a flower.

The young man asks me to take my hand off his wrist.

"It's hard to turn the wheel with one hand."

"Oh, I'm sorry."

"No problem."

"The strong smell of the leather made me think about riding horses."

"It's such a curvy road, that's all."

"When I was a girl I used to hold onto my dad's wrist while he drove."

"Oh?"

"A team of horses."

"My daughter rides horses."

"So you have a daughter?"

"Fifteen."

"Oh my goodness gracious."

"Years old. Fifteen years old."

"That's nice."

"And my son is six."

I see that the young man has already driven us to my daughter's neighborhood.

Here comes Anna Severinen, there comes Ville Muukkonen; they rush in with their own gravestones in their arms from different corners of the cemetery like children on the last day of school; now the endless summer begins. They gather at the gates of the cemetery, where an immense heavenly host of angels is blowing golden horns so loudly that the church collapses, and from the stones of the church and from the gravestones people start building a large boat with a sail a mile high flapping in the righteous wind of God. People board the boat, and it rises up to the sky; we sit side by side, my husband, Marzipan, and I and we watch how the earth becomes the size of a soccer ball and then disappears.

And Marzipan won't be afraid of heights anymore.

"I remember," I said.

"Excuse me?"

"Marzipan was afraid of heights."

"We knew each other as little twerps."

"Excuse me?"

"As kids. Then I went to college in Helsinki."

"I see."

"I dropped my northern dialect while I was there."

"I see."

"I came back this past winter."

"Did I know your father?"

"He sold cars. He died of cancer this past winter; I came back to settle up his estate. I'm an only kid."

"Aha."

"He died, he died of cancer."

"That's what I figured."

"I figured I'd stay here. I'm done with Helsinki."

"I see."

"I started my own business."

"You're not unemployed?"

"No, not at all."

"You knew my grandson?"

"Yeah. He was one of those wild boys around here. I kind of looked up to him."

"He was wild."

"I don't mean anything bad by that. I mean that he dared to do things others didn't—that's all. I used to think that's how I wanted to be when I grew up."

"Aha."

"But then I didn't want to when I did grow up."

"Not many did."

"I don't even know if he would've recognized me anymore. We hadn't seen each other in fifteen years."

"And still you came to his funeral. That was very nice of you."

"Well, I guess. If I was a chick, he might have remembered me."

"It's very nice of you to come."

"Gotta be with your buddy on his final voyage."

"Yes, that's our custom."

"There were a lot of peeps there."

"Oh?"

"A lot of people. I didn't know anyone except for Ensio. I remembered you. You made cardamom rolls for us once."

"Oh, my goodness. How can you remember that?"

"We were learning how to drink beer. You were baking."

"I'm glad you liked them."

"The cardamom rolls were delicious, and we had cold raspberry juice. That I remember. I haven't had cold raspberry juice since."

"I will give you some."

"That's not what I meant."

"I have dozens of bottles. I can't drink it all, and Sarlotta's children don't drink much of it."

"I can drop you off at your place after we have coffee."

"Thank you."

"It's my pleasure. You're Marzipan's grandma, after all."

I hear how the bottom of the car scrapes the bumps in the road that leads to my daughter's house. The young man has to park his car a ways off, because the yard is full of cars.

He helps me out of the car and holds my arm as we walk into the yard. The young man says that at this time of the year, even here in the north, there are leaves fluttering on the trees. I say that's the birch trees are just playing. He says he remembers that up here in the north, the leaves don't get to take up permanent residence; the leaves are playing house in the birch tree. He never used to think it was sad when the leaves fell off the trees. But since becoming an adult, he's been bothered by trees being chopped down.

When we go up the steps, I notice how tired I am. The young man helps me into the nearest armchair in the living room. I take off my hat and fluff up my thin hair. My forehead is covered in sweat. My daughter peeks out from the kitchen, and I ask her for a glass of water.

Funeral guests come from the kitchen to shake my hand. I find it hard to remember their names. Those who don't introduce themselves look familiar, but I can't remember many of their names. People used to talk louder—in the big farmhouse kitchen you had to in order to make yourself heard.

The water doesn't taste good. I put the glass on the edge of the table. While she's setting the table, Sarlotta asks me if I want more water. I want brandy.

"Grandma, not you, too," Sarlotta says, giving me a sad little smile. She opens the bar built into the bookcase and pours me a glass of brandy. She remembers to pour it into a regular glass, since I hate fishing brandy out of those tapered glasses.

The brandy hits me like electricity. I slowly empty my glass. I let myself slink back in the chair. I can hear and see, I understand what's happening around me, but I'm not participating in any way.

"Please go ahead and help yourselves."

I try to open my eyes, but I realize that they are open. I blink and try to make myself see sharper. My daughter asks everyone to help themselves to the buffet. Sarlotta comes and asks me if I'd like coffee and a piece of sandwich cake. I say I'd like some a little later.

Marzipan's son comes up beside me. He stares at me like a little rodent. What's his name? The same names get used from generation to generation so that soon no one will know who's who. I ask who's there. That's my old trick. The boy stares at me silently, making gestures and pointing to his mouth. I ask Sarlotta to give the boy some cake. The boy shows me his tongue. Sarlotta says that the boy's not asking for cake, he's playing mute. It's been going on for who knows how long now. I stroke the boy's head, the poor motherless boy. Laina's no mother. I hug the boy and he messes up the front of my dress.

It's Vertti, little Vertti.

The young man comes up to me, balancing his coffee and a plate with a slice of cake on it. He asks if I'm doing okay. I say that I'm quickly tiring out. He tells me he read somewhere that losing a child is the most painful

236

experience a person can endure in their life. He can't imagine how painful it is to lose a grandchild, probably even more difficult. He'd fear for his sanity if something were to happen to his Kimmo or Katariina. I nod. He supposes that I get some comfort from my faith. I nod again.

In the sky, the stone boat takes us to a planet that consists of a palace and a park. The palace is built out of pure marble that feels warm underfoot. The trees are all birches and palm trees, and the birches never lose their leaves. The sun glows, not in any specific place, but in the palace, the trees, the grass, the water, and in the precious people, who will never leave. Everything is made of light. Once a day they take us to the patio on the roof of the palace, and God's face shines down on us, the face that I've never seen in my dreams. I can't imagine what it looks like. Life there is comforting, like slowly rocking back and forth.

"You want to go home?"

My eyes were closed after all. I open them and look at the young man and the worried expression on his face. I say that the day has been tough and perhaps I'd better go back to the nursing home and rest. Sarlotta comes and asks if I'd like coffee or something. I want to go back to the nursing home.

My daughter whispers something to Sarlotta, and she goes into the kitchen. My daughter asks me if I'm feeling ill enough to need a doctor. I tell her that the home has a nurse who can evaluate whether I'm just tired or on my deathbed. The young man thinks talking about death is pointless. My daughter looks at him and then goes into the kitchen. Sarlotta comes out of the kitchen with a plastic container. She says she's packed up a piece of sandwich cake for me to take home. It's made of salmon, shrimp, and mayonnaise.

Sarlotta hands me the container. I give it to the young man and get up out of the chair. Without the brandy I would've conked out in the chair. I ask the young man if he can take me home right away. He says he's happy to, and he takes me by the arm. He's strong.

Sarlotta and my daughter hug me in the entryway. They're going to call me later in the evening. In the yard, Sarlotta's children run up to me shouting, "Grandma, Grandma, Grandma." They don't understand yet that my daughter is their grandma. They jump around me and tug at the hem of my coat. I'd fall if it weren't for the young man holding me up. The babysitter scoops the two smallest children into her arms. I kiss them, and the oldest one hugs my leg and whispers to me, "Where's Grandma going?" With his little fist he hits my sore knee. I don't dare say anything about it. Sarlotta comes to the top of the stairs and calls out to them; the children rush up the steps, jostling one another. It's my eighty-fourth spring.

We get to the car. The day is clear, just like in the courtyard of the palace. The young man helps me into the car. He goes around to the other side, gets behind the wheel, fastens my seatbelt first, then his, and looks at me. He says I look pale. I grab him by the wrist and say that there's only a small goblet of fresh blood still coursing through my veins, the rest is stale.

"You're tough," the young man says and starts the car. He drives slowly and says that he should definitely listen to grandmas more often, because after this road his butt will for sure be showing.

The young man is quiet for a little while, and then apologizes if he's used racy language. I start to laugh when I realize that he means the word "butt." I tell him I'd already heard shit, ass, and goddammit long before his father was born, and that my skin was pretty thick with respect to such things.

"My pop died a week before he turned sixty-three."

"Your father could have been my son."

"Not really. He was a tight ass."

"What kind of work did he do?"

"He was a car hustler."

"Ah…"

"He sold them; he didn't have his own dealership."

"I imagine you must've inherited some money."

"Yours truly here has made his own stack of cash, all by himself."

"I thought your father would've given you money and educated you."

"Well, he always gave me a couple hundred at the beginning of the semester."

"Mm-hmm."

"He wanted me to become an engineer."

"Uh-huh."

"I studied engineering for a year. Ensio started out at the same time, but he was in a different track."

"He's opened a new production line."

"What?"

"It's hard for the layperson to understand."

"The fuck if I understand anything about engineering. Magnesium burns with a clear flame, that's about it. Goddammit. Now when I think of it, I lost a year of my youth studying so that fifteen years later I can remember how something like magnesium burns."

"Mm-hmm."

"Well, now I'm swearing, since you gave me permission."

"It doesn't bother me."

"My pop would slap me on the side of the head if I swore. That's probably why I do it."

"I see."

"Now I don't get smacked on the side of the head. I say "fuck" for no reason at all."

"What did he die of?"

"Cancer."

"Many people go that way."

"I'm an idiot. Here I am taking Marzipan's grandma home from Marzipan's funeral, and I'm blabbing about croaking and stuff."

"It's all right."

"Do I take a left here?"

"Yes."

"I'm slowly starting to remember these roads here in Rovaniemi."

The young man smoothly brings the car to a stop. He's full of good qualities. I think about telling him about the palace and the park, but decide not to. He's young, he's decided to live forever; he wouldn't understand.

I tell him that I'll be fine from here. He won't hear of it, and so he takes me by the arm; it seems to me that if I were to get tired of walking, he'd carry me to my room. The girl at the front desk nods.

"We went to have a drink and then got a hotel room. What a tigress!"

The girl glances at me first as if to get permission, and then smiles at the young man's joke. I pat the man's round cheek in thanks. He urges me to call him if I need a dashing driver for a trip to town. He gives me his card, but the text is so small I can't read it. Later in the evening maybe, under the lamp.

The girl asks if I can make it to my room on my own. I say that I can. The young man waves from the door. I raise my hand.

I nod to the grandmas and grandpas in the hallway. Someone's singing "Silver Moon" in a high, creaky, old lady voice.

In my room I realize that I'm completely devoid of energy. I have to sit on the edge of the bed for a long time before I have the strength to take off my coat, hat, and shoes. The flower on my hat is dangling.

When I start to look for the photo album, I realize that I've been holding the container Sarlotta gave me in my hands the entire time. I put it on the table, then move it farther away once I find the album.

I look for the photo of Marzipan.

He's sitting on a swing, and it's obvious someone's told him to pose for the camera. He looks at me right in the eye. That's how he looked at me then, when I snapped the photo, and that's how he looks at me now, across many decades. It's summer, and he's wearing shorts. He's barefoot, and he's got a striped cap on, which I remember was blue and white.

There's a bandage stuck on his right leg. That moves me, it makes me so sad that my heart is about to stop. I sob uncontrollably; once I'm finished I go into the bathroom to wash my face. I look at my face in the mirror and wonder when a person stops fearing death.

It's not so terrible.

I sit in my chair and put my hands in my lap. They looked so ugly next to the young man's strong and good-smelling hands.

I remember that I haven't eaten since breakfast. I open the container, get a spoon and a glass of water, and take small bites of the sandwich cake. It tastes good. If food tastes good, so does life.

The cake is gone at the same time as my hunger.

I drink a second glass of water and lie down. Someone's singing "Silver Moon," coughs, and again "Silver Moon." My name is Manta.

Who was it that promised to call me this evening?

My grandson always ate the piece of marzipan on his birthday cake first.

27. Valde Åkerblom, Prison Warden

The guy seemed like he was carved out of oak—he wasn't going to be anyone's bitch here.

He had a dark complexion, and his hair was already sprinkled with gray. His face was impassive.

I asked him to sit down.

"Arkhipov?" I asked.

He nodded.

"Warden Åkerblom," I said.

He nodded.

I told him that he was in my prison for pre-trial detention. I asked if he understood what that meant.

He nodded.

"Nothing," I said. "That's what it means. You are being held here behind bars just like any convicted prisoner."

He nodded.

We stared at each other for a moment.

Outside my office, my young secretary was humming some pop song.

I asked if he was waiting for a speech.

He nodded.

I told him he'd be waiting for a long time. I was neither strict nor fair. I believed in discipline and order only if they happened to suit me.

He nodded.

We stared at each other for a while longer.

We started to laugh.

We shook hands. I asked if Russian crime bosses drank coffee or tea nowadays.

"Tea," he said.

"Too bad," I said and poured coffee for us and then put cream in it. I put three lumps of sugar on his saucer.

I handed him the cup and said I was sorry that he'd fallen into my trap.

"Huh?" he said.

"It was a trick, you admitted to being a Russian crime boss."

He looked at me, and said I was wrong. He added that if he'd gotten tea, he would've admitted to being one.

"In the old days, guys like you didn't even know how to read," I remarked aloud.

"Times change."

"Or we do," I said.

He nodded. "Or we do," he repeated.

"A reporter's coming to interview me this afternoon," I said.

"Why?" he said.

"Because I'm turning sixty," I said.

"Congratulations," he said.

"Have you spent thirty years in prison?" I asked.

"No," he said.

"And still you congratulate me," I said.

He finished his coffee. We shook hands. He left with the guard.

He was carved out of oak. He'd be able to withstand any prison for years, at least thirty.

I felt a diabolical kind of affection toward the old devil.

28. Aurora Arkhipova

There's no way I can hit those high notes. For the rest of the hymn I just lip-sync, and the choir director gives me a nasty look. What do I care, he knows I'm one of the best voices in the choir, and he's not gonna do anything about it.

After practice Kristiina asks if I want to go get some coffee or wine. I would've dragged her there by the hair if she hadn't asked me first.

We both order a large glass of white wine. Kristiina chooses it—it doesn't make any difference to me.

She talks about this and that, but I can tell she's got something on her mind. I politely ask what's wrong, but after a while I start on my own stuff. It's not often that she clams up and goes silent as if a plug has been pulled from the wall.

Since she won't talk, I will. I tell her that I need some spiritual advice. She immediately says she's no expert in the area; she just works in the parish office.

"I know, I know, Kristiina," I say. I add that I don't need to confess or receive forgiveness; I haven't done anything wrong.

"Those are Catholic things," Kristiina says with a distant smile. I wave my hand. As far as I'm concerned, all those robe wearers can fight among themselves as to who is the most devout.

"You know what I used to do for a living," I say. Kristiina says that's stayed between the two of us, and she's never said a word to anyone about it. I don't doubt that, I know she's not a gossipy bitch.

Kristiina blushes. She hisses that I should lower my voice. She wonders how I can sing like a nightingale, but everything else that comes out of my mouth sounds like it's straight from the boys' locker room.

I laugh, for the first time since the afternoon. I tell Kristiina again that I know she's kept my prostitute past a secret.

I remember the first time I talked about girl stuff with Kristiina. It had been pouring rain that entire day. I had to talk to somebody, because Arkady had asked me to marry him. Of course I couldn't talk to him about it.

I told Kristiina, because she looked like a friendly and decent woman. She was surprised by my invitation, but after choir practice she came with me. I told her I'd worked as a whore for five years in Stockholm, and then in Helsinki, when the Finno-Ugrians also finally figured out that an ass can be a bank, too.

Kristiina had raised her eyebrows almost as far as the back of her neck. And they stayed there for the rest of the evening. She asked if I needed a psychiatrist or a psychologist, as apparently I needed to confront my past.

"That's a load of bullshit," I said.

I didn't want to confront my past, fuck, I wanted to forget it. Kristiina took off her glasses and cleaned them for what felt like three years. She put them back on, and I said that Arkady had proposed to me, and did she think I should tell him what field of work I had been in? She then started cleaning her glasses again for at least as long as she had before.

Kristiina sighed. She complained that she never imagined she'd have to think about stuff like this.

"Well, think about it now; your head might come up with the right answer," I said.

For actually thinking about it I gave her ten points. She ordered some white wine instead of tea, stared at the few breaks in the pouring rain outside the window, sighed, looked me in the eye like I was an ailing guinea pig, and thought and thought.

"No," she finally said.

"What?" I exclaimed. I'd forgotten what I'd asked her. Kristiina went on a long discourse about how men

245

are made of a different fabric than us, they couldn't understand. They might be thieves and killers, but if they hear their wife has prostituted her ass, they can't handle it and start hurling whatever they can get their hands on against the wall, and sometimes it's their wife.

"Whored," I said.

"Prostituted," she hissed.

In the course of an hour I'd already learned that certain words hurt her ears.

"Whored," I said louder.

"Aurora," she pleaded with me.

You couldn't tease her for long. She was so sweet that if I liked girls, I'd like her.

She succeeded in convincing me that a sure way to stay an old maid was to talk about my hooker past with prospective husbands. I'm eternally grateful to her for that, so much so that I'd thrust my hand in a fire for her.

Kristiina looks at me when I thank her for having given me advice in the past. She still hasn't recovered from her blushing. It lasts half an hour. Now she has little red spots on her forehead and on her cheeks and on her neck.

"Yeah," Kristiina says.

"I was just reminding you," I say.

"Don't bother," she says. She orders some mineral water and pours it into her white wine. She offers me some, too, and I copy her, since I'm trying to keep my head clear tonight.

"Something happened to me today," I say.

"Go ahead and tell me, you can't surprise me anymore," she says.

"Don't be so sure."

"Try me."

"I have to go back a ways first."

"That's all right."

She spills her wine glass when I say that my husband Arkady's been arrested for murder. I tell her that

246

someone by the name of Marzipan Räikkönen has been killed and my Arkady has gotten mixed up in it.

The waitress comes to wipe up the table. I order each of us another large glass of white wine. Kristiina's in shock. She doesn't remember to stop me from ordering more, even though she never drinks more than one glass of white wine.

I comfort her by saying that I should be the one who's flipping out here, not her. I get scared, and ask her if she knows Marzipan. She smiles and asks me how she would know the crooks of Rovaniemi?

"How do you know he's a crook?" I ask.

She tells me she read it in the paper. The story mentioned the victim, but not Arkady.

I say that Marzipan definitely was the victim, but he wasn't Arkady's victim. Arkady's no saint, but I'm sure he hasn't killed anyone, because that's what he told me. I seem to be raising my voice a little.

Kristiina looks at the full glass of white wine in front of her like it's been belched up onto the red-checked tablecloth out of nowhere. She takes a sip of it and pours some mineral water into it. She says that she doesn't know many lawyers.

When I say that I don't need a fucking lawyer, Kristiina comes out of her trance. She looks at me with such a sad face that I get a tickle in my throat and my nostrils are burning.

I say that if she'll keep her sweet little trap shut for a while, I'll tell her all about it. Kristiina nods.

I was in the middle of painting my toenails, and as always, listening to Olavi Virta, the king. The phone growled. It always rang like that at our place, like an animal. I knew that Arkady was in the slammer, but I thought the cops were after him because of the booze deal.

It was some cop. He introduced himself. They're all shitheads in my opinion. He said his name was Detective Lieutenant Torsti Rautapää. "Say it again, Detective R-asshole?" I blurted out.

He laughed. He was cocky as fuck.

He told me that toward the end of the week he'd be interrogating Arkady, who was a murder suspect. "Your husband needs all the help he can get with respect to this case—you understand that, don't you?" he said, sucking up to me. He was talking so strangely that I got worried.

He wanted to meet me off the record, he said he didn't want to officially interrogate me and all that shit.

We met at the café in the Sampo Shopping Center. He bought me a chicken sandwich. I ate it. He rambled on about the weather, about how nowadays spring comes so early that the migratory birds return way ahead of time and then freeze; in the morning you can hear them going plunk, plunk as they fall frozen stiff from the trees to the ground. He tried some other poetic shit on me, too.

I asked him to get straight to the point.

He glanced at me angrily, and then said that my Arkady was in deep shit. He'd definitely be found guilty. The question was whether he'd be sentenced to life for murder, which in actuality meant he'd serve twelve years, or, if he was convicted of manslaughter he'd get eight years, in which case he'd get out in four as long as he hasn't done time in Finland before.

I was dumbstruck.

He put his paw on my hand. He said slowly and in a low voice that he could help Arkady by making sure the interrogation transcripts were written up the right way.

"Written up with the right tone," he purred.

Fuck, I recognized that tone—he was after my pussy. As a former hooker I knew what this game was all about.

I asked him what he thought he was doing. Who did he think I was?

He said it wasn't just him, but the vice squad as well. He'd dug up my record and found a couple of convictions for running a brothel in Helsinki. The fuck I'd run any kind of brothel. Paula and I lived in the same place together, but my name was on the lease. When Paula picked up some john and did stuff with him at our place, then apparently I was letting my apartment be used as a brothel; in other words, I was a madam.

Me, a madam? Imagine that. I was just a call girl.

That cop didn't even have to hint at what Arkady would conclude if he saw those documents. My head was swimming as I thought about it.

I asked him if all the cops in Rovaniemi were pricks like him. He laughed—he was a total sadist.

He said he figured it wouldn't be too much for an old whore to take on one more gig, especially if doing so would get her husband freed several years sooner.

I really wanted—I so wanted—to shove what was left of that chicken sandwich into that guy's face and grind it into a mush.

He could see from the expression on my face that he had me on the hook. All he had to do was reel me in.

He got up from the table and said that he'd be calling.

"Oh yeah?" I said. I didn't know what else to say.

He said we could maybe go catch a movie or go skating. He had to laugh again.

"You better take me up on the invitation," he taunted. "You better take me up on it."

He ambled off.

But then he came back and said that he really liked miniskirts.

"Minipricks like miniskirts," I said, since I was quickly approaching my fuck-you mode.

He looked at me and said, "Just remember, whore, you'll be wearing a skirt that just barely covers your ass the next time we see each other."

He looked at me in a really nasty way.

249

I stayed there at the table. I went to the counter and got another large Coke and sipped on it for a couple of hours.

What the fuck should I have done? Huh?

Should I have gone to the cop's supervisor and said, "Excuse me, this sounds crazy, but my husband's under suspicion for murder and now the cop who's investigating the case wants to fuck me; isn't that against some fucking regulation?"

If the supervisor believed me for some reason and had asked him, "Oh, so you're screwing suspects' wives, huh?" nothing would've come of it. The cop would've said, fuck, he had reason to suspect me of being an accessory to the crime, and that's why he was trying to find out what my deal was. I suppose that falls under a cop's duties.

The only thing that would've come of it would've been Arkady getting more time in the slammer. He'll for sure go nuts in jail anyway. He always thinks I'm preggers if my period is even three seconds late.

So I went and pissed out those Cokes in the bathroom and went home to wait and see what kinds of nasty things the cop wanted to do with me. I could tell he didn't want to just kiss and screw. His eyes were gleaming like a snake's.

He called after a couple of days and asked me to come to the station at such and such a time. I was about to shout out with joy; now he's changed his mind and he's going to interrogate me the normal way. He guessed what I was thinking and said that I was being asked to come there as a whore. And that I'd better keep that in mind.

I dug a twelve-inch-long skirt and high heels out of the closet and put on too much makeup. I took a taxi to the police station.

He was waiting for me in the entryway. He said that he didn't want whores shouting out his name throughout the department. We went into his office.

He walked behind his desk and put his feet up on it. He asked me to walk back and forth. I walked, turned around, leaned on the file cabinet, and bent over so that he could admire my ass and my black stockings.

I started thinking that he just wanted to look.

To hell with that.

He asked me to undress down to the waist. He stretched out his hand, and I threw him my jean jacket, my shirt, and my bra. Then I had to strut back and forth with my tits shaking.

He got up and took my breasts in his hands. He deliberately pinched my nipples so hard that I had to gasp.

"The whore's waking up," he said.

I was wondering what would happen next when he walked back behind his desk. He was already pitching a tent in his pants.

I was a little afraid, even though I've seen a little bit of this and fucking that.

In Stockholm, one john wanted to walk around the apartment in a diving suit, while I had to knit a sweater in bed. I had to prop myself up with my back against the pillow and the wall, and I had to be bare-breasted. My stomach could be under the covers, but the bottoms of my feet had to be outside the covers.

"Had to be, had to be, had to be." That's how he explained it to me every time.

He walked around and spoke French. At least it sounded like French through the snorkel. He didn't want to screw me or even touch me. Well, he did shake my hand when he arrived and when he left. I was knitting a sweater. He always brought it with him.

I told him once that he could get a sweater ten times cheaper from a store. He angrily barked something at me in French. After that, I didn't make any suggestions to him.

It's crazy, but the sweater guy scared me more than the usual horny drunk guy. The horny ones just wanted to shoot their loads unceremoniously all over the sheets. With the sweater guy, you couldn't really tell what he was all about.

I was afraid he'd suddenly grab a big hunting knife out of his bag and start slashing me. By the fifth time he came over, I knew the poor guy wasn't gonna kill anyone.

I looked at Detective Asshole and tried to guess what he wanted. He didn't quite look like he was into whipping or inflicting pain. Or water sports.

I figured he wanted to watch me touch myself as I moaned while he jacked off wearing shiny boots and a cop's hat and stuff like that. A fun half hour, come check out your local police force's daily routine. Or maybe he'd dig a rattan whip out of the closet and would want me to punish the bad boy.

I could live with anything like that. My tits started getting a little chilly.

The asshole said that I was a mischievous-looking whore. He told me to come and sit on his lap. I went over to him, sat on his lap and he kneaded my breasts and pinched my nipples. He panted a little. Suddenly he pushed me out of his lap and told me to walk back and forth.

After I'd walked around for a little while and had stuck my ass out at him, he said he'd be getting someone to interrogate soon. I asked if we were done.

"No, my dear whore," he said and laughed, "we're not even close to being done."

I asked him when the interrogation was gonna start. "Pretty soon," he said.

"Where should I go?" I asked. He asked how I liked his handsome desk.

"It's just a desk," I said.

He asked if I could see his legs underneath the desk.

"The side of the desk comes all the way down to the fucking floor," I said.

He snapped his fingers for me to come to him. He said that I could play hide-and-seek for a while.

I asked if I had to fucking crouch down underneath the desk.

"Please do, Miss Whore."

"What the fuck I am supposed to do down there?"

"Suck in some impressions," he said, opening his zipper and swinging his dick toward me.

What should I have done?

What the fucking fuck's fuck should I have done?

I started to take my shoes off, but the Asshole wouldn't let me. I crawled under the desk—it was surprisingly roomy down there. I accidentally kicked the side panel of the desk. The Asshole leaned over and growled at me that if I made any noise, I was screwed.

The Asshole stuck his dick in my face and flicked my forehead with his finger. He said that that was the sign for me to start sucking.

I got it. Even I figure things out sooner or later, even though I'm always the last one. Goddammit, he wanted me to give him a blowjob while he interrogated someone. Well, in any case this was a new one for me. You always learn new stuff. That's one thing I'd learned.

I got a flick on the forehead. I took his dick in my mouth and started. I tried to get it over with quickly, but the Asshole flicked me again, so I stopped. Well, at least he'd washed it.

I could hear people coming into the room. They were men. Their voices echoed so strangely under the table, however, that all I could make out was a word here and there.

The Asshole growled out something, and I could tell from his tone of voice that the shithead really was interrogating someone. When they'd chatted for fifteen minutes, the Asshole gave me another flick on the forehead. I took it in my mouth again and started sucking. It slipped out of my mouth accidentally and I let out a slurp.

I froze. It'd be a little more than embarrassing if I was caught with a cop's dick in my mouth.

I sucked him for quite a while until he gave me a flick. The guy was disgusting. I was sure you couldn't tell from his voice that he was getting sucked off. I started to think he'd conducted blowjob interrogations before.

Another flick.

I could tell I wasn't completely out of practice when I heard the Asshole's voice stiffen. Despite all the flicks on the forehead, I was just about to empty his pipe when I heard him say very clearly, "Aurora could've heard all kinds of things."

I stopped. He flicked me on the forehead right away. I took his dick in my mouth, but didn't do anything. I could hear better that way.

You just can't even imagine, I was about to die.

"Don't get Aurora mixed up in this."

I was about to die. I wanted to die.

The bastard was interrogating my Arkady. He was sick, sick goddammit.

What could I have done?

What the fucking goddamn hell could I have done?

I could've bitten his goddamn dick off, and he'd have gone running and screaming out the door with blood spewing all over, but what then? My Arkady.

He kept flicking me on the forehead. I sucked. Oh, I thought, forgive me, Arkady. My Arkady, please forgive me.

I continued and wondered what would happen if there was another cop in the room? Could I get up and say that the guy raped me?

It'd be hard to prove that he'd raped me.

But what if I said that he'd forced me to do it, that he's putting my husband behind bars? Forgive me, Arkady, you're the one I love, I thought, and I continued. In any case, if I got up, then Arkady would die on the spot.

That was for sure.

I've never given a blowjob while crying before.

You always learn new things.

I noticed that he was getting close. His dick was twitching. I took his seed in the palm of my hand and wiped it on his pants. He tried to flick me for that. I bit his finger.

"I have a bit of asthma," he fucking said to my Arkady.

I hunkered down under the desk until the interrogation was over. Everyone left, including the Asshole, but he soon returned. He pulled the chair away from the desk and asked the lady to come out.

"I'll bet that was something new for you," he said.

"Go fuck yourself," I said.

"But that's what whores are for," he laughed.

I asked what was going to happen to Arkady. The Asshole said that he'd probably be fine in prison as long as he didn't find out that his wife was sucking off cops during business hours. "During the cops' business hours," he added.

I told him this would all come back to haunt him one day if he didn't do something for Arkady. He cocked his ear and wondered if he'd heard correctly, a whore was threatening a highly-ranked police official?

"You heard right," I said.

He told me to get lost. He promised he'd be in touch when he needed his dick polished.

"Go fuck yourself," I said.

He raised his face from the papers he was supposedly examining. In his opinion, I wasn't good enough at using my tongue. He was surprised by that—with all my experience I should be able to catch flies with it.

I left. I went to the restroom to rinse out my mouth and wash my face. There was a woman in the restroom, and it felt like she was staring at me like she knew what I'd just done.

Kristiina pours some mineral water and misses her glass. I look in my pocket mirror to see how my face looks, it's swollen and my eyes are red.

Kristiina asks whether I can possibly be telling the truth. I look her in the eye, and she nods slowly.

The waitress comes and asks if we want anything more. I do. Kristiina shakes her head. Her hair is so short that only her bangs move.

"Fuck, he tricked me," I suddenly blurt.

"Aurora, Aurora," Kristiina whispers.

"Fuck, what a cop, what a damn pig," I sob.

"Aurora."

"I'm stupid, just stupid."

Kristiina takes me by the hand. She says that no one can do to anyone what that cop did to me.

"But he did it to me," I sob, and Kristiina looks away.

It's raining so hard that the lake seems like it's split in two—one of the lakes is in the sky, and the border between the two looks like a hazy war zone. I've seen it before.

"Rautapää?" Kristiina asks.

"Yeah," I say.

Kristiina doubts there's any way we can prove that he forced me to have sexual relations with him.

"I'm gonna kill him, I'm gonna kill him," I say.

"It's not worth going to prison for killing someone like that."

"I want revenge. He can't get off the hook just like that."

Kristiina says she doesn't think revenge will help or make me feel any better. I say that she wouldn't be talking like that if she'd crouched down under a desk with a cop's dick in her mouth.

We're both silent for a while. By now the light has changed into the kind of light that makes me melancholy, even on a good day.

I drink up the rest of the white wine. Kristiina asks what she can do for me. She asks me if I want to come stay at her place tonight.

"Yeah."

"Let's make paninis."

"If it's not too much trouble."

"Of course it isn't," she says, "we'll talk."

"He's the biggest asshole in the world."

"That's completely possible," Kristiina sighs.

29. Antero Rikkilä, Minister

I was thrilled that Marzipan was going to be buried, but I wish it would've been deeper than six feet.

But why did *I* have to officiate at his funeral? I could've gotten another minister to do it had I been paying any attention to the schedule.

A woman who was still young, but whose beauty was on the verge of fading, came to see me in the sacristy. She wanted me to perform part of the funeral service at the gravesite. Her grandmother didn't want to come into the church, but the young woman wanted her to hear the word of God, too.

She introduced herself as the sister of the deceased. I told her my name, and we shook hands. I expressed my condolences. Nice legs. Maybe five, seven years ago, that is.

I promised to conduct a service at the graveside. It looked windy out; maybe the wind would scatter my words into the air and they'd stay out of people's ears.

How many times had I wished for Marzipan's death? A thousand times would be an understatement. I prayed for it on my knees with my hands folded on my bed, my gaze fixed at the bedroom ceiling.

I put on my "Zorro costume" and solemnly walked toward my appointed spot. The mourners stopped their racket. I glanced up, which signified that I was contemplating why the Almighty saw fit to call his child to his side at precisely this time.

Why did he smash his child's head? Why did it happen so quickly? Why didn't he punish his child with a wasting disease that would've eaten away at him and humiliated him for years? He doesn't answer.

Father, receive the putrid soul of your child.

I started the ceremony, which, as agreed upon, was to be brief.

I observed the feigned grief and figured that this would turn out to be a good gig after all. I had developed a system whereby my mouth spoke the word of God, while my mind was occupied with more earthly matters.

Marriage is a good teacher for that skill. A bad marriage is an excellent teacher.

Marzipan's casket was moved onto the funeral carriage, and we sashayed along toward the cemetery. I kept my eyes fixed on my shoes forcing a sad expression on my face, because I felt like laughing so much.

The king of twats, the czar of pussies was making his final voyage. Now the entire guy was stiff.

In the churchyard the immense yellow disc in the sky was shining. Spring was in the air. Bile rose up into my mouth as I looked at these people, all dressed up in their Sunday best, these hypocritical dolts, these miserable bankrupt dwarves, pretending to be dignified in the magnificent spring air.

I wanted to scream at them.

Go into your caves, you animals, you smelly skunks…

You snake-shitting wolves, you screeching owls and hooting females…

You rapidly-reproducing pink vermin, you glowing cockroaches…

You insignificant devils…

You dung beetles, you screaming breeding mutants, you infected wounds. You crybabies…

You swine, you pigs, you herds of swine possessed with evil spirits. You horrible scourges of the earth…

You bleating rams, you tubfuls of raw meat rotting on the bone, you mannequins, you gigantic hairy-nostriled snot plugs, you boneless nightmares. You cheese-smacking scum, you reeking sewage-belching slime…

You decomposing corpses, you elementary school dropouts, you maggots, you brittle irons…

You flightless birds, you sunken graves, you suckers of rotting flesh, you drunken manure huggers, you bureaucrats, you politicians who get three votes in the parliamentary elections. You honorary degree holders in coffee drinking, you insistent sluts of political science…

You trainwrecks, you bums that dogs pee on, you veterans of charitable fundraising. You maniac motorsports fans, you Lapland dialect-speaking farters…

You frigid mares, you thin-haired ones, you discount coupon clippers…

You bloody stumps.

The casket was lowered into the grave. Before I could speak, we had to sing. My voice carries well.

I finally got a chance to rattle off about the life and merits of the deceased.

I swallowed.

I continued to engage the mourners, but it didn't prevent me from thinking.

I looked again, and I was absolutely certain. Kristiina was standing fifty yards away, alone, dressed in black, on the gravel pathway in the shade of a large tree.

I recognized her from her silhouette. It was both curvaceous and girlish. I pressed my hands together, my knuckles went white. That didn't prevent them from shaking.

I looked at Kristiina. It looked like she was looking straight into my eyes. She was looking right into my heart.

Why did you have to come?

Did you have to come to see Marzipan take his final voyage? Couldn't you have allowed me just this one beautiful moment of triumph and joy?

Kristiina's shadow merged with the shadow of the tree, and it became a giant that reached over toward me. Kristiina's arm turned into a tree branch, and when the sun moved, the branch grabbed onto me and ripped my heart out of my chest, and it stopped beating.

I felt dizzy.

An older lady glanced at me, who was it? Mrs. Räikkönen, the mother of the deceased, Marzipan's mother.

"We can contemplate on how fragile the thread is that connects a human soul to its mortal shell."

Kristiina didn't budge. She was just as quiet in the shade as in my mind. It had been two months since she'd replaced me with Marzipan.

Kristiina was my bliss.

I didn't know that yet when I approached her last fall. I just wanted someone new instead of the same old Hellevi.

Kristiina wasn't my first affair. I'd observed her for several weeks. I knew she couldn't be seduced unless she wanted to be. I knew that I had to cry to get her.

I talked about everything, my Lord how I talked about everything.

About life, women, children, the world, faith, refugees, demons, teenagers' anxieties, the formality and coldness of the Evangelical Lutheran Church compared to the forgiveness and community of the Catholic faith, feminism, ecumenism as a champion of world peace, Jesus' possible political leanings, the changing role of men, the role of sexuality as part of a person's overall personality, sexuality as a means of human communication, sexuality as one of the most beautiful expressions of divine love, sexuality as a means of power in today's valueless society, sexuality between men and women, sexuality between men and men, sexuality between women and women, sexuality in nursing homes, sexuality in the sacraments of the church, sexuality during puberty, sexuality within the universe, and about sexuality in Rovaniemi, here and now, immediately. Right now!

At home, in between these passionate discussions, I still had to play the role of a father, who every now and then banged his exhausted wife, taught his son how to hit a slapshot, and affectionately scolded his daughter for spending hours on the phone.

And all the while all I wanted was for Kristiina to take me to her bachelorette pad, offer me some wine, and then I'd screw her from behind so hard that her luscious mouth would open, ready to scream from pleasure, but instead my tool would pop out of it, having pierced her entire beautiful body with love; and right there in front of her brown eyes, dilated with joy, I'd shoot a magnificent splotch high up onto her bedroom wall next to her Magritte poster, something that'd be impossible to explain to her parents, who always visited unannounced.

And afterward Kristiina would be panting by my side, all covered in sweat, wanting and demanding that I divorce my wife.

When Kristiina finally gave in after I cried about my sense of inadequacy, I, the Preaching Stallion, immediately proved my inadequacy by going limp during foreplay. She understood the pressure I was under, or, as I later admitted to myself while cursing in the dark stairway of my house, my lack of pressure.

I took a week of sick leave, during which I lifted weights and took ginseng, China's entire fall harvest in fact. When I returned to work, Kristiina sent me an email saying she wanted to meet. We went to bed. She had a Miró poster on her wall. My back was sore from messing around with the weights, so the sex wasn't ecstasy, but later on it definitely became pure sextasy.

Because of my lust for her, I didn't realize I'd fallen in love.

I studied her.

When I was away from the congregation traveling, I'd look at the clock in my hotel room, call her at work and ask if she'd already gotten her coffee. She'd be stirring it at that very moment. That amazed her. At first my enthusiasm scared her, but then she began to be flattered by how I happened to know by the expression on her face that she wanted salmon soup. I just knew. If you love someone, you know things like that.

Her hair was blonde, golden.

When she got it cut short, I had to go into her office four times a day to stroke her hair. At home I could smell her shampoo on my hand. My wife looked at me. I gave her my hand and said that our female minister had sprayed on my hand the perfume we'd given her as a gift. My wife smelled it without saying anything.

Kristiina's breasts looked up. When I stood in front of her, they looked me in the eye, trustingly.

"Before you, Almighty Lord, today we commend unto you the soul of a member of your flock. Have mercy on him."

She always woke up startled.

She liked to sit in her easy chair with one leg on the floor and one leg draped over the arm of the chair, swinging to the beat of some movie soundtrack. It was so innocently provocative. She was as natural as a child, a fresh woman.

She'd get lipstick all over every glass she drank from. At restaurants she'd wipe the rim of her glass with a napkin, but at home she didn't bother; instead, she'd hold onto the glass by the rim so you couldn't see it. I'd tease her about it.

People would stare at the way she walked. She said it was because of volleyball, which she played well into her twenties. I encouraged her to wear high-heeled shoes or boots, but she didn't want to. "It's hard to walk in them," she said, "and besides, men don't like having to look up at a woman." She was five foot eleven.

I could draw a map of her body. I could travel all across that map without getting lost, from memory. Her triangle is golden yellow, and not very hairy. It oozed honey.

Her mouth, teeth, and saliva kept her lips constantly wet. It never got cold enough for her to need lip balm. It was incredible.

She was embarrassed when I asked her after work one day if I could have her shirt so I could smell her sweat. It intoxicated me. Sometimes just her smell would get me hard, just the slightest hint of her smell.

The light at the end of my tunnel was in the shape of her body.

I had to stroke her eyebrows with my fingers and then look at my fingers, but it was true, her eyebrows were naturally almost black.

She didn't like wearing jeans, because she thought her rear end was too wide. It was beautiful enough to eat.

The back of her neck was like the stem of a champagne glass.

"The Lord is the light of the world, we are his reflection. Just like the light of the moon is borrowed from the sun."

I met Marzipan when I officiated at his wedding. I believe Laina was one of the Korvenoja girls.

What a horrible wedding.

Everyone was embarrassed, except for Marzipan, who'd drunk himself beyond embarrassment. His pant legs were shiny from vomit and his face was swollen and sported a week's worth of stubble. Laina was irritable, and six months pregnant. But that was the least of the disgraces.

I tried to suggest to the bride that the veil in front of the bride's face symbolized virginity. She just didn't get it—she'd seen photos in the *Seura* magazine where celebrity brides wore veils. She had to have one, too.

Marzipan kept interrupting me as I tried to get through the ceremony. I had to whisper to him that as a minister, I could stop the proceedings if I believed the bride and groom weren't in complete possession of their physical and mental faculties. Marzipan showed me his bicep. He said that judging from the hardness of his bicep his mental faculties were just fine. He also had something else that was hard, and told Laina to feel it, right there at the altar. For a moment it looked like Laina was going to thrust her hand down Marzipan's pants, but she didn't.

We got through it. I didn't think I'd ever have to see Marzipan again, but he began to stop by my office at the church once or twice a year. He was always drunk, and said he'd come to get spiritual guidance. He knew I couldn't just throw him out.

Usually he wanted to argue about politics and would leave angry, because I refused to reveal who I was voting for. He claimed that he himself took politics seriously. He studied the candidates for weeks before making his final selection. He wanted to be absolutely sure his candidate got the fewest number of votes. He told me he often succeeded in doing so. Over the years I got used to his rants.

It was right at the beginning of last winter when he stopped by, pretending to look pensive.

He asked how to write an obituary. He said he was asking purely out of theoretical interest. I said that people usually put in a few stirring lines from a poem by Eino Leino or Saima Harmaja. Some self-declared writers insisted on seeing their own verses in the newspaper. People conformed to good manners; it wasn't considered in good taste to speak ill of the deceased.

Marzipan took a sip from his flask and told me in a sad voice that he'd heard his good friend Roisko-Mauri was on his deathbed. I expressed my condolences, and said that I didn't know the man. Marzipan went on and on about Roisko-Mauri's accomplishments. I had plans to see Kristiina, but I knew that if I started hustling

Marzipan out of there, I'd end up sitting in my office until midnight. Marzipan bragged that Roisko-Mauri held the Finnish record for the most dropped criminal charges. I said I admired men like him.

Marzipan asked whether it represented good manners for a man of God to mock one of his parishioners, especially one who was on his deathbed. I said that I didn't want to offend Roisko-Mauri.

Marzipan thought about that while taking swigs from his flask. He was chain-smoking so much that my eyes were burning as if I'd gotten soap in them. He walked around and snorted at the books in my office. He stopped to look out the window at the non-existent scenery and asked if it was okay to use "missing you like crazy" in an obituary and then list the names of those left behind.

I said that the church didn't control the content of obituaries. The church neither gave permission nor prohibited anything. As far as I understood, the newspaper ensured that illegal announcements didn't get published. I reminded him that although I wasn't a lawyer, I knew that there was a statute in the law that prohibited denigrating the memory of a deceased person. If Roisko-Mauri's relatives were of the opinion that the deceased had been defamed, they could file a lawsuit. Of course all of this was purely academic. I'd never heard of anyone who put the phrase "missing you like crazy" in an obituary, but to me it didn't sound illegal. Idiotic, yes.

Marzipan sat down and lit another cigarette. I opened the window and said I'd rather die from the cold than from cancer. He reminded me that the Lord didn't let us choose the way we go.

I was getting anxious. Once when I was late meeting her because of a long phone call, Kristiina came into my office to get me. I didn't want Kristiina to meet Marzipan; I didn't want to introduce the Beast to the Beauty. That's what I was actually thinking.

Marzipan said that as far as he knew, Roisko-Mauri didn't have any relatives. If he did, they wouldn't admit to being related. "Besides," Marzipan added, twisting his mouth from the swig of booze, "'missing you like crazy' is totally fitting to describe the grief of those left behind."

Marzipan stuck his tongue in his flask and licked the inside of it. He got up with a sigh and said that he'd stop by when spiritual anxiety struck again. I was so relieved, I gave him a smile. Someone knocked on the door. Kristiina walked in and stopped when she saw Marzipan.

"There are angels flitting around the church," Marzipan said. I patted him on the shoulder and steered him toward the door. I said we were about to have a meeting.

"Räikkönen," Marzipan said and stuck out his hand toward Kristiina. Kristiina squeezed it and introduced herself. Marzipan repeated her name to be sure he'd heard it correctly. He walked out the door without taking his eyes off her.

"Old classmates," he said to Kristiina, nodding toward me.

"Aha," Kristiina said.

A little over a month later Marzipan came by again. I wasn't happy that he was increasing the frequency of his visits.

As far as I could tell, he was sober.

He had thin leather gloves on. He regretted not being able to shake my hand because his rash had returned. That was nonsense, he'd never shaken my hand before, and I'd never taken offense at it.

He sat down and sighed that Roisko-Mauri had died. I offered my condolences. I asked if he'd thought about the final version of the obituary.

He looked at me, confused. After thinking for a long time, he said, "Yes."

We sat in silence, which bothered me.

I pointed out I had enough work for five ministers, and asked if he had anything else to say.

Marzipan said he wanted to commit suicide. I asked him to stop playing around—he was healthy and young.

He took a gun out of his jacket pocket. He was swinging it dangerously in my direction. I leapt out of my chair.

"Sit down," Marzipan said gently. I obeyed the tone in his voice.

I asked him to calm down, as this was no time to be reckless with guns. Marzipan told me not to wet my pants over something so trivial. If he wanted to kill me, he'd choose a different place and a different time, and probably also a different guy to pull the trigger.

I didn't understand what he was saying.

My room had especially big windows. I'd opened one just as Marzipan arrived in case he was smoking. I looked at the window and wondered how nimbly I could get over the sill and jump out. It was about a fifteen-foot drop.

Marzipan looked at me and got up.

He pointed his gun at the floor and pulled the trigger. The gun just clicked, it wasn't loaded. I was so relieved that tears welled up in my eyes.

Marzipan laughed. He said he only now realized how different our professions were.

"Oh really?" I asked, maybe a bit stupidly.

Marzipan explained that if he wanted to shoot me, knowing the business he's in, the potential victim should never relax until it was clear that all of the chambers of the gun were empty, not just the first one.

I didn't completely understand him.

He pointed the gun at the floor again and pulled the trigger maybe ten times. The gun kept clicking.

"Now you can be sure the thing's empty," Marzipan said, "Only now can you be sure."

He seemed to enjoy giving this lesson. I thanked him for taking the trouble. Now I knew how to act and what to think the next time someone tried to shoot me. Marzipan said he wasn't trying to shoot me, only enlighten me.

I was more than a little irritated.

I asked Marzipan if there was anything else on today's agenda: picking locks, counterfeiting, stealing cars, throwing rocks at windows? Marzipan shook his head.

Again there was silence.

I asked how Roisko-Mauri had died. I was amazed by what was coming out of my mouth. But I was raised this way, and I'd been doing it for years to earn my daily bread. You make conversation when you're stuck in someone's company.

"Suddenly," Marzipan said, "very suddenly."

I told him I'd gotten the impression that Roisko-Mauri had suffered from a disease.

Marzipan said that even so, death had come suddenly, like taxes. I didn't understand his metaphors, but I nodded to him and said that it was death's nature to arrive suddenly.

During our conversation Marzipan kept playing with the gun. Now that I knew it wasn't loaded, it looked like my son's toy. Marzipan threw it onto the table in front of me with a thud and told me to pick it up.

I refused.

Marzipan figured that at some point during my life I'd have to deal with a murderer. How could I even guess how a murderer felt, if I'd never held a gun in my hands?

He had a point. I reluctantly admitted it to myself, but not to him.

Marzipan urged me to pick up the gun and point it at him. I'd learn to understand the kind of power a gunman has. I picked it up. I was astounded by its weight.

I aimed the gun out the window, and voiced a gunshot sound.

I was a bit insulted because Marzipan seemed to be amused by it. He asked me to stop goofing off. I wouldn't be able to get into the right spirit unless I pulled the trigger.

I pointed the barrel at Marzipan. I looked him in the eye and pulled the trigger. Click. He didn't get shot in the head.

He asked how it felt. I told him I understood how a sick person could feel forbidden pleasure from handling a gun and shooting people.

"True," Marzipan said. I gave him back the gun and he put it in his pocket.

He left.

The next day I saw an article in the paper saying that the police were looking for a certain Mauri Hemminki Roisko's killer. He'd been shot in Sauvosaari.

An email message appeared in my inbox, in which Kristiina regretted that she couldn't see me anymore. She hoped I would understand.

She'd met someone new.

Someone new.

I got up then and there and went to look for Kristiina in the business office. They told me Kristiina was home sick. I went there.

From the outside, I saw a light on in her kitchen.

I ran up the steps and almost pushed the doorbell through the door.

Marzipan opened the door and asked me to come in. He asked me to wipe my shoes on the doormat. "Wet shoes can damage the parquet floor," he said.

In the kitchen, Kristiina was kneading dough. I was dumbfounded. We'd spent many evenings like that, with me sitting at the kitchen table and Kristiina cooking.

The scene was the same, except I wasn't the guy that she was cooking for.

Kristiina looked at me. She said she hoped I hadn't come to make a scene. She asked if Marzipan had explained the situation to me.

"We're not interested in theater," Marzipan joked from the doorway.

I asked Kristiina why.

She turned to roll out the dough. She was making pizza.

With her eyes on the dough, she said her heart had told her to.

"You traded me for a criminal," I said, "is that how little I meant to you?"

"Let's not call people names," Marzipan said, and told me to sit down. I did.

Kristiina turned, came and stood in front of me, and said that she respected me as a man and as a person but she was now in love with Marzipan and that was that. She had some flour on her cheek, it was adorable.

"You, a believer." I tried to get her to change her mind.

Marzipan went and stood behind Kristiina and asked me to guess which believer it was who'd been having a shameless extramarital affair lately? It wasn't Kristiina, because she wasn't married, so who could it be then?

I didn't respond.

Kristiina shrugged her shoulders.

I said I'd be taking the matter up with the church administration. I told her I could predict what the church council would think about the finance manager dating a known felon. It was questionable from the perspective of the financial security of the parish alone. On top of that, there were moral considerations.

"Oh my goodness gracious," Marzipan said.

My forehead burned when Marzipan stuck his hand under Kristiina's shirt from behind and groped her breasts. Kristiina snickered. Marzipan asked what he was leaving.

271

I didn't understand.

He kept repeating, "What am I leaving, what am I leaving?"

I told him I didn't understand.

"Fingerprints," Marzipan said slowly.

I got up and left. I went back to my office.

I thought to myself, how could I have been such an idiot as to handle a criminal's gun when he gave it to me wearing gloves?

It seemed impossible to think that Marzipan would have murdered a man in order to get Kristiina for himself. Yet a moment later it seemed possible. I knew with calm certainty that if I had to kill to get Kristiina back, I would.

But did Marzipan murder Roisko-Mauri? Or did he just use the situation to his advantage? It was a strange coincidence that I happened to be in Sauvosaari the day Roisko-Mauri was shot.

I couldn't do anything about it. I was innocent.

I asked myself which would be greater agony—losing Kristiina or doing life in prison? I didn't know, I really didn't.

Just thinking about it was the greatest agony, and Marzipan knew that.

"On the final day of judgment, this member of our congregation, whom we commend unto you, will be born again into God's grace and everlasting joy."

I raised my eyes and went on about the future happiness promised to Marzipan. I lauded his fate. I looked at these mourners. Every one of them, including the pale old lady shaking and babbling to herself on the chair, was rejoicing that Marzipan was the one rotting in the ground and not them.

As long as someone else is lying in the ground and not me.

You hypocrites…

You weathered pricks…

You timid pushovers, you seething buckets of shit...

You hardheaded quiz show participants, you hairy hemorrhoids, you whoopee cushions...

You shishkebabs...

You mediocre ones. You crying fans of Lasse Virén...

You laundry room gossips, you serious cows. You shitting seagulls...

You Supreme Court brownnosers, you interlibrary loaners, you closet masturbators. You demanders of good service...

You tangle-haired creatures, you wheelers and dealers. You emphasizers and underliners...

You fallen soldiers, you cabbage lovers. You pathetic hamsters...

You boombox-blasting fools at the campground...

You arthritic kleptos. You chapped sows' vulvas...

You masters of condom-free hazardous sex...

You limp ones fluttering in the slightest breeze...

You snake rapers. You whiners...

You fish guts. You Christmas fish...

You fuzzy heads, you dung beetles. You titterers...

You nit-pickers...

You squat jumps. You abscessed, flying humps. You holey-stockinged backcombers. You who wear wool socks with high heels...

You timid bulls...

You seals peering out of toilets...

You certified welders. You hymn slayers. You gamblers. You trash bag consultants. You evaluators of visual arts education. You theater festivals. You work spirits. You who shit into washing machines. You miserable rats. You young, pimply farts who carry a wet cell phone in the company car. You spry old folks. You pond scum. You elephants' horns. You warmongers...

You bedpans full of piss...

The mother of the deceased glared at me like a panther.

I realized I'd uttered the last insult aloud. I kept my composure, but I could tell that the woman believed her ears and not the expression on my face.

When I got to the end of the service, she turned her back to my outstretched hand. It was worse than getting spit at in the eye. I wasn't invited to the rotting carcass's funeral luncheon.

Suddenly I realized I was standing alone on the gravel path, mumbling to myself.

The mourners had gone. I looked at the big tree, but in its shade there was no Kristiina, only darkness. I hadn't seen her leave.

I looked around. I was the only living thing in the cemetery. I walked to Marzipan's grave, glanced around one more time and opened my fly. I tried, but nothing came out.

I went to change my clothes. I walked to my car and drove home.

"The night moon sings scooby-dooby-doo," the radio sang out. It felt significant to me.

At home I ate some gray meat. My son was teasing my daughter at the dinner table. My wife reprimanded them.

At six in the evening I realized I'd been sitting in the armchair for two hours, staring at the wall.

"So, what was her name this time?" my wife screamed.

When I started to cry, she panicked and scooped our son into her arms. My son wondered, "Where did Daddy get hurt?"

Part Four:

The face of Jesus Christ appeared on the ceiling

30. Arkady Wolfovich Arkhipov

I was lying on my bunk in my cell when the face of Jesus Christ appeared on the ceiling.

I touched my eyes to make sure they were open.

He looked like he was straight out of an icon, but larger and purer. And a magnificent light was shining behind his head.

"How are things going, Arkady Wolfovich?"

I tried to get up and throw myself on my knees, but Jesus Christ told me to stay where I was.

"How are things going, Arkady Wolfovich?"

"Things aren't going well, my Father. The Finns have arrested me and thrown me in jail. They think I've killed some Finnish scoundrel. Things aren't going well, my Father, Arkady Wolfovich is very sad and lonely."

"Who am I, then? You are not alone."

"Forgive me. I didn't realize who I was speaking to."

"Is your conscience clear?"

"What do you mean, Son of God?"

"Do you have a murder on your conscience?"

"I didn't murder Marzipan—that's the name of the Finn. I swear to you before all that is holy and dear to me that I did not murder him. I am innocent. I'm not guilty. The Finns are leading me, an innocent man, to slaughter. Before your Father, I assure you that I have no blood on my hands."

"Are you lying?"

"Me? Would I lie to Jesus Christ? What are you talking about?"

"Who killed him?"

"I don't know, Light of the World."

"Unless it was you."

"No, a thousand times no. You can rip the heart out of my chest, the eyes from my head, you can cast my soul into eternal damnation, but I didn't lay a hand on Marzipan."

"I don't travel the world ripping out hearts and piercing eyes, Arkady Wolfovich."

"If you ripped out my heart and pierced my eyes, but set me free, that would lessen my pain. Arkady Wolfovich has been left on a deserted planet."

"Who am I?"

"Forgive me, forgive me, my Father."

"That is why I travel the world."

I closed my eyes, but Jesus Christ didn't disappear from the ceiling of my cell. When I opened my eyes, he was smiling.

"What do you want to tell me, Arkady Wolfovich?"

"You came here. You're the one who should speak."

"You called me."

"Did I?"

"I come only when I'm called."

I was silent for a moment. I swallowed.

"My Father."

"Arkady Wolfovich."

"Don't misunderstand me."

"I won't."

"Are you sure?"

"On my word."

"I'm the victim of an injustice. I'm not the nicest person ever to roam the world, but I don't deserve this fate. Why am I being treated so wrongly that I'm being made out to be a murderer? That has never been my job in the gang's division of labor. Why am I being made out to be a murderer? Why not then make me into a murderer-rapist who tortures children and screws his mother? Why not, dammit? As long as we've already gone down this road, why not?"

"Is this what you wanted to tell me?"

"For starters, yes."

"Tell me everything."

"It's your turn. Otherwise our turns will get confused, my Father."

"Arkady Wolfovich. Is the world a department store?"

"You sure do ask the questions."

"Is the world a department store, where you can choose your punishment? You admit that you've trespassed against others. Yes, you have. Did they get to choose their punishment when you assaulted them, stole from them, disgraced them, or forced them into poverty? Did they get to choose the moment when you interfered in their lives? What were they guilty of for you to punish them? Are you the axis of the universe, around which the stars slowly dance? Why should you get to define who you are? You're a murderer."

"No, I'm not."

"But if that's what's been decided."

"But I'm not."

"You've now been booked for murder."

"I haven't been convicted yet."

"You know you'll be convicted."

"I don't know that. You know that."

"You'll be convicted."

"Goddammit! Fucking goddammit!"

"You'll be convicted."

"Why, tell me why!"

"I don't know. But you'll be convicted."

"Goddammit. There's no justice in this world."

"No, there isn't. But I am just."

"What good does that do me?"

"Your soul will have peace."

"It doesn't feel that way, it feels horrible. What will my mother think when she hears that her son has been convicted of murder?"

"Ask her."

"You're a big comfort, Son of God."

"You know that I am, Arkady Wolfovich."

"Jesus Christ, the Son of God."

"Arkady Wolfovich."

"Let's make a deal."

"I'm not a prosecutor."

"I'd take any punishment, any other kind of punishment."

"No, you wouldn't. You wouldn't take any other kind of punishment; you just want to choose your punishment."

"I'd go to prison for the same amount of time as for murder."

"Arkady Wolfovich, you can choose the punishment that you'll be given."

"What kind of choice is that?"

"The choice you have."

"You sound like a lawyer."

"I'm defending you."

"That's what my lawyer said, too."

"Bow your head and accept your punishment."

"Why is this happening? Why won't you play fair? Why are you punishing me when you know that it was the kid next to me who had the slingshot? You really do act like a teacher. Why must you do wrong, when you can do right?"

"Why did you do wrong, when you could have done right?"

"That's different. You have the power and the might. Why don't you punish me for stealing liquor, why don't you punish me for fraud, why don't you punish me for robbery, why don't you punish me for counterfeiting, why don't you punish me for pimping prostitutes?"

"I am punishing you."

"You're punishing me for a murder committed by someone else."

"You will be punished. It's not too harsh for the evil things you've done."

"When you punish, you don't grant any way to appeal."

"Yes, I do."

"Oh? How?"

"There are no appeals."

"My Father, my Father."

"Arkady Wolfovich."

"Am I really speaking to you?"

"Yes, you are."

"Your punishment is too harsh."

"No, it isn't."

"I'll die here."

"Everyone dies."

"I mean in prison, fuck, I mean in prison."

"As do I."

I fell silent. I showed Jesus Christ that I was sulking. I was covered in sweat. I pressed my forehead against the wall, which didn't dry it off, but felt cool.

I heard some clattering in the corridor. Someone peeked in through the door of my cell, but didn't say anything.

"Jesus Christ, the Light of the World."

"Arkady Wolfovich, my child."

"Do I nonetheless stand in good stead with you?"

"After you've endured your punishment, yes."

"Why didn't you make me a good person? Then you could be praising me now."

"I didn't make you."

"Your Father, then, why didn't your Father make me a good person? We could be enumerating my good deeds. We could be drinking tea."

"Ask Father."

"You ask him."

"I won't."

"You'll see him before I do."

"Arkady Wolfovich, humble yourself."

"I am not smart enough to understand why. Why your Father made me evil, and when I do evil deeds, he punishes me for it. He created me with his own hands. So he's punishing himself. Why does he need me for that? Why can't I live like a regular human and your Father could then punish himself every time he wanted to, without any intermediaries? Your Father touches the fire, but I'm the one who gets burned. It's wrong. My head creaks when I think about it."

"Don't think about it. Accept what you're given."

"Nothing's been given to me besides a beating."

"You're the one beating yourself."

"Your Father is nothing but a drill sergeant."

"Come on now."

"That's how he gets his orders carried out."

"You're upset."

"I'm being set up for life in prison. If my fellow countrymen don't kill me, then I'll suffocate from rage in here. In any case, I'll die. I'll die like a bedbug. Yes, I guess I'm a little upset."

"Calm down."

"That's easy for you to say."

"What do you mean?"

"You just show up on the ceilings of jail cells to dole out advice. Why don't you write a how-to guide to life, so you don't even have to show up? Those on the fringes of society could buy it from the store and burst out in boils while praising your Father, who in thanks would hit them up with a fresh scourge. Sometimes I really wonder."

"What?"

"Nothing."

"You forget."

"What?"

"That I was killed. And that I was nailed onto two-by-fours."

"I forgot, forgive me."

"You're forgiven."

"Really, for a moment there I forgot."

"It's okay."

"Don't take this the wrong way, but could you show me your hands?"

"So it's come to this?"

"Forget it, then."

"Arkady Wolfovich, you're better than that."

"It just popped into my head. I'm upset. Help me."

"Sure, why not."

"Grant me good judgment, forbearance, and patience."

"Oh?"

"Right now."

"Get up, Arkady Wolfovich."

"A moment ago I was supposed to lie down."

"Get up, you don't get to decide, listen to me."

"You're cruel to humans."

"Get up."

I got up and stood in the middle of the room. I looked up at the ceiling where Jesus Christ was shining down at me.

"On your knees, Arkady Wolfovich."

"Drill sergeant!"

"On your knees."

I went down on my knees. My side hurt. I looked up at the ceiling.

"Your sins have been forgiven."

"Thank you."

I stayed on my knees. Someone appeared at the door of my cell.

He asked what the fuck all the ruckus was about. It was Ivan Illich.

I told him I'd dropped my ring. His opinion was that I should be able to find it with less noise, as the entire corridor was echoing with my rants.

Ivan Illich said he'd help me. He came up alongside me and patted the floor.

We patted the floor a couple of times.

"Are you sure you dropped it, Arkady Wolfovich?"

"Yes, I'm sure I did."

"Maybe you dropped it, but not here."

"I dropped it just a minute ago."

"Is that right?"

"I heard a clink."

"You couldn't have heard anything with all that noise."

"Why would I lie?"

"You're starting to slip, Arkady Wolfovich."

"I'll be just fine."

"Have you gotten into your stash again?"

"What do you care about my stash?"

"It messes up your head, Arkady Wolfovich."

"Mind your own business."

"I do, but you're not minding your own."

"My sins have been forgiven."

"The court doesn't agree."

"What do you know about that?"

"I just know."

"Are you Jesus Christ?"

"You're starting to slip, Arkady Wolfovich."

"I'll be just fine."

"What ring was it?"

"It was a family ring."

"It's not here."

"Thanks for the help."

"You're welcome."

Ivan Illich got up off the floor and brushed off his knees.

I asked him if he'd taken a close look at the ceiling of his cell. Ivan Illich hadn't paid any special attention to it. In his opinion a ceiling was a ceiling.

I urged him to look at the ceiling again. It was a portal.

Ivan Illich looked at me. He put his hand on my shoulder. I didn't like the gentle look on his face.

"Arkady, Arkady, Arkady."

"What?"

"Have you been talking to Jesus Christ again?"

"What's it to you, Ivan Illich?"

"You're my friend."

"Yeah…"

"I'm worried about you."

"Your life would be in order if you'd start taking care of your soul."

"By looking at the ceiling?"

"Don't laugh."

"I'm not laughing, Arkady Wolfovich."

Ivan Illich wished me well and left. From the door he suggested that in a half hour I come get him, and we'd go to the gym. I said I would.

"For sure?"

"For sure, Ivan Illich. You're my friend."

He left.

I went to my bunk and lay down. I batted my eyes.

I examined every square inch of the ceiling.

Jesus Christ was gone.

I closed my eyes and pressed on my eyeballs through my eyelids. I saw shocking videos.

I tried to fall asleep. My eyes were pulsating.

I got up and looked for a mirror. I looked at my face up close.

My eyes were red. I had met Jesus Christ.

His light had hurt my eyes.

I stood in the middle of the cell. It was a good place. A hand came out of the wall and entered my chest without drawing any blood. It grabbed my heart and lifted it up in the air. My heart was glowing red, the wind galloped through it, and then the hand came down and put my heart back into my chest.

I had to sit down on my bunk. I was panting.

I'd been saved. I knew it. There was no question about it.

I stood up.

The bed, the ratty rug, the bottle of juice, the cigarette papers, and the bits of tobacco on the table were all swimming in the same certainty.

I kissed the wall. I kissed the bedspread, I kissed my clothes, I kissed the floor, I kissed my radio. I sang my mother's favorite hymn.

I praised the Lord, who had shown me the way.

Who had given me everlasting grace.

I laughed when I thought about the first court hearing. It was meaningless now, even though it had infuriated me so much. The next hearing would be at the end of next week.

I burst out laughing. I was so full of divine energy that I decided to go to the gym.

As I was bounding down the corridor I remembered that soon it'd be Midsummer, my favorite time of year.

31. Topi Räikkönen

Little Dlohačka was on her way to downtown Sarajevo with her mother on March 25, 1994. It was a beautiful day, and the sun was shining.

Little Dlohačka was holding onto her mother's hand and skipped around joyfully. Spring was early, and she could feel its joy in her young chest.

War was far away.

Little Dlohačka's father was at the front. They hadn't heard from him in a month. Her mother worked as a secretary for a big company. Fortunately she had a job—they had food every day. The meals were meager, but they were prepared with love.

Her mother was in a good mood as she'd gotten the afternoon off from work. She picked up Little Dlohačka from daycare, and they planned out a fun afternoon together in town. Mother had bought her daughter an ice cream cone.

Little Dlohačka was just five years old, but she was proud that she knew how to lick her ice cream cone without making a mess on her brand new jacket.

They were crossing the street when the murderer struck.

"Sniper" was too distinguished a military term for him; the rifleman was just a plain old murderer.

The bullet hit Little Dlohačka's mother in the forehead. She died instantly.

Little Dlohačka thought her mother had tripped. The girl laughed, because her mother had warned her about skipping around and falling. Now it was her mother herself who had tripped, even though she was an adult.

Soon Little Dlohačka stopped laughing.

Mother just wouldn't get up, no matter how hard little Dlohačka tugged on her sleeve. The girl started crying when she saw blood flowing from her mother's head.

Little Dlohačka's hands were stained with her mother's blood, and she cried for so long that her voice became a hoarse, pitiful wail.

People peered out of their houses along the street. They didn't dare go get Little Dlohačka out of the middle of the street for fear of the murderer.

Little Dlohačka cried next to her mother's cold body for seven hours before it got dark and a young man was brave enough to go save the little girl. The shocked girl didn't want to leave her mother's side.

Little Dlohačka was taken to an orphanage. For six months, none of the nurses or other children were able to establish any kind of human contact with her.

At Christmas Little Dlohačka started drawing. She's also started to speak, and the director of the orphanage believes that she'll start school in the fall.

The whereabouts of Little Dlohačka's father are unknown. Little Dlohačka is just an ordinary girl from Sarajevo.

I sighed and put the pencil away. A moment later I took it out and sharpened it. I thought about writing a bit more.

Keskilä showed up in the doorway of my cell and asked if I was busy.

"Nope," I said and asked him to have a seat. Keskilä squeezed his hand into a fist and pressed it against his forehead for a while. He's not like everyone else.

I had to snap at him to get him to sit down on the bunk.

He stared at the paper in front of me and asked if I'd been working. I said I had. He got excited, and demanded that I read to him what I'd written. I did, and it sounded really good. Keskilä stood up and shook my hand to thank me before darting out.

He returned five minutes later, as I knew he would. He had some paper and crayons with him.

He asked me to read it again. Keskilä was stubborn as a mule. He wouldn't leave until I did. He cheered me on as I read.

He drew the entire time I was reading.

When I was done, he stopped. Perplexed, he asked me what color crying was. I looked at the colors he had and said, "Blue."

He showed me his drawing. It was really bad.

I asked him if it was absolutely necessary to draw blood coming out of the woman's head and gushing up so high. He was surprised I didn't know there was enormous pressure in a person's head. If you get shot in the head, your head becomes a fountain.

He'd drawn the girl with one tooth. Her mouth was wide open and her expression was angry. I thought five-year-olds had more teeth. Keskilä claimed the Serbs had kicked them in.

I asked him to explain to me one more time what he did with these stupid stories. He paid me twenty euros apiece.

He told me he'd been convicted of negligent homicide and reckless driving. I said he didn't have to go back that far. He was finishing up his drawing with his tongue hanging out, not listening. He sniffed the snot back up into his nostrils at regular intervals and swallowed.

He said he was getting out in three weeks. I congratulated him.

He told me he was going to frame his drawings with my stories. Then he'd pack them in a large suitcase and go on a tour.

He'd go to small towns. He'd chat up librarians and say he represented the international organization

"Support the Children of Sarajevo." He'd ask for permission to exhibit drawings done by children from Sarajevo. The title of the exhibition would be "Mom, Why Do We Have War?"

The librarians would love it, but they'd get a bit suspicious. They'd ask how much the exhibition cost.

Keskilä would promise the exhibition for free, because it was the subject matter that counted, not the money. He wouldn't even charge admission. At the exhibition he'd put up an old wooden box with a photo of a small dirty-cheeked girl on it. On the side of the box, he'd write "Will you help me?"

He had a tried-and-true box for this purpose at home, all ready to go.

A week in each city would suffice before moving on to the next one.

I asked if people wouldn't start sniffing around. I doubted whether an organization named "Support the Children of Sarajevo" even existed. Keskilä said he'd had brochures and business cards printed up. Besides, people didn't think they were being swindled if they gave money voluntarily out of a guilty conscience.

He told me that for more than six months he ran an exhibition dedicated to the children of Ethiopia during the famine there. It was titled "Mom, I'm Hungry."

Some foofy art critic from one of the local papers sarcastically asked how those dirt-poor Africans even had crayons in the first place, but a group of feminists from Zonta International spoke up totally dismissing him. Keskilä usually tried to avoid interviews, because the police read newspapers, as did people in the embassies.

Keskilä enticed women's organizations to come to his exhibitions. They were the easiest to pry money from. Hunting associations weren't worth inviting. For school groups, he had to drop a hint to the teachers about donating money ahead of time, so the kids knew to ask their parents for money the night before.

In Äänekoski, Keskilä hit the jackpot.

The wife of a school board member regretted that she couldn't buy all the drawings, since she knew they had to be shown all over Finland. Keskilä quickly told her this was the exhibition's last stop. He promised to ask the organization's headquarters in Umeå, Sweden, if the drawings could be sold in order to advance the cause; the school board member's wife ended up getting the drawings for six thousand euros. To be on the safe side, Keskilä immediately traveled two hundred miles south to Salo, and in his hotel he drew more stick people with thick lips.

I asked him how much he made on one exhibition.

He was astonished that I was already badgering him for a raise after my first story.

I noted that I hadn't been paid a cent yet. He dug a crumpled hundred-euro bill out of his pocket and gave it to me. I was surprised he was walking around prison with his pockets full of money. He said he'd hire me full time when I got out.

I told him I'd think about it. Five seconds later I said I figured I'd be here so long that he'd return before I was released. He thought that was possible.

I asked him for the drawing, and looked at it carefully. It was bad, in fact it was really bad. Nonetheless, perhaps it would touch older women's souls. I didn't know a thing about the emotional lives of older women. I asked him if he thought the name of a Finnish paper company visible in the paper's watermark would raise people's suspicions—how would children from Sarajevo get Finnish paper?

"This is a draft."

"Are you going to redo them and make them better?"

"Of course."

"Good."

"Actually, I'll make them worse."

"Why?"

"They're not supposed to be good. They're drawn by traumatized children."

"How many are you going to draw?"

"Twenty or so. Thirty."

"That many?"

"Let's say forty."

"They'll all be similar."

"Traumatized kids are similar."

"Are they?"

"Yes. They're traumatized."

"Statistically, out of forty kids you should have a couple that can actually draw."

"Really?"

"At least a little."

"You draw a couple. Twenty euros each."

"Give me some paper."

I scribbled out a drawing in which two children have their arms around each other and in the background a car's burning. I made two drawings. Keskilä looked at me nervously.

"You think you're going to get paid for two identical drawings?"

"They're twins."

"These kids?"

"Yeah. They ended up in separate orphanages at first, but when their drawings were sent in to a competition, the judges realized they were twins."

"Goddammit. How did they end up in different orphanages?"

"How would I know?"

"What are their names?"

"How the fuck should I know?"

"Think about it."

"Fuckin' Haris and fuckin' Alija."

"Oh, yeah?"

"Yeah, for example. They could fuckin' be Kuuno and Kauno."

"Not if they're from Sarajevo."

"Alright. They're Haris and Alija."

"How do you spell that?"

"I'll write you a story."

"Do it now."

"No, you'll get it tonight."

"Are you sure?"

"Yeah, I'm sure."

"You should work for me. You're a genius."

Keskilä walked out. He left some paper and crayons in case I happened to come up with any other story lines. He came back right away. I usually couldn't get rid of him on the first attempt. He gave me two wadded up twenties. He was always good at paying up.

I went to lie down on my bunk.

I tried to think of some kind of story for Haris and Alija, but Marzipan squeezed himself into my mind.

If someone had told me two months ago that my cousin would soon be dead, I would've shrugged my shoulders and said too bad. I hadn't realized he was such an important guy to me.

I can only remember bits and pieces about him. It's been hard, because I haven't been able to recall exactly what he looked like.

Did he have a moustache? Sometimes he did.

His hair was light brown, almost blond.

He was a bit taller than me, husky and strong.

His eyetooth had been broken off by a beer mug. He said his stump of a tooth predicted the weather, but he was never right.

When he spoke he always sounded like he had a cold. When I mentioned it to him once, he asked me to come into the bathroom of the bar to listen to his farts, which he claimed were also hoarse. I didn't go.

The way he laughed always sounded like a bunch of mucus was rattling around in his lungs. It was from smoking, but not only from that, because I remember him cackling like that as a teenager.

He had a scar on his forehead, which was my fault.

We had swiped a truck that was supposed to have all kinds of goodies in it from precious jewels to smoked ham, but ended up only containing unsanded two-by-fours. As we were unloading the cargo, I handed him the end of a shaggy two-by-four, and it slipped and hit him in the forehead.

He bent over slowly, without making a sound.

He crouched down for probably a minute before he got up, a stream of blood spreading and glistening across his forehead.

"Occupational hazard," he said.

That elevated my status at the pub later on. When people asked him about the scarred and bulging bump on his forehead, he said, "Topi whacked me."

He said it with such a serious tone that people believed it for a while.

Who was there? Marzipan, Root Canal, Trampas, and my brother Aleksanteri, who disappeared during my first winter in prison.

I missed Marzipan.

I got up and started writing the story about the twins.

It didn't turn out right. Rage was seeping out of me and into the story.

I smoked a cigarette. I turned on the radio. I tried to focus on the twins again.

I'd asked Marzipan to find out what happened to Aleksanteri, but he didn't find out much. Aleksanteri left the pub one winter night and hasn't been heard from since.

I had my suspicions about the case, but I wasn't able to do anything about it from behind bars, from here inside the Jack-off Palace. I saw that I'd written that Haris and Alija were from the Jack-off Palace.

I ripped up the paper.

I went and lay down.

I was restless, even though I hadn't been sipping any prison moonshine and hadn't popped any pills. I doubted that I could still get mixed up with pills.

I'd felt like this before.

Lesonen came in. I sat up. He sat down next to me.

He told me that the Russian was in the gym.

I asked how he knew, who'd told him? He said he'd seen it himself.

The Russian was grunting in there all by himself.

I stood up, and so did Lesonen. He asked what we should do.

I asked if he had lifting gloves. He said he'd go get them. I put my hand on his shoulder and gave him my gloves. I took some spare gloves for myself.

"What now?" Lesonen asked.

"Let's go," I said.

32. Leo Kurppa

Someone's thrown a gay porn magazine on my bunk. Sweaty, muscled guys with huge dicks are pounding each other.

I take it to Kunis, who goes berserk and tries to hug me.

"Don't!" I say. "Not in your wildest dreams."

Kunis's eyes bulge as he thumbs the pages. He asks what makes prisoners' junk so valuable.

"Because it's handmade," I say.

He always asks the same thing. His first name is Gunnar.

I go back to my cell, swearing. I gotta do something about them fucking with me.

Pretty soon they'll have me licking their asses. This has gotta stop.

Well I *have* started something; I've been lifting weights.

I wait till 1:30—it's the quietest time, and walk to the gym.

I never wear gloves.

If they saw me there before I've had a chance to bulk up, they'd beat the shit outta me. I gotta thrash one of them, thrash the shit outta one.

I slip into the gym.

I'd close the door if there was one.

I go over to the back extension machine. It's the toughest one for me, and I always do it first.

I'm lying on my stomach when I hear a grunt.

Immediately I start sweating on the back of my neck.

I hear steps behind me, but I can't turn my head, since I'm belted to the machine.

"Try it this way," the voice says.

He puts a weight on top of my ankles. Then he tells me to start.

I do.

The weight's heavy. He's probably holding it on top of my ankles, so it won't fall off.

I get in ten reps before I'm out of breath.

The vinyl bench squeaks underneath me.

He takes the weight off, walks up next to me, and I turn my head.

"That give you rock-hard ass," the guy says.

I can't tell if he's part of the bunch that fucks with me. He doesn't hang out in the common areas much.

"Just trying help you," the guy says, and I realize now he sounds Russian. He says women like guys with rock-hard asses.

"Yeah," I say.

"Gives hips new rhythm," he says. He gyrates his hips.

It looks obscene.

I wonder what those fuckers would say if they walked into the gym right now, with the Russian swaying right in front of my nose.

He walks over to the weight bar laying on the ground. He piles on a bunch of twenty-five-pound plates.

Way too much for me.

The Russian's practicing Olympic snatch lifts. He does it ten times in a row. He's making quite a racket.

He's done this before.

He comes up in front of me, panting. I slither loose from the back machine. He tells me to put on a lifting belt. If I don't, I'll wreck my back.

I tell him I'm just throwing weights around to pass the time. The Russian says once you wreck your back, it's all over.

"Yeah," I say.

He cranks out fifteen snatches. The bar wobbles. He works up a sweat.

I'm embarrassed, but even so I can't leave.

I go get some fifteen-pound dumbbells. I curl them five times with each arm.

That's all I got, no matter how much I grimace. Fuck.

I set the weights down. I see the Russian staring at me and he can see that I'm breathing hard.

I tell him I got a cold that's sapped all my strength. The Russian says that happens.

He comes up in front of me and puts the palm of his hand on my forehead. "Tsk, tsk," he says.

I change position.

The Russian says I'm completely dry.

"It's over," I say, "my cold, that is."

The Russian laughs. He thinks I'm lifting the wrong way.

I ask him how you can lift the wrong way; you just pick them up off the ground—seems simple to me.

The Russian says I need to work up a sweat before I start lifting. Warm muscles get the biggest benefit, while cold muscles just get stiff and sore.

"Believe me," he says. He flexes his left pec and winks at me.

He tells me to jump rope first. There's a big pile of them in the back.

"Jump rope?" I ask, wondering who he's kidding.

The Russian says jumping rope is more fun than stretching, but they do the same thing.

"Believe me," he says.

I walk to the back of the gym and he motions for me to look farther back.

I find the ropes after a while, pull one out of the bunch and start jumping.

Standing up, the Russian presses the bar down to his chest and then straight over his head, at least ten times. A big vein appears on the side of his forehead.

I jump stiffly.

I can only jump over the rope once or twice before I trip and have to start all over.

It takes a while to get a sweat going.

I'm only a little out of breath when the Russian stops and comes over to me.

According to him, I'm pretty small for a man.

"Guys bigger than you have taken a fall," I respond. The Russian laughs.

"And stayed down," I add.

He laughs and says that's not what he's talking about. He thinks I oughta lift weights if I want to make it in prison.

He could teach me, if I wanted.

"Five foot four," I say.

The Russian says that real men are bigger than their dicks, and also a little smarter.

"Yeah," I say.

"Is that the deal with you?" he asks.

"Could be," I say.

He tells me to put the lifting belt on or he won't show me anything.

"Yeah," I say.

Someone peeks in, but not long enough for me to see his face.

The Russian glances toward the door, but the guy's gone. The Russian purses his lips and waves his hand toward me.

"The belt," he says.

"*Bay-elt*" is how he says it.

I ask where the belts are. He waves his hand around the gym.

They're supposed to be on the wall bars. They're not. These fucking convicts can't keep anything in order.

I walk toward the back of the gym and rummage around.

There are jump ropes, dumbbells, a couple of medicine balls, parallel bars, five hundred pounds of junk. And a couple of giant gymnastics horses that I remember from gym class in high school. They were big enough for a bunch of kids to hide inside.

We used to have to jump over them.

Being the smallest one in the class, I couldn't do it. I beat them all in floor hockey, though. We played it once. One time. Until the teacher realized I was good at it.

Later on we set his summer cabin on fire.

That's still the only crime I committed that I didn't get busted for.

I figure out that I have to lift up the leather cover on the gymnastics horse. Inside, in the darkness, I can see a stack of lifting belts.

I have to get a stool to climb over the edge of the horse to get inside it.

It's like a fort. Light's coming in through the slits on the sides.

I close the cover. It gets dark, which makes it seem even more like a fort.

I can almost stand up.

I choose a belt and struggle to put it on. I cinch it so tightly my eyes bulge out.

The Russian yells and asks if we're playing hide-and-seek now. He thought we were gonna lift weights.

I start to push on the leather cover of the horse when I hear something clanking.

I look out through a slit and see Topi Räikkönen by the door—he's flicked off the lights.

The room doesn't get any darker, though—it's a sunny midsummer day outside.

"What's going on?" asks the Russian.

"We're savin' electricity," Topi says.

"Fine with me," the Russian says.

From a standing position, the Russian lifts the bar off the ground up to his chest. His hands are close together on the bar. It looks heavy.

"We thought we'd lift a bit," Topi says.

"Put belt on," the Russian says.

"I'll think about it," Lesonen says.

"You just wreck your back," the Russian says.

I'm too afraid to come out. Lesonen's one of the guys who fucks with me. Go ahead, fucker, wreck your back.

"I'm Topi," Topi says.

"Topi who?" the Russian asks.

"My mama's own Topi," Topi says.

"Arkady," the Russian says.

"Lesonen," Lesonen says.

They shake hands, sorta embarrassed about it.

"Topi Lesonen?" Arkady asks.

"Whatcha mean?" Topi says.

"You look like each other."

"Gotta ask my old man," Topi says.

They laugh at that. I shift my feet, and my left foot hits the buckle on a lifting belt, and it clinks. The noise carries only a few feet, though.

The sweat's bubbling on my skin now. The horse is so airtight that I can smell my own sweat.

Topi and Lesonen are quietly lifting dumbbells. The Russian's banging snatch lifts again.

I decide to stay in the horse.

The Russian goes over to the wall bars, facing away from the wall. He lifts his legs up to a ninety-degree angle.

Topi and Lesonen are still lifting dumbbells.

The Russian walks back to the men. He asks if they wanna bench press.

"Yeah," Topi says.

"Me first," Lesonen says.

He lies down on the bench. Topi and the Russian load weights onto the bar.

Lesonen grunts and lifts the bar off the stand.

He lowers the bar to his chest five times and raises it five times.

On the last lift, Topi and the Russian take hold of the ends of the bar and guide it into the crutches.

"One more?" the Russian asks. He glances toward the back of the gym. I pray he doesn't holler out to me.

"In a bit," Lesonen says.

Topi gets on the bench. Lesonen and the Russian help him. Topi manages to do seven reps.

"Your turn," Lesonen says.

The Russian says he'll pass this set. He hasn't bench pressed in a while. He wants to take it easy.

"You can't even do ten," Topi says.

"I could, but I not feel like it right now," the Russian says.

"I could do twenty-five, but I don't feel like it," Lesonen says.

The Russian encourages him to feel like it; he says Lesonen might even make it to the Olympics. The inmates could sit in the TV room and cheer on their old pal.

"I can do twenty-five," Lesonen says.

"No way," the Russian says.

"You can't even do ten," Topi says.

"I can, but I not feel like it."

"Bet you a twenty," Topi says.

"You got cash?"

Topi digs around in the pocket of his sweatpants. He takes out something I can't see. The Russian nods.

He goes to the bench and lifts the bar off the crutches and onto his chest.

He lifts the bar easily ten times. He sighs and then lifts it again five times.

During the last rep, his arms are shaking.

Topi and Lesonen grab hold of the bar at both ends.

They slowly push the bar down.

"What? What going on?" the Russian panics.

Topi and Lesonen push the bar down on his chest so the Russian can't make a sudden move or slip out from under the bar.

"What going on?" the Russian wheezes. His upper body's quivering.

He's losing his strength.

"What...?" he tries to say. He can't take it much longer.

"Greetings from Marzipan," Topi says.

"No!" the Russian gasps.

"Actually, yes," Lesonen says.

Topi keeps glancing at the door. Nobody.

Topi and Lesonen kick the weight stand away. The bar's four inches above the Russian's throat.

"Guysss..." the Russian whispers. I can see his face turning blue.

"Tell us everything," Lesonen says.

"Jesus Christ speaks Russian."

His rattling voice carries to every corner of the gym. I'm afraid it'll carry beyond the gym as well.

"Possible, but I've never spoken to the guy," Topi says.

The Russian's strength gives out. Topi and Lesonen push the bar onto his throat.

It makes a crunching sound and the Russian's legs flop around.

I press my fist in front of my mouth so I don't scream.

I throw up. It's a horrible experience throwing up while trying not to make a sound.

"Let's get out of here," Lesonen hisses.

"Yeah," Topi says, "that was my first."

"Fuck, you wanna take him with you as a trophy or what?" Lesonen says.

I fall down onto the pile of belts.

Standing next to the bench, Topi freezes. In the doorway, Lesonen motions for Topi to come with him.

"You hear that?" Topi asks.

"No, let's go," Lesonen says.

"I heard something."

"You're hearin' shit; fuck, let's get outta here now," Lesonen says. He's pacing feverishly in the doorway.

Topi walks to the back of the gym. He drums his fingers on top of the horse.

"There ain't nobody there," Lesonen yells.

Topi bends over suddenly and peeks into the horse through a slit in the side. He'd be looking me straight in the eye if I weren't lying on the bottom in the stench of my own vomit.

"I'm goin', you fuckin' stay here," Lesonen yells.

"I'm comin'," Topi says.

I hear footsteps.

I have to catch my breath for a bit while staying on the bottom of the horse.

I gotta get out immediately.

I feel like throwing up the whole time, but I get up anyway. I take off the belt, throw the cover open, swing over the edge, and run to the door.

I don't even dare glance at the Russian.

I walk into the TV room and wipe my mouth on my sleeve.

I sit down in a chair, shaking.

Kunis comes in and sits down next to me. He's browsing through a magazine. I realize it ain't a porn mag.

Kunis says something. I hear him, but can't make out what he's saying.

Topi comes in. He messes around with the TV and roars and asks why the fuck Eurosport ain't on.

"Shapely black athletic asses," Kunis snickers.

"You and your bullshit," Topi says, and then sees me.

He looks me in the eyes as if he's slicing into them. He comes toward me.

He holds his stare the whole time he's walking toward me.

Kunis says that Topi's burning with the searing flame of either hate or love.

Topi stops in front of me.

He just stares.

"You, handsome boy, tell us how you feel," Kunis says. His voice sounds concerned.

"Kurppa," Topi says, "are you Kurppa?"

I say yes.

"You pissed your pants," he says. I look at my pants. He's right.

"Splashed back at me from the urinal," I say.

"Your piss made of rubber?" Topi asks and goes back to manhandling the TV. Kunis bursts out laughing.

I'm so relieved I almost piss my pants again.

33. Kristiina Mustamäki, Finance Manager

Aurora fell asleep on the couch.

I got a pillow for her and put it under her head. I covered her up with her jacket. Her breathing became regular.

She looked so calm; it was hard to believe what she'd been through the past few weeks.

She was completely beside herself when she got here.

She shook my hand at the door and said somberly that she was Aurora Arkhipova. I knew that something was very wrong when she didn't even notice me laughing when I responded, "I'm Ms. Kristiina Mustamäki, Finance Manager, just like I've always been. Hello, Mrs. Arkhipova."

She walked straight to the couch, threw her jacket on the arm of the chair, and talked incessantly. She was talking in order to keep herself afloat. She was clinging to the sound of her own voice.

She talked about the choir, about her sordid past, and about the curtains she'd seen at Sokos Department Store. They'd need to be shortened. She said she hadn't slept the previous night because she was thinking about how to redecorate her home. I made hot cocoa for us both. I crumbled a sleeping pill into her mug when she got to the part where the prison called and told her that Arkady was dead.

Fifteen minutes later she started telling me what Detective Lieutenant Rautapää had forced her to do under his desk. I didn't interrupt her, even though she'd told me about it before. It seemed to me like she'd crack if I interrupted her.

The sleeping pill started taking effect, but combined with her grief it propelled her into a scary trance.

She recounted the incident detail by detail, almost second by second.

I'd heard that under hypnosis people could remember with shocking precision events from years before. Grief, fatigue, and the medicine had hypnotized Aurora. Maybe she'd hypnotized herself. I kept listening.

She didn't even notice when I took a notebook off the shelf and wrote down a few things. I was sure she wouldn't remember a thing when she woke up from her spell.

When she told me about washing her face in the women's restroom at the police station, she tried to burst into tears, but none came.

She started moaning in a monotone, "If Arkady finds out, what if Arkady finds out? He can't find out."

I sat down next to her and let her rest her head on my shoulder.

She lifted her head. "You can't do that to another person, you just can't do that to another person."

She rested her head on my shoulder again. From there she fell into my lap.

She didn't hear me when I said, "No, you can't do that to another person."

On the couch, Aurora was sleeping soundly—she just heaved a few deep sighs. Sleeping, she looked twenty years younger than her age, but I knew the years would show up once she awoke.

I sipped my cocoa. It was cold and too sweet. I took some rum I'd received as a Christmas present out of the cupboard and splashed a little into my cocoa. That made it drinkable. I put the bottle back.

I walked onto the balcony, and the concrete felt warm under my bare feet. The birches in the yard reached up to the third floor, to my eye level. They were in full splendor. The sun took aim and hit every one of their leaves. I heard sounds from the river, at this hour they were still joyous and good-natured. A mildly intoxicated man, who looked like a country gentleman, raised his felt hat to me. It was Midsummer Eve, and people were grilling all over town. The bonfires were piled high and ready to be ignited later tonight.

Classic Midsummer, just like in the old Finnish movies directed by T.J. Särkkä.

I drank my rum cocoa and stayed out on the balcony, enjoying the sun. My legs were already covered with freckles. If we happened to get any real summer weather, my hair would get blonde streaks in it, looking like I'd bleached it. That's what my hair's like, the kind of hair Finnish women have. Marzipan used to stick his nose in my hair.

I walked into the bedroom. As I passed Aurora, I stroked her cheek and her hair.

I pulled Marzipan's leather jacket out from under the covers, smelled it, and put it on. I went and sat down in the armchair and tucked my legs underneath me.

The leather jacket was the only thing I had left of Marzipan, which was weird, because he was always leaving his things here. It was like he was subconsciously marking his territory. When I told him that he'd left his leather jacket at my place, he didn't care. Maybe it made him feel that now my apartment was part of his conquered domain.

As far as I was concerned, it would've been his domain without him leaving his things here.

Do you ever hear of love stories where the man makes the woman feel like an idiot? Not really.

When Antero introduced me to Marzipan, Marzipan told me he was one of Antero's buddies in the seminary. I thought to myself how these two school buddies couldn't be any more different from each other, but that was all that I thought.

Antero and I went to my place and spent the evening watching TV. I remember the three tenors were singing, and Antero was cracking jokes about Pavarotti's various diets. Suddenly I realized I'd asked him which parish his classmate worked in—or if in fact he worked in a parish at all. Antero looked at me and wanted to know which classmate I was talking about. Before I could brush aside the question, he started to laugh. He said that he considered himself an open-minded minister, but he sure was glad Marzipan didn't share his profession.

"Marzipan?" I asked, pretending to be surprised.

Antero told me he'd heard the guy's real name, but Marzipan was the name he was known by.

I asked what he did for a living.

"He's a criminal," Antero said. Chuckling, he asked me how it was possible that the finance manager of the parish couldn't tell a minister from a jailbird. "So much for a woman's instinct and knowledge of human nature," he snickered and asked me to guess how much Pavarotti weighed.

I suddenly remembered I had seen Marzipan first, before he made me feel like an idiot.

The next day my office phone rang, piercing the core of my being.

"Kristiina, come and have coffee with me," a male voice proposed.

Then he told me, cursing, that whatever I decided, he'd be having a beer.

I asked who was speaking. He said I knew full well who was speaking. He was right.

We met at Pub Pisto. He'd told me on the phone that it was a café downtown. From the entryway, I realized he'd used the term loosely.

The men sitting at the bar were intoxicated and rowdy. A large round table was full of drunken men. Marzipan came in, and, taking me by the hand, walked me to the dining room side. He greeted the people at the big round table, and they made crude comments to me.

"Regular churchgoers," Marzipan said. He took me to the back of the place, to a wooden picnic table with long benches on each side. A guy came up to us and wanted to talk about deodorant. I wasn't used to people just showing up at your table to talk.

At the bar, Marzipan got coffee for me and a pint of beer for himself. I couldn't think of anything to say to the deodorant guy. He was talking to himself.

When Marzipan returned, he moved the man to the other side of the table and sat next to me. He took off his jacket, raised his arm, and asked me to smell his armpit. He said he never used deodorant.

I smelled it and blushed nearly crimson with humiliation and anger. He was outrageous.

Marzipan wrapped his arm around my waist and said he was married. I got up, thanked him for his company, and left.

I felt so humiliated that when I got home I slammed pots and pans around and broke Dame Kiri Te Kanawa's LP. I took a shower. I let Antero say whatever he wanted to the answering machine.

I was horrified when I realized that my co-workers could have seen me with Marzipan.

I imagined him telling idiotic stories to all the drunks; I imagined him writing his signature with his tongue hanging out of the corner of his mouth; I imagined him licking his steak knife after a meal; I imagined him cussing out a referee; I imagined him rolling up his sleeves at his parents' dinner table so everyone could see his dirty blue-lettered LOVE tattoos; I imagined him acting remorseful while fondling his country-boy necklace; I imagined him drunk, feeling up his cheap and conceited wife's breasts; I imagined him roaring with laughter while watching morning cartoons.

I was sure his arms were covered with tattoos.

I was wrong.

Over the next few days I called all the Räikkönens in the phone book. When I asked if they had a Marzipan, one of the people said, "Not enough to give you some." I had to laugh, even though I was ready to snap.

By process of elimination I ended up at a number where the voice of an older woman answered the phone three days in a row. I kept thinking about it. Each time I hung up without saying a word.

After a week, he answered. I introduced myself.

"Who?" he asked, coughing. I think he did it on purpose. I asked if he had any tattoos on his arms.

"I can get some if that's what it takes," he answered after a long silence. I remember word for word what he said.

I asked if he'd bet his criminal friends that he could get a church office employee to meet him at a dumpy gangster bar. Marzipan said he didn't usually bet on such a sure thing.

Our story could have ended right then and there.

I held the receiver away from my ear.

I was about to slam the phone down, but decided not to. I don't know what stopped me. Was it my heart? If I had hung up on him, I'm sure I never would've heard from him again. I told Marzipan about it later and he assured me that he would've searched every corner of the globe for me, even if he had to travel on foot.

"You're just saying that," I said, but it made me happy.

We agreed to meet again. I chose the place.

I ordered an espresso and he had a bottle of beer. "Yech," he said, turning his nose up at the brand.

It was the dead of winter. I rubbed my hands together to get the blood flowing after being outside in the dark and cold. Marzipan took my hands, and they disappeared into his. He thought it was a natural thing to do, but to me it was scorchingly erotic. I warmed up quickly.

I don't remember anything else from the restaurant. I thought it was natural that we'd end up in bed. I'm not in the habit of jumping from bed to bed, but that night I would've shot my way into his. If anyone asked about my relationship with Antero, I would have said, "Who?"

His skin was very sensitive. He was surprised when I patted him on the butt.

A week after the first night, I knew he was in my life to stay. I wasn't sure how he felt, though.

I demanded that he use a condom even after he swore he was disease-free, and he felt hurt when I said it had nothing to do with his word.

I went through his wallet and threw his condoms in the garbage. That evening he got into bed, befuddled, and said he'd lost his hoods. He could never call them condoms or rubbers. I'd bought a variety of condoms, filled my nightstand drawer with them, from black to red, from ribbed to smooth. I opened the drawer and told him to choose one.

He chose one. Now I was hurt, because he didn't even ask why the finance manager of the parish needed two hundred hoods. It was impossible to make him jealous.

Afterward, I stood behind him as he was shaving and asked him what he thought of me. He flexed his pecs when he saw I was watching and said he didn't think anything special.

My anger surprised me.

I yelled at him to leave for good if he didn't think anything special about me.

Dumbfounded, he said, "Well, actually, I do."

"Oh yeah, what?" I screamed.

"You know," he said.

"No, I don't know!" I screamed.

Marzipan finished shaving and rinsed the shaving cream off his earlobes.

"Tell me!" I screamed louder.

He walked into the bedroom to get dressed. We'd been together for twelve days. I followed him from room to room and screamed, "Tell me, tell me, tell me!"

I ran into the kitchen and threw stuff around. When I went into the living room, Marzipan was sitting at the table, writing. I took a peek from behind him.

He wrote "Kristiina and Marzipan" and drew a heart around it.

I started to laugh. I saw myself laughing hysterically, as if I were outside my own body. I knew I was laughing, but I wasn't amused. I was horrified when I realized I couldn't stop. Marzipan left.

He came back at four in the morning, drunk. I was up, watching car chases on some movie channel. I heard him coming; I recognized the way he slammed the taxi door shut.

He was yelling outside, and made a terrible racket as he came up the stairs. All the way up to the third floor, he yelled, "Marzipan loves Kristiina. I, Marzipan Räikkönen, love Kristiina Mustamäki. Kristiina Mustamäki on the third floor," he yelled.

I was in heaven when I finally got to touch his hair.

He woke up in the afternoon, whining for some Coke. As I was making breakfast I asked him if he remembered coming back to my place. He took me by the shoulders, looked straight into my eyes, and asked if he should go back to the stairwell. I told him he could say it more softly from now on. He remembered to say it now and then, but I could tell it wasn't easy for him.

"You haven't said anything," he said.

An orange slice slipped out of my hands onto the floor. He was right.

"I love you," I said.

It came easily, though I'd never said it to any other man before. Not to Antero, and obviously not to my random partners.

I got up out of my chair. I walked into the kitchen quietly and closed my eyes. The leather jacket I was wearing squeaked, making me imagine Marzipan moving around the apartment. This was our home, our nest.

I made some more cocoa and poured a little splash of rum in it. I knew I'd start to cry if I got tipsy. Alcohol wasn't my drug.

Memories were.

After Marzipan's death, I'd spent the evenings sitting in the armchair, wearing his leather jacket and sipping gallons of cocoa. I went to work and avoided Antero. It was easy, as he only came to work a couple of days. The rest of the time he was on sick leave. I heard a rumor in the office that the reason was mental in nature. In the parish mental problems weren't considered a sickness, but laziness instead.

I kept doing my job, though at the end of the day I couldn't always remember what I'd done. The numbers jumped around, the lines marched on.

I lost weight. My mother complained when I didn't remember to call her on her birthday.

I was oblivious until one day the sweet old neighbor lady came over and brought me some pastries she'd baked. My apartment door lay wide open. She gave me the pastries at the door and said she wasn't going to come in since the young lady had company.

She said it good-naturedly, with a smile and a wink. She was referring to male company.

I was embarrassed when it dawned on me I'd been talking to myself.

I wondered if I'd been sitting alone for the last two months, babbling by myself and adding Marzipan's growls and absurd comments.

I put the leather jacket back in the closet. I wasn't going to sleep with it anymore. It was just leather. The man I loved wasn't there.

I checked on Aurora. Her arm was dangling off the couch, and I placed it on her chest.

I rummaged through the hat rack and was startled when I found Marzipan's gloves. I put them on. I took a sheet from the stack of copy paper and looked for a pen. I turned on the kitchen light, sat down at the table, and pulled out the notes I'd made while Aurora spewed out her story. I went to check one thing in the phone book.

It was awkward to write with my gloved left hand.

Mrs. Lemmikki Rautapää
Rovaniemi

You don't know me, and I hope you can forgive me for writing you this letter anonymously.

I'm writing about your husband, Detective Lieutenant Torsti Rautapää.

I know him intimately. I ask that you keep reading. My intention isn't to hurt you or to cause you any distress. I write to you with sisterly concern.

I'm sure after twenty or so years of marriage you know that our Torsti is a charming and passionate man. I've had the opportunity to feel his burning desire for five years now. Last month marked five years from the time he first started making his nocturnal visits to my place.

I'm afraid my story is the usual story of the so-called other woman.

At the beginning of our relationship, Torsti assured me that his marriage was nearing its end. He was ready for divorce and wanted to attempt a new relationship with me. That made me very happy.

You'll of course ask why a sensible woman would believe a man who obviously made up promises he didn't intend to keep. But a woman in love will believe anything. I'm sure you have experience with that.

A week ago he finally told me, swaggering and laughing, that he had no intention of tying the knot with

315

me. He'd never even seriously considered the option. His tone was obnoxious and condescending.

He also told me that he'd cheated on me over the course of our entire relationship. Naturally he didn't mean with you.

I want you to know this is the kind of man you've spent the best years of your life with.

I don't want to cause any trouble for you or your marriage, but I hope you can talk to your husband about the dynamics of relationships as adults, as mature people. I hope you can get your husband to understand that this is no way to treat women.

It's really not my wish to turn you against Torsti.

You might think I have mental issues or I'm writing this out of jealousy, but let me tell you this: Torsti wears black and yellow Batman boxers. He has a half-moon scar two inches below his navel, and he is uncircumcised with very tight foreskin.

Wishing you all the best and an enjoyable summer,

A friend

I read the letter through twice. It'll do. Written with my left hand the handwriting came out childish and sincere.

I went to the desk drawer and took out a stamp and an envelope from the middle of the stack. I moistened the tip of my gloved finger in a splash of water on the counter, wet the stamp and pressed it into place.

I felt I was doing a good deed.

No. With an evil and malicious deed, I was correcting an even greater evil. The world was a strange place.

I went into the kitchen and made some tea. I decided not to tell Aurora about the letter. During her diatribe, she said she was leaving for Helsinki the day after the Midsummer holiday. It was Arkady that had kept her in Rovaniemi, no one and nothing else.

I was surprised when I saw that the kitchen clock showed two in the morning. I walked out onto the balcony to look at the soft light. Distant shouts made it even more pristine. The birches were sleeping like young brides.

I sat down in the armchair.

I thought about what I was feeling.

There was a woman sleeping on the sofa whose husband had murdered the man I loved. I tried to search for hate and contempt within myself, but I couldn't find them. My grief didn't change, it stayed the same.

I didn't believe Aurora would ever be able to accept the fact that Arkady had murdered my Marzipan. I couldn't blame her. She loved her man, just as I did mine. I would've defended Marzipan tooth and nail, even though I knew he was a criminal. We never had time to discuss how Marzipan was going to arrange his life after I became a part of it. I don't think I could have lived with him getting sentenced to prison every couple of years.

I didn't rejoice in Arkady's death. I hadn't even asked Aurora how he died. From Marzipan's offhand comments I'd gotten an idea of what could happen in prison, but I thought some of it was just talk.

"Criminal, criminal, criminal."

That's all Antero could come up with in the only letter he sent me after our breakup. I wrote him and told him that if he sent me anything else, I'd show it to his wife. He was more afraid of Hellevi than he was of hell.

Antero wrote that he'd do everything in his power to see that I lost my job if I continued my liaisons with Marzipan. I thought he sounded pathetic. He claimed that Marzipan was a financial risk to the church, because I was the finance manager.

That was really mean.

Antero said he'd heard that Marzipan owed large debts to his other criminal friends. He insinuated that

Marzipan got me to fall for him so he could obtain access to the church's money. Antero maintained he remembered many stories of Casanovas pouncing on a woman from the church. After the money was stolen, the woman didn't dare report it to the police, but, fearing social disgrace, paid the money back herself.

Antero wrote that the cases destroyed the women's mental health. He insisted that he was worried about me.

I found Antero's insinuations and direct allegations cheap and offensive. He wasn't the same man I used to be smitten with. I used to enjoy his company, before I knew better.

Because my relationship with Marzipan was fresh, thoughts crept into my mind I later regretted upon reflection.

It wasn't that I was ashamed of Marzipan, but I didn't want him to come to my office, because that would've set tongues wagging. He didn't hide his profession—he wasn't even ashamed of it. After a couple of beers, he would happily tell anyone what he did for a living.

"I'm a P.H.O.," he'd say, and some people would nod their heads, impressed. They wondered how the computer industry always came up with new acronyms. They didn't realize he meant "Professional and Habitual Offender."

One time, however, I asked him to pick me up from work.

When he arrived, I told him I had to quickly do something on the other side of the building. I left the door to the safe wide open while I was gone for fifteen minutes. The safe held some papers and a five grand stack of hundred-euro notes clearly visible inside.

I returned. Marzipan had burned holes in his plastic cup with his cigarette. I scolded him for that and for smoking in the first place. I closed the safe and we left. The stack of bills had disappeared.

We went home. I didn't speak much and neither did Marzipan.

I made some food in the wok before I was overcome with shivers.

Marzipan was sitting at the table. I decided not to cry. I cursed Antero and his know-it-all attitude as I realized that I'd be repaying the church out of my own pocket. There went my emergency cash fund. And this was definitely an emergency.

I slammed the wok down on the table and sat down across from Marzipan. The stack of bills was on the table.

I stared at it completely still, for fear it would disappear.

"Girl, don't you ever test me again," Marzipan said.

I was so taken aback that I didn't even try to come up with white lies.

He was a little drunk, but calm. The calm didn't last.

He demanded that I count the money. I asked him to behave like an adult.

"Who's the one playing games here?" Marzipan asked. He told me to count the money immediately. He didn't want to be accused of stealing when he hadn't.

I begged him to calm down. I went over to touch him, but he pushed me away.

"Dammit, how much is supposed to be there?" Marzipan fumed. For the first time he looked scary.

"Five thousand euros," I said.

Marzipan started counting the money out loud, his voice breaking. He counted the money twice right in front of me. It added up to four thousand nine hundred euros.

Marzipan looked at me. I couldn't say anything. I started to sob. Marzipan cursed, took a fistful of chicken and rice out of the wok, screamed because it was hot, and threw it at the window. It made a thumping sound.

I remembered I'd given the receptionist a hundred euros to buy copy paper, and had the receipt. I told him that, spluttering.

"Goddammit," Marzipan said very slowly and very quietly.

"Forgive me, darling, forgive me," I begged.

"Goddammit," he said and left.

He returned a couple of hours later. I've never been so happy.

"Forgive me, darling."

"Forget about the whole thing."

"You love me?"

"Yeah."

"How much?"

"Like crazy."

"No, really."

"A lot."

"How much?"

"More than anyone else."

"That's wonderful."

"More than I love myself."

"It doesn't have to be that much."

"But that's how it is."

We went to bed. He left after midnight, but I didn't think anything of it, since he often did that. The next morning he was murdered.

Late in the evening on the day of the murder two policemen came and buzzed my doorbell. One was looking at the floor and the other at the ceiling, as they asked if I knew Marzipan. I regained consciousness in the armchair with the older policeman babbling at me like I was a baby. "Have some water... have some water, my dear, here you go." I didn't ask how they knew to come to my place to tell me about Marzipan's death.

I didn't want to get out of the armchair, and I didn't for two months.

I went to look at the kitchen clock, which now showed four in the morning.

I checked to make sure Aurora was still sleeping peacefully. I lifted her arm up again; it had slipped over the side of the couch.

That night, after the police had gone, I thought about calling Marzipan's wife. He hadn't told his wife about me, but he hadn't bothered to hide the affair, either. I couldn't figure out what I could say to her.

I was overcome with grief when it dawned on me that I couldn't call anyone to talk about Marzipan. Only Antero knew about our relationship. He would've misinterpreted things if I'd called him, and would've rushed over to comfort me.

I went out onto the balcony. The birches were waking up to a beautiful morning.

Suddenly I felt the same boundless joy as I did on the morning of the murder, when I had been walking around town repeating to myself that Marzipan Räikkönen was the most wonderful name in the world. The second most wonderful was Assar Vähänäkki, who just an hour earlier that morning had cleared his throat and told me I was pregnant.

I closed the balcony door.

I checked on Aurora, went into the bedroom, and fumbled my way under the blanket. Sleep took me with its soft-winged beats.

Come, my child.

A piece of a star shines within all of us.

34. Kaarle Hirttiö, Defense Attorney

I returned from the cabin the Wednesday after Midsummer. We'd decided that I'd work for the rest of the week and then go back to Marja and the children. I wasn't exactly sorry to leave.

We had just bought the cabin, and it needed a lot of work. I was very close to taking the seller to court. We paid twenty thousand euros for it. One of the neighbors, a contractor, came over and gave me an estimate for a remodel. Since I was a lawyer, he figured I could get it done for around ten thousand, under the table.

The message light was flashing on the home answering machine.

I returned a call to Prison Warden Valde Åkerblom. He took a while to answer.

"This is Åkerblom, but I'm not a Gypsy," he yelled into the receiver. I was used to his style.

He told me that my client Arkady Arkhipov was dead. The police were investigating, as was customary with suspicious prison deaths.

I asked if he'd been murdered.

"If you ask me…," Åkerblom sighed.

"Just tell me," I said.

"I'm positive someone killed him, but you didn't hear it from me."

"Of course I didn't."

He described how Arkhipov had died. It didn't sound like an accident to me. On the other hand, it was possible the strung-out junkie had lost his grip on the weight bar.

"Are they looking for a suspect?" I asked.

"They won't find shit," Åkerblom replied.

As far as he was concerned the police could investigate all they wanted in his jail, up to and including the second coming of Christ, but if they thought they were going to solve this one, they'd be sadly mistaken.

Åkerblom lamented that on the outside the boys squealed like little pigs, but in the slammer they always stood together so tight that if it didn't piss you off so much, you would've laughed about it. They kept quiet about everything, from petty theft to murder.

"Thanks for letting me know," I said.

"Uh…," Åkerblom said.

"Go ahead, say it," I said.

"Just to be clear, I never told you I suspected any kind of foul play here," Åkerblom said.

"Of course you didn't," I said.

Åkerblom wished me a good vacation and yelled at someone before the line went dead.

I walked into the garage and went to the safe. I keep thinking I should have the safe mounted on the wall in the house; it wasn't smart to keep it in the garage forever.

I took an envelope from the safe and went into my office. Arkhipov had it delivered to me after he hired me. He made me swear not to open it until he was cold in the ground.

I sat down in the dentist chair I'd bought at a liquidation sale. I adjusted the chair so I was lying down and wondered what I'd gotten myself into with this case.

Maybe I should've refused to take it. Actually, there was no doubt about that.

When I was offered the chance to defend Arkady Arkhipov, I opened my mouth, but couldn't even get a peep out.

Maybe I should've said that I was a friend of the man Arkhipov had killed. We were friends, though we hadn't seen each other for years, at least fifteen or so. I remembered a lot of things about Marzipan when I attended his funeral, and ended up driving his grandma around.

I thought about what would happen to my license to practice law if someone had seen me at Marzipan's funeral or if someone reported me to the presiding judge in the murder case, or to the Finnish Bar Association.

But of course everyone saw me, all of Marzipan's family and friends.

I kept thinking that it wouldn't have been in the family's best interest to tell the court that Marzipan's killer's defense attorney had been Marzipan's friend.

That's how I saw it, anyway.

It probably wasn't the most ethical thing to do, but I'd always been able to lie to myself. I convinced myself I was fulfilling a higher mission by ensuring that justice was served. Integrity itself wasn't so important.

I read through the interrogation reports and went to the prison to meet Arkhipov.

I was surprised he didn't ask the court to appoint free counsel for him. I figured he wanted everyone to see that his business made enough money to avoid attracting attention to his wealthy lifestyle.

Considering he was accused of murder, any other potential charges would be minor.

I wanted to know if he was going to stick to the story he told the interrogators. I made some notes and sketched out a defense. I was doing a professional job.

All of a sudden Arkhipov got up and stared at me.

"What now?"

"Everyone thinks I'm killer."

"What?"

"You think so."

"I don't."

"You do."

"Does it make a difference? I'm your defense attorney. I'm defending you."

"It make difference. I not kill."

"That has no effect on the defense."

"Why not?"

"Listen to me."

"Go ahead."

"The court doesn't care if the defense attorney believes his client or not. It also doesn't matter how many times in court the accused claims to be innocent. It's the evidence that decides the case."

"Do not take me for clown."

"Of course I don't."

"I want good defense."

"You have the right to get a different attorney."

"I know that."

"You could get one right away. It's fine by me."

"Not what I mean. You must believe."

"I do believe you."

"No, you don't."

Arkhipov calmed down, but looked at me dejectedly for the remainder of the conversation. I left the prison, which was always a relief. Arkhipov's attitude intrigued me.

The trial was a circus.

When Kassu Vartio shuffled into the courtroom, Arkhipov angrily grunted something in Russian.

I was aware of the facts, but Arkhipov mumbled to me that Vartio was definitely lying, because he had replaced the ammo in Vartio's gun with blanks.

The guy had tried to shoot himself in front of the police station, but the only thing he succeeded in doing was to end up deaf in one ear. Vartio wore a hearing aid, but everything that was said still had to be repeated over and over.

"Where were you on the morning of April 28?"

"What?"

"Where were you on the morning of April 28?"

"Kassu Vartio."

In the witness stand, Vartio looked like an angry owl, turning his good ear in every direction.

"Please tell us what happened after you went looking for Räikkönen down the trail near his house."

"Definitely not. Under no circumstances."

"Why not?"

"I'd like to tell you about what happened when we went after Marzipan in the woods."

"Go ahead."

"Why can't I?"

It took several minutes of hollering to ask every single question. The prosecutor loosened his tie and slammed a stack of papers on his table from three feet up in the air. Finally he let Vartio tell his story without interrupting him.

Vartio's message was clear: Arkhipov had murdered Marzipan.

"Liar," Arkhipov whispered to me. It didn't look like he had ever sat in court accused of anything before, even in Russia. He kept trying to win me over, like a little kid. I hissed back at him, saying he didn't need to try to convince me, since I was the only one in the room who was on his team.

According to Vartio, he had gone to Marzipan's place with Arkhipov and Ossi Kaukonen to discuss repaying the debt. Vartio was speaking so loudly that the prosecutor went over to turn off his microphone; the presiding judge nodded in agreement.

Vartio said they had been having a friendly chat with Mrs. Räikkönen, Marzipan's mother.

Mrs. Räikkönen said Marzipan had gone down the trail into the woods a moment before. Vartio said the men headed out after Marzipan. They ran into Marzipan sitting on a rock along the side of the trail. He wasn't surprised to see them.

Vartio had tried to have a constructive conversation with him about repaying the debt, but he grew concerned when Arkhipov became aggressive. Arkhipov called Marzipan all kinds of names and grabbed him by the collar. Marzipan swore he'd pay back the debt, but couldn't do it right away because he didn't have the money.

Arkhipov went wild with rage.

He was kicking rocks and bellowing in a fury. Vartio said he and Ossi had tried to calm him down. Arkhipov pulled out his gun, and the men scampered out of his way. Marzipan just sat on the rock and stared at Arkhipov pensively. He had warned Arkhipov that a dead man couldn't pay his debts.

Everyone had calmed down.

Vartio went on to say that he and Ossi had squatted by the rock to talk to Marzipan. Arkhipov was calm, but kept pacing around.

Vartio was silent for a moment. He stared at the back wall of the courtroom, and it looked like he was tearing up. The thug was a great actor.

According to Vartio, Marzipan was in the middle of discussing a debt repayment schedule when Arkhipov grabbed a rock and hurled it at the back of Marzipan's head. Marzipan groaned and fell over onto the trail. Arkhipov violently struck Marzipan in the head two more times.

Vartio recounted that he and Ossi had frozen as Arkhipov kicked Marzipan over onto his side, panting.

"I've never seen a man killed right in front of my eyes before," Vartio yelled.

"Lying, he lying, the scambag," Arkhipov said, shooting up from his chair.

"Scumbag," I said.

"Lying, he lying, the scumbag," Arkhipov ranted.

"You shouldn't mess with other people's guns," Vartio yelled.

The presiding judge pounded his gavel until it split in two. He commented that the Helsinki attorneys should advise their clients how to behave in court.

"My client apologizes for the outburst," I said, standing up.

"Who, me?" Arkhipov said, astonished.

"Shut the hell up," I said.

Vartio was staring at us, smiling.

I didn't know what had really happened in the woods, but I was ready to bet my law school diploma that Vartio's story was a far cry from the truth.

When my turn came to cross-examine, I asked Vartio what Arkhipov had done with the rock.

"Right around ten o'clock."

"You're wearing a hearing aid. How is it possible that you can't hear properly?"

"It don't always work."

"It's working now."

"Forty-two years."

"Knock it off. What did Arkhipov do with the rock?"

"With the rock?"

"Yes."

"Marzipan was sittin' on a rock."

"What did Arkhipov do with the rock?"

"He killed Marzipan. Murdered him."

"After that?"

"Nothing."

"How is it possible that no blood-stained rock was found at the crime scene?"

"Maybe he put it down on the ground with the bloody side facin' down."

"The police turn over stones at murder scenes."

"Well then I don't know."

"There are some big holes in your story. It's not credible."

"Every word of it's true."

"The police didn't find any blood on Arkhipov's clothing, except his own."

"Now I know."

"What?"

"He probably threw it into that pond."

"Did you see that?"

"No. But that's what happened."

"So you're guessing that's what happened?"

"I'm not claimin' I saw him throw it into the pond."

"There's a lot of other stuff you're claiming."

"That's what it musta been."

"But why was the only blood on Arkhipov's clothing his blood?"

"The blood didn't splatter."

"The entire crime scene was covered in blood within a radius of several feet."

"It probably spilled out afterward, while he was lyin' on the ground."

"Do you and Arkhipov have any disputes?"

"Maybe Marzipan turned over after we left, and the blood spilled out."

"Do you and Arkhipov have any disputes?"

"Yeah."

"About what?"

"Do you have a hearing aid? Can't you hear?"

"I'm asking you to answer the question. What kind of disputes?"

"I guess I'm holdin' a grudge against him for killin' a guy we know in cold blood. That ain't how we do things in Rovaniemi."

"Arkhipov changed the ammo in your gun to blanks before you went to see Räikkönen."

"I don't know nothin' about that."

"In his statement Arkhipov said he did. And the gun they found on you when you were arrested was loaded with blanks."

"Maybe I put them in there myself."

"Why would you do that?"

"I already said I wasn't gonna kill nobody. I'm just a hell-raiser. I just wanted to scare people with those blanks. Kildenstamm and that driver. I've been told I got a personality disorder."

"Isn't it true that you tried to commit suicide in the car in front of the police station, but you didn't succeed because Arkhipov had exchanged your ammo?"

"The gun went off by accident."

"Isn't it also true that you're furious with him about that?"

"That ain't true."

"Isn't it true that you get laughed at in prison because of what happened?"

"Nobody laughs at me."

"That's not what I've heard."

"You ain't the one with a screwed up ear."

"Let me pull together a few facts that have come to light."

"Why don't you pull on your own dick."

"After the events that occurred at the Räikkönens, you were in a car accident. You escaped from the hospital. You carjacked a vehicle. You believed the entire time that you had shot and killed an on-duty police officer. We have an affidavit from Auvo Root, the man you kidnapped. He said you thought you'd killed a man. Why? Because you thought your gun had real bullets in it. You ended up in front of the police station. You were trapped and thought you were a killer. You were desperate. Suicide was the only solution you saw, so you attempted it. But you couldn't even pull that off. Arkhipov robbed you of that opportunity, your only opportunity to save face, even in death. You therefore have every motive in the world to create as much misfortune for him as possible. And that's exactly what you're doing."

"There's a lot of bullshit in the world."

"No further questions."

Vartio wanted to stay in the courtroom to continue berating Arkhipov. His voice was hoarse from almost an hour of screaming. He sounded like a sick animal as the guards led him out of the room.

His final performance, insulting Arkhipov, suited me just fine. The fool proved my point; he was holding a grudge against Arkhipov.

After the first day of trial, I read through all the documents pertaining to the case. I was convinced something was wrong.

I went to check things out.

I drove to Marzipan's house. It was smaller and more dilapidated than I'd remembered from my childhood. As far as I could tell, the story-and-a-half house still had the same paint. A couple of loose bricks sat near the base of the chimney.

I knocked on the door. When no one answered, I stepped inside, calling out "Hello!"

Marzipan's mother came out of the kitchen, drying her hands. She looked at me, but didn't recognize me right away. A boy came and stood six feet away from me and gawked at me with an awkward intensity. I said hello to the mother.

"Hello."

"Uh…"

"You were at my son's funeral."

"Yes, I was. I'm…"

"Don't tell me…don't tell me. Kiikku!"

"Right. Marzi… Your son called me that."

"I hope you don't mind me calling a grown man by his childhood nickname."

"Not at all."

"It was nice of you to come to the funeral."

"He was my friend."

"Not all of his friends took the trouble."

"Um, how should I say this…"

"Please sit down."

"Thank you. Uh, I'm Arkhipov's defense attorney."

"Out. Get out of here, now."

She literally threw me out.

The enraged woman grabbed the lapels of my jacket and my arm, tossed me into the entryway, and onto the steps outside. The door slammed shut. The boy was looking at me in the window. The window fogged over and became sticky from his candy and his breath.

I felt my arm; it was throbbing with the beginnings of a bruise. The woman's fingers had grabbed me with a steel grip.

Instead of driving, which would've been the obvious choice, I ran from Marzipan's house toward town. The ground sucked up my legs, it was hard to lift them, and it didn't feel like I'd even get to the first curve in the road. I looked back and saw the lady jump into my car and lay on the gas with a lead foot.

I stupidly ran along the road. The engine was howling behind me. I turned my head and saw the car crash on top of me. I saw the lady's big yellow teeth.

I woke with a start. The dentist chair often makes me sleepy.

I went to the bathroom and rinsed off my face. I drank some water from the palm of my hand because I had a bad taste in my mouth.

I opened the envelope. It said, "To be opened after the death of Arkady Wolfovich Arkhipov." Inside were two envelopes. One of them clearly had money in it. I opened it first.

Inside was six thousand euros, in cash. It was an excellent way to pay attorney's fees—no withholding taxes.

The other envelope had the words "The Truth" written in Finnish on it.

I balanced the envelope on the tip of the letter opener and thought about Marzipan's friendship—what it meant to me. I wondered about the truth regarding his death, and about my reputation as a prominent criminal attorney.

Maybe I was still mixed up from the dream about running. I locked the money in the safe, then walked into the family room and threw the envelope into the fireplace without opening it. I watched to make sure it burned completely. Then I mixed the ashes. I went into the office and thought I could use the money to have the safe installed in the wall. Of course I wouldn't have anything left to put in it.

Rautapää had just woken up. The cop smelled like he'd been drinking the night before. Actually, he looked like he'd been drinking since Midsummer. I'd given him permission to crash in my office for the time being. Apparently Torsti was in the middle of the roughest storm in his twenty years of marriage. It looked like the guy was taking it hard.

I opened the windows and put coffee in the coffeemaker. I told him Arkhipov was dead. Rautapää wondered why his attorney hadn't been informed until now. I told him I'd been recharging my batteries at the cabin; there was no landline there and my cell phone was so new I hadn't yet given my number to everyone.

"Ah, I see," Rautapää sighed.

He asked if Arkhipov had left me any business to be settled.

"No. What do you mean?" I asked.

"Nothing," he said.

He looked so classically miserable that I got a beer out of the fridge and set it down in front of him with a bang.

"I also have some sparkling apple juice," I offered. I went back to the kitchen and looked for a bottle opener. I threw it to Rautapää before he had a chance to break a corner of the table.

Rautapää complained that in addition to all the bad stuff at home, he had to do everything at work. Everyone else was either on vacation or had gone insane. I asked him who in the department had lost their marbles to such an extent that it had to be documented. In my experience the police never bothered to waste paper on something like that. Rautapää glanced at me irritated, but then seemed to remember whose kindness his lodging depended on.

Rautapää sipped his beer suspiciously and told me that his subordinate, Detective Sergeant Nauris, had called him on Sunday evening and begged for a leave of absence. The guy had been on vacation for almost two months, and on the night before he was supposed to return to work he wanted a leave of absence.

"Have you ever heard of anything so crazy?" Rautapää swore that all of Nauris's time off had been used up long ago. Besides, Rautapää had an assignment for him. The police had gotten a tip about a stash of illegal alcohol. After a persistent stakeout, a couple of local schmucks had shown up on Sunday afternoon at the stash. It looked like the booze had come to Finland from Russia. Nauris would get to investigate the case. He didn't sound too excited about it. He'd called back fifteen minutes later to tender his resignation. Nauris said he was going to start eco-farming on some land his wife had inherited.

"Well, sounds like he's lost the taste for honest work," Rautapää said.

"You've got to do everything yourself if you want it done right," I commented.

"Goddammit," Rautapää said. He planned on calling in sick.

I asked how his wife was.

"Bad, really bad," Rautapää sighed.

He took a swig of beer, then got up stiffly, and sprinted into the bathroom.

"Was it bad beer?" I asked at the bathroom door. I closed the door in case any clients happened to come in.

Rautapää came out of the bathroom fifteen minutes later. He said he'd cleaned himself up and had decided to go to work after all. He was going to put up a "Do not disturb" sign and snooze in his office until he perked up. I wished him a good day at work.

With Rautapää gone, I sat for a good while in the most comfortable chair in my office. Then I went to the liquor cabinet and poured a tumbler full of Polish vodka.

I walked over to the window, and, feeling a little ridiculous, held the glass near my heart, lifted it to the window, and chugged down the vodka. It brought tears to my eyes.

That's how strong the vodka was.

The phone buzzed. I went over to answer it, still clearing my throat.

It was Rautapää. He wanted to chit-chat. I would've cut the call short had I been busy.

Laughing, he told me that the booze stash turned out to be a stash of bottled water. He said it was the only thing he'd found amusing in several days. He had fun thinking about how the stupid crooks here and in Russia stole, loaded, moved around, and stored all this water, while beating and killing each other.

Rautapää said he wouldn't mind seeing these kinds of things in the future. He also said he was happy to see such excellent cooperation between the police and the most prominent defense lawyer in the city. He felt this cooperation should be encouraged. He said he'd give me insider information any time it was possible during the course of an investigation.

I promised him—before he could ask—that he could crash at my office at least for the next week.

35. Vertti Räikkönen

Morning comes.

It's already inside the house, as little lights on the ceiling. Soon it'll be everywhere.

Vertti gets up. Vertti has to go potty.

The floor in the potty room is cold. Vertti lifts up one foot, then the other.

That way only one foot is cold.

Vertti goes into the kitchen. Does Vertti have to eat oatmeal?

Grandma comes in.

Grandma messes up Vertti's hair. Vertti feels embarrassed.

Grandma makes oatmeal. "Yellow stuff," Vertti says.

"Hush," Grandma says.

Grandma gets the yellow stuff out of the refrigerator. You put it in the oatmeal with a knife.

Vertti's not allowed to touch the knife.

If Vertti puts a knife in his mouth, he'll get a cut. The cut will bleed and hurt.

Vertti eats it all. Vertti shows his bowl to Grandma. Grandma's proud of Vertti.

Vertti goes to the potty room. One of Vertti's feet isn't cold at all.

There's a bandage on it. A glass hit it.

A glass can make a cut and hurt, too. Except if it has milk in it.

Daddy comes in.

Daddy's hair is messy. It's because Daddy's head hurts.

That's when Vertti can't yell.

Vertti wants a piece of candy. Grandma gives him a lot. Vertti eats it.

There's a flower in the window.

Vertti shows Daddy the flower.

Daddy says, "It's a tree, stupid."

But there's a flower inside the house. It's growing in a pot, not in the ground.

Grandma says the tree's a flower. Is it? Are trees big flowers?

Grandma's hair catches on fire. Vertti's not allowed to go near the stove. It burns. Grandma went near it.

Daddy lets out a funny sound. Daddy's like a cartoon.

Vertti laughs. Daddy's funny.

Daddy gives Vertti a little punch. But it's not the kind of punch you can drink, it stings Vertti's arm.

Grandma makes coffee. Grown-ups drink it. Daddy rips up the newspaper.

Grandma doesn't like it.

Daddy takes the candy away from Vertti. Vertti doesn't like that. Daddy takes the wrapper off the candy.

Vertti gets it back. The candy's good.

Daddy plays with Vertti. Vertti falls down on top of a toy.

Grandma hits Vertti on the back. The candy comes out of his mouth.

Daddy takes the candy wrapper off again. The old one was ruined. Vertti laughs.

Sonny comes and licks. He has such a little tongue. He takes a long time licking Vertti's face.

Daddy scares Sonny away. Sonny runs away.

Daddy takes the wrapper off a piece of candy for Vertti.

Daddy and Grandma are talking in loud voices.

They start playing.

Daddy throws a boot.

Grandma catches it. Grandma throws the boot out into the yard. Daddy goes to get it. Vertti isn't fast enough to go after him.

Daddy's so fast.

Vertti takes a squeaky toy. It knows how to squeak.

Vertti squeezes it, the toy squeaks. Grandma's walking around.

Grandma's mad. The game is over.

Vertti goes over to the window. Daddy's walking from the shed to the trail.

"Daddy trail," Vertti says.

Sonny comes, crouching. Sometimes he crouches.

He jumps into Grandma's lap. Grandma pets him.

He jumps out of her lap. He poops on the kitchen rug. It doesn't come out like a log.

Grandma yells out.

Grandma starts cleaning it up. Grandma's mad.

Grandma cleans up and sweeps. Sonny looks sad in the doorway.

Vertti presses the squeaky toy.

Grandma leaves and goes out into the yard. Vertti follows her.

From the start of the trail, Grandma looks behind her. Grandma doesn't see Vertti.

Grandma takes off running. Vertti runs. His foot hurts every time it hits the ground.

Daddy's sitting on a rock.

Daddy asks if they've been there already. Grandma asks, "Who?"

Vertti comes up beside Grandma. Grandma says, "Vertti, go back."

Vertti doesn't go.

Daddy says, "Have they been there yet?" Grandma says, "I was fooling you." Grandma says she didn't hear any cars.

Daddy says, "Shit, shit, shit." Grandma says, "That's what you are."

Daddy says, "I'm going to town." Grandma says, "Don't come back."

Daddy gets up and goes down the trail. Grandma picks up a rock from the ground. Grandma hits Daddy in the head from behind.

It makes a sound.

Daddy falls down on all fours. Daddy's crawling like a little baby.

Grandma hits Daddy again. Grandma says, "No more picking on Sonny."

Grandma says, "Are you done with that now?"

Daddy's just lying there. Daddy's not playing. Grandma's so mad because Daddy won't play.

Grandma says, "Are you done?"

Vertti says, "Why isn't Daddy playing?"

Grandma looks at Vertti. Grandma goes over to the pond. Grandma washes off the rock like it's a bowl.

Grandma puts the rock in the bushes on the shore. The bowl gets put back in the cupboard.

Vertti grabs Grandma by the dress.

Grandma says, "We're not going to talk about this." Vertti wants a piece of candy.

A piece of green candy. Grandma says that Vertti won't talk about this. Vertti won't ever talk about it.

Grandma comes up with another game.

Vertti goes up to Daddy and whispers to him that they have a new game now. But Vertti remembers that whispering's not allowed. Vertti's not whispering.

Daddy's done with the game. Daddy's just lying there. Daddy's head is always sore.

Grandma takes Vertti by the hand, Vertti walks home with Grandma.

Grandma gives Vertti a piece of candy. Grandma takes the wrapper off first.

Sonny comes back. Grandma says, "Vertti won't ever talk about this. It's a new game. A fun game."

Daddy's not talking. Vertti's not talking. Sonny's not talking.

Sometimes he purrs.

Also by Ice Cold Crime

Jarkko Sipila
Helsinki Homicide: Against the Wall
Winner of 2009 Best Finnish Crime Novel
ISBN: 978-0-9824449-0-0

Detective Lieutenant Kari Takamäki's trusted man Suhonen goes undercover as Suikkanen, a gangster full of action. In pursuit of a murderer, he must operate within the grey area of the law. But, will the end justify the means?

Jarkko Sipila
Helsinki Homicide: Vengeance
ISBN: 978-0-9824449-1-7

Tapani Larsson, a Finnish crime boss, walks out of prison with one thought on his mind: Vengeance. Larsson targets Suhonen, the undercover detective who put him in prison. With every string Suhonen pulls, he flirts with death itself.

Jarkko Sipila
Helsinki Homicide: Nothing but the Truth
ISBN: 978-0-9824449-3-1

A mother of a 12-year old girl is a witness in a murder case. After testifying in the trial, she finds herself the target of an escalating spiral of threats. As the threats mount, the witness is torn between her principles and her desire to keep her family safe. How much should an ordinary citizen sacrifice for the benefit of society as a whole?

Jarkko Sipila
Helsinki Homicide: Cold Trail
ISBN: 978-0-9824449-8-6

Amidst freezing rain, a convicted murderer escapes. Detective Lieutenant Kari Takamäki and his homicide team must return him back to prison. But as the manhunt begins, Takamäki's team starts digging into old evidence. Was he an innocent man unjustly sentenced to life in prison—and to losing his only son? The novel deliberates taking justice into your own hands.

Harri Nykanen
Raid and the Blackest Sheep
Winner of 2001 Best Finnish Crime Novel
ISBN: 978-0-9824449-2-4

Hard-nosed hit man Raid travels around Finland with Nygren, a career criminal in the twilight of his life, wreaking vengeance him and paying penance. Soon, Detective Lieutenant Jansson and his team as well as notorious criminals from Nygren's past are on the trail of the mysterious pair. In the end, the pilgrimage leaves a trail of wounded and dead in its wake.

Harri Nykanen
Raid and the Kid
ISBN: 978-0-9824449-4-8

Hard-nosed hit man Raid is reluctantly mixed up into the world of drug trafficking in this twisting tale of cops, criminals, and those who blur the lines, Detective Lieutenant Jansson and his team struggle to connect the dots behind a murder case. Were the killings the work of a jealous lover, the result of a theft racket gone awry, or something else entirely?

Seppo Jokinen
Wolves and Angels
Winner of 2002 Best Finnish Crime Novel
ISBN: 978-0-9824449-5-5

With attacks on the disabled and ailing, Detective Sakari Koskinen and his eccentric team spring into action in a gripping story about the struggles of the disabled coping with their new lives and the strains on those who care for them. Nuanced depictions of interpersonal relationships and personal challenges make Jokinen's characters come to life on the page.

Scott Stevenson
Decay Time – A Wall Street Murder and Morality Tale
ISBN: 978-0-9824449-7-9

A dead man is found in the penthouse suite of an opulent midtown Manhattan hotel. Who is he? Was he murdered or was it suicide, and would it make yet another headline about the financial meltdown rocking Wall Street? *Decay Time*, written by a former investment banker, is a story about people, not products, and illuminates the world of the Wall Street trading floor before, during, and following the 2008 financial crisis.

Anja Snellman
Pet Shop Girls
ISBN: 978-0-9824449-6-2

Twelve years ago, on a December Sunday, Jasmin Martin disappeared. Despite the best efforts of the police, her trail quickly went cold. How could the child of a comfortable, middle-class family be swept into a world mothers and fathers fear deepest in their hearts, a global network of pornographers and drug smugglers, pedophiles and pimps? Where is she now and with whom? Jasmin's tale is told from multiple perspectives in this beautifully crafted and suspenseful novel.

Website: www.icecoldcrime.com

Phone: +1 952 353 4804